All Around the Moon

All Around the Moon

Jules Verne

MINT EDITIONS

All Around the Moon was first published in 1871.

This edition published by Mint Editions 2021.

ISBN 9781513270449 | E-ISBN 9781513275444

Published by Mint Editions®

 MINT
EDITIONS

minteditionbooks.com

Publishing Director: Jennifer Newens
Design & Production: Rachel Lopez Metzger
Translation: Edward Roth
Typesetting: Westchester Publishing Services

Contents

Preliminary Chapter

Resuming the First Part of the Work and Serving as an Introduction to the Second

A few years ago the world was suddenly astounded by hearing of an experiment of a most novel and daring nature, altogether unprecedented in the annals of science. The BALTIMORE GUN CLUB, a society of artillerymen started in America during the great Civil War, had conceived the idea of nothing less than establishing direct communication with the Moon by means of a projectile! President Barbican, the originator of the enterprise, was strongly encouraged in its feasibility by the astronomers of Cambridge Observatory, and took upon himself to provide all the means necessary to secure its success. Having realized by means of a public subscription the sum of nearly five and a half millions of dollars, he immediately set himself to work at the necessary gigantic labors.

In accordance with the Cambridge men's note, the cannon intended to discharge the projectile was to be planted in some country not further than 28° north or south from the equator, so that it might be aimed vertically at the Moon in the zenith. The bullet was to be animated with an initial velocity of 12,000 yards to the second. It was to be fired off on the night of December 1st, at thirteen minutes and twenty seconds before eleven o'clock, precisely. Four days afterwards it was to hit the Moon, at the very moment that she reached her *perigee*, that is to say, her nearest point to the Earth, about 228,000 miles distant.

The leading members of the Club, namely President Barbican, Secretary Marston, Major Elphinstone and General Morgan, forming the executive committee, held several meetings to discuss the shape and material of the bullet, the nature and position of the cannon, and the quantity and quality of the powder. The decision soon arrived at was as follows: 1st—The bullet was to be a hollow aluminium shell, its diameter nine feet, its walls a foot in thickness, and its weight 19,250 pounds; 2nd—The cannon was to be a columbiad 900 feet in length, a well of that depth forming the vertical mould in which it was to be cast, and 3rd—The powder was to be 400 thousand pounds of gun cotton, which, by developing more than 200 thousand millions of cubic feet of gas under the projectile, would easily send it as far as our satellite.

These questions settled, Barbican, aided by Murphy, the Chief Engineer of the Cold Spring Iron Works, selected a spot in Florida, near the 27th degree north latitude, called Stony Hill, where after the performance of many wonderful feats in mining engineering, the Columbiad was successfully cast.

Things had reached this state when an incident occurred which excited the general interest a hundred fold.

A Frenchman from Paris, Michel Ardan by name, eccentric, but keen and shrewd as well as daring, demanded, by the Atlantic telegraph, permission to be enclosed in the bullet so that he might be carried to the Moon, where he was curious to make certain investigations. Received in America with great enthusiasm, Ardan held a great meeting, triumphantly carried his point, reconciled Barbican to his mortal foe, a certain Captain M'Nicholl, and even, by way of clinching the reconciliation, induced both the newly made friends to join him in his contemplated trip to the Moon.

The bullet, so modified as to become a hollow conical cylinder with plenty of room inside, was further provided with powerful water-springs and readily-ruptured partitions below the floor, intended to deaden the dreadful concussion sure to accompany the start. It was supplied with provisions for a year, water for a few months, and gas for nearly two weeks. A self-acting apparatus, of ingenious construction, kept the confined atmosphere sweet and healthy by manufacturing pure oxygen and absorbing carbonic acid. Finally, the Gun Club had constructed, at enormous expense, a gigantic telescope, which, from the summit of Long's Peak, could pursue the Projectile as it winged its way through the regions of space. Everything at last was ready.

On December 1st, at the appointed moment, in the midst of an immense concourse of spectators, the departure took place, and, for the first time in the world's history, three human beings quitted our terrestrial globe with some possibility in their favor of finally reaching a point of destination in the inter-planetary spaces. They expected to accomplish their journey in 97 hours, 13 minutes and 20 seconds, consequently reaching the Lunar surface precisely at midnight on December 5–6, the exact moment when the Moon would be full.

Unfortunately, the instantaneous explosion of such a vast quantity of gun-cotton, by giving rise to a violent commotion in the atmosphere, generated so much vapor and mist as to render the Moon invisible for several nights to the innumerable watchers in the Western Hemisphere, who vainly tried to catch sight of her.

In the meantime, J.T. Marston, the Secretary of the Gun Club, and a most devoted friend of Barbican's, had started for Long's Peak, Colorado, on the summit of which the immense telescope, already alluded to, had been erected; it was of the reflecting kind, and possessed power sufficient to bring the Moon within a distance of five miles. While Marston was prosecuting his long journey with all possible speed, Professor Belfast, who had charge of the telescope, was endeavoring to catch a glimpse of the Projectile, but for a long time with no success. The hazy, cloudy weather lasted for more than a week, to the great disgust of the public at large. People even began to fear that further observation would have to be deferred to the 3d of the following month, January, as during the latter half of December the waning Moon could not possibly give light enough to render the Projectile visible.

At last, however, to the unbounded satisfaction of all, a violent tempest suddenly cleared the sky, and on the 13th of December, shortly after midnight, the Moon, verging towards her last quarter, revealed herself sharp and bright on the dark background of the starry firmament.

That same morning, a few hours before Marston's arrival at the summit of Long's Peak, a very remarkable telegram had been dispatched by Professor Belfast to the Smithsonian Institute, Washington. It announced:

That on December 13th, at 2 o'clock in the morning, the Projectile shot from Stony Hill had been perceived by Professor Belfast and his assistants; that, deflected a little from its course by some unknown cause, it had not reached its mark, though it had approached near enough to be affected by the Lunar attraction; and that, its rectilineal motion having become circular, it should henceforth continue to describe a regular orbit around the Moon, of which in fact it had become the Satellite. The dispatch went on further to state:

That the *elements* of the new heavenly body had not yet been calculated, as at least three different observations, taken at different times, were necessary to determine them. The distance of the Projectile from the Lunar surface, however, might be set down roughly at roughly 2833 miles.

The dispatch concluded with the following hypotheses, positively pronounced to be the only two possible: Either, 1, The Lunar attraction would finally prevail, in which case the travellers would reach their destination; or 2, The Projectile, kept whirling forever in an immutable orbit, would go on revolving around the Moon till time should be no more.

In either alternative, what should be the lot of the daring adventurers? They had, it is true, abundant provisions to last them for some time, but even supposing that they did reach the Moon and thereby completely establish the practicability of their daring enterprise, how were they ever to get back? *Could* they ever get back? or ever even be heard from? Questions of this nature, freely discussed by the ablest pens of the day, kept the public mind in a very restless and excited condition.

We must be pardoned here for making a little remark which, however, astronomers and other scientific men of sanguine temperament would do well to ponder over. An observer cannot be too cautious in announcing to the public his discovery when it is of a nature purely speculative. Nobody is obliged to discover a planet, or a comet, or even a satellite, but, before announcing to the world that you have made such a discovery, first make sure that such is really the fact. Because, you know, should it afterwards come out that you have done nothing of the kind, you make yourself a butt for the stupid jokes of the lowest newspaper scribblers. Belfast had never thought of this. Impelled by his irrepressible rage for discovery—the *furor inveniendi* ascribed to all astronomers by Aurelius Priscus—he had therefore been guilty of an indiscretion highly un-scientific when his famous telegram, launched to the world at large from the summit of the Rocky Mountains, pronounced so dogmatically on the only possible issues of the great enterprise.

The truth was that his telegram contained *two* very important errors: 1. Error of *observation*, as facts afterwards proved; the Projectile *was* not seen on the 13th and *could* not have been on that day, so that the little black spot which Belfast professed to have seen was most certainly not the Projectile; 2. Error of *theory* regarding the final fate of the Projectile, since to make it become the Moon's satellite was flying in the face of one of the great fundamental laws of Theoretical Mechanics.

Only one, therefore, the first, of the hypotheses so positively announced, was capable of realization. The travellers—that is to say if they still lived—might so combine and unite their own efforts with those of the Lunar attraction as actually to succeed at last in reaching the Moon's surface.

Now the travellers, those daring but cool-headed men who knew very well what they were about, *did* still live, they *had* survived the frightful concussion of the start, and it is to the faithful record of their wonderful trip in the bullet-car, with all its singular and dramatic details, that the present volume is devoted. The story may destroy many illusions, prejudices and conjectures; but it will at least give correct ideas of the strange incidents to which such an enterprise is exposed, and it will certainly bring out in strong colors the effects of Barbican's scientific conceptions, M'Nicholl's mechanical resources, and Ardan's daring, eccentric, but brilliant and effective combinations.

Besides, it will show that J.T. Marston, their faithful friend and a man every way worthy of the friendship of such men, was only losing his time while mirroring the Moon in the speculum of the gigantic telescope on that lofty peak of the mountains.

I

From 10 p.m. to 10 46' 40"

The moment that the great clock belonging to the works at Stony Hill had struck ten, Barbican, Ardan and M'Nicholl began to take their last farewells of the numerous friends surrounding them. The two dogs intended to accompany them had been already deposited in the Projectile. The three travellers approached the mouth of the enormous cannon, seated themselves in the flying car, and once more took leave for the last time of the vast throng standing in silence around them. The windlass creaked, the car started, and the three daring men disappeared in the yawning gulf.

The trap-hole giving them ready access to the interior of the Projectile, the car soon came back empty; the great windlass was presently rolled away; the tackle and scaffolding were removed, and in a short space of time the great mouth of the Columbiad was completely rid of all obstructions.

M'Nicholl took upon himself to fasten the door of the trap on the inside by means of a powerful combination of screws and bolts of his own invention. He also covered up very carefully the glass lights with strong iron plates of extreme solidity and tightly fitting joints.

Ardan's first care was to turn on the gas, which he found burning rather low; but he lit no more than one burner, being desirous to economize as much as possible their store of light and heat, which, as he well knew, could not at the very utmost last them longer than a few weeks.

Under the cheerful blaze, the interior of the Projectile looked like a comfortable little chamber, with its circular sofa, nicely padded walls, and dome shaped ceiling.

All the articles that it contained, arms, instruments, utensils, etc., were solidly fastened to the projections of the wadding, so as to sustain the least injury possible from the first terrible shock. In fact, all precautions possible, humanly speaking, had been taken to counteract this, the first, and possibly one of the very greatest dangers to which the courageous adventurers would be exposed.

Ardan expressed himself to be quite pleased with the appearance of things in general.

"It's a prison, to be sure," said he "but not one of your ordinary prisons that always keep in the one spot. For my part, as long as I can have the privilege of looking out of the window, I am willing to lease it for a hundred years. Ah! Barbican, that brings out one of your stony smiles. You think our lease may last longer than that! Our tenement may become our coffin, eh? Be it so. I prefer it anyway to Mahomet's; it may indeed float in the air, but it won't be motionless as a milestone!"

Barbican, having made sure by personal inspection that everything was in perfect order, consulted his chronometer, which he had carefully set a short time before with Chief Engineer Murphy's, who had been charged to fire off the Projectile.

"Friends," he said, "it is now twenty minutes past ten. At 10 46' 40", precisely, Murphy will send the electric current into the gun-cotton. We have, therefore, twenty-six minutes more to remain on earth."

"Twenty-six minutes and twenty seconds," observed Captain M'Nicholl, who always aimed at mathematical precision.

"Twenty-six minutes!" cried Ardan, gaily. "An age, a cycle, according to the use you make of them. In twenty-six minutes how much can be done! The weightiest questions of warfare, politics, morality, can be discussed, even decided, in twenty-six minutes. Twenty-six minutes well spent are infinitely more valuable than twenty-six lifetimes wasted! A few seconds even, employed by a Pascal, or a Newton, or a Barbican, or any other profoundly intellectual being Whose thoughts wander through eternity—"

"As mad as Marston! Every bit!" muttered the Captain, half audibly.

"What do you conclude from this rigmarole of yours?" interrupted Barbican.

"I conclude that we have twenty-six good minutes still left—"

"Only twenty-four minutes, ten seconds," interrupted the Captain, watch in hand.

"Well, twenty-four minutes, Captain," Ardan went on; "now even in twenty-four minutes, I maintain—"

"Ardan," interrupted Barbican, "after a very little while we shall have plenty of time for philosophical disputations. Just now let us think of something far more pressing."

"More pressing! what do you mean? are we not fully prepared?"

"Yes, fully prepared, as far at least as we have been able to foresee. But we may still, I think, possibly increase the number of precautions to be taken against the terrible shock that we are so soon to experience."

"What? Have you any doubts whatever of the effectiveness of your brilliant and extremely original idea? Don't you think that the layers of water, regularly disposed in easily-ruptured partitions beneath this floor, will afford us sufficient protection by their elasticity?"

"I hope so, indeed, my dear friend, but I am by no means confident."

"He hopes! He is by no means confident! Listen to that, Mac! Pretty time to tell us so! Let me out of here!"

"Too late!" observed the Captain quietly. "The trap-hole alone would take ten or fifteen minutes to open."

"Oh then I suppose I must make the best of it," said Ardan, laughing. "All aboard, gentlemen! The train starts in twenty minutes!"

"In nineteen minutes and eighteen seconds," said the Captain, who never took his eye off the chronometer.

The three travellers looked at each other for a little while, during which even Ardan appeared to become serious. After another careful glance at the several objects lying around them, Barbican said, quietly:

"Everything is in its place, except ourselves. What we have now to do is to decide on the position we must take in order to neutralize the shock as much as possible. We must be particularly careful to guard against a rush of blood to the head."

"Correct!" said the Captain.

"Suppose we stood on our heads, like the circus tumblers!" cried Ardan, ready to suit the action to the word.

"Better than that," said Barbican; "we can lie on our side. Keep clearly in mind, dear friends, that at the instant of departure it makes very little difference to us whether we are inside the bullet or in front of it. There is, no doubt, *some* difference," he added, seeing the great eyes made by his friends, "but it is exceedingly little."

"Thank heaven for the *some*!" interrupted Ardan, fervently.

"Don't you approve of my suggestion, Captain?" asked Barbican.

"Certainly," was the hasty reply. "That is to say, absolutely. Seventeen minutes twenty-seven seconds!"

"Mac isn't a human being at all!" cried Ardan, admiringly. "He is a repeating chronometer, horizontal escapement, London-made lever, capped, jewelled,—"

His companions let him run on while they busied themselves in making their last arrangements, with the greatest coolness and most systematic method. In fact, I don't think of anything just now to compare them to except a couple of old travellers who, having to pass the night in the train, are trying to make themselves as comfortable as possible for their long journey. In your profound astonishment, you may naturally ask me of what strange material can the hearts of these Americans be made, who can view without the slightest semblance of a flutter the approach of the most appalling dangers? In your curiosity I fully participate, but, I'm sorry to say, I can't gratify it. It is one of those things that I could never find out.

Three mattresses, thick and well wadded, spread on the disc forming the false bottom of the Projectile, were arranged in lines whose parallelism was simply perfect. But Ardan would never think of occupying his until the very last moment. Walking up and down, with the restless nervousness of a wild beast in a cage, he kept up a continuous fire of talk; at one moment with his friends, at another with the dogs, addressing the latter by the euphonious and suggestive names of Diana and Satellite.

"Ho, pets!" he would exclaim as he patted them gently, "you must not forget the noble part you are to play up there. You must be models of canine deportment. The eyes of the whole Selenitic world will be upon you. You are the standard bearers of your race. From you they will receive their first impression regarding its merits. Let it be a favorable one. Compel those Selenites to acknowledge, in spite of themselves, that the terrestrial race of canines is far superior to that of the very best Moon dog among them!"

"Dogs in the Moon!" sneered M'Nicholl, "I like that!"

"Plenty of dogs!" cried Ardan, "and horses too, and cows, and sheep, and no end of chickens!"

"A hundred dollars to one there isn't a single chicken within the whole Lunar realm, not excluding even the invisible side!" cried the Captain, in an authoritative tone, but never taking his eye off the chronometer.

"I take that bet, my son," coolly replied Ardan, shaking the Captain's hand by way of ratifying the wager; "and this reminds me, by the way, Mac, that you have lost three bets already, to the pretty little tune of six thousand dollars."

"And paid them, too!" cried the captain, monotonously; "ten, thirty-six, six!"

"Yes, and in a quarter of an hour you will have to pay nine thousand dollars more; four thousand because the Columbiad will not burst, and five thousand because the Projectile will rise more than six miles from the Earth."

"I have the money ready," answered the Captain, touching his breeches pocket. "When I lose I pay. Not sooner. Ten, thirty-eight, ten!"

"Captain, you're a man of method, if there ever was one. I think, however, that you made a mistake in your wagers."

"How so?" asked the Captain listlessly, his eye still on the dial.

"Because, by Jove, if you win there will be no more of you left to take the money than there will be of Barbican to pay it!"

"Friend Ardan," quietly observed Barbican, "my stakes are deposited in the *Wall Street Bank*, of New York, with orders to pay them over to the Captain's heirs, in case the Captain himself should fail to put in an appearance at the proper time."

"Oh! you rhinoceroses, you pachyderms, you granite men!" cried Ardan, gasping with surprise; "you machines with iron heads, and iron hearts! I may admire you, but I'm blessed if I understand you!"

"Ten, forty-two, ten!" repeated M'Nicholl, as mechanically as if it was the chronometer itself that spoke.

"Four minutes and a half more," said Barbican.

"Oh! four and a half little minutes!" went on Ardan. "Only think of it! We are shut up in a bullet that lies in the chamber of a cannon nine hundred feet long. Underneath this bullet is piled a charge of 400 thousand pounds of gun-cotton, equivalent to 1600 thousand pounds of ordinary gunpowder! And at this very instant our friend Murphy, chronometer in hand, eye on dial, finger on discharger, is counting the last seconds and getting ready to launch us into the limitless regions of planetary—"

"Ardan, dear friend," interrupted Barbican, in a grave tone, "a serious moment is now at hand. Let us meet it with some interior recollection. Give me your hands, my dear friends."

"Certainly," said Ardan, with tears in his voice, and already at the other extreme of his apparent levity.

The three brave men united in one last, silent, but warm and impulsively affectionate pressure.

"And now, great God, our Creator, protect us! In Thee we trust!" prayed Barbican, the others joining him with folded hands and bowed heads.

"Ten, forty-six!" whispered the Captain, as he and Ardan quietly took their places on the mattresses.

Only forty seconds more!

Barbican rapidly extinguishes the gas and lies down beside his companions.

The deathlike silence now reigning in the Projectile is interrupted only by the sharp ticking of the chronometer as it beats the seconds.

Suddenly, a dreadful shock is felt, and the Projectile, shot up by the instantaneous development of 200,000 millions of cubic feet of gas, is flying into space with inconceivable rapidity!

II

The First Half Hour

What had taken place within the Projectile? What effect had been produced by the frightful concussion? Had Barbican's ingenuity been attended with a fortunate result? Had the shock been sufficiently deadened by the springs, the buffers, the water layers, and the partitions so readily ruptured? Had their combined effect succeeded in counteracting the tremendous violence of a velocity of 12,000 yards a second, actually sufficient to carry them from London to New York in six minutes? These, and a hundred other questions of a similar nature were asked that night by the millions who had been watching the explosion from the base of Stony Hill. Themselves they forgot altogether for the moment; they forgot everything in their absorbing anxiety regarding the fate of the daring travellers. Had one among them, our friend Marston, for instance, been favored with a glimpse at the interior of the projectile, what would he have seen?

Nothing at all at first, on account of the darkness; except that the walls had solidly resisted the frightful shock. Not a crack, nor a bend, nor a dent could be perceived; not even the slightest injury had the admirably constructed piece of mechanical workmanship endured. It had not yielded an inch to the enormous pressure, and, far from melting and falling back to earth, as had been so seriously apprehended, in showers of blazing aluminium, it was still as strong in every respect as it had been on the very day that it left the Cold Spring Iron Works, glittering like a silver dollar.

Of real damage there was actually none, and even the disorder into which things had been thrown in the interior by the violent shock was comparatively slight. A few small objects lying around loose had been furiously hurled against the ceiling, but the others appeared not to have suffered the slightest injury. The straps that fastened them up were unfrayed, and the fixtures that held them down were uncracked.

The partitions beneath the disc having been ruptured, and the water having escaped, the false floor had been dashed with tremendous violence against the bottom of the Projectile, and on this disc at this moment three human bodies could be seen lying perfectly still and motionless.

Were they three corpses? Had the Projectile suddenly become a great metallic coffin bearing its ghastly contents through the air with the rapidity of a lightning flash?

In a very few minutes after the shock, one of the bodies stirred a little, the arms moved, the eyes opened, the head rose and tried to look around; finally, with some difficulty, the body managed to get on its knees. It was the Frenchman! He held his head tightly squeezed between his hands for some time as if to keep it from splitting. Then he felt himself rapidly all over, cleared his throat with a vigorous "hem!" listened to the sound critically for an instant, and then said to himself in a relieved tone, but in his native tongue:

"One man all right! Call the roll for the others!"

He tried to rise, but the effort was too great for his strength. He fell back again, his brain swimming, his eyes bursting, his head splitting. His state very much resembled that of a young man waking up in the morning after his first tremendous "spree."

"Br—rr!" he muttered to himself, still talking French; "this reminds me of one of my wild nights long ago in the *Quartier Latin*, only decidedly more so!"

Lying quietly on his back for a while, he could soon feel that the circulation of his blood, so suddenly and violently arrested by the terrific shock, was gradually recovering its regular flow; his heart grew more normal in its action; his head became clearer, and the pain less distracting.

"Time to call that roll," he at last exclaimed in a voice with some pretensions to firmness; "Barbican! MacNicholl!"

He listens anxiously for a reply. None comes. A snow-wrapt grave at midnight is not more silent. In vain does he try to catch even the faintest sound of breathing, though he listens intently enough to hear the beating of their hearts; but he hears only his own.

"Call that roll again!" he mutters in a voice far less assured than before; "Barbican! MacNicholl!"

The same fearful unearthly stillness.

"The thing is getting decidedly monotonous!" he exclaimed, still speaking French. Then rapidly recovering his consciousness as the full horror of the situation began to break on his mind, he went on muttering audibly: "Have they really hopped the twig? Bah! Fudge! what has not been able to knock the life out of one little Frenchman can't have killed two Americans! They're all right! But first and foremost, let us enlighten the situation!"

So saying, he contrived without much difficulty to get on his feet. Balancing himself then for a moment, he began groping about for the gas. But he stopped suddenly.

"Hold on a minute!" he cried; "before lighting this match, let us see if the gas has been escaping. Setting fire to a mixture of air and hydrogen would make a pretty how-do-you-do! Such an explosion would infallibly burst the Projectile, which so far seems all right, though I'm blest if I can tell whether we're moving or not."

He began sniffing and smelling to discover if possible the odor of escaped gas. He could not detect the slightest sign of anything of the kind. This gave him great courage. He knew of course that his senses were not yet in good order, still he thought he might trust them so far as to be certain that the gas had not escaped and that consequently all the other receptacles were uninjured.

At the touch of the match, the gas burst into light and burned with a steady flame. Ardan immediately bent anxiously over the prostrate bodies of his friends. They lay on each other like inert masses, M'Nicholl stretched across Barbican.

Ardan first lifted up the Captain, laid him on the sofa, opened his clenched hands, rubbed them, and slapped the palms vigorously. Then he went all over the body carefully, kneading it, rubbing it, and gently patting it. In such intelligent efforts to restore suspended circulation, he seemed perfectly at home, and after a few minutes his patience was rewarded by seeing the Captain's pallid face gradually recover its natural color, and by feeling his heart gradually beat with a firm pulsation.

At last M'Nicholl opened his eyes, stared at Ardan for an instant, pressed his hand, looked around searchingly and anxiously, and at last whispered in a faint voice:

"How's Barbican?"

"Barbican is all right, Captain," answered Ardan quietly, but still speaking French. "I'll attend to him in a jiffy. He had to wait for his turn. I began with you because you were the top man. We'll see in a minute what we can do for dear old Barby (*ce cher Barbican*)!"

In less than thirty seconds more, the Captain not only was able to sit up himself, but he even insisted on helping Ardan to lift Barbican, and deposit him gently on the sofa.

The poor President had evidently suffered more from the concussion than either of his companions. As they took off his coat they were at first terribly shocked at the sight of a great patch of blood staining his shirt bosom, but they were inexpressibly relieved at finding that it proceeded from a slight contusion of the shoulder, little more than skin deep.

Every approved operation that Ardan had performed for the Captain, both now repeated for Barbican, but for a long time with nothing like a favorable result.

Ardan at first tried to encourage the Captain by whispers of a lively and hopeful nature, but not yet understanding why M'Nicholl did not deign to make a single reply, he grew reserved by degrees and at last would not speak a single word. He worked at Barbican, however, just as before.

M'Nicholl interrupted himself every moment to lay his ear on the breast of the unconscious man. At first he had shaken his head quite despondingly, but by degrees he found himself more and more encouraged to persist.

"He breathes!" he whispered at last.

"Yes, he has been breathing for some time," replied Ardan, quietly, still unconsciously speaking French. "A little more rubbing and pulling and pounding will make him as spry as a young grasshopper."

They worked at him, in fact, so vigorously, intelligently and perseveringly, that, after what they considered a long hour's labor, they had the delight of seeing the pale face assume a healthy hue, the inert limbs give signs of returning animation, and the breathing become strong and regular.

At last, Barbican suddenly opened his eyes, started into an upright position on the sofa, took his friends by the hands, and, in a voice showing complete consciousness, demanded eagerly:

"Ardan, M'Nicholl, are we moving?"

His friends looked at each other, a little amused, but more perplexed. In their anxiety regarding their own and their friend's recovery, they had never thought of asking such a question. His words recalled them at once to a full sense of their situation.

"Moving? Blessed if I can tell!" said Ardan, still speaking French.

"We may be lying fifty feet deep in a Florida marsh, for all I know," observed M'Nicholl.

"Or, likely as not, in the bottom of the Gulf of Mexico," suggested Ardan, still in French.

"Suppose we find out," observed Barbican, jumping up to try, his voice as clear and his step as firm as ever.

But trying is one thing, and finding out another. Having no means of comparing themselves with external objects, they could not possibly tell whether they were moving, or at an absolute stand-still. Though our Earth is whirling us continually around the Sun at the tremendous speed of 500 miles a minute, its inhabitants are totally unconscious of the slightest motion. It was the same with our travellers. Through their own personal consciousness they could tell absolutely nothing. Were they shooting through space like a meteor? They could not tell. Had they fallen back and buried themselves deep in the sandy soil of Florida, or, still more likely, hundreds of fathoms deep beneath the waters of the Gulf of Mexico? They could not form the slightest idea.

Listening evidently could do no good. The profound silence proved nothing. The padded walls of the Projectile were too thick to admit any sound whether of wind, water, or human beings. Barbican, however, was soon struck forcibly by one circumstance. He felt himself to be very uncomfortably warm, and his friend's faces looked very hot and flushed. Hastily removing the cover that protected the thermometer, he closely inspected it, and in an instant uttered a joyous exclamation.

"Hurrah!" he cried. "We're moving! There's no mistake about it. The thermometer marks 113 degrees Fahrenheit. Such a stifling heat could not come from the gas. It comes from the exterior walls of our projectile, which atmospheric friction must have made almost red hot. But this heat must soon diminish, because we are already far beyond the regions of the atmosphere, so that instead of smothering we shall be shortly in danger of freezing."

"What?" asked Ardan, much bewildered. "We are already far beyond the limits of the terrestrial atmosphere! Why do you think so?"

M'Nicholl was still too much flustered to venture a word.

"If you want me to answer your question satisfactorily, my dear Ardan," replied Barbican, with a quiet smile, "you will have the kindness to put your questions in English."

"What do you mean, Barbican!" asked Ardan, hardly believing his ears.

"Hurrah!" cried M'Nicholl, in the tone of a man who has suddenly made a welcome but most unexpected discovery.

"I don't know exactly how it is with the Captain," continued Barbican, with the utmost tranquillity, "but for my part the study of the languages never was my strong point, and though I always admired the French, and even understood it pretty well, I never could converse in it without giving myself more trouble than I always find it convenient to assume."

"You don't mean to say that I have been talking French to you all this time!" cried Ardan, horror-stricken.

"The most elegant French I ever heard, backed by the purest Parisian accent," replied Barbican, highly amused; "Don't you think so, Captain?" he added, turning to M'Nicholl, whose countenance still showed the most comical traces of bewilderment.

"Well, I swan to man!" cried the Captain, who always swore a little when his feelings got beyond his control; "Ardan, the Boss has got the rig on both of us this time, but rough as it is on you it is a darned sight more so on me. Be hanged if I did not think you were talking English the whole time, and I put the whole blame for not understanding you on the disordered state of my brain!"

Ardan only stared, and scratched his head, but Barbican actually—no, not *laughed*, that serene nature could not *laugh*. His cast-iron features puckered into a smile of the richest drollery, and his eyes twinkled with the wickedest fun; but no undignified giggle escaped the portal of those majestic lips.

"It *sounds* like French, I'd say to myself," continued the Captain, "but I *know* it's English, and by and by, when this whirring goes out of my head, I shall easily understand it."

Ardan now looked as if he was beginning to see the joke.

"The most puzzling part of the thing to me," went on M'Nicholl, giving his experience with the utmost gravity, "was why English sounded so like *French*. If it was simple incomprehensible gibberish, I could readily blame the state of my ears for it. But the idea that my bothered ears could turn a mere confused, muzzled, buzzing reverberation into a sweet, harmonious, articulate, though unintelligible, human language, made me sure that I was fast becoming crazy, if I was not so already."

"Ha! ha! ha!" roared Ardan, laughing till the tears came. "Now I understand why the poor Captain made me no reply all the time, and looked at me with such a hapless woe-begone expression of countenance. The fact is, Barbican, that shock was too much both for M'Nicholl and myself. You are the only man among us whose head is fire-proof, blast-proof, and powder-proof. I really believe a burglar would have greater difficulty in blowing your head-piece open than in bursting one of those famous American safes your papers make such a fuss about. A wonderful head, the Boss's, isn't it M'Nicholl?"

"Yes," said the Captain, as slowly as if every word were a gem of the profoundest thought, "the Boss has a fearful and a wonderful head!"

"But now to business!" cried the versatile Ardan, "Why do you think, Barbican, that we are at present beyond the limits of the terrestrial atmosphere?"

"For a very simple reason," said Barbican, pointing to the chronometer; "it is now more than seven minutes after 11. We must, therefore, have been in motion more than twenty minutes. Consequently, unless our initial velocity has been very much diminished by the friction, we must have long before this completely cleared the fifty miles of atmosphere enveloping the earth."

"Correct," said the Captain, cool as a cucumber, because once more in complete possession of all his senses; "but how much do you think the initial velocity to have been diminished by the friction?"

"By a third, according to my calculations," replied Barbican, "which I think are right. Supposing our initial velocity, therefore, to have been 12,000 yards per second, by the time we quitted the atmosphere it must have been reduced to 8,000 yards per second. At that rate, we must have gone by this time—"

"Then, Mac, my boy, you've lost your two bets!" interrupted Ardan. "The Columbiad has not burst, four thousand dollars; the Projectile has risen at least six miles, five thousand dollars; come, Captain, bleed!"

"Let me first be sure we're right," said the Captain, quietly. "I don't deny, you see, that friend Barbican's arguments are quite right, and, therefore, that I have lost my nine thousand dollars. But there is another view of the case possible, which might annul the bet."

"What other view?" asked Barbican, quickly.

"Suppose," said the Captain, very drily, "that the powder had not caught, and that we were still lying quietly at the bottom of the Columbiad!"

"By Jove!" laughed Ardan, "there's an idea truly worthy of my own nondescript brain! We must surely have changed heads during that concussion! No matter, there is some sense left in us yet. Come now, Captain, consider a little, if you can. Weren't we both half-killed by the shock? Didn't I rescue you from certain death with these two hands? Don't you see Barbican's shoulder still bleeding by the violence of the shock?"

"Correct, friend Michael, correct in every particular," replied the Captain, "But one little question."

"Out with it!"

"Friend Michael, you say we're moving?"

"Yes."

"In consequence of the explosion?"

"Certainly!"

"Which must have been attended with a tremendous report?"

"Of course!"

"Did you hear that report, friend Michael?"

"N—o," replied Ardan, a little disconcerted at the question. "Well, no; I can't say that I did hear any report."

"Did you, friend Barbican?"

"No," replied Barbican, promptly. "I heard no report whatever."

His answer was ready, but his look was quite as disconcerted as Ardan's.

"Well, friend Barbican and friend Michael," said the Captain, very drily as he leered wickedly at both, "put that and that together and tell me what you make of it."

"It's a fact!" exclaimed Barbican, puzzled, but not bewildered. "Why did we not hear that report?"

"Too hard for me," said Ardan. "Give it up!"

The three friends gazed at each other for a while with countenances expressive of much perplexity. Barbican appeared to be the least self-possessed of the party. It was a complete turning of the tables from the state of things a few moments ago. The problem was certainly simple enough, but for that very reason the more inexplicable. If they were moving the explosion must have taken place; but if the explosion had taken place, why had they not heard the report?

Barbican's decision soon put an end to speculation.

"Conjecture being useless," said he, "let us have recourse to facts. First, let us see where we are. Drop the deadlights!"

This operation, simple enough in itself and being immediately undertaken by the whole three, was easily accomplished. The screws fastening the bolts by which the external plates of the deadlights were solidly pinned, readily yielded to the pressure of a powerful wrench. The bolts were then driven outwards, and the holes which had contained them were immediately filled with solid plugs of India rubber. The bolts once driven out, the external plates dropped by their own weight, turning on a hinge, like portholes, and the strong plate-glass forming the light immediately showed itself. A second light exactly similar, could be cleared away on the opposite side of the Projectile; a third, on the summit of the dome, and a fourth, in the centre of the bottom. The travellers could thus take observations in four different directions, having an opportunity of gazing at the firmament through the side lights, and at the Earth and the Moon through the lower and the upper lights of the Projectile.

Ardan and the Captain had commenced examining the floor, previous to operating on the bottom light. But Barbican was the first to get through his work at one of the side lights, and M'Nicholl and Ardan soon heard him shouting:

"No, my friends!" he exclaimed, in tones of decided emotion; "we have *not* fallen back to Earth; nor are we lying in the bottom of the Gulf of Mexico. No! We are driving through space! Look at the stars glittering all around! Brighter, but smaller than we have ever seen them before! We have left the Earth and the Earth's atmosphere far behind us!"

"Hurrah! Hurrah!" cried M'Nicholl and Ardan, feeling as if electric shocks were coursing through them, though they could see nothing, looking down from the side light, but the blackest and profoundest obscurity.

Barbican soon convinced them that this pitchy blackness proved that they were not, and could not be, reposing on the surface of the Earth, where at that moment, everything was illuminated by the bright moonlight; also that they had passed the different layers of the atmosphere, where the diffused and refracted rays would be also sure to reveal themselves through the lights of the Projectile. They were, therefore, certainly moving. No doubt was longer possible.

"It's a fact!" observed the Captain, now quite convinced. "Then I've lost!"

"Let me congratulate you!" cried Ardan, shaking his hand.

"Here is your nine thousand dollars, friend Barbican," said the Captain, taking a roll of greenbacks of high denomination out of his porte-monnaie.

"You want a receipt, don't you, Captain?" asked Barbican, counting the money.

"Yes, I should prefer one, if it is not too much trouble," answered M'Nicholl; "it saves dispute."

Coolly and mechanically, as if seated at his desk, in his office, Barbican opened his memorandum book, wrote a receipt on a blank page, dated, signed and sealed it, and then handed it to the Captain, who put it away carefully among the other papers of his portfolio.

Ardan, taking off his hat, made a profound bow to both of his companions, without saying a word. Such formality, under such extraordinary circumstances, actually paralysed his tongue for the moment. No wonder that he could not understand those Americans. Even Indians would have surprised him by an exhibition of such stoicism. After indulging in silent wonder for a minute or two, he joined his companions who were now busy looking out at the starry sky.

"Where is the Moon?" he asked. "How is it that we cannot see her?"

"The fact of our not seeing her," answered Barbican, "gives me very great satisfaction in one respect; it shows that our Projectile was shot so rapidly out of the Columbiad that it had not time to be impressed with the slightest revolving motion—for us a most fortunate matter. As for the rest—see, there is *Cassiopeia*, a little to the left is *Andromeda*, further down is the great square of *Pegasus*, and to the southwest *Fomalhaut* can be easily seen swallowing the *Cascade*. All this shows we are looking west and consequently cannot see the Moon, which is approaching the zenith from the east. Open the other light—But hold on! Look here! What can this be?"

The three travellers, looking westwardly in the direction of *Alpherat*, saw a brilliant object rapidly approaching them. At a distance, it looked like a dusky moon, but the side turned towards the Earth blazed with a bright light, which every moment became more intense. It came towards them with prodigious velocity and, what was worse, its path lay so directly in the course of the Projectile that a collision seemed inevitable. As it moved onward, from west to east, they could easily see that it rotated on its axis, like all heavenly bodies; in fact, it somewhat resembled a Moon on a small scale, describing its regular orbit around the Earth.

"*Mille tonerres!*" cried Ardan, greatly excited; "what is that? Can it be another projectile?" M'Nicholl, wiping his spectacles, looked again, but made no reply. Barbican looked puzzled and uneasy. A collision was quite possible, and the results, even if not frightful in the highest degree, must be extremely deplorable. The Projectile, if not absolutely dashed to pieces, would be diverted from its own course and dragged along in a new one in obedience to the irresistible attraction of this furious asteroid.

Barbican fully realized that either alternative involved the complete failure of their enterprise. He kept perfectly still, but, never losing his presence of mind, he curiously looked on the approaching object with a gladiatorial eye, as if seeking to detect some unguarded point in his terrible adversary. The Captain was equally silent; he looked like a man who had fully made up his mind to regard every possible contingency with the most stoical indifference. But Ardan's tongue, more fluent than ever, rattled away incessantly.

"Look! Look!" he exclaimed, in tones so perfectly expressive of his rapidly alternating feelings as to render the medium of words totally unnecessary. "How rapidly the cursed thing is nearing us! Plague take your ugly phiz, the more I know you, the less I like you! Every second she doubles in size! Come, Madame Projectile! Stir your stumps a little livelier, old lady! He's making for you as straight as an arrow! We're going right in his way, or he's coming in ours, I can't say which. It's taking a mean advantage of us either way. As for ourselves—what can *we* do! Before such a monster as that we are as helpless as three men in a little skiff shooting down the rapids to the brink of Niagara! Now for it!"

Nearer and nearer it came, but without noise, without sparks, without a trail, though its lower part was brighter than ever. Its path lying little above them, the nearer it came the more the collision seemed inevitable. Imagine yourself caught on a narrow railroad bridge at midnight with an express train approaching at full speed, its reflector already dazzling you with its light, the roar of the cars rattling in your ears, and you may conceive the feelings of the travellers. At last it was so near that the travellers started back in affright, with eyes shut, hair on end, and fully believing their last hour had come. Even then Ardan had his *mot*.

"We can neither switch off, down brakes, nor clap on more steam! Hard luck!"

In an instant all was over. The velocity of the Projectile was fortunately great enough to carry it barely above the dangerous point; and in a flash the terrible bolide disappeared rapidly several hundred yards beneath the affrighted travellers.

"Good bye! And may you never come back!" cried Ardan, hardly able to breathe. "It's perfectly outrageous! Not room enough in infinite space to let an unpretending bullet like ours move about a little without incurring the risk of being run over by such a monster as that! What is it anyhow? Do you know, Barbican?"

"I do," was the reply.

"Of course, you do! What is it that he don't know? Eh, Captain?"

"It is a simple bolide, but one of such enormous dimensions that the Earth's attraction has made it a satellite."

"What!" cried Ardan, "another satellite besides the Moon? I hope there are no more of them!"

"They are pretty numerous," replied Barbican; "but they are so small and they move with such enormous velocity that they are very seldom seen. Petit, the Director of the Observatory of Toulouse, who these last years has devoted much time and care to the observation of bolides, has calculated that the very one we have just encountered moves with such astonishing swiftness that it accomplishes its revolution around the Earth in about 3 hours and 20 minutes!"

"Whew!" whistled Ardan, "where should we be now if it had struck us!"

"You don't mean to say, Barbican," observed M'Nicholl, "that Petit has seen this very one?"

"So it appears," replied Barbican.

"And do all astronomers admit its existence?" asked the Captain.

"Well, some of them have their doubts," replied Barbican—

"If the unbelievers had been here a minute or two ago," interrupted Ardan, "they would never express a doubt again."

"If Petit's calculation is right," continued Barbican, "I can even form a very good idea as to our distance from the Earth."

"It seems to me Barbican can do what he pleases here or elsewhere," observed Ardan to the Captain.

"Let us see, Barbican," asked M'Nicholl; "where has Petit's calculation placed us?"

"The bolide's distance being known," replied Barbican, "at the moment we met it we were a little more than 5 thousand miles from the Earth's surface."

"Five thousand miles already!" cried Ardan, "why we have only just started!"

"Let us see about that," quietly observed the Captain, looking at his chronometer, and calculating with his pencil. "It is now 10 minutes past eleven; we have therefore been 23 minutes on the road. Supposing our initial velocity of 10,000 yards or nearly seven miles a second, to have been kept up, we should by this time be about 9,000 miles from the Earth; but by allowing for friction and gravity, we can hardly be more than 5,500 miles. Yes, friend Barbican, Petit does not seem to be very wrong in his calculations."

But Barbican hardly heard the observation. He had not yet answered the puzzling question that had already presented itself to them for solution; and until he had done so he could not attend to anything else.

"That's all very well and good, Captain," he replied in an absorbed manner, "but we have not yet been able to account for a very strange phenomenon. Why didn't we hear the report?"

No one replying, the conversation came to a stand-still, and Barbican, still absorbed in his reflections, began clearing the second light of its external shutter. In a few minutes the plate dropped, and the Moon beams, flowing in, filled the interior of the Projectile with her brilliant light. The Captain immediately put out the gas, from motives of economy as well as because its glare somewhat interfered with the observation of the interplanetary regions.

The Lunar disc struck the travellers as glittering with a splendor and purity of light that they had never witnessed before. The beams, no longer strained through the misty atmosphere of the Earth, streamed copiously in through the glass and coated the interior walls of the Projectile with a brilliant silvery plating. The intense blackness of the sky enhanced the dazzling radiance of the Moon. Even the stars blazed with a new and unequalled splendor, and, in the absence of a refracting atmosphere, they flamed as bright in the close proximity of the Moon as in any other part of the sky.

You can easily conceive the interest with which these bold travellers gazed on the Starry Queen, the final object of their daring journey. She was now insensibly approaching the zenith, the mathematical point which she was to reach four days later. They presented their telescopes, but her mountains, plains, craters and general characteristics hardly came out a particle more sharply than if they had been viewed from the Earth. Still, her light, unobstructed by air or vapor, shimmered with a lustre actually transplendent. Her disc shone like a mirror of polished platins. The travellers remained for some time absorbed in the silent contemplation of the glorious scene.

"How they're gazing at her this very moment from Stony Hill!" said the Captain at last to break the silence.

"By Jove!" cried Ardan; "It's true! Captain you're right. We were near forgetting our dear old Mother, the Earth. What ungrateful children! Let me feast my eyes once more on the blessed old creature!"

Barbican, to satisfy his companion's desire, immediately commenced to clear away the disc which covered the floor of the Projectile and prevented them from getting at the lower light. This disc, though it had been dashed to the bottom of the Projectile with great violence, was still as strong as ever, and, being made in compartments fastened by screws, to dismount it was no easy matter. Barbican, however, with the help of the others, soon had it all taken apart, and put away the pieces carefully, to serve again in case of need. A round hole about a foot and a half in diameter appeared, bored through the floor of the Projectile. It was closed by a circular pane of plate-glass, which was about six inches thick, fastened by a ring of copper. Below, on the outside, the glass was protected by an aluminium plate, kept in its place by strong bolts and nuts. The latter being unscrewed, the bolts slipped out by their own weight, the shutter fell, and a new communication was established between the interior and the exterior.

Ardan knelt down, applied his eye to the light, and tried to look out. At first everything was quite dark and gloomy.

"I see no Earth!" he exclaimed at last.

"Don't you see a fine ribbon of light?" asked Barbican, "right beneath us? A thin, pale, silvery crescent?"

"Of course I do. Can that be the Earth?"

"*Terra Mater* herself, friend Ardan. That fine fillet of light, now hardly visible on her eastern border, will disappear altogether as soon as the Moon is full. Then, lying as she will be between the Sun and the Moon, her illuminated face will be turned away from us altogether, and for several days she will be involved in impenetrable darkness."

"And that's the Earth!" repeated Ardan, hardly able to believe his eyes, as he continued to gaze on the slight thread of silvery white light, somewhat resembling the appearance of the "Young May Moon" a few hours after sunset.

Barbican's explanation was quite correct. The Earth, in reference to the Moon or the Projectile, was in her last phase, or octant as it is called, and showed a sharp-horned, attenuated, but brilliant crescent strongly relieved by the black background of the sky. Its light, rendered a little bluish by the density of the atmospheric envelopes, was not quite as brilliant as the Moon's. But the Earth's crescent, compared to the Lunar, was of dimensions much greater, being fully 4 times larger. You would have called it a vast, beautiful, but very thin bow extending over the sky. A few points, brighter than the rest, particularly in its concave part, revealed the presence of lofty mountains, probably the Himalayahs. But they disappeared every now and then under thick vapory spots, which are never seen on the Lunar disc. They were the thin concentric cloud rings that surround the terrestrial sphere.

However, the travellers' eyes were soon able to trace the rest of the Earth's surface not only with facility, but even to follow its outline with absolute delight. This was in consequence of two different phenomena, one of which they could easily account for; but the other they could not explain without Barbican's assistance. No wonder. Never before had mortal eye beheld such a sight. Let us take each in its turn.

We all know that the ashy light by means of which we perceive what is called the *Old Moon in the Young Moon's arms* is due to the Earth-shine, or the reflection of the solar rays from the Earth to the Moon. By a phenomenon exactly identical, the travellers could now see that portion of the Earth's surface which was unillumined by the Sun; only, as, in consequence of the different areas of the respective surfaces, the *Earthlight* is thirteen times more intense than the *Moonlight*, the dark portion of the Earth's disc appeared considerably more adumbrated than the *Old Moon*.

But the other phenomenon had burst on them so suddenly that they uttered a cry loud enough to wake up Barbican from his problem. They had discovered a true starry ring! Around the Earth's outline, a ring, of internally well defined thickness, but somewhat hazy on the outside, could easily be traced by its surpassing brilliancy. Neither the *Pleiades*, the *Northern Crown*, the *Magellanic Clouds* nor the great nebulas of *Orion*, or of *Argo*, no sparkling cluster, no corona, no group of glittering star-dust that the travellers had ever gazed at, presented such attractions as the diamond ring they now saw encompassing the Earth, just as the brass meridian encompasses a terrestrial globe. The resplendency of its light enchanted them, its pure softness delighted them, its perfect regularity astonished them. What was it? they asked Barbican. In a few words he explained it. The beautiful luminous ring was simply an optical illusion, produced by the refraction of the terrestrial atmosphere. All the stars in the neighborhood of the Earth, and many actually behind it, had their rays refracted, diffused, radiated, and finally converged to a focus by the atmosphere, as if by a double convex lens of gigantic power.

Whilst the travellers were profoundly absorbed in the contemplation of this wondrous sight, a sparkling shower of shooting stars suddenly flashed over the Earth's dark surface, making it for a moment as bright as the external ring. Hundreds of bolides, catching fire from contact with the atmosphere, streaked the darkness with their luminous trails, overspreading it occasionally with sheets of electric flame. The Earth was just then in her perihelion, and we all know that the months of November and December are so highly favorable to the appearance of these meteoric showers that at the famous display of November, 1866, astronomers counted as many as 8,000 between midnight and four o'clock.

Barbican explained the whole matter in a few words. The Earth, when nearest to the sun, occasionally plunges into a group of countless meteors travelling like comets, in eccentric orbits around the grand centre of our solar system. The atmosphere strikes the rapidly moving bodies with such violence as to set them on fire and render them visible to us in beautiful star showers. But to this simple explanation of the famous November meteors Ardan would not listen. He preferred believing that Mother Earth, feeling that her three daring children were still looking at her, though five thousand miles away, shot off her best rocket-signals to show that she still thought of them and would never let them out of her watchful eye.

For hours they continued to gaze with indescribable interest on the faintly luminous mass so easily distinguishable among the other heavenly bodies. Jupiter blazed on their right, Mars flashed his ruddy light on their left, Saturn with his rings looked like a round white spot on a black wall; even Venus they could see almost directly under them, easily recognizing her by her soft, sweetly scintillant light. But no planet or constellation possessed any attraction for the travellers, as long as their eyes could trace that shadowy, crescent-edged, diamond-girdled, meteor-furrowed spheroid, the theatre of their existence, the home of so many undying desires, the mysterious cradle of their race!

Meantime the Projectile cleaved its way upwards, rapidly, unswervingly, though with a gradually retarding velocity. As the Earth sensibly grew darker, and the travellers' eyes grew dimmer, an irresistible somnolency slowly stole over their weary frames. The extraordinary excitement they had gone through during the last four or five hours, was naturally followed by a profound reaction.

"Captain, you're nodding," said Ardan at last, after a longer silence than usual; "the fact is, Barbican is the only wake man of the party, because he is puzzling over his problem. *Dum vivimus vivamus*! As we are asleep let us be asleep!"

So saying he threw himself on the mattress, and his companions immediately followed the example.

They had been lying hardly a quarter of an hour, when Barbican started up with a cry so loud and sudden as instantly to awaken his companions.

The bright moonlight showed them the President sitting up in his bed, his eye blazing, his arms waving, as he shouted in a tone reminding them of the day they had found him in St. Helena wood.

"*Eureka!* I've got it! I know it!"

"What have you got?" cried Ardan, bouncing up and seizing him by the right hand.

"What do you know?" cried the Captain, stretching over and seizing him by the left.

"The reason why we did not hear the report!"

"Well, why did not we hear it!" asked both rapidly in the same breath.

"Because we were shot up 30 times faster than sound can travel!"

III

They Make Themselves at Home and Feel Quite Comfortable

This curious explanation given, and its soundness immediately recognized, the three friends were soon fast wrapped in the arms of Morpheus. Where in fact could they have found a spot more favorable for undisturbed repose? On land, where the dwellings, whether in populous city or lonely country, continually experience every shock that thrills the Earth's crust? At sea, where between waves or winds or paddles or screws or machinery, everything is tremor, quiver or jar? In the air, where the balloon is incessantly twirling, oscillating, on account of the ever varying strata of different densities, and even occasionally threatening to spill you out? The Projectile alone, floating grandly through the absolute void, in the midst of the profoundest silence, could offer to its inmates the possibility of enjoying slumber the most complete, repose the most profound.

There is no telling how long our three daring travellers would have continued to enjoy their sleep, if it had not been suddenly terminated by an unexpected noise about seven o'clock in the morning of December 2nd, eight hours after their departure.

This noise was most decidedly of barking.

"The dogs! It's the dogs!" cried Ardan, springing up at a bound.

"They must be hungry!" observed the Captain.

"We have forgotten the poor creatures!" cried Barbican.

"Where can they have gone to?" asked Ardan, looking for them in all directions.

At last they found one of them hiding under the sofa. Thunderstruck and perfectly bewildered by the terrible shock, the poor animal had kept close in its hiding place, never daring to utter a sound, until at last the pangs of hunger had proved too strong even for its fright.

They readily recognized the amiable Diana, but they could not allure the shivering, whining animal from her retreat without a good deal of coaxing. Ardan talked to her in his most honeyed and seductive accents, while trying to pull her out by the neck.

"Come out to your friends, charming Diana," he went on, "come out, my beauty, destined for a lofty niche in the temple of canine glory! Come out, worthy scion of a race deemed worthy by the Egyptians to be a companion of the great god, Anubis, by the Christians, to be a friend of the good Saint Roch! Come out and partake of a glory before which the stars of Montargis and of St. Bernard shall henceforward pale their ineffectual fire! Come out, my lady, and let me think o'er the countless multiplication of thy species, so that, while sailing through the interplanetary spaces, we may indulge in endless flights of fancy on the number and variety of thy descendants who will ere long render the Selenitic atmosphere vocal with canine ululation!"

Diana, whether flattered or not, allowed herself to be dragged out, still uttering short, plaintive whines. A hasty examination satisfying her friends that she was more frightened than hurt and more hungry than either, they continued their search for her companion.

"Satellite! Satellite! Step this way, sir!" cried Ardan. But no Satellite appeared and, what was worse, not the slightest sound indicated his presence. At last he was discovered on a ledge in the upper portion of the Projectile, whither he had been shot by the terrible concussion. Less fortunate than his female companion, the poor fellow had received a frightful shock and his life was evidently in great danger.

"The acclimatization project looks shaky!" cried Ardan, handing the animal very carefully and tenderly to the others. Poor Satellite's head had been crushed against the roof, but, though recovery seemed hopeless, they laid the body on a soft cushion, and soon had the satisfaction of hearing it give vent to a slight sigh.

"Good!" said Ardan, "while there's life there's hope. You must not die yet, old boy. We shall nurse you. We know our duty and shall not shirk the responsibility. I should rather lose the right arm off my body than be the cause of your death, poor Satellite! Try a little water?"

The suffering creature swallowed the cool draught with evident avidity, then sunk into a deep slumber.

The friends, sitting around and having nothing more to do, looked out of the window and began once more to watch the Earth and the Moon with great attention. The glittering crescent of the Earth was evidently narrower than it had been the preceding evening, but its volume was still enormous when compared to the Lunar crescent, which was now rapidly assuming the proportions of a perfect circle.

"By Jove," suddenly exclaimed Ardan, "why didn't we start at the moment of Full Earth?—that is when our globe and the Sun were in opposition?"

"Why *should* we!" growled M'Nicholl.

"Because in that case we should be now looking at the great continents and the great seas in a new light—the former glittering under the solar rays, the latter darker and somewhat shaded, as we see them on certain maps. How I should like to get a glimpse at those poles of the Earth, on which the eye of man has never yet lighted!"

"True," replied Barbican, "but if the Earth had been Full, the Moon would have been New, that is to say, invisible to us on account of solar irradiation. Of the two it is much preferable to be able to keep the point of arrival in view rather than the point of departure."

"You're right, Barbican," observed the Captain; "besides, once we're in the Moon, the long Lunar night will give us plenty of time to gaze our full at yonder great celestial body, our former home, and still swarming with our fellow beings."

"Our fellow beings no longer, dear boy!" cried Ardan. "We inhabit a new world peopled by ourselves alone, the Projectile! Ardan is Barbican's fellow being, and Barbican M'Nicholl's. Beyond us, outside us, humanity ends, and we are now the only inhabitants of this microcosm, and so we shall continue till the moment when we become Selenites pure and simple."

"Which shall be in about eighty-eight hours from now," replied the Captain.

"Which is as much as to say—?" asked Ardan.

"That it is half past eight," replied M'Nicholl.

"My regular hour for breakfast," exclaimed Ardan, "and I don't see the shadow of a reason for changing it now."

The proposition was most acceptable, especially to the Captain, who frequently boasted that, whether on land or water, on mountain summits or in the depths of mines, he had never missed a meal in all his life. In escaping from the Earth, our travellers felt that they had by no means escaped from the laws of humanity, and their stomachs now called on them lustily to fill the aching void. Ardan, as a Frenchman, claimed the post of chief cook, an important office, but his companions yielded it with alacrity. The gas furnished the requisite heat, and the provision chest supplied the materials for their first repast. They commenced with three plates of excellent soup, extracted from *Liebig's* precious tablets, prepared from the best beef that ever roamed over the Pampas.

To this succeeded several tenderloin beefsteaks, which, though reduced to a small bulk by the hydraulic engines of the *American Dessicating Company*, were pronounced to be fully as tender, juicy and savory as if they had just left the gridiron of a London Club House. Ardan even swore that they were "bleeding," and the others were too busy to contradict him.

Preserved vegetables of various kinds, "fresher than nature," according to Ardan, gave an agreeable variety to the entertainment, and these were followed by several cups of magnificent tea, unanimously allowed to be the best they had ever tasted. It was an odoriferous young hyson gathered that very year, and presented to the Emperor of Russia by the famous rebel chief Yakub Kushbegi, and of which Alexander had expressed himself as very happy in being able to send a few boxes to his friend, the distinguished President of the Baltimore Gun Club. To crown the meal, Ardan unearthed an exquisite bottle of *Chambertin*, and, in glasses sparkling with the richest juice of the *Cote d'or,* the travellers drank to the speedy union of the Earth and her satellite.

And, as if his work among the generous vineyards of Burgundy had not been enough to show his interest in the matter, even the Sun wished to join the party. Precisely at this moment, the Projectile beginning to leave the conical shadow cast by the Earth, the rays of the glorious King of Day struck its lower surface, not obliquely, but perpendicularly, on account of the slight obliquity of the Moon's orbit with that of the Earth.

"The Sun," cried Ardan.

"Of course," said Barbican, looking at his watch, "he's exactly up to time."

"How is it that we see him only through the bottom light of our Projectile?" asked Ardan.

"A moment's reflection must tell you," replied Barbican, "that when we started last night, the Sun was almost directly below us; therefore, as we continue to move in a straight line, he must still be in our rear."

"That's clear enough," said the Captain, "but another consideration, I'm free to say, rather perplexes me. Since our Earth lies between us and the Sun, why don't we see the sunlight forming a great ring around the globe, in other words, instead of the full Sun that we plainly see there below, why do we not witness an annular eclipse?"

"Your cool, clear head has not yet quite recovered from the shock, my dear Captain;" replied Barbican, with a smile. "For two reasons we can't see the ring eclipse: on account of the angle the Moon's orbit makes with the Earth, the three bodies are not at present in a direct line; we, therefore, see the Sun a little to the west of the earth; secondly, even if they were exactly in a straight line, we should still be far from the point whence an annular eclipse would be visible."

"That's true," said Ardan; "the cone of the Earth's shadow must extend far beyond the Moon."

"Nearly four times as far," said Barbican; "still, as the Moon's orbit and the Earth's do not lie in exactly the same plane, a Lunar eclipse can occur only when the nodes coincide with the period of the Full Moon, which is generally twice, never more than three times in a year. If we had started about four days before the occurrence of a Lunar eclipse, we should travel all the time in the dark. This would have been obnoxious for many reasons."

"One, for instance?"

"An evident one is that, though at the present moment we are moving through a vacuum, our Projectile, steeped in the solar rays, revels in their light and heat. Hence great saving in gas, an important point in our household economy."

In effect, the solar rays, tempered by no genial medium like our atmosphere, soon began to glare and glow with such intensity, that the Projectile under their influence, felt like suddenly passing from winter to summer. Between the Moon overhead and the Sun beneath it was actually inundated with fiery rays.

"One feels good here," cried the Captain, rubbing his hands.

"A little too good," cried Ardan. "It's already like a hot-house. With a little garden clay, I could raise you a splendid crop of peas in twenty-four hours. I hope in heaven the walls of our Projectile won't melt like wax!"

"Don't be alarmed, dear friend," observed Barbican, quietly. "The Projectile has seen the worst as far as heat is concerned; when tearing through the atmosphere, she endured a temperature with which what she is liable to at present stands no comparison. In fact, I should not be astonished if, in the eyes of our friends at Stony Hill, it had resembled for a moment or two a red-hot meteor."

"Poor Marston must have looked on us as roasted alive!" observed Ardan.

"What could have saved us I'm sure I can't tell," replied Barbican. "I must acknowledge that against such a danger, I had made no provision whatever."

"I knew all about it," said the Captain, "and on the strength of it, I had laid my fifth wager."

"Probably," laughed Ardan, "there was not time enough to get grilled in: I have heard of men who dipped their fingers into molten iron with impunity."

Whilst Ardan and the Captain were arguing the point, Barbican began busying himself in making everything as comfortable as if, instead of a four days' journey, one of four years was contemplated. The reader, no doubt, remembers that the floor of the Projectile contained about 50 square feet; that the chamber was nine feet high; that space was economized as much as possible, nothing but the most absolute necessities being admitted, of which each was kept strictly in its own place; therefore, the travellers had room enough to move around in with a certain liberty. The thick glass window in the floor was quite as solid as any other part of it; but the Sun, streaming in from below, lit up the Projectile strangely, producing some very singular and startling effects of light appearing to come in by the wrong way.

The first thing now to be done was to see after the water cask and the provision chest. They were not injured in the slightest respect, thanks to the means taken to counteract the shock. The provisions were in good condition, and abundant enough to supply the travellers for a whole year—Barbican having taken care to be on the safe side, in case the Projectile might land in a deserted region of the Moon. As for the water and the other liquors, the travellers had enough only for two months. Relying on the latest observations of astronomers, they had convinced themselves that the Moon's atmosphere, being heavy, dense and thick in the deep valleys, springs and streams of water could hardly fail to show themselves there. During the journey, therefore, and for the first year of their installation on the Lunar continent, the daring travellers would be pretty safe from all danger of hunger or thirst.

The air supply proved also to be quite satisfactory. The *Reiset* and *Regnault* apparatus for producing oxygen contained a supply of chlorate of potash sufficient for two months. As the productive material had to be maintained at a temperature of between 7 and 8 hundred degrees Fahr., a steady consumption of gas was required; but here too the supply far exceeded the demand. The whole arrangement worked charmingly, requiring only an odd glance now and then. The high temperature changing the chlorate into a chloride, the oxygen was disengaged gradually but abundantly, every eighteen pounds of chlorate of potash, furnishing the seven pounds of oxygen necessary for the daily consumption of the inmates of the Projectile.

Still—as the reader need hardly be reminded—it was not sufficient to renew the exhausted oxygen; the complete purification of the air required the absorption of the carbonic acid, exhaled from the lungs. For nearly 12 hours the atmosphere had been gradually becoming more and more charged with this deleterious gas, produced from the combustion of the blood by the inspired oxygen. The Captain soon saw this, by noticing with what difficulty Diana was panting. She even appeared to be smothering, for the carbonic acid—as in the famous *Grotto del Cane* on the banks of Lake Agnano, near Naples—was collecting like water on the floor of the Projectile, on account of its great specific gravity. It already threatened the poor dog's life, though not yet endangering that of her masters. The Captain, seeing this state of things, hastily laid on the floor one or two cups containing caustic potash and water, and stirred the mixture gently: this substance, having a powerful affinity for carbonic acid, greedily absorbed it, and after a few moments the air was completely purified.

The others had begun by this time to check off the state of the instruments. The thermometer and the barometer were all right, except one self-recorder of which the glass had got broken. An excellent aneroid barometer, taken safe and sound out of its wadded box, was carefully hung on a hook in the wall. It marked not only the pressure of the air in the Projectile, but also the quantity of the watery vapor that it contained. The needle, oscillating a little beyond thirty, pointed pretty steadily at "*Fair*."

The mariner's compasses were also found to be quite free from injury. It is, of course, hardly necessary to say that the needles pointed in no particular direction, the magnetic pole of the Earth being unable at such a distance to exercise any appreciable influence on them. But when brought to the Moon, it was expected that these compasses, once more subjected to the influence of the current, would attest certain phenomena. In any case, it would be interesting to verify if the Earth and her satellite were similarly affected by the magnetic forces.

A hypsometer, or instrument for ascertaining the heights of the Lunar mountains by the barometric pressure under which water boils, a sextant to measure the altitude of the Sun, a theodolite for taking horizontal or vertical angles, telescopes, of indispensable necessity when the travellers should approach the Moon,—all these instruments, carefully examined, were found to be still in perfect working order, notwithstanding the violence of the terrible shock at the start.

As to the picks, spades, and other tools that had been carefully selected by the Captain; also the bags of various kinds of grain and the bundles of various kinds of shrubs, which Ardan expected to transplant to the Lunar plains—they were all still safe in their places around the upper corners of the Projectile.

Some other articles were also up there which evidently possessed great interest for the Frenchman. What they were nobody else seemed to know, and he seemed to be in no hurry to tell. Every now and then, he would climb up, by means of iron pins fixed in the wall, to inspect his treasures; whatever they were, he arranged them and rearranged them with evident pleasure, and as he rapidly passed a careful hand through certain mysterious boxes, he joyfully sang in the falsest possible of false voices the lively piece from *Nicolo*:

> *Le temps est beau, la route est belle,*
> *La promenade est un plaisir.*

{The day is bright, our hearts are light.}
{How sweet to rove through wood and dell.}

or the well known air in *Mignon*:

> *Legères hirondelles,*
> *Oiseaux bénis de Dieu,*
> *Ouvrez-ouvrez vos ailes,*
> *Envolez-vous! adieu!*

{Farewell, happy Swallows, farewell!}
{With summer for ever to dwell}
{Ye leave our northern strand}
{For the genial southern land}
{Balmy with breezes bland.}
{Return? Ah, who can tell?}
{Farewell, happy Swallows, farewell!}

Barbican was much gratified to find that his rockets and other fireworks had not received the least injury. He relied upon them for the performance of a very important service as soon as the Projectile, having passed the point of neutral attraction between the Earth and the Moon, would begin to fall with accelerated velocity towards the Lunar surface. This descent, though—thanks to the respective volumes of the attracting bodies—six times less rapid than it would have been on the surface of the Earth, would still be violent enough to dash the Projectile into a thousand pieces. But Barbican confidently expected by means of his powerful rockets to offer very considerable obstruction to the violence of this fall, if not to counteract its terrible effects altogether.

The inspection having thus given general satisfaction, the travellers once more set themselves to watching external space through the lights in the sides and the floor of the Projectile.

Everything still appeared to be in the same state as before. Nothing was changed. The vast arch of the celestial dome glittered with stars, and constellations blazed with a light clear and pure enough to throw an astronomer into an ecstasy of admiration. Below them shone the Sun, like the mouth of a white-hot furnace, his dazzling disc defined sharply on the pitch-black back-ground of the sky. Above them the Moon, reflecting back his rays from her glowing surface, appeared to stand motionless in the midst of the starry host.

A little to the east of the Sun, they could see a pretty large dark spot, like a hole in the sky, the broad silver fringe on one edge fading off into a faint glimmering mist on the other—it was the Earth. Here and there in all directions, nebulous masses gleamed like large flakes of star dust, in which, from nadir to zenith, the eye could trace without a break that vast ring of impalpable star powder, the famous *Milky Way*, through the midst of which the beams of our glorious Sun struggle with the dusky pallor of a star of only the fourth magnitude.

Our observers were never weary of gazing on this magnificent and novel spectacle, of the grandeur of which, it is hardly necessary to say, no description can give an adequate idea. What profound reflections it suggested to their understandings! What vivid emotions it enkindled in their imaginations! Barbican, desirous of commenting the story of the journey while still influenced by these inspiring impressions, noted carefully hour by hour every fact that signalized the beginning of his enterprise. He wrote out his notes very carefully and systematically, his round full hand, as business-like as ever, never betraying the slightest emotion.

The Captain was quite as busy, but in a different way. Pulling out his tablets, he reviewed his calculations regarding the motion of projectiles, their velocities, ranges and paths, their retardations and their accelerations, jotting down the figures with a rapidity wonderful to behold. Ardan neither wrote nor calculated, but kept up an incessant fire of small talk, now with Barbican, who hardly ever answered him, now with M'Nicholl, who never heard him, occasionally with Diana, who never understood him, but oftenest with himself, because, as he said, he liked not only to talk to a sensible man but also to hear what a sensible man had to say. He never stood still for a moment, but kept "bobbing around" with the effervescent briskness of a bee, at one time roosting at the top of the ladder, at another peering through the floor light, now to the right, then to the left, always humming scraps from the *Opera Bouffe*, but never changing the air. In the small space which was then a whole world to the travellers, he represented to the life the animation and loquacity of the French, and I need hardly say he played his part to perfection.

The eventful day, or, to speak more correctly, the space of twelve hours which with us forms a day, ended for our travellers with an abundant supper, exquisitely cooked. It was highly enjoyed.

No incident had yet occurred of a nature calculated to shake their confidence. Apprehending none therefore, full of hope rather and already certain of success, they were soon lost in a peaceful slumber, whilst the Projectile, moving rapidly, though with a velocity uniformly retarding, still cleaved its way through the pathless regions of the empyrean.

IV

A Chapter for the Cornell Girls

No incident worth recording occurred during the night, if night indeed it could be called. In reality there was now no night or even day in the Projectile, or rather, strictly speaking, it was always *night* on the upper end of the bullet, and always *day* on the lower. Whenever, therefore, the words *night* and *day* occur in our story, the reader will readily understand them as referring to those spaces of time that are so called in our Earthly almanacs, and were so measured by the travellers' chronometers.

The repose of our friends must indeed have been undisturbed, if absolute freedom from sound or jar of any kind could secure tranquillity. In spite of its immense velocity, the Projectile still seemed to be perfectly motionless. Not the slightest sign of movement could be detected. Change of locality, though ever so rapid, can never reveal itself to our senses when it takes place in a vacuum, or when the enveloping atmosphere travels at the same rate as the moving body. Though we are incessantly whirled around the Sun at the rate of about seventy thousand miles an hour, which of us is conscious of the slightest motion? In such a case, as far as sensation is concerned, motion and repose are absolutely identical. Neither has any effect one way or another on a material body. Is such a body in motion? It remains in motion until some obstacle stops it. Is it at rest? It remains at rest until some superior force compels it to change its position. This indifference of bodies to motion or rest is what physicists call *inertia*.

Barbican and his companions, therefore, shut up in the Projectile, could readily imagine themselves to be completely motionless. Had they been outside, the effect would have been precisely the same. No rush of air, no jarring sensation would betray the slightest movement. But for the sight of the Moon gradually growing larger above them, and of the Earth gradually growing smaller beneath them, they could safely swear that they were fast anchored in an ocean of deathlike immobility.

Towards the morning of next day (December 3), they were awakened by a joyful, but quite unexpected sound.

"Cock-a-doodle! doo!" accompanied by a decided flapping of wings.

The Frenchman, on his feet in one instant and on the top of the ladder in another, attempted to shut the lid of a half open box, speaking in an angry but suppressed voice:

"Stop this hullabaloo, won't you? Do you want me to fail in my great combination!"

"Hello?" cried Barbican and M'Nicholl, starting up and rubbing their eyes.

"What noise was that?" asked Barbican.

"Seems to me I heard the crowing of a cock," observed the Captain.

"I never thought your ears could be so easily deceived, Captain," cried Ardan, quickly, "Let us try it again," and, flapping his ribs with his arms, he gave vent to a crow so loud and natural that the lustiest chanticleer that ever saluted the orb of day might be proud of it.

The Captain roared right out, and even Barbican snickered, but as they saw that their companion evidently wanted to conceal something, they immediately assumed straight faces and pretended to think no more about the matter.

"Barbican," said Ardan, coming down the ladder and evidently anxious to change the conversation, "have you any idea of what I was thinking about all night?"

"Not the slightest."

"I was thinking of the promptness of the reply you received last year from the authorities of Cambridge University, when you asked them about the feasibility of sending a bullet to the Moon. You know very well by this time what a perfect ignoramus I am in Mathematics. I own I have been often puzzled when thinking on what grounds they could form such a positive opinion, in a case where I am certain that the calculation must be an exceedingly delicate matter."

"The feasibility, you mean to say," replied Barbican, "not exactly of sending a bullet to the Moon, but of sending it to the neutral point between the Earth and the Moon, which lies at about nine-tenths of the journey, where the two attractions counteract each other. Because that point once passed, the Projectile would reach the Moon's surface by virtue of its own weight."

"Well, reaching that neutral point be it;" replied Ardan, "but, once more, I should like to know how they have been able to come at the necessary initial velocity of 12,000 yards a second?"

"Nothing simpler," answered Barbican.

"Could you have done it yourself?" asked the Frenchman.

"Without the slightest difficulty. The Captain and myself could have readily solved the problem, only the reply from the University saved us the trouble."

"Well, Barbican, dear boy," observed Ardan, "all I've got to say is, you might chop the head off my body, beginning with my feet, before you could make me go through such a calculation."

"Simply because you don't understand Algebra," replied Barbican, quietly.

"Oh! that's all very well!" cried Ardan, with an ironical smile. "You great $x+y$ men think you settle everything by uttering the word *Algebra*!"

"Ardan," asked Barbican, "do you think people could beat iron without a hammer, or turn up furrows without a plough?"

"Hardly."

"Well, Algebra is an instrument or utensil just as much as a hammer or a plough, and a very good instrument too if you know how to make use of it."

"You're in earnest?"

"Quite so."

"And you can handle the instrument right before my eyes?"

"Certainly, if it interests you so much."

"You can show me how they got at the initial velocity of our Projectile?"

"With the greatest pleasure. By taking into proper consideration all the elements of the problem, viz.: (1) the distance between the centres of the Earth and the Moon, (2) the Earth's radius, (3) its volume, and (4) the Moon's volume, I can easily calculate what must be the initial velocity, and that too by a very simple formula."

"Let us have the formula."

"In one moment; only I can't give you the curve really described by the Projectile as it moves between the Earth and the Moon; this is to be obtained by allowing for their combined movement around the Sun. I will consider the Earth and the Sun to be motionless, that being sufficient for our present purpose."

"Why so?"

"Because to give you that exact curve would be to solve a point in the 'Problem of the Three Bodies,' which Integral Calculus has not yet reached."

"What!" cried Ardan, in a mocking tone, "is there really anything that Mathematics can't do?"

"Yes," said Barbican, "there is still a great deal that Mathematics can't even attempt."

"So far, so good;" resumed Ardan. "Now then what is this Integral Calculus of yours?"

"It is a branch of Mathematics that has for its object the summation of a certain infinite series of indefinitely small terms: but for the solution of which, we must generally know the function of which a given function is the differential coefficient. In other words," continued Barbican, "in it we return from the differential coefficient, to the function from which it was deduced."

"Clear as mud!" cried Ardan, with a hearty laugh.

"Now then, let me have a bit of paper and a pencil," added Barbican, "and in half an hour you shall have your formula; meantime you can easily find something interesting to do."

In a few seconds Barbican was profoundly absorbed in his problem, while M'Nicholl was watching out of the window, and Ardan was busily employed in preparing breakfast.

The morning meal was not quite ready, when Barbican, raising his head, showed Ardan a page covered with algebraic signs at the end of which stood the following formula:—

$$\frac{1}{2}\left(v'^2 - v^2\right) = gr\left\{\frac{r}{x} - 1 + \frac{m'}{m}\left(\frac{r}{d-x} - \frac{r}{d-r}\right)\right\}$$

"Which means?" asked Ardan.

"It means," said the Captain, now taking part in the discussion, "that the half of v prime squared minus v squared equals gr multiplied by r over x minus one plus m prime over m multiplied by r over d minus x minus r over d minus r. . . that is—"

"That is," interrupted Ardan, in a roar of laughter, "x stradlegs on y, making for z and jumping over p! Do *you* mean to say you understand the terrible jargon, Captain?"

"Nothing is clearer, Ardan."

"You too, Captain! Then of course I must give in gracefully, and declare that the sun at noon-day is not more palpably evident than the sense of Barbican's formula."

"You asked for Algebra, you know," observed Barbican.

"Rock crystal is nothing to it!"

"The fact is, Barbican," said the Captain, who had been looking over the paper, "you have worked the thing out very well. You have the integral equation of the living forces, and I have no doubt it will give us the result sought for."

"Yes, but I should like to understand it, you know," cried Ardan: "I would give ten years of the Captain's life to understand it!"

"Listen then," said Barbican. "Half of v prime squared less v squared, is the formula giving us the half variation of the living force."

"Mac pretends he understands all that!"

"You need not be a *Solomon* to do it," said the Captain. "All these signs that you appear to consider so cabalistic form a language the clearest, the shortest, and the most logical, for all those who can read it."

"You pretend, Captain, that, by means of these hieroglyphics, far more incomprehensible than the sacred Ibis of the Egyptians, you can discover the velocity at which the Projectile should start?"

"Most undoubtedly," replied the Captain, "and, by the same formula I can even tell you the rate of our velocity at any particular point of our journey."

"You can?"

"I can."

"Then you're just as deep a one as our President."

"No, Ardan; not at all. The really difficult part of the question Barbican has done. That is, to make out such an equation as takes into account all the conditions of the problem. After that, it's a simple affair of Arithmetic, requiring only a knowledge of the four rules to work it out."

"Very simple," observed Ardan, who always got muddled at any kind of a difficult sum in addition.

"Captain," said Barbican, "*you* could have found the formulas too, if you tried."

"I don't know about that," was the Captain's reply, "but I do know that this formula is wonderfully come at."

"Now, Ardan, listen a moment," said Barbican, "and you will see what sense there is in all these letters."

"I listen," sighed Ardan with the resignation of a martyr.

"d is the distance from the centre of the Earth to the centre of the Moon, for it is from the centres that we must calculate the attractions."

"That I comprehend."

"r is the radius of the Earth."

"That I comprehend."

"m is the mass or volume of the Earth; m prime that of the Moon. We must take the mass of the two attracting bodies into consideration, since attraction is in direct proportion to their masses."

"That I comprehend."

"g is the gravity or the velocity acquired at the end of a second by a body falling towards the centre of the Earth. Clear?"

"That I comprehend."

"Now I represent by x the varying distance that separates the Projectile from the centre of the Earth, and by v prime its velocity at that distance."

"That I comprehend."

"Finally, v is its velocity when quitting our atmosphere."

"Yes," chimed in the Captain, "it is for this point, you see, that the velocity had to be calculated, because we know already that the initial velocity is exactly the three halves of the velocity when the Projectile quits the atmosphere."

"That I don't comprehend," cried the Frenchman, energetically.

"It's simple enough, however," said Barbican.

"Not so simple as a simpleton," replied the Frenchman.

"The Captain merely means," said Barbican, "that at the instant the Projectile quitted the terrestrial atmosphere it had already lost a third of its initial velocity."

"So much as a third?"

"Yes, by friction against the atmospheric layers: the quicker its motion, the greater resistance it encountered."

"That of course I admit, but your v squared and your v prime squared rattle in my head like nails in a box!"

"The usual effect of Algebra on one who is a stranger to it; to finish you, our next step is to express numerically the value of these several symbols. Now some of them are already known, and some are to be calculated."

"Hand the latter over to me," said the Captain.

"First," continued Barbican: "r, the Earth's radius is, in the latitude of Florida, about 3,921 miles. d, the distance from the centre of the Earth to the centre of the Moon is 56 terrestrial radii, which the Captain calculates to be. . .?"

"To be," cried M'Nicholl working rapidly with his pencil, "219,572 miles, the moment the Moon is in her *perigee*, or nearest point to the Earth."

"Very well," continued Barbican. "Now m prime over m, that is the ratio of the Moon's mass to that of the Earth is about the 1/81. g gravity being at Florida about 32-1/4 feet, of course $g \times r$ must be—how much, Captain?"

"38,465 miles," replied M'Nicholl.

"Now then?" asked Ardan.

"Now then," replied Barbican, "the expression having numerical values, I am trying to find v, that is to say, the initial velocity which the Projectile must possess in order to reach the point where the two attractions neutralize each other. Here the velocity being null, v prime becomes zero, and x the required distance of this neutral point must be represented by the nine-tenths of d, the distance between the two centres."

"I have a vague kind of idea that it must be so," said Ardan.

"I shall, therefore, have the following result;" continued Barbican, figuring up; "x being nine-tenths of d, and v prime being zero, my formula becomes:—

$$v^2 = gr\left\{1 - \frac{10r}{d} - \frac{1}{81}\left(\frac{10r}{d} - \frac{r}{d-r}\right)\right\}$$ "

The Captain read it off rapidly.

"Right! that's correct!" he cried.

"You think so?" asked Barbican.

"As true as Euclid!" exclaimed M'Nicholl.

"Wonderful fellows," murmured the Frenchman, smiling with admiration.

"You understand now, Ardan, don't you?" asked Barbican.

"Don't I though?" exclaimed Ardan, "why my head is splitting with it!"

"Therefore," continued Barbican,

$$" 2v^2 = 2gr\left\{1 - \frac{10r}{d} - \frac{1}{81}\left(\frac{10r}{d} - \frac{r}{d-r}\right)\right\}$$ "

"And now," exclaimed M'Nicholl, sharpening his pencil; "in order to obtain the velocity of the Projectile when leaving the atmosphere, we have only to make a slight calculation."

The Captain, who before clerking on a Mississippi steamboat had been professor of Mathematics in an Indiana university, felt quite at home at the work. He rained figures from his pencil with a velocity that would have made Marston stare. Page after page was filled with his multiplications and divisions, while Barbican looked quietly on, and Ardan impatiently stroked his head and ears to keep down a rising head-ache.

"Well?" at last asked Barbican, seeing the Captain stop and throw a somewhat hasty glance over his work.

"Well," answered M'Nicholl slowly but confidently, "the calculation is made, I think correctly; and v, that is, the velocity of the Projectile when quitting the atmosphere, sufficient to carry it to the neutral point, should be at least. . ."

"How much?" asked Barbican, eagerly.

"Should be at least 11,972 yards the first second."

"What!" cried Barbican, jumping off his seat. "How much did you say?"

"11,972 yards the first second it quits the atmosphere."

"Oh, malediction!" cried Barbican, with a gesture of terrible despair.

"What's the matter?" asked Ardan, very much surprised.

"Enough is the matter!" answered Barbican excitedly. "This velocity having been diminished by a third, our initial velocity should have been at least. . ."

"17,958 yards the first second!" cried M'Nicholl, rapidly flourishing his pencil.

"But the Cambridge Observatory having declared that 12,000 yards the first second were sufficient, our Projectile started with no greater velocity!"

"Well?" asked M'Nicholl.

"Well, such a velocity will never do!"

"How??"
"How!!" } cried the Captain and Ardan in one voice.

"We can never reach the neutral point!"

"Thunder and lightning"

"Fire and Fury!"

"We can't get even halfway!"

"Heaven and Earth!"

Mille noms d'un boulet! cried Ardan, wildly gesticulating.

"And we shall fall back to the Earth!"

"Oh!"

"Ah!"

They could say no more. This fearful revelation took them like a stroke of apoplexy.

V

The Colds of Space

How could they imagine that the Observatory men had committed such a blunder? Barbican would not believe it possible. He made the Captain go over his calculation again and again; but no flaw was to be found in it. He himself carefully examined it, figure after figure, but he could find nothing wrong. They both took up the formula and subjected it to the strongest tests; but it was invulnerable. There was no denying the fact. The Cambridge professors had undoubtedly blundered in saying that an initial velocity of 12,000 yards a second would be enough to carry them to the neutral point. A velocity of nearly 18,000 yards would be the very lowest required for such a purpose. They had simply forgotten to allow a third for friction.

The three friends kept profound silence for some time. Breakfast now was the last thing thought of. Barbican, with teeth grating, fingers clutching, and eye-brows closely contracting, gazed grimly through the window. The Captain, as a last resource, once more examined his calculations, earnestly hoping to find a figure wrong. Ardan could neither sit, stand nor lie still for a second, though he tried all three. His silence, of course, did not last long.

"Ha! ha! ha!" he laughed bitterly. "Precious scientific men! Villainous old hombogues! The whole set not worth a straw! I hope to gracious, since we must fall, that we shall drop down plumb on Cambridge Observatory, and not leave a single one of the miserable old women, called professors, alive in the premises!"

A certain expression in Ardan's angry exclamation had struck the Captain like a shot, and set his temples throbbing violently.

"*Must* fall!" he exclaimed, starting up suddenly. "Let us see about that! It is now seven o'clock in the morning. We must have, therefore, been at least thirty-two hours on the road, and more than half of our passage is already made. If we are going to fall at all, we must be falling now! I'm certain we're not, but, Barbican, you have to find it out!"

Barbican caught the idea like lightning, and, seizing a compass, he began through the floor window to measure the visual angle of the distant Earth. The apparent immobility of the Projectile allowed him to do this with great exactness. Then laying aside the instrument, and wiping off the thick drops of sweat that bedewed his forehead, he began jotting down some figures on a piece of paper. The Captain looked on with keen interest; he knew very well that Barbican was calculating their distance from the Earth by the apparent measure of the terrestrial diameter, and he eyed him anxiously.

Pretty soon his friends saw a color stealing into Barbican's pale face, and a triumphant light glittering in his eye.

"No, my brave boys!" he exclaimed at last throwing down his pencil, "we're not falling! Far from it, we are at present more than 150 thousand miles from the Earth!"

"Hurrah!" } "Bravo!" } cried M'Nicholl and Ardan, in a breath.

"We have passed the point where we should have stopped if we had had no more initial velocity than the Cambridge men allowed us!"

"Hurrah! hurrah!"

"Bravo, Bravissimo!"

"And we're still going up!"

"Glory, glory, hallelujah!" sang M'Nicholl, in the highest excitement.

"*Vive ce cher Barbican!*" cried Ardan, bursting into French as usual whenever his feelings had the better of him.

"Of course we're marching on!" continued M'Nicholl, "and I know the reason why, too. Those 400,000 pounds of gun-cotton gave us greater initial velocity than we had expected!"

"You're right, Captain!" added Barbican; "besides, you must not forget that, by getting rid of the water, the Projectile was relieved of considerable weight!"

"Correct again!" cried the Captain. "I had not thought of that!"

"Therefore, my brave boys," continued Barbican, with some excitement; "away with melancholy! We're all right!"

"Yes; everything is lovely and the goose hangs high!" cried the Captain, who on grand occasions was not above a little slang.

"Talking of goose reminds me of breakfast," cried Ardan; "I assure you, my fright has not taken away my appetite!"

"Yes," continued Barbican. "Captain, you're quite right. Our initial velocity very fortunately was much greater than what our Cambridge friends had calculated for us!"

"Hang our Cambridge friends and their calculations!" cried Ardan, with some asperity; "as usual with your scientific men they've more brass than brains! If we're not now bed-fellows with the oysters in the

Gulf of Mexico, no thanks to our kind Cambridge friends. But talking of oysters, let me remind you again that breakfast is ready."

The meal was a most joyous one. They ate much, they talked more, but they laughed most. The little incident of Algebra had certainly very much enlivened the situation.

"Now, my boys," Ardan went on, "all things thus turning out quite comfortable, I would just ask you why we should not succeed? We are fairly started. No breakers ahead that I can see. No rock on our road. It is freer than the ships on the raging ocean, aye, freer than the balloons in the blustering air. But the ship arrives at her destination; the balloon, borne on the wings of the wind, rises to as high an altitude as can be endured; why then should not our Projectile reach the Moon?"

"It *will* reach the Moon!" nodded Barbican.

"We shall reach the Moon or know for what!" cried M'Nicholl, enthusiastically.

"The great American nation must not be disappointed!" continued Ardan. "They are the only people on Earth capable of originating such an enterprise! They are the only people capable of producing a Barbican!"

"Hurrah!" cried M'Nicholl.

"That point settled," continued the Frenchman, "another question comes up to which I have not yet called your attention. When we get to the Moon, what shall we do there? How are we going to amuse ourselves? I'm afraid our life there will be awfully slow!"

His companions emphatically disclaimed the possibility of such a thing.

"You may deny it, but I know better, and knowing better, I have laid in my stores accordingly. You have but to choose. I possess a varied assortment. Chess, draughts, cards, dominoes—everything in fact, but a billiard table?"

"What!" exclaimed Barbican; "cumbered yourself with such gimcracks?"

"Such gimcracks are not only good to amuse ourselves with, but are eminently calculated also to win us the friendship of the Selenites."

"Friend Michael," said Barbican, "if the Moon is inhabited at all, her inhabitants must have appeared several thousand years before the advent of Man on our Earth, for there seems to be very little doubt that Luna is considerably older than Terra in her present state. Therefore, Selenites, if their brain is organized like our own, must have by this time invented all that we are possessed of, and even much which we are still to invent in the course of ages. The probability is that, instead of their learning from us, we shall have much to learn from them."

"What!" asked Ardan, "you think they have artists like Phidias, Michael Angelo and Raphael?"

"Certainly."

"And poets like Homer, Virgil, Dante, Shakspeare, Göthe and Hugo?"

"Not a doubt of it."

"And philosophers like Plato, Aristotle, Descartes, Bacon, Kant?"

"Why not?"

"And scientists like Euclid, Archimedes, Copernicus, Newton, Pascal?"

"I should think so."

"And famous actors, and singers, and composers, and—and photographers?"

"I could almost swear to it."

"Then, dear boy, since they have gone ahead as far as we and even farther, why have not those great Selenites tried to start a communication with the Earth? Why have they not fired a projectile from the regions lunar to the regions terrestrial?"

"Who says they have not done so?" asked Barbican, coolly.

"Attempting such a communication," observed the Captain, "would certainly be much easier for them than for us, principally for two reasons. First, attraction on the Moon's surface being six times less than on the Earth's, a projectile could be sent off more rapidly; second, because, as this projectile need be sent only 24 instead of 240 thousand miles, they could do it with a quantity of powder ten times less than what we should require for the same purpose."

"Then I ask again," said the Frenchman; "why haven't they made such an attempt?"

"And I reply again," answered Barbican. "How do you know that they have not made such an attempt?"

"Made it? When?"

"Thousands of years ago, before the invention of writing, before even the appearance of Man on the Earth."

"But the bullet?" asked Ardan, triumphantly; "Where's the bullet? Produce the bullet!"

"Friend Michael," answered Barbican, with a quiet smile, "you appear to forget that the 5/6 of the surface of our Earth is water. 5 to 1, therefore, that the bullet is more likely to be lying this moment at the bottom of the Atlantic or the Pacific than anywhere else on the surface of our globe. Besides, it may have sunk into some weak point of the surface, at the early epoch when the crust of the Earth had not acquired sufficient solidity."

"Captain," said Ardan, turning with a smile to M'Nicholl; "no use in trying to catch Barby; slippery as an eel, he has an answer for everything. Still I have a theory on the subject myself, which I think it no harm to ventilate. It is this: The Selenites have never sent us any projectile at all, simply because they had no gunpowder: being older and wiser than we, they were never such fools as to invent any.—But, what's that? Diana howling for her breakfast! Good! Like genuine scientific men, while squabbling over nonsense, we let the poor animals die of hunger. Excuse us, Diana; it is not the first time the little suffer from the senseless disputes of the great."

So saying he laid before the animal a very toothsome pie, and contemplated with evident pleasure her very successful efforts towards its hasty and complete disappearance.

"Looking at Diana," he went on, "makes me almost wish we had made a Noah's Ark of our Projectile by introducing into it a pair of all the domestic animals!"

"Not room enough," observed Barbican.

"No doubt," remarked the Captain, "the ox, the cow, the horse, the goat, all the ruminating animals would be very useful in the Lunar continent. But we couldn't turn our Projectile into a stable, you know."

"Still, we might have made room for a pair of poor little donkeys!" observed Ardan; "how I love the poor beasts. Fellow feeling, you will say. No doubt, but there really is no animal I pity more. They are the most ill-treated brutes in all creation. They are not only banged during life; they are banged worse after death!"

"Hey! How do you make that out?" asked his companions, surprised.

"Because we make their skins into drum heads!" replied Ardan, with an air, as if answering a conundrum.

Barbican and M'Nicholl could hardly help laughing at the absurd reply of their lively companion, but their hilarity was soon stopped by the expression his face assumed as he bent over Satellite's body, where it lay stretched on the sofa.

"What's the matter now?" asked Barbican.

"Satellite's attack is over," replied Ardan.

"Good!" said M'Nicholl, misunderstanding him.

"Yes, I suppose it is good for the poor fellow," observed Ardan, in melancholy accents. "Life with one's skull broken is hardly an enviable possession. Our grand acclimatization project is knocked sky high, in more senses than one!"

There was no doubt of the poor dog's death. The expression of Ardan's countenance, as he looked at his friends, was of a very rueful order.

"Well," said the practical Barbican, "there's no help for that now; the next thing to be done is to get rid of the body. We can't keep it here with us forty-eight hours longer."

"Of course not," replied the Captain, "nor need we; our lights, being provided with hinges, can be lifted back. What is to prevent us from opening one of them, and flinging the body out through it!"

The President of the Gun Club reflected a few minutes; then he spoke:

"Yes, it can be done; but we must take the most careful precautions."

"Why so?" asked Ardan.

"For two simple reasons;" replied Barbican; "the first refers to the air enclosed in the Projectile, and of which we must be very careful to lose only the least possible quantity."

"But as we manufacture air ourselves!" objected Ardan.

"We manufacture air only partly, friend Michael," replied Barbican. "We manufacture only oxygen; we can't supply nitrogen—By the bye, Ardan, won't you watch the apparatus carefully every now and then to see that the oxygen is not generated too freely. Very serious consequences would attend an immoderate supply of oxygen—No, we can't manufacture nitrogen, which is so absolutely necessary for our air and which might escape readily through the open windows."

"What! the few seconds we should require for flinging out poor Satellite?"

"A very few seconds indeed they should be," said Barbican, very gravely.

"Your second reason?" asked Ardan.

"The second reason is, that we must not allow the external cold, which must be exceedingly great, to penetrate into our Projectile and freeze us alive."

"But the Sun, you know—"

"Yes, the Sun heats our Projectile, but it does not heat the vacuum through which we are now floating. Where there is no air there can neither be heat nor light; just as wherever the rays of the Sun do not arrive directly, it must be both cold and dark. The temperature around us, if there be anything that can be called temperature, is produced solely by stellar radiation. I need not say how low that is in the scale, or that it would be the temperature to which our Earth should fall, if the Sun were suddenly extinguished."

"Little fear of that for a few more million years," said M'Nicholl.

"Who can tell?" asked Ardan. "Besides, even admitting that the Sun will not soon be extinguished, what is to prevent the Earth from shooting away from him?"

"Let friend Michael speak," said Barbican, with a smile, to the Captain; "we may learn something."

"Certainly you may," continued the Frenchman, "if you have room for anything new. Were we not struck by a comet's tail in 1861?"

"So it was said, anyhow," observed the Captain. "I well remember what nonsense there was in the papers about the 'phosphorescent auroral glare.'"

"Well," continued the Frenchman, "suppose the comet of 1861 influenced the Earth by an attraction superior to the Sun's. What would be the consequence? Would not the Earth follow the attracting body, become its satellite, and thus at last be dragged off to such a distance that the Sun's rays could no longer excite heat on her surface?"

"Well, that might possibly occur," said Barbican slowly, "but even then I question if the consequences would be so terrible as you seem to apprehend."

"Why not?"

"Because the cold and the heat might still manage to be nearly equalized on our globe. It has been calculated that, had the Earth been carried off by the comet of '61, when arrived at her greatest distance, she would have experienced a temperature hardly sixteen times greater than the heat we receive from the Moon, which, as everybody knows, produces no appreciable effect, even when concentrated to a focus by the most powerful lenses."

"Well then," exclaimed Ardan, "at such a temperature—"

"Wait a moment," replied Barbican. "Have you never heard of the principle of compensation? Listen to another calculation. Had the Earth been dragged along with the comet, it has been calculated that at her perihelion, or nearest point to the Sun, she would have to endure a heat 28,000 times greater than our mean summer temperature. But this heat, fully capable of turning the rocks into glass and the oceans into vapor, before proceeding to such extremity, must have first formed a thick interposing ring of clouds, and thus considerably modified the excessive temperature. Therefore, between the extreme cold of the aphelion and the excessive heat of the perihelion, by the great law of compensation, it is probable that the mean temperature would be tolerably endurable."

"At how many degrees is the temperature of the interplanetary space estimated?" asked M'Nicholl.

"Some time ago," replied Barbican, "this temperature was considered to be very low indeed—millions and millions of degrees below zero. But Fourrier of Auxerre, a distinguished member of the *Académie des Sciences*, whose *Mémoires* on the temperature of the Planetary spaces appeared about 1827, reduced these figures to considerably diminished proportions. According to his careful estimation, the temperature of space is not much lower than 70 or 80 degrees Fahr. below zero."

"No more?" asked Ardan.

"No more," answered Barbican, "though I must acknowledge we have only his word for it, as the *Mémoire* in which he had recorded all the elements of that important determination, has been lost somewhere, and is no longer to be found."

"I don't attach the slightest importance to his, or to any man's words, unless they are sustained by reliable evidence," exclaimed M'Nicholl. "Besides, if I'm not very much mistaken, Pouillet—another countryman of yours, Ardan, and an Academician as well as Fourrier—esteems the temperature of interplanetary spaces to be at least 256° Fahr. below zero. This we can easily verify for ourselves this moment by actual experiment."

"Not just now exactly," observed Barbican, "for the solar rays, striking our Projectile directly, would give us a very elevated instead of a very low temperature. But once arrived at the Moon, during those nights fifteen days long, which each of her faces experiences alternately, we shall have plenty of time to make an experiment with every condition in our favor. To be sure, our Satellite is at present moving in a vacuum."

"A vacuum?" asked Ardan; "a perfect vacuum?"

"Well, a perfect vacuum as far as air is concerned."

"But is the air replaced by nothing?"

"Oh yes," replied Barbican. "By ether."

"Ah, ether! and what, pray, is ether?"

"Ether, friend Michael, is an elastic gas consisting of imponderable atoms, which, as we are told by works on molecular physics, are, in proportion to their size, as far apart as the celestial bodies are from each other in space. This distance is less than the $1/3000000 \times 1/1000'$, or the one trillionth of a foot. The vibrations of the molecules of this ether produce the sensations of light and heat, by making 430 trillions of undulations per second, each undulation being hardly more than the one ten-millionth of an inch in width."

"Trillions per second! ten-millionths of an inch in width!" cried Ardan. "These oscillations have been very neatly counted and ticketed, and checked off! Ah, friend Barbican," continued the Frenchman, shaking his head, "these numbers are just tremendous guesses, frightening the ear but revealing nothing to the intelligence."

"To get ideas, however, we must calculate—"

"No, no!" interrupted Ardan: "not calculate, but compare. A trillion tells you nothing—Comparison, everything. For instance, you say, the volume of *Uranus* is 76 times greater than the Earth's; *Saturn's* 900 times greater; *Jupiter's* 1300 times greater; the Sun's 1300 thousand times greater—You may tell me all that till I'm tired hearing it, and I shall still be almost as ignorant as ever. For my part I prefer to be told one of those simple comparisons that I find in the old almanacs: The Sun is a globe two feet in diameter; *Jupiter*, a good sized orange; *Saturn*, a smaller orange; *Neptune*, a plum; *Uranus*, a good sized cherry; the Earth, a pea; *Venus*, also a pea but somewhat smaller; *Mars*, a large pin's head; *Mercury*, a mustard seed; *Juno*, *Ceres*, *Vesta*, *Pallas*, and the other asteroids so many grains of sand. Be told something like that, and you have got at least the tail of an idea!"

This learned burst of Ardan's had the natural effect of making his hearers forget what they had been arguing about, and they therefore proceeded at once to dispose of Satellite's body. It was a simple matter enough—no more than to fling it out of the Projectile into space, just as the sailors get rid of a dead body by throwing it into the sea. Only in this operation they had to act, as Barbican recommended, with the utmost care and dispatch, so as to lose as little as possible of the internal air, which, by its great elasticity, would violently strive to escape. The bolts of the floor-light, which was more than a foot in diameter, were carefully unscrewed, while Ardan, a good deal affected, prepared to launch his dog's body into space. The glass, worked by a powerful lever which enabled it to overcome the pressure of the enclosed air, turned quickly on its hinges, and poor Satellite was dropped out. The whole operation was so well managed that very little air escaped, and ever afterwards Barbican employed the same means to rid the Projectile of all the litter and other useless matter by which it was occasionally encumbered.

The evening of this third of December wore away without further incident. As soon as Barbican had announced that the Projectile was still winging its way, though with retarded velocity, towards the lunar disc, the travellers quietly retired to rest.

VI

INSTRUCTIVE CONVERSATION

On the fourth of December, the Projectile chronometers marked five o'clock in the morning, just as the travellers woke up from a pleasant slumber. They had now been 54 hours on their journey. As to lapse of *time*, they had passed not much more than half of the number of hours during which their trip was to last; but, as to lapse of *space*, they had already accomplished very nearly the seven-tenths of their passage. This difference between time and distance was due to the regular retardation of their velocity.

They looked at the earth through the floor-light, but it was little more than visible—a black spot drowned in the solar rays. No longer any sign of a crescent, no longer any sign of ashy light. Next day, towards midnight, the Earth was to be *new*, at the precise moment when the Moon was to be *full*. Overhead, they could see the Queen of Night coming nearer and nearer to the line followed by the Projectile, and evidently approaching the point where both should meet at the appointed moment. All around, the black vault of heaven was dotted with luminous points which seemed to move somewhat, though, of course, in their extreme distance their relative size underwent no change. The Sun and the stars looked exactly as they had appeared when observed from the Earth. The Moon indeed had become considerably enlarged in size, but the travellers' telescopes were still too weak to enable them to make any important observation regarding the nature of her surface, or that might determine her topographical or geological features.

Naturally, therefore, the time slipped away in endless conversation. The Moon, of course, was the chief topic. Each one contributed his share of peculiar information, or peculiar ignorance, as the case might be. Barbican and M'Nicholl always treated the subject gravely, as became learned scientists, but Ardan preferred to look on things with the eye of fancy. The Projectile, its situation, its direction, the incidents possible to occur, the precautions necessary to take in order to break the fall on the Moon's surface—these and many other subjects furnished endless food for constant debate and inexhaustible conjectures.

For instance, at breakfast that morning, a question of Ardan's regarding the Projectile drew from Barbican an answer curious enough to be reported.

"Suppose, on the night that we were shot up from Stony Hill," said Ardan, "suppose the Projectile had encountered some obstacle powerful enough to stop it—what would be the consequence of the sudden halt?"

"But," replied Barbican, "I don't understand what obstacle it could have met powerful enough to stop it."

"Suppose some obstacle, for the sake of argument," said Ardan.

"Suppose what can't be supposed," replied the matter-of-fact Barbican, "what cannot possibly be supposed, unless indeed the original impulse proved too weak. In that case, the velocity would have decreased by degrees, but the Projectile itself would not have suddenly stopped."

"Suppose it had struck against some body in space."

"What body, for instance?"

"Well, that enormous bolide which we met."

"Oh!" hastily observed the Captain, "the Projectile would have been dashed into a thousand pieces and we along with it."

"Better than that," observed Barbican; "we should have been burned alive."

"Burned alive!" laughed Ardan. "What a pity we missed so interesting an experiment! How I should have liked to find out how it felt!"

"You would not have much time to record your observations, friend Michael, I assure you," observed Barbican. "The case is plain enough. Heat and motion are convertible terms. What do we mean by heating water? Simply giving increased, in fact, violent motion to its molecules."

"Well!" exclaimed the Frenchman, "that's an ingenious theory any how!"

"Not only ingenious but correct, my dear friend, for it completely explains all the phenomena of caloric. Heat is nothing but molecular movement, the violent oscillation of the particles of a body. When you apply the brakes to the train, the train stops. But what has become of its motion? It turns into heat and makes the brakes hot. Why do people grease the axles? To hinder them from getting too hot, which they assuredly would become if friction was allowed to obstruct the motion. You understand, don't you?"

"Don't I though?" replied Ardan, apparently in earnest. "Let me show you how thoroughly. When I have been running hard and long, I feel myself perspiring like a bull and hot as a furnace. Why am I then forced to stop? Simply because my motion has been transformed into heat! Of course, I understand all about it!"

Barbican smiled a moment at this comical illustration of his theory and then went on:

"Accordingly, in case of a collision it would have been all over instantly with our Projectile. You have seen what becomes of the bullet that strikes the iron target. It is flattened out of all shape; sometimes it is even melted into a thin film. Its motion has been turned into heat. Therefore, I maintain that if our Projectile had struck that bolide, its velocity, suddenly checked, would have given rise to a heat capable of completely volatilizing it in less than a second."

"Not a doubt of it!" said the Captain. "President," he added after a moment, "haven't they calculated what would be the result, if the Earth were suddenly brought to a stand-still in her journey, through her orbit?"

"It has been calculated," answered Barbican, "that in such a case so much heat would be developed as would instantly reduce her to vapor."

"Hm!" exclaimed Ardan; "a remarkably simple way for putting an end to the world!"

"And supposing the Earth to fall into the Sun?" asked the Captain.

"Such a fall," answered Barbican, "according to the calculations of Tyndall and Thomson, would develop an amount of heat equal to that produced by sixteen hundred globes of burning coal, each globe equal in size to the earth itself. Furthermore such a fall would supply the Sun with at least as much heat as he expends in a hundred years!"

"A hundred years! Good! Nothing like accuracy!" cried Ardan. "Such infallible calculators as Messrs. Tyndall and Thomson I can easily excuse for any airs they may give themselves. They must be of an order much higher than that of ordinary mortals like us!"

"I would not answer myself for the accuracy of such intricate problems," quietly observed Barbican; "but there is no doubt whatever regarding one fact: motion suddenly interrupted always develops heat. And this has given rise to another theory regarding the maintenance of the Sun's temperature at a constant point. An incessant rain of bolides falling on his surface compensates sufficiently for the heat that he is continually giving forth. It has been calculated—"

"Good Lord deliver us!" cried Ardan, putting his hands to his ears: "here comes Tyndall and Thomson again!"

—"It has been calculated," continued Barbican, not heeding the interruption, "that the shock of every bolide drawn to the Sun's surface by gravity, must produce there an amount of heat equal to that of the combustion of four thousand blocks of coal, each the same size as the falling bolide."

"I'll wager another cent that our bold savants calculated the heat of the Sun himself," cried Ardan, with an incredulous laugh.

"That is precisely what they have done," answered Barbican referring to his memorandum book; "the heat emitted by the Sun," he continued, "is exactly that which would be produced by the combustion of a layer of coal enveloping the Sun's surface, like an atmosphere, 17 miles in thickness."

"Well done! and such heat would be capable of—?"

"Of melting in an hour a stratum of ice 2400 feet thick, or, according to another calculation, of raising a globe of ice-cold water, 3 times the size of our Earth, to the boiling point in an hour."

"Why not calculate the exact fraction of a second it would take to cook a couple of eggs?" laughed Ardan. "I should as soon believe in one calculation as in the other.—But—by the by—why does not such extreme heat cook us all up like so many beefsteaks?"

"For two very good and sufficient reasons," answered Barbican. "In the first place, the terrestrial atmosphere absorbs the 4/10 of the solar heat. In the second, the quantity of solar heat intercepted by the Earth is only about the two billionth part of all that is radiated."

"How fortunate to have such a handy thing as an atmosphere around us," cried the Frenchman; "it not only enables us to breathe, but it actually keeps us from sizzling up like griskins."

"Yes," said the Captain, "but unfortunately we can't say so much for the Moon."

"Oh pshaw!" cried Ardan, always full of confidence. "It's all right there too! The Moon is either inhabited or she is not. If she is, the inhabitants must breathe. If she is not, there must be oxygen enough left for we, us and co., even if we should have to go after it to the bottom of the ravines, where, by its gravity, it must have accumulated! So much the better! we shall not have to climb those thundering mountains!"

So saying, he jumped up and began to gaze with considerable interest on the lunar disc, which just then was glittering with dazzling brightness.

"By Jove!" he exclaimed at length; "it must be pretty hot up there!"

"I should think so," observed the Captain; "especially when you remember that the day up there lasts 360 hours!"

"Yes," observed Barbican, "but remember on the other hand that the nights are just as long, and, as the heat escapes by radiation, the mean temperature cannot be much greater than that of interplanetary space."

"A high old place for living in!" cried Ardan. "No matter! I wish we were there now! Wouldn't it be jolly, dear boys, to have old Mother Earth for our Moon, to see her always on our sky, never rising, never setting, never undergoing any change except from New Earth to Last Quarter! Would not it be fun to trace the shape of our great Oceans and Continents, and to say: 'there is the Mediterranean! there is China! there is the gulf of Mexico! there is the white line of the Rocky Mountains where old Marston is watching for us with his big telescope!' Then we should see every line, and brightness, and shadow fade away by degrees, as she came nearer and nearer to the Sun, until at last she sat completely lost in his dazzling rays! But—by the way—Barbican, are there any eclipses in the Moon?"

"O yes; solar eclipses" replied Barbican, "must always occur whenever the centres of the three heavenly bodies are in the same line, the Earth occupying the middle place. However, such eclipses must always be annular, as the Earth, projected like a screen on the solar disc, allows more than half of the Sun to be still visible."

"How is that?" asked M'Nicholl, "no total eclipses in the Moon? Surely the cone of the Earth's shadow must extend far enough to envelop her surface?"

"It does reach her, in one sense," replied Barbican, "but it does not in another. Remember the great refraction of the solar rays that must be produced by the Earth's atmosphere. It is easy to show that this refraction prevents the Sun from ever being totally invisible. See here!" he continued, pulling out his tablets, "Let a represent the horizontal parallax, and b the half of the Sun's apparent diameter—"

"Ouch!" cried the Frenchman, making a wry face, "here comes Mr. x square riding to the mischief on a pair of double zeros again! Talk English, or Yankee, or Dutch, or Greek, and I'm your man! Even a little Arabic I can digest! But hang me, if I can endure your Algebra!"

"Well then, talking Yankee," replied Barbican with a smile, "the mean distance of the Moon from the Earth being sixty terrestrial radii, the length of the conic shadow, in consequence of atmospheric refraction, is reduced to less than forty-two radii. Consequently, at the moment of an eclipse, the Moon is far beyond the reach of the real shadow, so that she can see not only the border rays of the Sun, but even those proceeding from his very centre."

"Oh then," cried Ardan with a loud laugh, "we have an eclipse of the Sun at the moment when the Sun is quite visible! Isn't that very like a bull, Mr. Philosopher Barbican?"

"Yet it is perfectly true notwithstanding," answered Barbican. "At such a moment the Sun is not eclipsed, because we can see him: and then again he is eclipsed because we see him only by means of a few of his rays, and even these have lost nearly all their brightness in their passage through the terrestrial atmosphere!"

"Barbican is right, friend Michael," observed the Captain slowly: "the same phenomenon occurs on earth every morning at sunrise, when refraction shows us

'the Sun new ris'n
Looking through the horizontal misty air,
Shorn of his beams.'"

"He must be right," said Ardan, who, to do him justice, though quick at seeing a reason, was quicker to acknowledge its justice: "yes, he must be right, because I begin to understand at last very clearly what he really meant. However, we can judge for ourselves when we get there.—But, apropos of nothing, tell me, Barbican, what do you think of the Moon being an ancient comet, which had come so far within the sphere of the Earth's attraction as to be kept there and turned into a satellite?"

"Well, that *is* an original idea!" said Barbican with a smile.

"My ideas generally are of that category," observed Ardan with an affectation of dry pomposity.

"Not this time, however, friend Michael," observed M'Nicholl.

"Oh! I'm a plagiarist, am I?" asked the Frenchman, pretending to be irritated.

"Well, something very like it," observed M'Nicholl quietly. "Apollonius Rhodius, as I read one evening in the Philadelphia Library, speaks of the Arcadians of Greece having a tradition that their ancestors were so ancient that they inhabited the Earth long before the Moon had ever become our satellite. They therefore called them *Proselênoi* or *Ante-lunarians*. Now starting with some such wild notion as this, certain scientists have looked on the Moon as an ancient comet brought close enough to the Earth to be retained in its orbit by terrestrial attraction."

"Why may not there be something plausible in such a hypothesis?" asked Ardan with some curiosity.

"There is nothing whatever in it," replied Barbican decidedly: "a simple proof is the fact that the Moon does not retain the slightest trace of the vaporous envelope by which comets are always surrounded."

"Lost her tail you mean," said Ardan. "Pooh! Easy to account for that! It might have got cut off by coming too close to the Sun!"

"It might, friend Michael, but an amputation by such means is not very likely."

"No? Why not?"

"Because—because—By Jove, I can't say, because I don't know," cried Barbican with a quiet smile on his countenance.

"Oh what a lot of volumes," cried Ardan, "could be made out of what we don't know!"

"At present, for instance," observed M'Nicholl, "I don't know what o'clock it is."

"Three o'clock!" said Barbican, glancing at his chronometer.

"No!" cried Ardan in surprise. "Bless us! How rapidly the time passes when we are engaged in scientific conversation! Ouf! I'm getting decidedly too learned! I feel as if I had swallowed a library!"

"I feel," observed M'Nicholl, "as if I had been listening to a lecture on Astronomy in the *Star* course."

"Better stir around a little more," said the Frenchman; "fatigue of body is the best antidote to such severe mental labor as ours. I'll run up the ladder a bit." So saying, he paid another visit to the upper portion of the Projectile and remained there awhile whistling *Malbrouk*, whilst his companions amused themselves in looking through the floor window.

Ardan was coming down the ladder, when his whistling was cut short by a sudden exclamation of surprise.

"What's the matter?" asked Barbican quickly, as he looked up and saw the Frenchman pointing to something outside the Projectile.

Approaching the window, Barbican saw with much surprise a sort of flattened bag floating in space and only a few yards off. It seemed perfectly motionless, and, consequently, the travellers knew that it must be animated by the same ascensional movement as themselves.

"What on earth can such a consarn be, Barbican?" asked Ardan, who every now and then liked to ventilate his stock of American slang. "Is it one of those particles of meteoric matter you were speaking of just now, caught within the sphere of our Projectile's attraction and accompanying us to the Moon?"

"What I am surprised at," observed the Captain, "is that though the specific gravity of that body is far inferior to that of our Projectile, it moves with exactly the same velocity."

"Captain," said Barbican, after a moment's reflection, "I know no more what that object is than you do, but I can understand very well why it keeps abreast with the Projectile."

"Very well then, why?"

"Because, my dear Captain, we are moving through a vacuum, and because all bodies fall or move—the same thing—with equal velocity through a vacuum, no matter what may be their shape or their specific gravity. It is the air alone that makes a difference of weight. Produce an artificial vacuum in a glass tube and you will see that all objects whatever falling through, whether bits of feather or grains of shot, move with precisely the same rapidity. Up here, in space, like cause and like effect."

"Correct," assented M'Nicholl. "Everything therefore that we shall throw out of the Projectile is bound to accompany us to the Moon."

"Well, we *were* smart!" cried Ardan suddenly.

"How so, friend Michael?" asked Barbican.

"Why not have packed the Projectile with ever so many useful objects, books, instruments, tools, et cetera, and fling them out into space once we were fairly started! They would have all followed us safely! Nothing would have been lost! And—now I think on it—why not fling ourselves out through the window? Shouldn't we be as safe out there as that bolide? What fun it would be to feel ourselves sustained and upborne in the ether, more highly favored even than the birds, who must keep on flapping their wings continually to prevent themselves from falling!"

"Very true, my dear boy," observed Barbican; "but how could we breathe?"

"It's a fact," exclaimed the Frenchman. "Hang the air for spoiling our fun! So we must remain shut up in our Projectile?"

"Not a doubt of it!"

—"Oh Thunder!" roared Ardan, suddenly striking his forehead.

"What ails you?" asked the Captain, somewhat surprised.

"Now I know what that bolide of ours is! Why didn't we think of it before? It is no asteroid! It is no particle of meteoric matter! Nor is it a piece of a shattered planet!"

"What is it then?" asked both of his companions in one voice.

"It is nothing more or less than the body of the dog that we threw out yesterday!"

So in fact it was. That shapeless, unrecognizable mass, melted, expunged, flat as a bladder under an unexhausted receiver, drained of its air, was poor Satellite's body, flying like a rocket through space, and rising higher and higher in close company with the rapidly ascending Projectile!

VII

A High Old Time

A new phenomenon, therefore, strange but logical, startling but admitting of easy explanation, was now presented to their view, affording a fresh subject for lively discussion. Not that they disputed much about it. They soon agreed on a principle from which they readily deducted the following general law: *Every object thrown out of the Projectile should partake of the Projectile's motion: it should therefore follow the same path, and never cease to move until the Projectile itself came to a stand-still.*

But, in sober truth, they were at anything but a loss of subjects of warm discussion. As the end of their journey began to approach, their senses became keener and their sensations vivider. Steeled against surprise, they looked for the unexpected, the strange, the startling; and the only thing at which they would have wondered would be to be five minutes without having something new to wonder at. Their excited imaginations flew far ahead of the Projectile, whose velocity, by the way, began to be retarded very decidedly by this time, though, of course, the travellers had as yet no means to become aware of it. The Moon's size on the sky was meantime getting larger and larger; her apparent distance was growing shorter and shorter, until at last they could almost imagine that by putting their hands out they could nearly touch her.

Next morning, December 5th, all were up and dressed at a very early hour. This was to be the last day of their journey, if all calculations were correct. That very night, at 12 o'clock, within nineteen hours at furthest, at the very moment of Full Moon, they were to reach her resplendent surface. At that hour was to be completed the most extraordinary journey ever undertaken by man in ancient or modern times. Naturally enough, therefore, they found themselves unable to sleep after four o'clock in the morning; peering upwards through the windows now visibly glittering under the rays of the Moon, they spent some very exciting hours in gazing at her slowly enlarging disc, and shouting at her with confident and joyful hurrahs.

The majestic Queen of the Stars had now risen so high in the spangled heavens that she could hardly rise higher. In a few degrees more she would reach the exact point of space where her junction with the Projectile was to be effected. According to his own observations, Barbican calculated that they should strike her in the northern hemisphere, where her plains, or *seas* as they are called, are immense, and her mountains are comparatively rare. This, of course, would be so much the more favorable, if, as was to be apprehended, the lunar atmosphere was confined exclusively to the low lands.

"Besides," as Ardan observed, "a plain is a more suitable landing place than a mountain. A Selenite deposited on the top of Mount Everest or even on Mont Blanc, could hardly be considered, in strict language, to have arrived on Earth."

"Not to talk," added M'Nicholl, "of the comfort of the thing! When you land on a plain, there you are. When you land on a peak or on a steep mountain side, where are you? Tumbling over an embankment with the train going forty miles an hour, would be nothing to it."

"Therefore, Captain Barbican," cried the Frenchman, "as we should like to appear before the Selenites in full skins, please land us in the snug though unromantic North. We shall have time enough to break our necks in the South."

Barbican made no reply to his companions, because a new reflection had begun to trouble him, to talk about which would have done no good. There was certainly something wrong. The Projectile was evidently heading towards the northern hemisphere of the Moon. What did this prove? Clearly, a deviation resulting from some cause. The bullet, lodged, aimed, and fired with the most careful mathematical precision, had been calculated to reach the very centre of the Moon's disc. Clearly it was not going to the centre now. What could have produced the deviation? This Barbican could not tell; nor could he even determine its extent, having no points of sight by which to make his observations. For the present he tried to console himself with the hope that the deviation of the Projectile would be followed by no worse consequence than carrying them towards the northern border of the Moon, where for several reasons it would be comparatively easier to alight. Carefully avoiding, therefore, the use of any expression which might needlessly alarm his companions, he continued to observe the Moon as carefully as he could, hoping every moment to find some grounds for believing that the deviation from the centre was only a slight one. He almost shuddered at the thought of what would be their situation, if the bullet, missing its aim, should pass the Moon, and plunge into the interplanetary space beyond it.

As he continued to gaze, the Moon, instead of presenting the usual flatness of her disc, began decidedly to show a surface somewhat convex. Had the Sun been shining on her obliquely, the shadows would have certainly thrown the great mountains into strong relief. The eye could then bury itself deep in the yawning chasms of the craters, and easily follow the cracks, streaks, and ridges which stripe, flecker, and bar the immensity of her plains. But for the present all relief was lost in the dazzling glare. The Captain could hardly distinguish even those dark spots that impart to the full Moon some resemblance to the human face.

"Face!" cried Ardan: "well, a very fanciful eye may detect a face, though, for the sake of Apollo's beauteous sister, I regret to say, a terribly pockmarked one!"

The travellers, now evidently approaching the end of their journey, observed the rapidly increasing world above them with newer and greater curiosity every moment. Their fancies enkindled at the sight of the new and strange scenes dimly presented to their view. In imagination they climbed to the summit of this lofty peak. They let themselves down to the abyss of that yawning crater. Here they imagined they saw vast seas hardly kept in their basins by a rarefied atmosphere; there they thought they could trace mighty rivers bearing to vast oceans the tribute of the snowy mountains. In the first promptings of their eager curiosity, they peered greedily into her cavernous depths, and almost expected, amidst the deathlike hush of inaudible nature, to surprise some sound from the mystic orb floating up there in eternal silence through a boundless ocean of never ending vacuum.

This last day of their journey left their memories stored with thrilling recollections. They took careful note of the slightest details. As they neared their destination, they felt themselves invaded by a vague, undefined restlessness. But this restlessness would have given way to decided uneasiness, if they had known at what a slow rate they were travelling. They would have surely concluded that their present velocity would never be able to take them as far as the neutral point, not to talk of passing it. The reason of such considerable retardation was, that by this time the Projectile had reached such a great distance from the Earth that it had hardly any weight. But even this weight, such as it was, was to be diminished still further, and finally, to vanish altogether as soon as the bullet reached the neutral point, where the two attractions, terrestrial and lunar, should counteract each other with new and surprising effects.

Notwithstanding the absorbing nature of his observations, Ardan never forgot to prepare breakfast with his usual punctuality. It was eaten readily and relished heartily. Nothing could be more exquisite than his calf's foot jelly liquefied and prepared by gas heat, except perhaps his meat biscuits of preserved Texas beef and Southdown mutton. A bottle of Château Yquem and another of Clos de Vougeot, both of superlative excellence in quality and flavor, crowned the repast. Their vicinity to the Moon and their incessant glancing at her surface did not prevent the travellers from touching each other's glasses merrily and often. Ardan took occasion to remark that the lunar vineyards—if any existed—must be magnificent, considering the intense solar heat they continually experienced. Not that he counted on them too confidently, for he told his friends that to provide for the worst he had supplied himself with a few cases of the best vintages of Médoc and the Côte d'Or, of which the bottles, then under discussion, might be taken as very favorable specimens.

The Reiset and Regnault apparatus for purifying the air worked splendidly, and maintained the atmosphere in a perfectly sanitary condition. Not an atom of carbonic acid could resist the caustic potash; and as for the oxygen, according to M'Nicholl's expression, "it was A prime number one!"

The small quantity of watery vapor enclosed in the Projectile did no more harm than serving to temper the dryness of the air: many a splendid *salon* in New York, London, or Paris, and many an auditorium, even of theatre, opera house or Academy of Music, could be considered its inferior in what concerned its hygienic condition.

To keep it in perfect working order, the apparatus should be carefully attended to. This, Ardan looked on as his own peculiar occupation. He was never tired regulating the tubes, trying the taps, and testing the heat of the gas by the pyrometer. So far everything had worked satisfactorily, and the travellers, following the example of their friend Marston on a previous occasion, began to get so stout that their own mothers would not know them in another month, should their imprisonment last so long. Ardan said they all looked so sleek and thriving that he was reminded forcibly of a nice lot of pigs fattening in a pen for a country fair. But how long was this good fortune of theirs going to last?

Whenever they took their eyes off the Moon, they could not help noticing that they were still attended outside by the spectre of Satellite's corpse and by the other refuse of the Projectile. An occasional melancholy howl also attested Diana's recognition of her companion's unhappy fate. The travellers saw with surprise that these waifs still seemed perfectly motionless in space, and kept their respective distances apart as mathematically as if they had been fastened with nails to a stone wall.

"I tell you what, dear boys;" observed Ardan, commenting on this curious phenomenon; "if the concussion had been a little too violent for one of us that night, his survivors would have been seriously embarrassed in trying to get rid of his remains. With no earth to cover him up, no sea to plunge him into, his corpse would never disappear from view, but would pursue us day and night, grim and ghastly like an avenging ghost!"

"Ugh!" said the Captain, shuddering at the idea.

"But, by the bye, Barbican!" cried the Frenchman, dropping the subject with his usual abruptness; "you have forgotten something else! Why didn't you bring a scaphander and an air pump? I could then venture out of the Projectile as readily and as safely as the diver leaves his boat and walks about on the bottom of the river! What fun to float in the midst of that mysterious ether! to steep myself, aye, actually to revel in the pure rays of the glorious sun! I should have ventured out on the very point of the Projectile, and there I should have danced and postured and kicked and bobbed and capered in a style that Taglioni never dreamed of!"

"Shouldn't I like to see you!" cried the Captain grimly, smiling at the idea.

"You would not see him long!" observed Barbican quietly. "The air confined in his body, freed from external pressure, would burst him like a shell, or like a balloon that suddenly rises to too great a height in the air! A scaphander would have been a fatal gift. Don't regret its absence, friend Michael; never forget this axiom: *As long as we are floating in empty space, the only spot where safety is possible is inside the Projectile!*"

The words "possible" and "impossible" always grated on Ardan's ears. If he had been a lexicographer, he would have rigidly excluded them from his dictionary, both as meaningless and useless. He was preparing an answer for Barbican, when he was cut out by a sudden observation from M'Nicholl.

"See here, friends!" cried the Captain; "this going to the Moon is all very well, but how shall we get back?"

His listeners looked at each other with a surprised and perplexed air. The question, though a very natural one, now appeared to have presented itself to their consideration absolutely for the first time.

"What do you mean by such a question, Captain?" asked Barbican in a grave judicial tone.

"Mac, my boy," said Ardan seriously, "don't it strike you as a little out of order to ask how you are to return when you have not got there yet?"

"I don't ask the question with any idea of backing out," observed the Captain quietly; "as a matter of purely scientific inquiry, I repeat my question: how are we to return?"

"I don't know," replied Barbican promptly.

"For my part," said Ardan; "if I had known how to get back, I should have never come at all!"

"Well! of all the answers!" said the Captain, lifting his hands and shaking his head.

"The best under the circumstances;" observed Barbican; "and I shall further observe that such a question as yours at present is both useless and uncalled for. On some future occasion, when we shall consider it advisable to return, the question will be in order, and we shall discuss it with all the attention it deserves. Though the Columbiad is at Stony Hill, the Projectile will still be in the Moon."

"Much we shall gain by that! A bullet without a gun!"

"The gun we can make and the powder too!" replied Barbican confidently. "Metal and sulphur and charcoal and saltpetre are likely enough to be present in sufficient quantities beneath the Moon's surface. Besides, to return is a problem of comparatively easy solution: we should have to overcome the lunar attraction only—a slight matter— the rest of the business would be readily done by gravity."

"Enough said on the subject!" exclaimed Ardan curtly; "how to get back is indefinitely postponed! How to communicate with our friends on the Earth, is another matter, and, as it seems to me, an extremely easy one."

"Let us hear the very easy means by which you propose to communicate with our friends on Earth," asked the Captain, with a sneer, for he was by this time a little out of humor.

"By means of bolides ejected from the lunar volcanoes," replied the Frenchman without an instant's hesitation.

"Well said, friend Ardan," exclaimed Barbican. "I am quite disposed to acknowledge the feasibility of your plan. Laplace has calculated that a force five times greater than that of an ordinary cannon would be sufficient to send a bolide from the Moon to the Earth. Now there is no cannon that can vie in force with even the smallest volcano."

"Hurrah!" cried Ardan, delighted at his success; "just imagine the pleasure of sending our letters postage free! But—oh! what a splendid idea!—Dolts that we were for not thinking of it sooner!"

"Let us have the splendid idea!" cried the Captain, with some of his old acrimony.

"Why didn't we fasten a wire to the Projectile?" asked Ardan, triumphantly, "It would have enabled us to exchange telegrams with the Earth!"

"Ho! ho! ho!" roared the Captain, rapidly recovering his good humor; "decidedly the best joke of the season! Ha! ha! ha! Of course you have calculated the weight of a wire 240 thousand miles long?"

"No matter about its weight!" cried the Frenchman impetuously; "we should have laughed at its weight! We could have tripled the charge of the Columbiad; we could have quadrupled it!—aye, quintupled it, if necessary!" he added in tones evidently increasing in loudness and violence.

"Yes, friend Michael," observed Barbican; "but there is a slight and unfortunately a fatal defect in your project. The Earth, by its rotation, would have wrapped our wire around herself, like thread around a spool, and dragged us back almost with the speed of lightning!"

"By the Nine gods of Porsena!" cried Ardan, "something is wrong with my head to-day! My brain is out of joint, and I am making as nice a mess of things as my friend Marston was ever capable of! By the bye—talking of Marston—if we never return to the Earth, what is to prevent him from following us to the Moon?"

"Nothing!" replied Barbican; "he is a faithful friend and a reliable comrade. Besides, what is easier? Is not the Columbiad still at Stony Hill? Cannot gun-cotton be readily manufactured on any occasion? Will not the Moon again pass through the zenith of Florida? Eighteen years from now, will she not occupy exactly the same spot that she does to-day?"

"Certainly!" cried Ardan, with increasing enthusiasm, "Marston will come! and Elphinstone of the torpedo! and the gallant Bloomsbury, and Billsby the brave, and all our friends of the Baltimore Gun Club!

And we shall receive them with all the honors! And then we shall establish projectile trains between the Earth and the Moon! Hurrah for J.T. Marston!"

"Hurrah for Secretary Marston!" cried the Captain, with an enthusiasm almost equal to Ardan's.

"Hurrah for my dear friend Marston!" cried Barbican, hardly less excited than his comrades.

Our old acquaintance, Marston, of course could not have heard the joyous acclamations that welcomed his name, but at that moment he certainly must have felt his ears most unaccountably tingling. What was he doing at the time? He was rattling along the banks of the Kansas River, as fast as an express train could take him, on the road to Long's Peak, where, by means of the great Telescope, he expected to find some traces of the Projectile that contained his friends. He never forgot them for a moment, but of course he little dreamed that his name at that very time was exciting their vividest recollections and their warmest applause.

In fact, their recollections were rather too vivid, and their applause decidedly too warm. Was not the animation that prevailed among the guests of the Projectile of a very unusual character, and was it not becoming more and more violent every moment? Could the wine have caused it? No; though not teetotallers, they never drank to excess. Could the Moon's proximity, shedding her subtle, mysterious influence over their nervous systems, have stimulated them to a degree that was threatening to border on frenzy? Their faces were as red as if they were standing before a hot fire; their breathing was loud, and their lungs heaved like a smith's bellows; their eyes blazed like burning coals; their voices sounded as loud and harsh as that of a stump speaker trying to make himself heard by an inattentive or hostile crowd; their words popped from their lips like corks from Champagne bottles; their gesticulating became wilder and in fact more alarming—considering the little room left in the Projectile for muscular displays of any kind.

But the most extraordinary part of the whole phenomenon was that neither of them, not even Barbican, had the slightest consciousness of any strange or unusual ebullition of spirits either on his own part or on that of the others.

"See here, gentlemen!" said the Captain in a quick imperious manner—the roughness of his old life on the Mississippi would still break out—"See here, gentlemen! It seems I'm not to know if we are to return from the Moon. Well!—Pass that for the present! But there is one thing I *must* know!"

"Hear! hear the Captain!" cried Barbican, stamping with his foot, like an excited fencing master. "There is one thing he *must* know!"

"I want to know what we're going to do when we get there!"

"He wants to know what we're going to do when we get there! A sensible question! Answer it, Ardan!"

"Answer it yourself, Barbican! You know more about the Moon than I do! You know more about it than all the Nasmyths that ever lived!"

"I'm blessed if I know anything at all about it!" cried Barbican, with a joyous laugh. "Ha, ha, ha! The first eastern shore Marylander or any other simpleton you meet in Baltimore, knows as much about the Moon as I do! Why we're going there, I can't tell! What we're going to do when we get there, can't tell either! Ardan knows all about it! He can tell! He's taking us there!"

"Certainly I can tell! should I have offered to take you there without a good object in view?" cried Ardan, husky with continual roaring. "Answer me that!"

"No conundrums!" cried the Captain, in a voice sourer and rougher than ever; "tell us if you can in plain English, what the demon we have come here for!"

"I'll tell you if I feel like it," cried Ardan, folding his arms with an aspect of great dignity; "and I'll not tell you if I don't feel like it!"

"What's that?" cried Barbican. "You'll not give us an answer when we ask you a reasonable question?"

"Never!" cried Ardan, with great determination. "I'll never answer a question reasonable or unreasonable, unless it is asked in a proper manner!"

"None of your French airs here!" exclaimed M'Nicholl, by this time almost completely out of himself between anger and excitement. "I don't know where I am; I don't know where I'm going; I don't know why I'm going; *you* know all about it, Ardan, or at least you think you do! Well then, give me a plain answer to a plain question, or by the Thirty-eight States of our glorious Union, I shall know what for!"

"Listen, Ardan!" cried Barbican, grappling with the Frenchman, and with some difficulty restraining him from flying at M'Nicholl's throat; "You ought to tell him! It is only your duty! One day you found us both in St. Helena woods, where we had no more idea of going to the Moon than of sailing to the South Pole! There you twisted us both around your finger, and induced us to follow you blindly on the most formidable journey ever undertaken by man! And now you refuse to tell us what it was all for!"

"I don't refuse, dear old Barbican! To you, at least, I can't refuse anything!" cried Ardan, seizing his friend's hands and wringing them violently. Then letting them go and suddenly starting back, "you wish to know," he continued in resounding tones, "why we have followed out the grandest idea that ever set a human brain on fire! Why we have undertaken a journey that for length, danger, and novelty, for fascinating, soul-stirring and delirious sensations, for all that can attract man's burning heart, and satisfy the intensest cravings of his intellect, far surpasses the vividest realities of Dante's passionate dream! Well, I will tell you! It is to annex another World to the New One! It is to take possession of the Moon in the name of the United States of America! It is to add a thirty-ninth State to the glorious Union! It is to colonize the lunar regions, to cultivate them, to people them, to transport to them some of our wonders of art, science, and industry! It is to civilize the Selenites, unless they are more civilized already than we are ourselves! It is to make them all good Republicans, if they are not so already!"

"Provided, of course, that there are Selenites in existence!" sneered the Captain, now sourer than ever, and in his unaccountable excitement doubly irritating.

"Who says there are no Selenites?" cried Ardan fiercely, with fists clenched and brows contracted.

"I do!" cried M'Nicholl stoutly; "I deny the existence of anything of the kind, and I denounce every one that maintains any such whim as a visionary, if not a fool!"

Ardan's reply to this taunt was a desperate facer, which, however, Barbican managed to stop while on its way towards the Captain's nose. M'Nicholl, seeing himself struck at, immediately assumed such a posture of defence as showed him to be no novice at the business. A battle seemed unavoidable; but even at this trying moment Barbican showed himself equal to the emergency.

"Stop, you crazy fellows! you ninnyhammers! you overgrown babies!" he exclaimed, seizing his companions by the collar, and violently swinging them around with his vast strength until they stood back to back; "what are you going to fight about? Suppose there are Lunarians in the Moon! Is that a reason why there should be Lunatics in the Projectile! But, Ardan, why do you insist on Lunarians? Are we so shiftless that we can't do without them when we get to the Moon?"

"I don't insist on them!" cried Ardan, who submitted to Barbican like a child. "Hang the Lunarians! Certainly, we can do without them! What do I care for them? Down with them!"

"Yes, down with the Lunarians!" cried M'Nicholl as spitefully as if he had even the slightest belief in their existence.

"We shall take possession of the Moon ourselves!" cried Ardan. "Lunarians or no Lunarians!"

"We three shall constitute a Republic!" cried M'Nicholl.

"I shall be the House!" cried Ardan.

"And I the Senate!" answered the Captain.

"And Barbican our first President!" shrieked the Frenchman.

"Our first and last!" roared M'Nicholl.

"No objections to a third term!" yelled Ardan.

"He's welcome to any number of terms he pleases!" vociferated M'Nicholl.

"Hurrah for President Barbican of the Lunatic—I mean of the Lunar Republic!" screamed Ardan.

"Long may he wave, and may his shadow never grow less!" shouted Captain M'Nicholl, his eyes almost out of their sockets.

Then with voices reminding you of sand fiercely blown against the window panes, the *President* and the *Senate* chanted the immortal *Yankee Doodle*, whilst the *House* delivered itself of the *Marseillaise*, in a style which even the wildest Jacobins in Robespierre's day could hardly have surpassed.

But long before either song was ended, all three broke out into a dance, wild, insensate, furious, delirious, paroxysmatical. No Orphic festivals on Mount Cithaeron ever raged more wildly. No Bacchic revels on Mount Parnassus were ever more corybantic. Diana, demented by the maddening example, joined in the orgie, howling and barking frantically in her turn, and wildly jumping as high as the ceiling of the Projectile. Then came new accessions to the infernal din. Wings suddenly began to flutter, cocks to crow, hens to cluck; and five or six chickens, managing to escape out of their coop, flew backwards and forwards blindly, with frightened screams, dashing against each other and against the walls of the Projectile, and altogether getting up as demoniacal a hullabaloo as could be made by ten thousand bats that you suddenly disturbed in a cavern where they had slept through the winter.

Then the three companions, no longer able to withstand the overpowering influence of the mysterious force that mastered them, intoxicated, more than drunk, burned by the air that scorched their organs of respiration, dropped at last, and lay flat, motionless, senseless as dabs of clay, on the floor of the Projectile.

VIII

The Neutral Point

What had taken place? Whence proceeded this strange intoxication whose consequences might have proved so disastrous? A little forgetfulness on Ardan's part had done the whole mischief, but fortunately M'Nicholl was able to remedy it in time.

After a regular fainting spell several minutes long, the Captain was the first man to return to consciousness and the full recovery of his intellectual faculties. His first feelings were far from pleasant. His stomach gnawed him as if he had not eaten for a week, though he had taken breakfast only a few hours before; his eyes were dim, his brain throbbing, and his limbs shaking. In short, he presented every symptom usually seen in a man dying of starvation. Picking himself up with much care and difficulty, he roared out to Ardan for something to eat. Seeing that the Frenchman was unable or unwilling to respond, he concluded to help himself, by beginning first of all to prepare a little tea. To do this, fire was necessary; so, to light his lamp, he struck a match.

But what was his surprise at seeing the sulphur tip of the match blazing with a light so bright and dazzling that his eyes could hardly bear it! Touching it to the gas burner, a stream of light flashed forth equal in its intensity to the flame of an electric lamp. Then he understood it all in an instant. The dazzling glare, his maddened brain, his gnawing stomach—all were now clear as the noon-day Sun.

"The oxygen!" he cried, and, suddenly stooping down and examining the tap of the air apparatus, he saw that it had been only half turned off. Consequently the air was gradually getting more and more impregnated with this powerful gas, colorless, odorless, tasteless, infinitely precious, but, unless when strongly diluted with nitrogen, capable of producing fatal disorders in the human system. Ardan, startled by M'Nicholl's question about the means of returning from the Moon, had turned the cock only half off.

The Captain instantly stopped the escape of the oxygen, but not one moment too soon. It had completely saturated the atmosphere. A few minutes more and it would have killed the travellers, not like carbonic acid, by smothering them, but by burning them up, as a strong draught burns up the coals in a stove.

It took nearly an hour for the air to become pure enough to allow the lungs their natural play. Slowly and by degrees, the travellers recovered from their intoxication; they had actually to sleep off the fumes of the oxygen as a drunkard has to sleep off the effects of his brandy. When Ardan learned that he was responsible for the whole trouble, do you think the information disconcerted him? Not a bit of it. On the contrary, he was rather proud of having done something startling, to break the monotony of the journey; and to put a little life, as he said, into old Barbican and the grim Captain, so as to get a little fun out of such grave philosophers.

After laughing heartily at the comical figure cut by his two friends capering like crazy students at the *Closerie des Lilas*, he went on moralizing on the incident:

"For my part, I'm not a bit sorry for having partaken of this fuddling gas. It gives me an idea, dear boys. Would it not be worth some enterprising fellow's while to establish a sanatorium provided with oxygen chambers, where people of a debilitated state of health could enjoy a few hours of intensely active existence! There's money in it, as you Americans say. Just suppose balls or parties given in halls where the air would be provided with an extra supply of this enrapturing gas! Or, theatres where the atmosphere would be maintained in a highly oxygenated condition. What passion, what fire in the actors! What enthusiasm in the spectators! And, carrying the idea a little further, if, instead of an assembly or an audience, we should oxygenize towns, cities, a whole country—what activity would be infused into the whole people! What new life would electrify a stagnant community! Out of an old used-up nation we could perhaps make a bran-new one, and, for my part, I know more than one state in old Europe where this oxygen experiment might be attended with a decided advantage, or where, at all events, it could do no harm!"

The Frenchman spoke so glibly and gesticulated so earnestly that M'Nicholl once more gravely examined the stop-cock; but Barbican damped his enthusiasm by a single observation.

"Friend Michael," said he, "your new and interesting idea we shall discuss at a more favorable opportunity. At present we want to know where all these cocks and hens have come from."

"These cocks and hens?"

"Yes."

Ardan threw a glance of comical bewilderment on half a dozen or so of splendid barn-yard fowls that were now beginning to recover from the effects of the oxygen. For an instant he could not utter a word; then, shrugging his shoulders, he muttered in a low voice:

"Catastrophe prematurely exploded!"

"What are you going to do with these chickens?" persisted Barbican.

"Acclimatize them in the Moon, by Jove! what else?" was the ready reply.

"Why conceal them then?"

"A hoax, a poor hoax, dear President, which proves a miserable failure! I intended to let them loose on the Lunar Continent at the first favorable opportunity. I often had a good laugh to myself, thinking of your astonishment and the Captain's at seeing a lot of American poultry scratching for worms on a Lunar dunghill!"

"Ah! wag, jester, incorrigible *farceur!*" cried Barbican with a smile; "you want no nitrous oxide to put a bee in your bonnet! He is always as bad as you and I were for a short time, M'Nicholl, under the laughing gas! He's never had a sensible moment in his life!"

"I can't say the same of you," replied Ardan; "you had at least one sensible moment in all your lives, and that was about an hour ago!"

Their incessant chattering did not prevent the friends from at once repairing the disorder of the interior of the Projectile. Cocks and hens were put back in their cages. But while doing so, the friends were astonished to find that birds, though good sized creatures, and now pretty fat and plump, hardly felt heavier in their hands than if they had been so many sparrows. This drew their interested attention to a new phenomenon.

From the moment they had left the Earth, their own weight, and that of the Projectile and the objects therein contained, had been undergoing a progressive diminution. They might never be able to ascertain this fact with regard to the Projectile, but the moment was now rapidly approaching when the loss of weight would become perfectly sensible, both regarding themselves and the tools and instruments surrounding them. Of course, it is quite clear, that this decrease could not be indicated by an ordinary scales, as the weight to balance the object would have lost precisely as much as the object itself. But a spring balance, for instance, in which the tension of the coil is independent of attraction, would have readily given the exact equivalent of the loss.

Attraction or weight, according to Newton's well known law, acting in direct proportion to the mass of the attracting body and in inverse proportion to the square of the distance, this consequence clearly follows: Had the Earth been alone in space, or had the other heavenly bodies been suddenly annihilated, the further from the Earth the Projectile would be, the less weight it would have. However, it would never *entirely* lose its weight, as the terrestrial attraction would have always made itself felt at no matter what distance. But as the Earth is not the only celestial body possessing attraction, it is evident that there may be a point in space where the respective attractions may be entirely annihilated by mutual counteraction. Of this phenomenon the present instance was a case in point. In a short time, the Projectile and its contents would for a few moments be absolutely and completely deprived of all weight whatsoever.

The path described by the Projectile was evidently a line from the Earth to the Moon averaging somewhat less than 240,000 miles in length. According as the distance between the Projectile and the Earth was increasing, the terrestrial attraction was diminishing in the ratio of the square of the distance, and the lunar attraction was augmenting in the same proportion.

As before observed, the point was not now far off where, the two attractions counteracting each other, the bullet would actually weigh nothing at all. If the masses of the Earth and the Moon had been equal, this should evidently be found half way between the two bodies. But by making allowance for the difference of the respective masses, it was easy to calculate that this point would be situated at the 9/10 of the total distance, or, in round numbers, at something less than 216,000 miles from the Earth.

At this point, a body that possessed no energy or principle of movement within itself, would remain forever, relatively motionless, suspended like Mahomet's coffin, being equally attracted by the two orbs and nothing impelling it in one direction rather than in the other.

Now the Projectile at this moment was nearing this point; if it reached it, what would be the consequence?

To this question three answers presented themselves, all possible under the circumstances, but very different in their results.

1. Suppose the Projectile to possess velocity enough to pass the neutral point. In such case, it would undoubtedly proceed onward to the Moon, being drawn thither by Lunar attraction.

2. Suppose it lacked the requisite velocity for reaching the neutral point. In such a case it would just as certainly fall back to the Earth, in obedience to the law of Terrestrial attraction.

3. Suppose it to be animated by just sufficient velocity to reach the neutral point, but not to pass it. In that case, the Projectile would remain forever in the same spot, perfectly motionless as far as regards the Earth and the Moon, though of course following them both in their annual orbits round the Sun.

Such was now the state of things, which Barbican tried to explain to his friends, who, it need hardly be said, listened to his remarks with the most intense interest. How were they to know, they asked him, the precise instant at which the Projectile would reach the neutral point? That would be an easy matter, he assured them. It would be at the very moment when both themselves and all the other objects contained in the Projectile would be completely free from every operation of the law of gravity; in other words, when everything would cease to have weight.

This gradual diminution of the action of gravity, the travellers had been for some time noticing, but they had not yet witnessed its total cessation. But that very morning, about an hour before noon, as the Captain was making some little experiment in Chemistry, he happened by accident to overturn a glass full of water. What was his surprise at seeing that neither the glass nor the water fell to the floor! Both remained suspended in the air almost completely motionless.

"The prettiest experiment I ever saw!" cried Ardan; "let us have more of it!"

And seizing the bottles, the arms, and the other objects in the Projectile, he arranged them around each other in the air with some regard to symmetry and proportion. The different articles, keeping strictly each in its own place, formed a very attractive group wonderful to behold. Diana, placed in the apex of the pyramid, would remind you of those marvellous suspensions in the air performed by Houdin, Herman, and a few other first class wizards. Only being kept in her place without being hampered by invisible strings, the animal rather seemed to enjoy the exhibition, though in all probability she was hardly conscious of any thing unusual in her appearance.

Our travellers had been fully prepared for such a phenomenon, yet it struck them with as much surprise as if they had never uttered a scientific reason to account for it. They saw that, no longer subject to the ordinary laws of nature, they were now entering the realms of the marvellous. They felt that their bodies were absolutely without weight. Their arms, fully extended, no longer sought their sides. Their heads oscillated unsteadily on their shoulders. Their feet no longer rested on the floor. In their efforts to hold themselves straight, they looked like drunken men trying to maintain the perpendicular. We have all read stories of some men deprived of the power of reflecting light and of others who could not cast a shadow. But here reality, no fantastic story, showed you men who, through the counteraction of attractive forces, could tell no difference between light substances and heavy substances, and who absolutely had no weight whatever themselves!

"Let us take graceful attitudes!" cried Ardan, "and imagine we are playing *tableaux*! Let us, for instance, form a grand historical group of the three great goddesses of the nineteenth century. Barbican will represent Minerva or *Science*; the Captain, Bellona or *War*; while I, as Madre Natura, the newly born goddess of *Progress*, floating gracefully over you both, extend my hands so, fondly patronizing the one, but grandly ordering off the other, to the regions of eternal night! More on your toe, Captain! Your right foot a little higher! Look at Barbican's admirable pose! Now then, prepare to receive orders for a new tableau! Form group *à la Jardin Mabille!* Presto! Change!"

In an instant, our travellers, changing attitudes, formed the new group with tolerable success. Even Barbican, who had been to Paris in his youth, yielding for a moment to the humor of the thing, acted the *naif Anglais* to the life. The Captain was frisky enough to remind you of a middle-aged Frenchman from the provinces, on a hasty visit to the capital for a few days' fun. Ardan was in raptures.

"Oh! if Raphael could only see us!" he exclaimed in a kind of ecstasy. "He would paint such a picture as would throw all his other masterpieces in the shade!"

"Knock spots out of the best of them by fifty per cent!" cried the Captain, gesticulating well enough *à l'étudiant*, but rather mixing his metaphors.

"He should be pretty quick in getting through the job," observed Barbican, the first as usual to recover tranquillity. "As soon as the Projectile will have passed the neutral point—in half an hour at longest—lunar attraction will draw us to the Moon."

"We shall have to crawl on the ceiling then like flies," said Ardan.

"Not at all," said the Captain; "the Projectile, having its centre of gravity very low, will turn upside down by degrees."

"Upside down!" cried Ardan. "That will be a nice mess! everything higgledy-piggledy!"

"No danger, friend Michael," said M'Nicholl; "there shall be no disorder whatever; nothing will quit its place; the movement of the Projectile will be effected by such slow degrees as to be imperceptible."

"Yes," added Barbican, "as soon as we shall have passed the neutral point, the base of the Projectile, its heaviest part, will swing around gradually until it faces the Moon. Before this phenomenon, however, can take place, we must of course cross the line."

"Cross the line!" cried the Frenchman; "then let us imitate the sailors when they do the same thing in the Atlantic Ocean! Splice the main brace!"

A slight effort carried him sailing over to the side of the Projectile. Opening a cupboard and taking out a bottle and a few glasses, he placed them on a tray. Then setting the tray itself in the air as on a table in front of his companions, he filled the glasses, passed them around, and, in a lively speech interrupted with many a joyous hurrah, congratulated his companions on their glorious achievement in being the first that ever crossed the lunar line.

This counteracting influence of the attractions lasted nearly an hour. By that time the travellers could keep themselves on the floor without much effort. Barbican also made his companions remark that the conical point of the Projectile diverged a little from the direct line to the Moon, while by an inverse movement, as they could notice through the window of the floor, the base was gradually turning away from the Earth. The Lunar attraction was evidently getting the better of the Terrestrial. The fall towards the Moon, though still almost insensible, was certainly beginning.

It could not be more than the eightieth part of an inch in the first second. But by degrees, as the attractive force would increase, the fall would be more decided, and the Projectile, overbalanced by its base, and presenting its cone to the Earth, would descend with accelerated velocity to the Lunar surface. The object of their daring attempt would then be successfully attained. No further obstacle, therefore, being likely to stand in the way of the complete success of the enterprise, the Captain and the Frenchman cordially shook hands with Barbican, all kept congratulating each other on their good fortune as long as the bottle lasted.

They could not talk enough about the wonderful phenomenon lately witnessed; the chief point, the neutralization of the law of gravity, particularly, supplied them with an inexhaustible subject. The Frenchman, as usual, as enthusiastic in his fancy, as he was fanciful in his enthusiasm, got off some characteristic remarks.

"What a fine thing it would be, my boys," he exclaimed, "if on Earth we could be so fortunate as we have been here, and get rid of that weight that keeps us down like lead, that rivets us to it like an adamantine chain! Then should we prisoners become free! Adieu forever to all weariness of arms or feet! At present, in order to fly over the surface of the Earth by the simple exertion of our muscles or even to sustain ourselves in the air, we require a muscular force fifty times greater than we possess; but if attraction did not exist, the simplest act of the will, our slightest whim even, would be sufficient to transport us to whatever part of space we wished to visit."

"Ardan, you had better invent something to kill attraction," observed M'Nicholl drily; "you can do it if you try. Jackson and Morton have killed pain by sulphuric ether. Suppose you try your hand on attraction!"

"It would be worth a trial!" cried Ardan, so full of his subject as not to notice the Captain's jeering tone; "attraction once destroyed, there is an end forever to all loads, packs and burdens! How the poor omnibus horses would rejoice! Adieu forever to all cranes, derricks, capstans, jackscrews, and even hotel-elevators! We could dispense with all ladders, door steps, and even stair-cases!"

"And with all houses too," interrupted Barbican; "or, at least, we *should* dispense with them because we could not have them. If there was no weight, you could neither make a wall of bricks nor cover your house with a roof. Even your hat would not stay on your head. The cars would not stay on the railway nor the boats on the water. What do I say? We could not have any water. Even the Ocean would leave its bed and float away into space. Nay, the atmosphere itself would leave us, being detained in its place by terrestrial attraction and by nothing else."

"Too true, Mr. President," replied Ardan after a pause. "It's a fact. I acknowledge the corn, as Marston says. But how you positive fellows do knock holes into our pretty little creations of fancy!"

"Don't feel so bad about it, Ardan;" observed M'Nicholl; "though there may be no orb from which gravity is excluded altogether, we shall soon land in one, where it is much less powerful than on the Earth."

"You mean the Moon!"

"Yes, the Moon. Her mass being 1/89 of the Earth's, her attractive power should be in the same proportion; that is, a boy 10 years old, whose weight on Earth is about 90 lbs., would weigh on the Moon only about 1 pound, if nothing else were to be taken into consideration. But when standing on the surface of the Moon, he is relatively 4 times nearer to the centre than when he is standing on the surface of the Earth. His weight, therefore, having to be increased by the square of the distance, must be sixteen times greater. Now 16 times 1/89 being less than 1/5, it is clear that my weight of 150 pounds will be cut down to nearly 30 as soon as we reach the Moon's surface."

"And mine?" asked Ardan.

"Yours will hardly reach 25 pounds, I should think," was the reply.

"Shall my muscular strength diminish in the same proportion?" was the next question.

"On the contrary, it will be relatively so much the more increased that you can take a stride 15 feet in width as easily as you can now take one of ordinary length."

"We shall be all Samsons, then, in the Moon!" cried Ardan.

"Especially," replied M'Nicholl, "if the stature of the Selenites is in proportion to the mass of their globe."

"If so, what should be their height?"

"A tall man would hardly be twelve inches in his boots!"

"They must be veritable Lilliputians then!" cried Ardan; "and we are all to be Gullivers! The old myth of the Giants realized! Perhaps the Titans that played such famous parts in the prehistoric period of our Earth, were adventurers like ourselves, casually arrived from some great planet!"

"Not from such planets as *Mercury*, *Venus* or *Mars* anyhow, friend Michael," observed Barbican. "But the inhabitants of *Jupiter*, *Saturn*, *Uranus*, or *Neptune*, if they bear the same proportion to their planet that we do ours, must certainly be regular Brobdignagians."

"Let us keep severely away from all planets of the latter class then," said Ardan. "I never liked to play the part of Lilliputian myself. But how about the Sun, Barbican? I always had a hankering after the Sun!"

"The Sun's volume is about 1-1/3 million times greater than that of the Earth, but his density being only about 1/4, the attraction on his surface is hardly 30 times greater than that of our globe. Still, every proportion observed, the inhabitants of the Sun can't be much less than 150 or 160 feet in height."

"*Mille tonnerres!*" cried Ardan, "I should be there like Ulysses among the Cyclops! I'll tell you what it is, Barbican; if we ever decide on going to the Sun, we must provide ourselves before hand with a few of your Rodman's Columbiads to frighten off the Solarians!"

"Your Columbiads would not do great execution there," observed M'Nicholl; "your bullet would be hardly out of the barrel when it would drop to the surface like a heavy stone pushed off the wall of a house."

"Oh! I like that!" laughed the incredulous Ardan.

"A little calculation, however, shows the Captain's remark to be perfectly just," said Barbican. "Rodman's ordinary 15 inch Columbiad requires a charge of 100 pounds of mammoth powder to throw a ball of 500 pounds weight. What could such a charge do with a ball weighing 30 times as much or 15,000 pounds? Reflect on the enormous weight everything must have on the surface of the Sun! Your hat, for instance, would weigh 20 or 30 pounds. Your cigar nearly a pound. In short, your own weight on the Sun's surface would be so great, more than two tons, that if you ever fell you should never be able to pick yourself up again!"

"Yes," added the Captain, "and whenever you wanted to eat or drink you should rig up a set of powerful machinery to hoist the eatables and drinkables into your mouth."

"Enough of the Sun to-day, boys!" cried Ardan, shrugging his shoulders; "I don't contemplate going there at present. Let us be satisfied with the Moon! There, at least, we shall be of some account!"

IX

A Little off the Track

Barbican's mind was now completely at rest at least on one subject. The original force of the discharge had been great enough to send the Projectile beyond the neutral line. Therefore, there was no longer any danger of its falling back to the Earth. Therefore, there was no longer any danger of its resting eternally motionless on the point of the counteracting attractions. The next subject to engage his attention was the question: would the Projectile, under the influence of lunar attraction, succeed in reaching its destination?

The only way in which it *could* succeed was by falling through a space of nearly 24,000 miles and then striking the Moon's surface. A most terrific fall! Even taking the lunar attraction to be only the one-sixth of the Earth's, such a fall was simply bewildering to think of. The greatest height to which a balloon ever ascended was seven miles (Glaisher, 1862). Imagine a fall from even that distance! Then imagine a fall from a height of four thousand miles!

Yet it was for a fall of this appalling kind on the surface of the Moon that the travellers had now to prepare themselves. Instead of avoiding it, however, they eagerly desired it and would be very much disappointed if they missed it. They had taken the best precautions they could devise to guard against the terrific shock. These were mainly of two kinds: one was intended to counteract as much as possible the fearful results to be expected the instant the Projectile touched the lunar surface; the other, to retard the velocity of the fall itself, and thereby to render it less violent.

The best arrangement of the first kind was certainly Barbican's water-contrivance for counteracting the shock at starting, which has been so fully described in our former volume. (See *Baltimore Gun Club*, page 353.) But unfortunately it could be no longer employed. Even if the partitions were in working order, the water—two thousand pounds in weight had been required—was no longer to be had. The little still left in the tanks was of no account for such a purpose. Besides, they had not a single drop of the precious liquid to spare, for they were as yet anything but sanguine regarding the facility of finding water on the Moon's surface.

Fortunately, however, as the gentle reader may remember, Barbican, besides using water to break the concussion, had provided the movable disc with stout pillars containing a strong buffing apparatus, intended to protect it from striking the bottom too violently after the destruction of the different partitions. These buffers were still good, and, gravity being as yet almost imperceptible, to put them once more in order and adjust them to the disc was not a difficult task.

The travellers set to work at once and soon accomplished it. The different pieces were put together readily—a mere matter of bolts and screws, with plenty of tools to manage them. In a short time the repaired disc rested on its steel buffers, like a table on its legs, or rather like a sofa seat on its springs. The new arrangement was attended with at least one disadvantage. The bottom light being covered up, a convenient view of the Moon's surface could not be had as soon as they should begin to fall in a perpendicular descent. This, however, was only a slight matter, as the side lights would permit the adventurers to enjoy quite as favorable a view of the vast regions of the Moon as is afforded to balloon travellers when looking down on the Earth over the sides of their car.

The disc arrangement was completed in about an hour, but it was not till past twelve o'clock before things were restored to their usual order. Barbican then tried to make fresh observations regarding the inclination of the Projectile; but to his very decided chagrin he found that it had not yet turned over sufficiently to commence the perpendicular fall: on the contrary, it even seemed to be following a curve rather parallel with that of the lunar disc. The Queen of the Stars now glittered with a light more dazzling than ever, whilst from an opposite part of the sky the glorious King of Day flooded her with his fires.

The situation began to look a little serious.

"Shall we ever get there!" asked the Captain.

"Let us be prepared for getting there, any how," was Barbican's dubious reply.

"You're a pretty pair of suspenders," said Ardan cheerily (he meant of course doubting hesitators, but his fluent command of English sometimes led him into such solecisms). "Certainly we shall get there—and perhaps a little sooner than will be good for us."

This reply sharply recalled Barbican to the task he had undertaken, and he now went to work seriously, trying to combine arrangements to break the fall. The reader may perhaps remember Ardan's reply to the Captain on the day of the famous meeting in Tampa.

"Your fall would be violent enough," the Captain had urged, "to splinter you like glass into a thousand fragments."

"And what shall prevent me," had been Ardan's ready reply, "from breaking my fall by means of counteracting rockets suitably disposed, and let off at the proper time?"

The practical utility of this idea had at once impressed Barbican. It could hardly be doubted that powerful rockets, fastened on the outside to the bottom of the Projectile, could, when discharged, considerably retard the velocity of the fall by their sturdy recoil. They could burn in a vacuum by means of oxygen furnished by themselves, as powder burns in the chamber of a gun, or as the volcanoes of the Moon continue their action regardless of the absence of a lunar atmosphere.

Barbican had therefore provided himself with rockets enclosed in strong steel gun barrels, grooved on the outside so that they could be screwed into corresponding holes already made with much care in the bottom of the Projectile. They were just long enough, when flush with the floor inside, to project outside by about six inches. They were twenty in number, and formed two concentric circles around the dead light. Small holes in the disc gave admission to the wires by which each of the rockets was to be discharged externally by electricity. The whole effect was therefore to be confined to the outside. The mixtures having been already carefully deposited in each barrel, nothing further need be done than to take away the metallic plugs which had been screwed into the bottom of the Projectile, and replace them by the rockets, every one of which was found to fit its grooved chamber with rigid exactness.

This evidently should have been all done before the disc had been finally laid on its springs. But as this had to be lifted up again in order to reach the bottom of the Projectile, more work was to be done than was strictly necessary. Though the labor was not very hard, considering that gravity had as yet scarcely made itself felt, M'Nicholl and Ardan were not sorry to have their little joke at Barbican's expense. The Frenchman began humming

"Aliquandoque bonus dormitat Homerus,"

to a tune from *Orphée aux Enfers*, and the Captain said something about the Philadelphia Highway Commissioners who pave a street one day, and tear it up the next to lay the gas pipes. But his friends' humor was all lost on Barbican, who was so wrapped up in his work that he probably never heard a word they said.

Towards three o'clock every preparation was made, every possible precaution taken, and now our bold adventurers had nothing more to do than watch and wait.

The Projectile was certainly approaching the Moon. It had by this time turned over considerably under the influence of attraction, but its own original motion still followed a decidedly oblique direction. The consequence of these two forces might possibly be a tangent, line approaching the edge of the Moon's disc. One thing was certain: the Projectile had not yet commenced to fall directly towards her surface; its base, in which its centre of gravity lay, was still turned away considerably from the perpendicular.

Barbican's countenance soon showed perplexity and even alarm. His Projectile was proving intractable to the laws of gravitation. The *unknown* was opening out dimly before him, the great boundless unknown of the starry plains. In his pride and confidence as a scientist, he had flattered himself with having sounded the consequence of every possible hypothesis regarding the Projectile's ultimate fate: the return to the Earth; the arrival at the Moon; and the motionless dead stop at the neutral point. But here, a new and incomprehensible fourth hypothesis, big with the terrors of the mystic infinite, rose up before his disturbed mind, like a grim and hollow ghost. After a few seconds, however, he looked at it straight in the face without wincing. His companions showed themselves just as firm. Whether it was science that emboldened Barbican, his phlegmatic stoicism that propped up the Captain, or his enthusiastic vivacity that cheered the irrepressible Ardan, I cannot exactly say. But certainly they were all soon talking over the matter as calmly as you or I would discuss the advisability of taking a sail on the lake some beautiful evening in July.

Their first remarks were decidedly peculiar and quite characteristic. Other men would have asked themselves where the Projectile was taking them to. Do you think such a question ever occurred to them? Not a bit of it. They simply began asking each other what could have been the cause of this new and strange state of things.

"Off the track, it appears," observed Ardan. "How's that?"

"My opinion is," answered the Captain, "that the Projectile was not aimed true. Every possible precaution had been taken, I am well aware, but we all know that an inch, a line, even the tenth part of a hair's breadth wrong at the start would have sent us thousands of miles off our course by this time."

"What have you to say to that, Barbican?" asked Ardan.

"I don't think there was any error at the start," was the confident reply; "not even so much as a line! We took too many tests proving the absolute perpendicularity of the Columbiad, to entertain the slightest doubt on that subject. Its direction towards the zenith being incontestable, I don't see why we should not reach the Moon when she comes to the zenith."

"Perhaps we're behind time," suggested Ardan.

"What have you to say to that, Barbican?" asked the Captain. "You know the Cambridge men said the journey had to be done in 97 hours 13 minutes and 20 seconds. That's as much as to say that if we're not up to time we shall miss the Moon."

"Correct," said Barbican. "But we *can't* be behind time. We started, you know, on December 1st, at 13 minutes and 20 seconds before 11 o'clock, and we were to arrive four days later at midnight precisely. To-day is December 5th Gentlemen, please examine your watches. It is now half past three in the afternoon. Eight hours and a half are sufficient to take us to our journey's end. Why should we not arrive there?"

"How about being ahead of time?" asked the Captain.

"Just so!" said Ardan. "You know we have discovered the initial velocity to have been greater than was expected."

"Not at all! not at all!" cried Barbican "A slight excess of velocity would have done no harm whatever had the direction of the Projectile been perfectly true. No. There must have been a digression. We must have been switched off!"

"Switched off? By what?" asked both his listeners in one breath.

"I can't tell," said Barbican curtly.

"Well!" said Ardan; "if Barbican can't tell, there is an end to all further talk on the subject. We're switched off—that's enough for me. What has done it? I don't care. Where are we going to? I don't care. What is the use of pestering our brains about it? We shall soon find out. We are floating around in space, and we shall end by hauling up somewhere or other."

But in this indifference Barbican was far from participating. Not that he was not prepared to meet the future with a bold and manly heart. It was his inability to answer his own question that rendered him uneasy. What *had* switched them off? He would have given worlds for an answer, but his brain sorely puzzled sought one in vain.

In the mean time, the Projectile continued to turn its side rather than its base towards the Moon; that is, to assume a lateral rather than a direct movement, and this movement was fully participated in by the multitude of the objects that had been thrown outside. Barbican could even convince himself by sighting several points on the lunar surface, by this time hardly more than fifteen or eighteen thousand miles distant, that the velocity of the Projectile instead of accelerating was becoming more and more uniform. This was another proof that there was no perpendicular fall. However, though the original impulsive force was still superior to the Moon's attraction, the travellers were evidently approaching the lunar disc, and there was every reason to hope that they would at last reach a point where, the lunar attraction at last having the best of it, a decided fall should be the result.

The three friends, it need hardly be said, continued to make their observations with redoubled interest, if redoubled interest were possible. But with all their care they could as yet determine nothing regarding the topographical details of our radiant satellite. Her surface still reflected the solar rays too dazzlingly to show the relief necessary for satisfactory observation.

Our travellers kept steadily on the watch looking out of the side lights, till eight o'clock in the evening, by which time the Moon had grown so large in their eyes that she covered up fully half the sky. At this time the Projectile itself must have looked like a streak of light, reflecting, as it did, the Sun's brilliancy on the one side and the Moon's splendor on the other.

Barbican now took a careful observation and calculated that they could not be much more than 2,000 miles from the object of their journey. The velocity of the Projectile he calculated to be about 650 feet per second or 450 miles an hour. They had therefore still plenty of time to reach the Moon in about four hours. But though the bottom of the Projectile continued to turn towards the lunar surface in obedience to the law of centripetal force, the centrifugal force was still evidently strong enough to change the path which it followed into some kind of curve, the exact nature of which would be exceedingly difficult to calculate.

The careful observations that Barbican continued to take did not however prevent him from endeavoring to solve his difficult problem. What *had* switched them off? The hours passed on, but brought no result. That the adventurers were approaching the Moon was evident, but it was just as evident that they should never reach her. The nearest point the Projectile could ever possibly attain would only be the result of two opposite forces, the attractive and the repulsive, which, as was now clear, influenced its motion. Therefore, to land in the Moon was an utter impossibility, and any such idea was to be given up at once and for ever.

"*Quand même*! What of it!" cried Ardan; after some moments' silence. "We're not to land in the Moon! Well! let us do the next best thing—pass close enough to discover her secrets!"

But M'Nicholl could not accept the situation so coolly. On the contrary, he decidedly lost his temper, as is occasionally the case with even phlegmatic men. He muttered an oath or two, but in a voice hardly loud enough to reach Barbican's ear. At last, impatient of further restraint, he burst out:

"Who the deuce cares for her secrets? To the hangman with her secrets! We started to land in the Moon! That's what's got to be done! That I want or nothing! Confound the darned thing, I say, whatever it was, whether on the Earth or off it, that shoved us off the track!"

"On the Earth or off it!" cried Barbican, striking his head suddenly; "now I see it! You're right, Captain! Confound the bolide that we met the first night of our journey!"

"Hey?" cried Ardan.

"What do you mean?" asked M'Nicholl.

"I mean," replied Barbican, with a voice now perfectly calm, and in a tone of quiet conviction, "that our deviation is due altogether to that wandering meteor."

"Why, it did not even graze us!" cried Ardan.

"No matter for that," replied Barbican. "Its mass, compared to ours, was enormous, and its attraction was undoubtedly sufficiently great to influence our deviation."

"Hardly enough to be appreciable," urged M'Nicholl.

"Right again, Captain," observed Barbican. "But just remember an observation of your own made this very afternoon: an inch, a line, even the tenth part of a hair's breadth wrong at the beginning, in a journey of 240 thousand miles, would be sufficient to make us miss the Moon!"

X

The Observers of the Moon

B arbican's happy conjecture had probably hit the nail on the head. The divergency even of a second may amount to millions of miles if you only have your lines long enough. The Projectile had certainly gone off its direct course; whatever the cause, the fact was undoubted. It was a great pity. The daring attempt must end in a failure due altogether to a fortuitous accident, against which no human foresight could have possibly taken precaution. Unless in case of the occurrence of some other most improbable accident, reaching the Moon was evidently now impossible. To failure, therefore, our travellers had to make up their minds.

But was nothing to be gained by the trip? Though missing actual contact with the Moon, might they not pass near enough to solve several problems in physics and geology over which scientists had been for a long time puzzling their brains in vain? Even this would be some compensation for all their trouble, courage, and intelligence. As to what was to be their own fate, to what doom were themselves to be reserved— they never appeared to think of such a thing. They knew very well that in the midst of those infinite solitudes they should soon find themselves without air. The slight supply that kept them from smothering could not possibly last more than five or six days longer. Five or six days! What of that? *Quand même*! as Ardan often exclaimed. Five or six days were centuries to our bold adventurers! At present every second was a year in events, and infinitely too precious to be squandered away in mere preparations for possible contingencies. The Moon could never be reached, but was it not possible that her surface could be carefully observed? This they set themselves at once to find out.

The distance now separating them from our Satellite they estimated at about 400 miles. Therefore relatively to their power of discovering the details of her disc, they were still farther off from the Moon than some of our modern astronomers are to-day, when provided with their powerful telescopes.

We know, for example, that Lord Rosse's great telescope at Parsonstown, possessing a power of magnifying 6000 times, brings the

Moon to within 40 miles of us; not to speak of Barbican's great telescope on the summit of Long's Peak, by which the Moon, magnified 48,000 times, was brought within 5 miles of the Earth, where it therefore could reveal with sufficient distinctness every object above 40 feet in diameter.

Therefore our adventurers, though at such a comparatively small distance, could not make out the topographical details of the Moon with any satisfaction by their unaided vision. The eye indeed could easily enough catch the rugged outline of these vast depressions improperly called "Seas," but it could do very little more. Its powers of adjustability seemed to fail before the strange and bewildering scene. The prominence of the mountains vanished, not only through the foreshortening, but also in the dazzling radiation produced by the direct reflection of the solar rays. After a short time therefore, completely foiled by the blinding glare, the eye turned itself unwillingly away, as if from a furnace of molten silver.

The spherical surface, however, had long since begun to reveal its convexity. The Moon was gradually assuming the appearance of a gigantic egg with the smaller end turned towards the Earth. In the earlier days of her formation, while still in a state of mobility, she had been probably a perfect sphere in shape, but, under the influence of terrestrial gravity operating for uncounted ages, she was drawn at last so much towards the centre of attraction as to resemble somewhat a prolate spheriod. By becoming a satellite, she had lost the native perfect regularity of her outline; her centre of gravity had shifted from her real centre; and as a result of this arrangement, some scientists have drawn the conclusion that the Moon's air and water have been attracted to that portion of her surface which is always invisible to the inhabitants of the Earth.

The convexity of her outline, this bulging prominence of her surface, however, did not last long. The travellers were getting too near to notice it. They were beginning to survey the Moon as balloonists survey the Earth. The Projectile was now moving with great rapidity—with nothing like its initial velocity, but still eight or nine times faster than an express train. Its line of movement, however, being oblique instead of direct, was so deceptive as to induce Ardan to flatter himself that they might still reach the lunar surface. He could never persuade himself to believe that they should get so near their aim and still miss it. No; nothing might, could, would or should induce him to believe it, he repeated again and again. But Barbican's pitiless logic left him no reply.

"No, dear friend, no. We can reach the Moon only by a fall, and we don't fall. Centripetal force keeps us at least for a while under the lunar influence, but centrifugal force drives us away irresistibly."

These words were uttered in a tone that killed Ardan's last and fondest hope.

THE PORTION OF THE MOON they were now approaching was her northern hemisphere, found usually in the lower part of lunar maps. The lens of a telescope, as is well known, gives only the inverted image of the object; therefore, when an upright image is required, an additional glass must be used. But as every additional glass is an additional obstruction to the light, the object glass of a Lunar telescope is employed without a corrector; light is thereby saved, and in viewing the Moon, as in viewing a map, it evidently makes very little difference whether we see her inverted or not. Maps of the Moon therefore, being drawn from the image formed by the telescope, show the north in the lower part, and *vice versa*. Of this kind was the *Mappa Selenographica*, by Beer and Maedler, so often previously alluded to and now carefully consulted by Barbican. The northern hemisphere, towards which they were now rapidly approaching, presented a strong contrast with the southern, by its vast plains and great depressions, checkered here and there by very remarkable isolated mountains.

At midnight the Moon was full. This was the precise moment at which the travellers would have landed had not that unlucky bolide drawn them off the track. The Moon was therefore strictly up to time, arriving at the instant rigidly determined by the Cambridge Observatory. She occupied the exact point, to a mathematical nicety, where our 28th parallel crossed the perigee. An observer posted in the bottom of the Columbiad at Stony Hill, would have found himself at this moment precisely under the Moon. The axis of the enormous gun, continued upwards vertically, would have struck the orb of night exactly in her centre.

It is hardly necessary to tell our readers that, during this memorable night of the 5th and 6th of December, the travellers had no desire to close their eyes. Could they do so, even if they had desired? No! All their faculties, thoughts, and desires, were concentrated in one single word: "Look!" Representatives of the Earth, and of all humanity past and present, they felt that it was with their eyes that the race of man contemplated the lunar regions and penetrated the secrets of our satellite! A certain indescribable emotion therefore, combined with an undefined sense of responsibility, held possession of their hearts, as they moved silently from window to window.

Their observations, recorded by Barbican, were vigorously remade, revised, and re-determined, by the others. To make them, they had telescopes which they now began to employ with great advantage. To regulate and investigate them, they had the best maps of the day.

Whilst occupied in this silent work, they could not help throwing a short retrospective glance on the former Observers of the Moon.

The first of these was Galileo. His slight telescope magnified only thirty times, still, in the spots flecking the lunar surface, like the eyes checkering a peacock's tail, he was the first to discover mountains and even to measure their heights. These, considering the difficulties under which he labored, were wonderfully accurate, but unfortunately he made no map embodying his observations.

A few years afterwards, Hevel of Dantzic, (1611–1688) a Polish astronomer—more generally known as Hevelius, his works being all written in Latin—undertook to correct Galileo's measurements. But as his method could be strictly accurate only twice a month—the periods of the first and second quadratures—his rectifications could be hardly called successful.

Still it is to the labors of this eminent astronomer, carried on uninterruptedly for fifty years in his own observatory, that we owe the first map of the Moon. It was published in 1647 under the name of *Selenographia*. He represented the circular mountains by open spots somewhat round in shape, and by shaded figures he indicated the vast plains, or, as he called them, the *seas*, that occupied so much of her surface. These he designated by names taken from our Earth. His map shows you a *Mount Sinai* the midst of an *Arabia*, an *Ætna* in the centre of a *Sicily*, *Alps*, *Apennines*, *Carpathians*, a *Mediterranean*, a *Palus Mæolis*, a *Pontus Euxinus*, and a *Caspian Sea*. But these names seem to have been given capriciously and at random, for they never recall any resemblance existing between themselves and their namesakes on our globe. In the wide open spot, for instance, connected on the south with vast continents and terminating in a point, it would be no easy matter to recognize the reversed image of the *Indian Peninsula*, the *Bay of Bengal*, and *Cochin China*. Naturally, therefore, these names were nearly all soon dropped; but another system of nomenclature, proposed by an astronomer better acquainted with the human heart, met with a success that has lasted to the present day.

This was Father Riccioli, a Jesuit, and (1598–1671) a contemporary of Hevelius. In his *Astronomia Reformata*, (1665), he published a rough and incorrect map of the Moon, compiled from observations made by Grimaldi of Ferrara; but in designating the mountains, he named them after eminent astronomers, and this idea of his has been carefully carried out by map makers of later times.

A third map of the Moon was published at Rome in 1666 by Dominico Cassini of Nice (1625–1712), the famous discoverer of Saturn's satellites. Though somewhat incorrect regarding measurements, it was superior to Riccioli's in execution, and for a long time it was considered a standard work. Copies of this map are still to be found, but Cassini's original copper-plate, preserved for a long time at the *Imprimerie Royale* in Paris, was at last sold to a brazier, by no less a personage than the Director of the establishment himself, who, according to Arago, wanted to get rid of what he considered useless lumber!

La Hire (1640–1718), professor of astronomy in the *Collège de France*, and an accomplished draughtsman, drew a map of the Moon which was thirteen feet in diameter. This map could be seen long afterwards in the library of St. Genevieve, Paris, but it was never engraved.

About 1760, Mayer, a famous German astronomer and the director of the observatory of Göttingen, began the publication of a magnificent map of the Moon, drawn after lunar measurements all rigorously verified by himself. Unfortunately his death in 1762 interrupted a work which would have surpassed in accuracy every previous effort of the kind.

Next appears Schroeter of Erfurt (1745–1816), a fine observer (he first discovered the Lunar *Rills*), but a poor draughtsman: his maps are therefore of little value. Lohrman of Dresden published in 1838 an excellent map of the Moon, 15 inches in diameter, accompanied by descriptive text and several charts of particular portions on a larger scale.

But this and all other maps were thrown completely into the shade by Beer and Maedler's famous *Mappa Selenographica*, so often alluded to in the course of this work. This map, projected orthographically— that is, one in which all the rays proceeding from the surface to the eye are supposed to be parallel to each other—gives a reproduction of the lunar disc exactly as it appears. The representation of the mountains and plains is therefore correct only in the central portion; elsewhere, north, south, east, or west, the features, being foreshortened, are crowded together, and cannot be compared in measurement with those in the centre. It is more than three feet square; for convenient reference it is divided into four parts, each having a very full index; in short, this map is in all respects a master piece of lunar cartography.

After Beer and Maedler, we should allude to Julius Schmitt's (of Athens) excellent selenographic reliefs: to Doctor Draper's, and to Father Secchi's successful application of photography to lunar representation; to De La Rue's (of London) magnificent stereographs of the Moon, to be had at every optician's; to the clear and correct map prepared by Lecouturier and Chapuis in 1860; to the many beautiful pictures of the Moon in various phases of illumination obtained by the Messrs. Bond of Harvard University; to Rutherford's (of New York) unparalleled lunar photographs; and finally to Nasmyth and Carpenter's wonderful work on the Moon, illustrated by photographs of her surface in detail, prepared from models at which they had been laboring for more than a quarter of the century.

Of all these maps, pictures, and projections, Barbican had provided himself with only two—Beer and Maedler's in German, and Lecouturier and Chapuis' in French. These he considered quite sufficient for all purposes, and certainly they considerably simplified his labors as an observer.

His best optical instruments were several excellent marine telescopes, manufactured especially under his direction. Magnifying the object a hundred times, on the surface of the Earth they would have brought the Moon to within a distance of somewhat less than 2400 miles. But at the point to which our travellers had arrived towards three o'clock in the morning, and which could hardly be more than 12 or 1300 miles from the Moon, these telescopes, ranging through a medium disturbed by no atmosphere, easily brought the lunar surface to within less than 13 miles' distance from the eyes of our adventurers.

Therefore they should now see objects in the Moon as clearly as people can see the opposite bank of a river that is about 12 miles wide.

XI

Fact and Fancy

H ave you ever seen the Moon?" said a teacher ironically one day in class to one of his pupils.

"No, sir;" was the pert reply; "but I think I can safely say I've heard it spoken about."

Though saying what he considered a smart thing, the pupil was probably perfectly right. Like the immense majority of his fellow beings, he had looked at the Moon, heard her talked of, written poetry about her, but, in the strict sense of the term, he had probably never seen her—that is—scanned her, examined her, surveyed her, inspected her, reconnoitred her—even with an opera glass! Not one in a thousand, not one in ten thousand, has ever examined even the map of our only Satellite. To guard our beloved and intelligent reader against this reproach, we have prepared an excellent reduction of Beer and Maedler's *Mappa*, on which, for the better understanding of what is to follow, we hope he will occasionally cast a gracious eye.

When you look at any map of the Moon, you are struck first of all with one peculiarity. Contrary to the arrangement prevailing in Mars and on our Earth, the continents occupy principally the southern hemisphere of the lunar orb. Then these continents are far from presenting such sharp and regular outlines as distinguish the Indian Peninsula, Africa, and South America. On the contrary, their coasts, angular, jagged, and deeply indented, abound in bays and peninsulas. They remind you of the coast of Norway, or of the islands in the Sound, where the land seems to be cut up into endless divisions. If navigation ever existed on the Moon's surface, it must have been of a singularly difficult and dangerous nature, and we can scarcely say which of the two should be more pitied—the sailors who had to steer through these dangerous and complicated passes, or the map-makers who had to designate them on their charts.

You will also remark that the southern pole of the Moon is much more *continental* than the northern. Around the latter, there exists only a slight fringe of lands separated from the other continents by vast "seas." This word "seas"—a term employed by the first lunar map constructors—is still retained to designate those vast depressions on the Moon's surface, once perhaps covered with water, though they are now only enormous plains. In the south, the continents cover nearly the whole hemisphere. It is therefore possible that the Selenites have planted their flag on at least one of their poles, whereas the Parrys and Franklins of England, the Kanes and the Wilkeses of America, the Dumont d'Urvilles and the Lamberts of France, have so far met with obstacles completely insurmountable, while in search of those unknown points of our terrestrial globe.

The islands—the next feature on the Moon's surface—are exceedingly numerous. Generally oblong or circular in shape and almost as regular in outline as if drawn with a compass, they form vast archipelagoes like the famous group lying between Greece and Asia Minor, which mythology has made the scene of her earliest and most charming legends. As we gaze at them, the names of Naxos, Tenedos, Milo, and Carpathos rise up before our mind's eye, and we begin looking around for the Trojan fleet and Jason's Argo. This, at least, was Ardan's idea, and at first his eyes would see nothing on the map but a Grecian archipelago. But his companions, sound practical men, and therefore totally devoid of sentiment, were reminded by these rugged coasts of the beetling cliffs of New Brunswick and Nova Scotia; so that, where the Frenchman saw the tracks of ancient heroes, the Americans saw only commodious shipping points and favorable sites for trading posts—all, of course, in the purest interest of lunar commerce and industry.

To end our hasty sketch of the continental portion of the Moon, we must say a few words regarding her orthography or mountain systems. With a fair telescope you can distinguish very readily her mountain chains, her isolated mountains, her circuses or ring formations, and her rills, cracks and radiating streaks. The character of the whole lunar relief is comprised in these divisions. It is a surface prodigiously reticulated, upheaved and depressed, apparently without the slightest order or system. It is a vast Switzerland, an enormous Norway, where everything is the result of direct plutonic action. This surface, so rugged, craggy and wrinkled, seems to be the result of successive contractions of the crust, at an early period of the planet's existence. The examination of the lunar disc is therefore highly favorable for the study of the great geological phenomena of our own globe. As certain astronomers have remarked, the Moon's surface, though older than the Earth's, has remained younger. That is, it has undergone less change. No water has broken through its rugged elevations, filled up its scowling cavities, and by incessant action tended continuously to the production of a general level. No atmosphere, by its disintegrating, decomposing influence has softened off the rugged features of the plutonic mountains. Volcanic action alone, unaffected by either aqueous or atmospheric forces, can here be seen in all its glory. In other words the Moon looks now as our Earth did endless ages ago, when "she was void and empty and when darkness sat upon the face of the deep;" eons of ages ago, long before the tides of the ocean and the winds of the atmosphere had begun to strew her rough surface with sand and clay, rock and coal, forest and meadow, gradually preparing it, according to the laws of our beneficent Creator, to be at last the pleasant though the temporary abode of Man!

Having wandered over vast continents, your eye is attracted by the "seas" of dimensions still vaster. Not only their shape, situation, and look, remind us of our own oceans, but, again like them, they occupy the greater part of the Moon's surface. The "seas," or, more correctly, plains, excited our travellers' curiosity to a very high degree, and they set themselves at once to examine their nature.

The astronomer who first gave names to those "seas" in all probability was a Frenchman. Hevelius, however, respected them, even Riccioli did not disturb them, and so they have come down to us. Ardan laughed heartily at the fancies which they called up, and said the whole thing reminded him of one of those "maps of matrimony" that he had once seen or read of in the works of Scudéry or Cyrano de Bergerac.

"However," he added, "I must say that this map has much more reality in it than could be found in the sentimental maps of the 17th century. In fact, I have no difficulty whatever in calling it the *Map of Life!* very neatly divided into two parts, the east and the west, the masculine and the feminine. The women on the right, and the men on the left!"

At such observations, Ardan's companions only shrugged their shoulders. A map of the Moon in their eyes was a map of the Moon, no more, no less; their romantic friend might view it as he pleased. Nevertheless, their romantic friend was not altogether wrong. Judge a little for yourselves.

What is the first "sea" you find in the hemisphere on the left? The *Mare Imbrium* or the Rainy Sea, a fit emblem of our human life, beaten by many a pitiless storm. In a corresponding part of the southern hemisphere you see *Mare Nubium*, the Cloudy Sea, in which our poor human reason so often gets befogged. Close to this lies *Mare Humorum*, the Sea of Humors, where we sail about, the sport of each fitful breeze, "everything by starts and nothing long." Around all, embracing all, lies *Oceanus Procellarum*, the Ocean of Tempests, where, engaged in one continuous struggle with the gusty whirlwinds, excited by our own passions or those of others, so few of us escape shipwreck. And, when disgusted by the difficulties of life, its deceptions, its treacheries and all the other miseries "that flesh is heir to," where do we too often fly to avoid them? To the *Sinus Iridium* or the *Sinus Roris*, that is Rainbow Gulf and Dewy Gulf whose glittering lights, alas! give forth no real illumination to guide our stumbling feet, whose sun-tipped pinnacles have less substance than a dream, whose enchanting waters all evaporate before we can lift a cup-full to our parched lips! Showers, storms, fogs, rainbows—is not the whole mortal life of man comprised in these four words?

Now turn to the hemisphere on the right, the women's side, and you also discover "seas," more numerous indeed, but of smaller dimensions and with gentler names, as more befitting the feminine temperament. First comes *Mare Serenitatis*, the Sea of Serenity, so expressive of the calm, tranquil soul of an innocent maiden. Near it is *Lacus Somniorum*, the Lake of Dreams, in which she loves to gaze at her gilded and rosy future. In the southern division is seen *Mare Nectaris*, the Sea of Nectar, over whose soft heaving billows she is gently wafted by Love's caressing winds, "Youth on the prow and Pleasure at the helm." Not far off is *Mare Fecunditatis*, the Sea of Fertility, in which she becomes the happy mother of rejoicing children. A little north is *Mare Crisium*, the Sea of Crises where her life and happiness are sometimes exposed to sudden, and unexpected dangers which fortunately, however, seldom end fatally. Far to the left, near the men's side, is *Mare Vaporum*, the Sea of Vapors, into which, though it is rather small, and full of sunken rocks, she sometimes allows herself to wander, moody, and pouting, and not exactly knowing where she wants to go or what she wants to do. Between the two last expands the great *Mare Tranquillitatis*, the Sea of Tranquillity, into whose quiet depths are at last absorbed all her simulated passions, all her futile aspirations, all her unglutted desires, and whose unruffled waters are gliding on forever in noiseless current towards *Lacus Mortis*, the Lake of Death, whose misty shores

"In ruthless, vast, and gloomy woods are girt."

So at least Ardan mused as he stooped over Beer and Maedler's map. Did not these strange successive names somewhat justify his flights of fancy? Surely they had a wonderful variety of meaning. Was it by accident or by forethought deep that the two hemispheres of the Moon had been thus so strangely divided, yet, as man to woman, though divided still united, and thus forming even in the cold regions of space a perfect image of our terrestrial existence? Who can say that our romantic French friend was altogether wrong in thus explaining the astute fancies of the old astronomers?

His companions, however, it need hardly be said, never saw the "seas" in that light. They looked on them not with sentimental but with geographical eyes. They studied this new world and tried to get it by heart, working at it like a school boy at his lessons. They began by measuring its angles and diameters.

To their practical, common sense vision *Mare Nubium*, the Cloudy Sea, was an immense depression of the surface, sprinkled here and there with a few circular mountains. Covering a great portion of that part of the southern hemisphere which lies east of the centre, it occupied a space of about 270 thousand square miles, its central point lying in 15° south latitude and 20° east longitude. Northeast from this lay *Oceanus Procellarum*, the Ocean of Tempests, the most extensive of all the plains on the lunar disc, embracing a surface of about half a million of square miles, its centre being in 10° north and 45° east. From its bosom those wonderful mountains *Kepler* and *Aristarchus* lifted their vast ramparts glittering with innumerable streaks radiating in all directions.

To the north, in the direction of *Mare Frigoris*, extends *Mare Imbrium*, the Sea of Rains, its central point in 35° north and 20° east. It is somewhat circular in shape, and it covers a space of about 300 thousand square miles. South of *Oceanus Procellarum* and separated from *Mare Nubium* by a goodly number of ring mountains, lies the little basin of *Mare Humorum*, the Sea of Humors, containing only about 66 thousand square miles, its central point having a latitude of 25° south and a longitude of 40° east.

On the shores of these great seas three "Gulfs" are easily found: *Sinus Aestuum*, the Gulf of the Tides, northeast of the centre; *Sinus Iridium*, the Gulf of the Rainbows, northeast of the *Mare Imbrium*; and *Sinus Roris*, the Dewy Gulf, a little further northeast. All seem to be small plains enclosed between chains of lofty mountains.

The western hemisphere, dedicated to the ladies, according to Ardan, and therefore naturally more capricious, was remarkable for "seas" of smaller dimensions, but much more numerous. These were principally:

Mare Serenitatis, the Sea of Serenity, 25° north and 20° west, comprising a surface of about 130 thousand square miles; *Mare Crisium*, the Sea of Crises, a round, well defined, dark depression towards the northwestern edge, 17° north 55° west, embracing a surface of 60 thousand square miles, a regular Caspian Sea in fact, only that the plateau in which it lies buried is surrounded by a girdle of much higher mountains. Then towards the equator, with a latitude of 5° north and a longitude of 25° west, appears *Mare Tranquillitatis*, the Sea of Tranquillity, occupying about 180 thousand square miles. This communicates on the south with *Mare Nectaris*, the Sea of Nectar, embracing an extent of about 42 thousand square miles, with a mean latitude of 15° south and a longitude of 35° west. Southwest from *Mare Tranquillitatis*, lies *Mare Fecunditatis*, the Sea of Fertility, the greatest in this hemisphere, as it occupies an extent of more than 300 thousand square miles, its latitude being 3° south and its longitude 50° west. For away to the north, on the borders of the *Mare Frigoris*, or Icy Sea, is seen the small *Mare Humboldtianum*, or Humboldt Sea, with a surface of about 10 thousand square miles. Corresponding to this in the southern hemisphere lies the *Mare Australe*, or South Sea, whose surface, as it extends along the western rim, is rather difficult to calculate. Finally, right in the centre of the lunar disc, where the equator intersects the first meridian, can be seen *Sinus Medii*, the Central Gulf, the common property therefore of all the hemispheres, the northern and southern, as well as of the eastern and western.

Into these great divisions the surface of our satellite resolved itself before the eyes of Barbican and M'Nicholl. Adding up the various measurements, they found that the surface of her visible hemisphere was about 7-1/2 millions of square miles, of which about the two thirds comprised the volcanoes, the mountain chains, the rings, the islands— in short, the land portion of the lunar surface; the other third comprised the "seas," the "lakes," the "marshes," the "bays" or "gulfs," and the other divisions usually assigned to water.

To all this deeply interesting information, though the fruit of observation the closest, aided and confirmed by calculation the profoundest, Ardan listened with the utmost indifference. In fact, even his French politeness could not suppress two or three decided yawns, which of course the mathematicians were too absorbed to notice.

In their enthusiasm they tried to make him understand that though the Moon is 13-1/2 times smaller than our Earth, she can show more than 50 thousand craters, which astronomers have already counted and designated by specific names.

"To conclude this portion of our investigation therefore," cried Barbican, clearing his throat, and occupying Aldan's right ear,—"the Moon's surface is a honey combed, perforated, punctured—"

"A fistulous, a rugose, salebrous,—" cut in the Captain, close on the left.

—"And highly cribriform superficies—" cried Barbican.

—"A sieve, a riddle, a colander—" shouted the Captain.

—"A skimming dish, a buckwheat cake, a lump of green cheese—" went on Barbican—.

—In fact, there is no knowing how far they would have proceeded with their designations, comparisons, and scientific expressions, had not Ardan, driven to extremities by Barbican's last profanity, suddenly jumped up, broken away from his companions, and clapped a forcible extinguisher on their eloquence by putting his hands on their lips and keeping them there awhile. Then striking a grand attitude, he looked towards the Moon and burst out in accents of thrilling indignation:

"Pardon, O beautiful Diana of the Ephesians! Pardon, O Phoebe, thou pearl-faced goddess of night beloved of Greece! O Isis, thou sympathetic queen of Nile-washed cities! O Astarte, thou favorite deity of the Syrian hills! O Artemis, thou symbolical daughter of Jupiter and Latona, that is of light and darkness! O brilliant sister of the radiant Apollo! enshrined in the enchanting strains of Virgil and Homer, which I only half learned at college, and therefore unfortunately forget just now! Otherwise what pleasure I should have had in hurling them at the heads of Barbican, M'Nicholl, and every other barbarous iconoclast of the nineteenth century!—"

Here he stopped short, for two reasons: first he was out of breath; secondly, he saw that the irrepressible scientists had been too busy making observations of their own to hear a single word of what he had uttered, and were probably totally unconscious that he had spoken at all. In a few seconds his breath came back in full blast, but the idea of talking when only deaf men were listening was so disconcerting as to leave him actually unable to get off another syllable.

XII

A Bird's Eye View of the Lunar Mountains

I am rather inclined to believe myself that not one word of Ardan's rhapsody had been ever heard by Barbican or M'Nicholl. Long before he had spoken his last words, they had once more become mute as statues, and now were both eagerly watching, pencil in hand, spyglass to eye, the northern lunar hemisphere towards which they were rapidly but indirectly approaching. They had fully made up their minds by this time that they were leaving far behind them the central point which they would have probably reached half an hour ago if they had not been shunted off their course by that inopportune bolide.

About half past twelve o'clock, Barbican broke the dead silence by saying that after a careful calculation they were now only about 875 miles from the Moon's surface, a distance two hundred miles less in length than the lunar radius, and which was still to be diminished as they advanced further north. They were at that moment ten degrees north of the equator, almost directly over the ridge lying between the *Mare Serenitatis* and the *Mare Tranquillitatis*. From this latitude all the way up to the north pole the travellers enjoyed a most satisfactory view of the Moon in all directions and under the most favorable conditions. By means of their spyglasses, magnifying a hundred times, they cut down this distance of 875 miles to about 9. The great telescope of the Rocky Mountains, by its enormous magnifying power of 48,000, brought the Moon, it is true, within a distance of 5 miles, or nearly twice as near; but this advantage of nearness was considerably more than counterbalanced by a want of clearness, resulting from the haziness and refractiveness of the terrestrial atmosphere, not to mention those fatal defects in the reflector that the art of man has not yet succeeded in remedying. Accordingly, our travellers, armed with excellent telescopes—of just power enough to be no injury to clearness,—and posted on unequalled vantage ground, began already to distinguish certain details that had probably never been noticed before by terrestrial observers. Even Ardan, by this time quite recovered from his fit of sentiment and probably infected a little by the scientific enthusiasm of his companions, began to observe and note and observe and note, alternately, with all the *sangfroid* of a veteran astronomer.

"Friends," said Barbican, again interrupting a silence that had lasted perhaps ten minutes, "whither we are going I can't say; if we shall ever revisit the Earth, I can't tell. Still, it is our duty so to act in all respects as if these labors of ours were one day to be of service to our fellow-creatures. Let us keep our souls free from every distraction. We are now astronomers. We see now what no mortal eye has ever gazed on before. This Projectile is simply a work room of the great Cambridge Observatory lifted into space. Let us take observations!"

With these words, he set to work with a renewed ardor, in which his companions fully participated. The consequence was that they soon had several of the outline maps covered with the best sketches they could make of the Moon's various aspects thus presented under such favorable circumstances. They could now remark not only that they were passing the tenth degree of north latitude, but that the Projectile followed almost directly the twentieth degree of east longitude.

"One thing always puzzled me when examining maps of the Moon," observed Ardan, "and I can't say that I see it yet as clearly as if I had thought over the matter. It is this. I could understand, when looking through a lens at an object, why we get only its reversed image—a simple law of optics explains *that*. Therefore, in a map of the Moon, as the bottom means the north and the top the south, why does not the right mean the west and the left the east? I suppose I could have made this out by a little thought, but thinking, that is reflection, not being my forte, it is the last thing I ever care to do. Barbican, throw me a word or two on the subject."

"I can see what troubles you," answered Barbican, "but I can also see that one moment's reflection would have put an end to your perplexity. On ordinary maps of the Earth's surface when the north is the top, the right hand must be the east, the left hand the west, and so on. That is simply because we look *down* from *above*. And such a map seen through a lens will appear reversed in all respects. But in looking at the Moon, that is *up* from *down*, we change our position so far that our right hand points west and our left east. Consequently, in our reversed map, though the north becomes south, the right remains east, and—"

"Enough said! I see it at a glance! Thank you, Barbican. Why did not they make you a professor of astronomy? Your hint will save me a world of trouble."

Aided by the *Mappa Selenographica*, the travellers could easily recognize the different portions of the Moon over which they were now moving. An occasional glance at our reduction of this map, given as a frontispiece, will enable the gentle reader to follow the travellers on the line in which they moved and to understand the remarks and observations in which they occasionally indulged.

"Where are we now?" asked Ardan.

"Over the northern shores of the *Mare Nubium*," replied Barbican. "But we are still too far off to see with any certainty what they are like. What is the *Mare* itself? A sea, according to the early astronomers? a plain of solid sand, according to later authority? or an immense forest, according to De la Rue of London, so far the Moon's most successful photographer? This gentleman's authority, Ardan, would have given you decided support in your famous dispute with the Captain at the meeting near Tampa, for he says very decidedly that the Moon has an atmosphere, very low to be sure but very dense. This, however, we must find out for ourselves; and in the meantime let us affirm nothing until we have good grounds for positive assertion."

Mare Nubium, though not very clearly outlined on the maps, is easily recognized by lying directly east of the regions about the centre. It would appear as if this vast plain were sprinkled with immense lava blocks shot forth from the great volcanoes on the right, *Ptolemaeus*, *Alphonse*, *Alpetragius* and *Arzachel*. But the Projectile advanced so rapidly that these mountains soon disappeared, and the travellers were not long before they could distinguish the great peaks that closed the "Sea" on its northern boundary. Here a radiating mountain showed a summit so dazzling with the reflection of the solar rays that Ardan could not help crying out:

"It looks like one of the carbon points of an electric light projected on a screen! What do you call it, Barbican?"

"*Copernicus*," replied the President. "Let us examine old *Copernicus*!"

This grand crater is deservedly considered one of the greatest of the lunar wonders. It lifts its giant ramparts to upwards of 12,000 feet above the level of the lunar surface. Being quite visible from the Earth and well situated for observation, it is a favorite object for astronomical study; this is particularly the case during the phase existing between Last Quarter and the New Moon, when its vast shadows, projected boldly from the east towards the west, allow its prodigious dimensions to be measured.

After *Tycho*, which is situated in the southern hemisphere, *Copernicus* forms the most important radiating mountain in the lunar disc. It looms up, single and isolated, like a gigantic light-house, on the peninsula separating *Mare Nubium* from *Oceanus Procellarum* on one side and from *Mare Imbrium* on the other; thus illuminating with its splendid radiation three "Seas" at a time. The wonderful complexity of its bright streaks diverging on all sides from its centre presented a scene alike splendid and unique. These streaks, the travellers thought, could be traced further north than in any other direction: they fancied they could detect them even in the *Mare Imbrium*, but this of course might be owing to the point from which they made their observations. At one o'clock in the morning, the Projectile, flying through space, was exactly over this magnificent mountain.

In spite of the brilliant sunlight that was blazing around them, the travellers could easily recognize the peculiar features of *Copernicus*. It belongs to those ring mountains of the first class called Circuses. Like *Kepler* and *Aristarchus*, who rule over *Oceanus Procellarum*, *Copernicus*, when viewed through our telescopes, sometimes glistens so brightly through the ashy light of the Moon that it has been frequently taken for a volcano in full activity. Whatever it may have been once, however, it is certainly nothing more now than, like all the other mountains on the visible side of the Moon, an extinct volcano, only with a crater of such exceeding grandeur and sublimity as to throw utterly into the shade everything like it on our Earth. The crater of Etna is at most little more than a mile across. The crater of *Copernicus* has a diameter of at least 50 miles. Within it, the travellers could easily discover by their glasses an immense number of terraced ridges, probably landslips, alternating with stratifications resulting from successive eruptions. Here and there, but particularly in the southern side, they caught glimpses of shadows of such intense blackness, projected across the plateau and lying there like pitch spots, that they could not tell them from yawning chasms of incalculable depth. Outside the crater the shadows were almost as deep, whilst on the plains all around, particularly in the west, so many small craters could be detected that the eye in vain attempted to count them.

"Many circular mountains of this kind," observed Barbican, "can be seen on the lunar surface, but *Copernicus*, though not one of the greatest, is one of the most remarkable on account of those diverging streaks of bright light that you see radiating from its summit. By looking steadily into its crater, you can see more cones than mortal eye ever lit on before. They are so numerous as to render the interior plateau quite rugged, and were formerly so many openings giving vent to fire and volcanic matter. A curious and very common arrangement of this internal plateau of lunar craters is its lying at a lower level than the external plains, quite the contrary to a terrestrial crater, which generally has its bottom much higher than the level of the surrounding country. It follows therefore that the deep lying curve of the bottom of these ring mountains would give a sphere with a diameter somewhat smaller than the Moon's."

"What can be the cause of this peculiarity?" asked M'Nicholl.

"I can't tell;" answered Barbican, "but, as a conjecture, I should say that it is probably to the comparatively smaller area of the Moon and the more violent character of her volcanic action that the extremely rugged character of her surface is mainly due."

"Why, it's the *Campi Phlegraei* or the Fire Fields of Naples over again!" cried Ardan suddenly. "There's *Monte Barbaro*, there's the *Solfatara*, there is the crater of *Astroni*, and there is the *Monte Nuovo*, as plain as the hand on my body!"

"The great resemblance between the region you speak of and the general surface of the Moon has been often remarked;" observed Barbican, "but it is even still more striking in the neighborhood of *Theophilus* on the borders of *Mare Nectaris*."

"That's *Mare Nectaris*, the gray spot over there on the southwest, isn't it?" asked M'Nicholl; "is there any likelihood of our getting a better view of it?"

"Not the slightest," answered Barbican, "unless we go round the Moon and return this way, like a satellite describing its orbit."

By this time they had arrived at a point vertical to the mountain centre. *Copernicus's* vast ramparts formed a perfect circle or rather a pair of concentric circles. All around the mountain extended a dark grayish plain of savage aspect, on which the peak shadows projected themselves in sharp relief. In the gloomy bottom of the crater, whose dimensions are vast enough to swallow Mont Blanc body and bones, could be distinguished a magnificent group of cones, at least half a mile in height and glittering like piles of crystal. Towards the north several breaches could be seen in the ramparts, due probably to a caving in of immense masses accumulated on the summit of the precipitous walls.

As already observed, the surrounding plains were dotted with numberless craters mostly of small dimensions, except *Gay Lussac* on the north, whose crater was about 12 miles in diameter. Towards the southwest and the immediate east, the plain appeared to be very flat, no protuberance, no prominence of any kind lifting itself above the general dead level. Towards the north, on the contrary, as far as where the peninsula jutted on *Oceanus Procellarum*, the plain looked like a sea of lava wildly lashed for a while by a furious hurricane and then, when its waves and breakers and driving ridges were at their wildest, suddenly frozen into solidity. Over this rugged, rumpled, wrinkled surface and in all directions, ran the wonderful streaks whose radiating point appeared to be the summit of *Copernicus*. Many of them appeared to be ten miles wide and hundreds of miles in length.

The travellers disputed for some time on the origin of these strange radii, but could hardly be said to have arrived at any conclusion more satisfactory than that already reached by some terrestrial observers.

To M'Nicholl's question:

"Why can't these streaks be simply prolonged mountain crests reflecting the sun's rays more vividly by their superior altitude and comparative smoothness?"

Barbican readily replied:

"These streaks *can't* be mountain crests, because, if they were, under certain conditions of solar illumination they should project *shadows*—a thing which they have never been known to do under any circumstances whatever. In fact, it is only during the period of the full Moon that these streaks are seen at all; as soon as the sun's rays become oblique, they disappear altogether—a proof that their appearance is due altogether to peculiar advantages in their surface for the reflection of light."

"Dear boys, will you allow me to give my little guess on the subject?" asked Ardan.

His companions were profuse in expressing their desire to hear it.

"Well then," he resumed, "seeing that these bright streaks invariably start from a certain point to radiate in all directions, why not suppose them to be streams of lava issuing from the crater and flowing down the mountain side until they cooled?"

"Such a supposition or something like it has been put forth by Herschel," replied Barbican; "but your own sense will convince you that it is quite untenable when you consider that lava, however hot and liquid it may be at the commencement of its journey, cannot flow on for hundreds of miles, up hills, across ravines, and over plains, all the time in streams of almost exactly equal width."

"That theory of yours holds no more water than mine, Ardan," observed M'Nicholl.

"Correct, Captain," replied the Frenchman; "Barbican has a trick of knocking the bottom out of every weaker vessel. But let us hear what he has to say on the subject himself. What is your theory. Barbican?"

"My theory," said Barbican, "is pretty much the same as that lately presented by an English astronomer, Nasmyth, who has devoted much study and reflection to lunar matters. Of course, I only formulate my theory, I don't affirm it. These streaks are cracks, made in the Moon's surface by cooling or by shrinkage, through which volcanic matter has been forced up by internal pressure. The sinking ice of a frozen lake, when meeting with some sharp pointed rock, cracks in a radiating manner: every one of its fissures then admits the water, which immediately spreads laterally over the ice pretty much as the lava spreads itself over the lunar surface. This theory accounts for the radiating nature of the streaks, their great and nearly equal thickness, their immense length, their inability to cast a shadow, and their invisibility at any time except at or near the Full Moon. Still it is nothing but a theory, and I don't deny that serious objections may be brought against it."

"Do you know, dear boys," cried Ardan, led off as usual by the slightest fancy, "do you know what I am thinking of when I look down on the great rugged plains spread out beneath us?"

"I can't say, I'm sure," replied Barbican, somewhat piqued at the little attention he had secured for his theory.

"Well, what are you thinking of?" asked M'Nicholl.

"Spillikins!" answered Ardan triumphantly.

"Spillikins?" cried his companions, somewhat surprised.

"Yes, Spillikins! These rocks, these blocks, these peaks, these streaks, these cones, these cracks, these ramparts, these escarpments,—what are they but a set of spillikins, though I acknowledge on a grand scale? I wish I had a little hook to pull them one by one!"

"Oh, do be serious, Ardan!" cried Barbican, a little impatiently.

"Certainly," replied Ardan. "Let us be serious, Captain, since seriousness best befits the subject in hand. What do you think of another comparison? Does not this plain look like an immense battle field piled with the bleaching bones of myriads who had slaughtered each other to a man at the bidding of some mighty Caesar? What do you think of that lofty comparison, hey?"

"It is quite on a par with the other," muttered Barbican.

"He's hard to please, Captain," continued Ardan, "but let us try him again! Does not this plain look like—?"

"My worthy friend," interrupted Barbican, quietly, but in a tone to discourage further discussion, "what you think the plain *looks like* is of very slight import, as long as you know no more than a child what it really *is*!"

"Bravo, Barbican! well put!" cried the irrepressible Frenchman. "Shall I ever realize the absurdity of my entering into an argument with a scientist!"

But this time the Projectile, though advancing northward with a pretty uniform velocity, had neither gained nor lost in its nearness to the lunar disc. Each moment altering the character of the fleeting landscape beneath them, the travellers, as may well be imagined, never thought of taking an instant's repose. At about half past one, looking to their right on the west, they saw the summits of another mountain; Barbican, consulting his map, recognized *Eratosthenes*.

This was a ring mountain, about 33 miles in diameter, having, like *Copernicus*, a crater of immense profundity containing central cones. Whilst they were directing their glasses towards its gloomy depths, Barbican mentioned to his friends Kepler's strange idea regarding the formation of these ring mountains. "They must have been constructed," he said, "by mortal hands."

"With what object?" asked the Captain.

"A very natural one," answered Barbican. "The Selenites must have undertaken the immense labor of digging these enormous pits at places of refuge in which they could protect themselves against the fierce solar rays that beat against them for 15 days in succession!"

"Not a bad idea, that of the Selenites!" exclaimed Ardan.

"An absurd idea!" cried M'Nicholl. "But probably Kepler never knew the real dimensions of these craters. Barbican knows the trouble and time required to dig a well in Stony Hill only nine hundred feet deep. To dig out a single lunar crater would take hundreds and hundreds of years, and even then they should be giants who would attempt it!"

"Why so?" asked Ardan. "In the Moon, where gravity is six times less than on the Earth, the labor of the Selenites can't be compared with that of men like us."

"But suppose a Selenite to be six times smaller than a man like us!" urged M'Nicholl.

"And suppose a Selenite never had an existence at all!" interposed Barbican with his usual success in putting an end to the argument. "But never mind the Selenites now. Observe *Eratosthenes* as long as you have the opportunity."

"Which will not be very long," said M'Nicholl. "He is already sinking out of view too far to the right to be carefully observed."

"What are those peaks beyond him?" asked Ardan.

"The *Apennines*," answered Barbican; "and those on the left are the *Carpathians*."

"I have seen very few mountain chains or ranges in the Moon," remarked Ardan, after some minutes' observation.

"Mountains chains are not numerous in the Moon," replied Barbican, "and in that respect her oreographic system presents a decided contrast with that of the Earth. With us the ranges are many, the craters few; in the Moon the ranges are few and the craters innumerable."

Barbican might have spoken of another curious feature regarding the mountain ranges: namely, that they are chiefly confined to the northern hemisphere, where the craters are fewest and the "seas" the most extensive.

For the benefit of those interested, and to be done at once with this part of the subject, we give in the following little table a list of the chief lunar mountain chains, with their latitude, and respective heights in English feet.

	Name.	Degrees of Latitude.	Height.
Southern Hemisphere.	Altai Mountains	17° to 28	13,000ft.
	Cordilleras	10 to 20	12,000
	Pyrenees	8 to 18	12,000
	Riphean	5 to 10	2,600
Northern Hemisphere.	Haemus	10 to 20	6,300
	Carpathian	15 to 19	6,000
	Apennines	14 to 27	18,000
	Taurus	25 to 34	8,500
	Hercynian	17 to 29	3,400
	Caucasus	33 to 40	17,000
	Alps	42 to 30	10,000

Of these different chains, the most important is that of the *Apennines*, about 450 miles long, a length, however, far inferior to that of many of the great mountain ranges of our globe. They skirt the western shores of the *Mare Imbrium*, over which they rise in immense cliffs, 18 or 20 thousand feet in height, steep as a wall and casting over the plain intensely black shadows at least 90 miles long. Of Mt. *Huyghens*, the highest in the group, the travellers were just barely able to distinguish the sharp angular summit in the far west. To the east, however, the *Carpathians*, extending from the 18th to 30th degrees of east longitude, lay directly under their eyes and could be examined in all the peculiarities of their distribution.

Barbican proposed a hypothesis regarding the formation of those mountains, which his companions thought at least as good as any other. Looking carefully over the *Carpathians* and catching occasional glimpses of semi-circular formations and half domes, he concluded that the chain must have formerly been a succession of vast craters. Then had come some mighty internal discharge, or rather the subsidence to which *Mare Imbrium* is due, for it immediately broke off or swallowed up one half of those mountains, leaving the other half steep as a wall on one side and sloping gently on the other to the level of the surrounding plains. The *Carpathians* were therefore pretty nearly in the same condition as the crater mountains *Ptolemy*, *Alpetragius* and *Arzachel* would find themselves in, if some terrible cataclysm, by tearing away their eastern ramparts, had turned them into a chain of mountains whose towering cliffs would nod threateningly over the western shores of *Mare Nubium*. The mean height of the *Carpathians* is about 6,000 feet, the altitude of certain points in the Pyrenees such as the *Port of Pineda*, or *Roland's Breach*, in the shadow of *Mont Perdu*. The northern slopes of the *Carpathians* sink rapidly towards the shores of the vast *Mare Imbrium*.

Towards two o'clock in the morning, Barbican calculated the Projectile to be on the 20th northern parallel, and therefore almost immediately over the little ring mountain called *Pytheas*, about 4600 feet in height. The distance of the travellers from the Moon at this point could not be more than about 750 miles, reduced to about 7 by means of their excellent telescopes.

Mare Imbrium, the Sea of Rains here revealed itself in all its vastness to the eyes of the travellers, though it must be acknowledged that the immense depression so called, did not afford them a very clear idea regarding its exact boundaries. Right ahead of them rose *Lambert* about a mile in height; and further on, more to the left, in the direction of *Oceanus Procellarum*, *Euler* revealed itself by its glittering radiations. This mountain, of about the same height as *Lambert*, had been the object of very interesting calculations on the part of Schroeter of Erfurt. This keen observer, desirous of inquiring into the probable origin of the lunar mountains, had proposed to himself the following question: Does the volume of the crater appear to be equal to that of the surrounding ramparts? His calculations showing him that this was generally the case, he naturally concluded that these ramparts must therefore have been the product of a single eruption, for successive eruptions of volcanic matter would have disturbed this correlation. *Euler* alone, he found, to be an exception to this general law, as the volume of its crater appeared to be twice as great as that of the mass surrounding it. It must therefore have been formed by several eruptions in succession, but in that case what had become of the ejected matter?

Theories of this nature and all manner of scientific questions were, of course, perfectly permissible to terrestrial astronomers laboring under the disadvantage of imperfect instruments. But Barbican could not think of wasting his time in any speculation of the kind, and now, seeing that his Projectile perceptibly approached the lunar disc, though he despaired of ever reaching it, he was more sanguine than ever of being soon able to discover positively and unquestionably some of the secrets of its formation.

XIII

LUNAR LANDSCAPES

At half past two in the morning of December 6th, the travellers crossed the 30th northern parallel, at a distance from the lunar surface of 625 miles, reduced to about 6 by their spy-glasses. Barbican could not yet see the least probability of their landing at any point of the disc. The velocity of the Projectile was decidedly slow, but for that reason extremely puzzling. Barbican could not account for it. At such a proximity to the Moon, the velocity, one would think, should be very great indeed to be able to counteract the lunar attraction. Why did it not fall? Barbican could not tell; his companions were equally in the dark. Ardan said he gave it up. Besides they had no time to spend in investigating it. The lunar panorama was unrolling all its splendors beneath them, and they could not bear to lose one of its slightest details.

The lunar disc being brought within a distance of about six miles by the spy-glasses, it is a fair question to ask, what *could* an aeronaut at such an elevation from our Earth discover on its surface? At present that question can hardly be answered, the most remarkable balloon ascensions never having passed an altitude of five miles under circumstances favorable for observers. Here, however, is an account, carefully transcribed from notes taken on the spot, of what Barbican and his companions *did* see from their peculiar post of observation.

Varieties of color, in the first place, appeared here and there upon the disc. Selenographers are not quite agreed as to the nature of these colors. Not that such colors are without variety or too faint to be easily distinguished. Schmidt of Athens even says that if our oceans on earth were all evaporated, an observer in the Moon would hardly find the seas and continents of our globe even so well outlined as those of the Moon are to the eye of a terrestrial observer. According to him, the shade of color distinguishing those vast plains known as "seas" is a dark gray dashed with green and brown,—a color presented also by a few of the great craters.

This opinion of Schmidt's, shared by Beer and Maedler, Barbican's observations now convinced him to be far better founded than that of certain astronomers who admit of no color at all being visible on the

Moon's surface but gray. In certain spots the greenish tint was quite decided, particularly in *Mare Serenitatis* and *Mare Humorum,* the very localities where Schmidt had most noticed it. Barbican also remarked that several large craters, of the class that had no interior cones, reflected a kind of bluish tinge, somewhat like that given forth by a freshly polished steel plate. These tints, he now saw enough to convince him, proceeded really from the lunar surface, and were not due, as certain astronomers asserted, either to the imperfections of the spy-glasses, or to the interference of the terrestrial atmosphere. His singular opportunity for correct observation allowed him to entertain no doubt whatever on the subject. Hampered by no atmosphere, he was free from all liability to optical illusion. Satisfied therefore as to the reality of these tints, he considered such knowledge a positive gain to science. But that greenish tint—to what was it due? To a dense tropical vegetation maintained by a low atmosphere, a mile or so in thickness? Possibly. But this was another question that could not be answered at present.

Further on he could detect here and there traces of a decidedly ruddy tint. Such a shade he knew had been already detected in the *Palus Somnii*, near *Mare Crisium*, and in the circular area of *Lichtenberg*, near the *Hercynian Mountains*, on the eastern edge of the Moon. To what cause was this tint to be attributed? To the actual color of the surface itself? Or to that of the lava covering it here and there? Or to the color resulting from the mixture of other colors seen at a distance too great to allow of their being distinguished separately? Impossible to tell.

Barbican and his companions succeeded no better at a new problem that soon engaged their undivided attention. It deserves some detail.

Having passed *Lambert*, being just over *Timocharis*, all were attentively gazing at the magnificent crater of *Archimedes* with a diameter of 52 miles across and ramparts more than 5000 feet in height, when Ardan startled his companions by suddenly exclaiming:

"Hello! Cultivated fields as I am a living man!"

"What do you mean by your cultivated fields?" asked M'Nicholl sourly, wiping his glasses and shrugging his shoulders.

"Certainly cultivated fields!" replied Ardan. "Don't you see the furrows? They're certainly plain enough. They are white too from glistening in the sun, but they are quite different from the radiating streaks of *Copernicus*. Why, their sides are perfectly parallel!"

"Where are those furrows?" asked M'Nicholl, putting his glasses to his eye and adjusting the focus.

"You can see them in all directions," answered Ardan; "but two are particularly visible: one running north from *Archimedes*, the other south towards the *Apennines*."

M'Nicholl's face, as he gazed, gradually assumed a grin which soon developed into a snicker, if not a positive laugh, as he observed to Ardan:

"Your Selenites must be Brobdignagians, their oxen Leviathans, and their ploughs bigger than Marston's famous cannon, if these are furrows!"

"How's that, Barbican?" asked Ardan doubtfully, but unwilling to submit to M'Nicholl.

"They're not furrows, dear friend," said Barbican, "and can't be, either, simply on account of their immense size. They are what the German astronomers called *Rillen*; the French, *rainures*, and the English, *grooves*, *canals*, *clefts*, *cracks*, *chasms*, or *fissures*."

"You have a good stock of names for them anyhow," observed Ardan, "if that does any good."

"The number of names given them," answered Barbican, "shows how little is really known about them. They have been observed in all the level portion of the Moon's surface. Small as they appear to us, a little calculation must convince you that they are in some places hundreds of miles in length, a mile in width and probably in many points several miles in depth. Their width and depth, however, vary, though their sides, so far as observed, are always rigorously parallel. Let us take a good look at them."

Putting the glass to his eye, Barbican examined the clefts for some time with close attention. He saw that their banks were sharp edged and extremely steep. In many places they were of such geometrical regularity that he readily excused Gruithuysen's idea of deeming them to be gigantic earthworks thrown up by the Selenite engineers. Some of them were as straight as if laid out with a line, others were curved a little here and there, though still maintaining the strict parallelism of their sides. These crossed each other; those entered craters and came out at the other side. Here, they furrowed annular plateaus, such as *Posidonius* or *Petavius*. There, they wrinkled whole seas, for instance, *Mare Serenitatis*.

These curious peculiarities of the lunar surface had interested the astronomic mind to a very high degree at their first discovery, and have proved to be very perplexing problems ever since. The first observers do not seem to have noticed them. Neither Hevelius, nor Cassini, nor La Hire, nor Herschel, makes a single remark regarding their nature.

It was Schroeter, in 1789, who called the attention of scientists to them for the first time. He had only 11 to show, but Lohrmann soon recorded 75 more. Pastorff, Gruithuysen, and particularly Beer and Maedler were still more successful, but Julius Schmidt, the famous astronomer of Athens, has raised their number up to 425, and has even published their names in a catalogue. But counting them is one thing, determining their nature is another. They are not fortifications, certainly: and cannot be ancient beds of dried up rivers, for two very good and sufficient reasons: first, water, even under the most favorable circumstances on the Moon's surface, could have never ploughed up such vast channels; secondly, these chasms often traverse lofty craters through and through, like an immense railroad cutting.

At these details, Ardan's imagination became unusually excited and of course it was not without some result. It even happened that he hit on an idea that had already suggested itself to Schmidt of Athens.

"Why not consider them," he asked, "to be the simple phenomena of vegetation?"

"What do you mean?" asked Barbican.

"Rows of sugar cane?" suggested M'Nicholl with a snicker.

"Not exactly, my worthy Captain," answered Ardan quietly, "though you were perhaps nearer to the mark than you expected. I don't mean exactly rows of sugar cane, but I do mean vast avenues of trees—poplars, for instance—planted regularly on each side of a great high road."

"Still harping on vegetation!" said the Captain. "Ardan, what a splendid historian was spoiled in you! The less you know about your facts, the readier you are to account for them."

"*Ma foi*," said Ardan simply, "I do only what the greatest of your scientific men do—that is, guess. There is this difference however between us—I call my guesses, guesses, mere conjecture;—they dignify theirs as profound theories or as astounding discoveries!"

"Often the case, friend Ardan, too often the case," said Barbican.

"In the question under consideration, however," continued the Frenchman, "my conjecture has this advantage over some others: it explains why these rills appear and seem to disappear at regular intervals."

"Let us hear the explanation," said the Captain.

"They become invisible when the trees lose their leaves, and they reappear when they resume them."

"His explanation is not without ingenuity," observed Barbican to M'Nicholl, "but, my dear friend," turning to Ardan, "it is hardly admissible."

"Probably not," said Ardan, "but why not?"

"Because as the Sun is nearly always vertical to the lunar equator, the Moon can have no change of seasons worth mentioning; therefore her vegetation can present none of the phenomena that you speak of."

This was perfectly true. The slight obliquity of the Moon's axis, only 1-1/2°, keeps the Sun in the same altitude the whole year around. In the equatorial regions he is always vertical, and in the polar he is never higher than the horizon. Therefore, there can be no change of seasons; according to the latitude, it is a perpetual winter, spring, summer, or autumn the whole year round. This state of things is almost precisely similar to that which prevails in Jupiter, who also stands nearly upright in his orbit, the inclination of his axis being only about 3°.

But how to account for the *grooves*? A very hard nut to crack. They must certainly be a later formation than the craters and the rings, for they are often found breaking right through the circular ramparts. Probably the latest of all lunar features, the results of the last geological epochs, they are due altogether to expansion or shrinkage acting on a large scale and brought about by the great forces of nature, operating after a manner altogether unknown on our earth. Such at least was Barbican's idea.

"My friends," he quietly observed, "without meaning to put forward any pretentious claims to originality, but by simply turning to account some advantages that have never before befallen contemplative mortal eye, why not construct a little hypothesis of our own regarding the nature of these grooves and the causes that gave them birth? Look at that great chasm just below us, somewhat to the right. It is at least fifty or sixty miles long and runs along the base of the *Apennines* in a line almost perfectly straight. Does not its parallelism with the mountain chain suggest a causative relation? See that other mighty *rill*, at least a hundred and fifty miles long, starting directly north of it and pursuing so true a course that it cleaves *Archimedes* almost cleanly into two. The nearer it lies to the mountain, as you perceive, the greater its width; as it recedes in either direction it grows narrower. Does not everything point out to one great cause of their origin? They are simple crevasses, like those so often noticed on Alpine glaciers, only that these tremendous cracks in the surface are produced by the shrinkage of the crust consequent on cooling. Can we point out some analogies to this on the Earth? Certainly. The defile of the Jordan, terminating in the awful depression of the Dead Sea, no doubt occurs to you on the moment. But the *Yosemite Valley*, as I saw it ten years ago, is an apter comparison. There I stood on the brink of a tremendous chasm with perpendicular walls, a mile in width, a mile in depth and eight miles in length. Judge if I was astounded! But how should we feel it, when travelling on the lunar surface, we should suddenly find ourselves on the brink of a yawning chasm two miles wide, fifty miles long, and so fathomless in sheer vertical depth as to leave its black profundities absolutely invisible in spite of the dazzling sunlight!"

"I feel my flesh already crawling even in the anticipation!" cried Ardan.

"I shan't regret it much if we never get to the Moon," growled M'Nicholl; "I never hankered after it anyhow!"

By this time the Projectile had reached the fortieth degree of lunar latitude, and could hardly be further than five hundred miles from the surface, a distance reduced to about 5 miles by the travellers' glasses. Away to their left appeared *Helicon*, a ring mountain about 1600 feet high; and still further to the left the eye could catch a glimpse of the cliffs enclosing a semi-elliptical portion of *Mare Imbrium*, called the *Sinus Iridium*, or Bay of the Rainbows.

In order to allow astronomers to make complete observations on the lunar surface, the terrestrial atmosphere should possess a transparency seventy times greater than its present power of transmission. But in the void through which the Projectile was now floating, no fluid whatever interposed between the eye of the observer and the object observed. Besides, the travellers now found themselves at a distance that had never before been reached by the most powerful telescopes, including even Lord Rosse's and the great instrument on the Rocky Mountains. Barbican was therefore in a condition singularly favorable to resolve the great question concerning the Moon's inhabitableness. Nevertheless, the solution still escaped him. He could discover nothing around him but a dreary waste of immense plains, and towards the north, beneath him, bare mountains of the aridest character.

Not the slightest vestige of man's work could be detected over the vast expanse. Not the slightest sign of a ruin spoke of his ever having been there. Nothing betrayed the slightest trace of the development of animal life, even in an inferior degree. No movement. Not the least glimpse of vegetation. Of the three great kingdoms that hold dominion on the surface of the globe, the mineral, the vegetable and the animal, one alone was represented on the lunar sphere: the mineral, the whole mineral, and nothing but the mineral.

"Why!" exclaimed Ardan, with a disconcerted look, after a long and searching examination, "I can't find anybody. Everything is as motionless as a street in Pompeii at 4 o'clock in the morning!"

"Good comparison, friend Ardan;" observed M'Nicholl. "Lava, slag, volcanic eminences, vitreous matter glistening like ice, piles of scoria, pitch black shadows, dazzling streaks, like rivers of light breaking over jagged rocks—these are now beneath my eye—these alone I can detect—not a man—not an animal—not a tree. The great American Desert is a land of milk and honey in comparison with the joyless orb over which we are now moving. However, even yet we can predicate nothing positive. The atmosphere may have taken refuge in the depths of the chasms, in the interior of the craters, or even on the opposite side of the Moon, for all we know!"

"Still we must remember," observed Barbican, "that even the sharpest eye cannot detect a man at a distance greater than four miles and a-half, and our glasses have not yet brought us nearer than five."

"Which means to say," observed Ardan, "that though we can't see the Selenites, they can see our Projectile!"

But matters had not improved much when, towards four o'clock in the morning, the travellers found themselves on the 50th parallel, and at a distance of only about 375 miles from the lunar surface. Still no trace of the least movement, or even of the lowest form of life.

"What peaked mountain is that which we have just passed on our right?" asked Ardan. "It is quite remarkable, standing as it does in almost solitary grandeur in the barren plain."

"That is *Pico*," answered Barbican. "It is at least 8000 feet high and is well known to terrestrial astronomers as well by its peculiar shadow as on account of its comparative isolation. See the collection of perfectly formed little craters nestling around its base."

"Barbican," asked M'Nicholl suddenly, "what peak is that which lies almost directly south of *Pico*? I see it plainly, but I can't find it on my map."

"I have remarked that pyramidal peak myself," replied Barbican; "but I can assure you that so far it has received no name as yet, although it is likely enough to have been distinguished by the terrestrial astronomers. It can't be less than 4000 feet in height."

"I propose we called it *Barbican*!" cried Ardan enthusiastically.

"Agreed!" answered M'Nicholl, "unless we can find a higher one."

"We must be before-hand with Schmidt of Athens!" exclaimed Ardan. "He will leave nothing unnamed that his telescope can catch a glimpse of."

"Passed unanimously!" cried M'Nicholl.

"And officially recorded!" added the Frenchman, making the proper entry on his map.

"*Salve, Mt. Barbican!*" then cried both gentlemen, rising and taking off their hats respectfully to the distant peak.

"Look to the west!" interrupted Barbican, watching, as usual, while his companions were talking, and probably perfectly unconscious of what they were saying; "directly to the west! Now tell me what you see!"

"I see a vast valley!" answered M'Nicholl.

"Straight as an arrow!" added Ardan.

"Running through lofty mountains!" cried M'Nicholl.

"Cut through with a pair of saws and scooped out with a chisel!" cried Ardan.

"See the shadows of those peaks!" cried M'Nicholl catching fire at the sight. "Black, long, and sharp as if cast by cathedral spires!"

"Oh! ye crags and peaks!" burst forth Ardan; "how I should like to catch even a faint echo of the chorus you could chant, if a wild storm roared over your beetling summits! The pine forests of Norwegian mountains howling in midwinter would not be an accordeon in comparison!"

"Wonderful instance of subsidence on a grand scale!" exclaimed the Captain, hastily relapsing into science.

"Not at all!" cried the Frenchman, still true to his colors; "no subsidence there! A comet simply came too close and left its mark as it flew past."

"Fanciful exclamations, dear friends," observed Barbican; "but I'm not surprised at your excitement. Yonder is the famous *Valley of the Alps*, a standing enigma to all selenographers. How it could have been formed, no one can tell. Even wilder guesses than yours, Ardan, have been hazarded on the subject. All we can state positively at present regarding this wonderful formation, is what I have just recorded in my note-book: the *Valley of the Alps* is about 5 mile wide and 70 or 80 long: it is remarkably flat and free from *debris*, though the mountains on each side rise like walls to the height of at least 10,000 feet.—Over the whole surface of our Earth I know of no natural phenomenon that can be at all compared with it."

"Another wonder almost in front of us!" cried Ardan. "I see a vast lake black as pitch and round as a crater; it is surrounded by such lofty mountains that their shadows reach clear across, rendering the interior quite invisible!"

"That's *Plato*," said M'Nicholl; "I know it well; it's the darkest spot on the Moon: many a night I gazed at it from my little observatory in Broad Street, Philadelphia."

"Right, Captain," said Barbican; "the crater *Plato*, is, indeed, generally considered the blackest spot on the Moon, but I am inclined to consider the spots *Grimaldi* and *Riccioli* on the extreme eastern edge to be somewhat darker. If you take my glass, Ardan, which is of somewhat greater power than yours, you will distinctly see the bottom of the crater. The reflective power of its plateau probably proceeds from the exceedingly great number of small craters that you can detect there."

"I think I see something like them now," said Ardan. "But I am sorry the Projectile's course will not give us a vertical view."

"Can't be helped!" said Barbican; "we must go where it takes us. The day may come when man can steer the projectile or the balloon in which he is shut up, in any way he pleases, but that day has not come yet!"

Towards five in the morning, the northern limit of *Mare Imbrium* was finally passed, and *Mare Frigoris* spread its frost-colored plains far to the right and left. On the east the travellers could easily see the ring-mountain *Condamine*, about 4000 feet high, while a little ahead on the right they could plainly distinguish *Fontenelle* with an altitude nearly twice as great. *Mare Frigoris* was soon passed, and the whole lunar surface beneath the travellers, as far as they could see in all directions, now bristled with mountains, crags, and peaks. Indeed, at the 70th parallel the "Seas" or plains seem to have come to an end. The spy-glasses now brought the surface to within about three miles, a distance less than that between the hotel at Chamouni and the summit of Mont Blanc. To the left, they had no difficulty in distinguishing the ramparts of *Philolaus*, about 12,000 feet high, but though the crater had a diameter of nearly thirty miles, the black shadows prevented the slightest sign of its interior from being seen. The Sun was now sinking very low, and the illuminated surface of the Moon was reduced to a narrow rim.

By this time, too, the bird's eye view to which the observations had so far principally confined, decidedly altered its character. They could now look back at the lunar mountains that they had been just sailing over—a view somewhat like that enjoyed by a tourist standing on the summit of Mt. St. Gothard as he sees the sun setting behind the peaks of the Bernese Oberland. The lunar landscapes however, though seen under these new and ever varying conditions, "hardly gained much by the change," according to Ardan's expression. On the contrary, they looked, if possible, more dreary and inhospitable than before.

The Moon having no atmosphere, the benefit of this gaseous envelope in softening off and nicely shading the approaches of light and darkness, heat and cold, is never felt on her surface. There, no twilight ever softly ushers in the brilliant sun, or sweetly heralds the near approach of night's dark shadow. Night follows day, and day night, with the startling suddenness of a match struck or a lamp extinguished in a cavern. Nor can it present any gradual transition from either extreme of temperature. Hot jumps to cold, and cold jumps to hot. A moment after a glacial midnight, it is a roasting noon. Without an instant's warning the temperature falls from 212° Fahrenheit to the icy winter of interstellar space. The surface is all dazzling glare, or pitchy gloom. Wherever the direct rays of the sun do not fall, darkness reigns supreme. What we call diffused light on Earth, the grateful result of refraction, the luminous matter held in suspension by the air, the mother of our dawns and our dusks, of our blushing mornings and our dewy eyes, of our shades, our penumbras, our tints and all the other magical effects of *chiaro-oscuro*—this diffused light has absolutely no existence on the surface of the Moon. Nothing is there to break the inexorable contrast between intense white and intense black. At mid-day, let a Selenite shade his eyes and look at the sky: it will appear to him as black as pitch, while the stars still sparkle before him as vividly as they do to us on the coldest and darkest night in winter.

From this you can judge of the impression made on our travellers by those strange lunar landscapes. Even their decided novelty and very strange character produced any thing but a pleasing effect on the organs of sight. With all their enthusiasm, the travellers felt their eyes "get out of gear," as Ardan said, like those of a man blind from his birth and suddenly restored to sight. They could not adjust them so as to be able to realize the different plains of vision. All things seemed in a heap.

Foreground and background were indistinguishably commingled. No painter could ever transfer a lunar landscape to his canvas.

"Landscape," Ardan said; "what do you mean by a landscape? Can you call a bottle of ink intensely black, spilled over a sheet of paper intensely white, a landscape?"

At the eightieth degree, when the Projectile was hardly 100 miles distant from the Moon, the aspect of things underwent no improvement. On the contrary, the nearer the travellers approached the lunar surface, the drearier, the more inhospitable, and the more *unearthly*, everything seem to look. Still when five o'clock in the morning brought our travellers to within 50 miles of *Mount Gioja*—which their spy-glasses rendered as visible as if it was only about half a mile off, Ardan could not control himself.

"Why, we're there" he exclaimed; "we can touch her with our hands! Open the windows and let me out! Don't mind letting me go by myself. It is not very inviting quarters I admit. But as we are come to the jumping off place, I want to see the whole thing through. Open the lower window and let me out. I can take care of myself!"

"That's what's more than any other man can do," said M'Nicholl drily, "who wants to take a jump of 50 miles!"

"Better not try it, friend Ardan," said Barbican grimly: "think of Satellite! The Moon is no more attainable by your body than by our Projectile. You are far more comfortable in here than when floating about in empty space like a bolide."

Ardan, unwilling to quarrel with his companions, appeared to give in; but he secretly consoled himself by a hope which he had been entertaining for some time, and which now looked like assuming the appearance of a certainty. The Projectile had been lately approaching the Moon's surface so rapidly that it at last seemed actually impossible not to finally touch it somewhere in the neighborhood of the north pole, whose dazzling ridges now presented themselves in sharp and strong relief against the black sky. Therefore he kept silent, but quietly bided his time.

The Projectile moved on, evidently getting nearer and nearer to the lunar surface. The Moon now appeared to the travellers as she does to us towards the beginning of her Second Quarter, that is as a bright crescent instead of a hemisphere. On one side, glaring dazzling light; on the other, cavernous pitchy darkness. The line separating both was broken into a thousand bits of protuberances and concavities, dented, notched, and jagged.

At six o'clock the travellers found themselves exactly over the north pole. They were quietly gazing at the rapidly shifting features of the wondrous view unrolling itself beneath them, and were silently wondering what was to come next, when, suddenly, the Projectile passed the dividing line. The Sun and Moon instantly vanished from view. The next moment, without the slightest warning the travellers found themselves plunged in an ocean of the most appalling darkness!

XIV

A NIGHT OF FIFTEEN DAYS

The Projectile being not quite 30 miles from the Moon's north pole when the startling phenomenon, recorded in our last chapter, took place, a few seconds were quite sufficient to launch it at once from the brightest day into the unknown realms of night. The transition was so abrupt, so unexpected, without the slightest shading off, from dazzling effulgence to Cimmerian gloom, that the Moon seemed to have been suddenly extinguished like a lamp when the gas is turned off.

"Where's the Moon?" cried Ardan in amazement.

"It appears as if she had been wiped out of creation!" cried M'Nicholl.

Barbican said nothing, but observed carefully. Not a particle, however, could he see of the disc that had glittered so resplendently before his eyes a few moments ago. Not a shadow, not a gleam, not the slightest vestige could he trace of its existence. The darkness being profound, the dazzling splendor of the stars only gave a deeper blackness to the pitchy sky. No wonder. The travellers found themselves now in a night that had plenty of time not only to become black itself, but to steep everything connected with it in palpable blackness. This was the night 354-1/4 hours long, during which the invisible face of the Moon is turned away from the Sun. In this black darkness the Projectile now fully participated. Having plunged into the Moon's shadow, it was as effectually cut off from the action of the solar rays as was every point on the invisible lunar surface itself.

The travellers being no longer able to see each other, it was proposed to light the gas, though such an unexpected demand on a commodity at once so scarce and so valuable was certainly disquieting. The gas, it will be remembered, had been intended for heating alone, not illumination, of which both Sun and Moon had promised a never ending supply. But here both Sun and Moon, in a single instant vanished from before their eyes and left them in Stygian darkness.

"It's all the Sun's fault!" cried Ardan, angrily trying to throw the blame on something, and, like every angry man in such circumstances, bound to be rather nonsensical.

"Put the saddle on the right horse, Ardan," said M'Nicholl patronizingly, always delighted at an opportunity of counting a point off the Frenchman. "You mean it's all the Moon's fault, don't you, in setting herself like a screen between us and the Sun?"

"No, I don't!" cried Ardan, not at all soothed by his friend's patronizing tone, and sticking like a man to his first assertion right or wrong. "I know what I say! It will be all the Sun's fault if we use up our gas!"

"Nonsense!" said M'Nicholl. "It's the Moon, who by her interposition has cut off the Sun's light."

"The Sun had no business to allow it to be cut off," said Ardan, still angry and therefore decidedly loose in his assertions.

Before M'Nicholl could reply, Barbican interposed, and his even voice was soon heard pouring balm on the troubled waters.

"Dear friends," he observed, "a little reflection on either side would convince you that our present situation is neither the Moon's fault nor the Sun's fault. If anything is to be blamed for it, it is our Projectile which, instead of rigidly following its allotted course, has awkwardly contrived to deviate from it. However, strict justice must acquit even the Projectile. It only obeyed a great law of nature in shifting its course as soon as it came within the sphere of that inopportune bolide's influence."

"All right!" said Ardan, as usual in the best of humor after Barbican had laid down the law. "I have no doubt it is exactly as you say; and, now that all is settled, suppose we take breakfast. After such a hard night spent in work, a little refreshment would not be out of place!"

Such a proposition being too reasonable even for M'Nicholl to oppose, Ardan turned on the gas, and had everything ready for the meal in a few minutes. But, this time, breakfast was consumed in absolute silence. No toasts were offered, no hurrahs were uttered. A painful uneasiness had seized the hearts of the daring travellers. The darkness into which they were so suddenly plunged, told decidedly on their spirits. They felt almost as if they had been suddenly deprived of their sight. That thick, dismal savage blackness, which Victor Hugo's pen is so fond of occasionally revelling in, surrounded them on all sides and crushed them like an iron shroud.

It was felt worse than ever when, breakfast being over, Ardan carefully turned off the gas, and everything within the Projectile was as dark as without. However, though they could not see each other's faces, they could hear each other's voices, and therefore they soon began to talk. The most natural subject of conversation was this terrible night 354 hours long, which the laws of nature have imposed on the Lunar inhabitants. Barbican undertook to give his friends some explanation regarding the cause of the startling phenomenon, and the consequences resulting from it.

"Yes, startling is the word for it," observed Barbican, replying to a remark of Ardan's; "and still more so when we reflect that not only are both lunar hemispheres deprived, by turns, of sun light for nearly 15 days, but that also the particular hemisphere over which we are at this moment floating is all that long night completely deprived of earth-light. In other words, it is only one side of the Moon's disc that ever receives any light from the Earth. From nearly every portion of one side of the Moon, the Earth is always as completely absent as the Sun is from us at midnight. Suppose an analogous case existed on the Earth; suppose, for instance, that neither in Europe, Asia or North America was the Moon ever visible—that, in fact, it was to be seen only at our antipodes. With what astonishment should we contemplate her for the first time on our arrival in Australia or New Zealand!"

"Every man of us would pack off to Australia to see her!" cried Ardan.

"Yes," said M'Nicholl sententiously; "for a visit to the South Sea a Turk would willingly forego Mecca; and a Bostonian would prefer Sidney even to Paris."

"Well," resumed Barbican, "this interesting marvel is reserved for the Selenite that inhabits the side of the Moon which is always turned away from our globe."

"And which," added the Captain, "we should have had the unspeakable satisfaction of contemplating if we had only arrived at the period when the Sun and the Earth are not at the same side of the Moon—that is, 15 days sooner or later than now."

"For my part, however," continued Barbican, not heeding these interruptions, "I must confess that, notwithstanding the magnificent splendor of the spectacle when viewed for the first time by the Selenite who inhabits the dark side of the Moon, I should prefer to be a resident on the illuminated side. The former, when his long, blazing, roasting, dazzling day is over, has a night 354 hours long, whose darkness, like that, just now surrounding us, is ever unrelieved save by the cold cheerless rays of the stars. But the latter has hardly seen his fiery sun sinking on one horizon when he beholds rising on the opposite one an orb, milder, paler, and colder indeed than the Sun, but fully as large as thirteen of our full Moons, and therefore shedding thirteen times as much light. This would be our Earth. It would pass through all its phases too, exactly like our Satellite. The Selenites would have their New Earth, Full Earth, and Last Quarter. At midnight, grandly illuminated, it would shine with the greatest glory. But that is almost as much as can be said for it. Its futile heat would but poorly compensate for its superior radiance. All the calorie accumulated in the lunar soil during the 354 hours day would have by this time radiated completely into space. An intensity of cold would prevail, in comparison to which a Greenland winter is tropical. The temperature of interstellar space, 250° below zero, would be reached. Our Selenite, heartily tired of the cold pale Earth, would gladly see her sink towards the horizon, waning as she sank, till at last she appeared no more than half full. Then suddenly a faint rim of the solar orb reveals itself on the edge of the opposite sky. Slowly, more than 14 times more slowly than with us, does the Sun lift himself above the lunar horizon. In half an hour, only half his disc is revealed, but that is more than enough to flood the lunar landscape with a dazzling intensity of light, of which we have no counterpart on Earth. No atmosphere refracts it, no hazy screen softens it, no enveloping vapor absorbs it, no obstructing medium colors it. It breaks on the eye, harsh, white, dazzling, blinding, like the electric light seen a few yards off. As the hours wear away, the more blasting becomes the glare; and the higher he rises in the black sky, but slowly, slowly. It takes him seven of our days to reach the meridian. By that time the heat has increased from an arctic temperature to double the boiling water point, from 250° below zero to 500° above it, or the point at which tin melts. Subjected to these extremes, the glassy rocks crack, shiver and crumble away; enormous land slides occur; peaks topple over; and tons of debris, crashing down the mountains, are swallowed up forever in the yawing chasms of the bottomless craters."

"Bravo!" cried Ardan, clapping his hands softly: "our President is sublime! He reminds me of the overture of *Guillaume Tell*!"

"Souvenir de Marston!" growled M'Nicholl.

"These phenomena," continued Barbican, heedless of interruption and his voice betraying a slight glow of excitement, "these phenomena going on without interruption from month to month, from year to year, from age to age, from *eon* to *eon*, have finally convinced me that—what?" he asked his hearers, interrupting himself suddenly.

—"That the existence at the present time—" answered M'Nicholl.

—"Of either animal or vegetable life—" interrupted Ardan.

—"In the Moon is hardly possible!" cried both in one voice.

"Besides?" asked Barbican: "even if there *is* any life—?"

—"That to live on the dark side would be much more inconvenient than on the light side!" cried M'Nicholl promptly.

—"That there is no choice between them!" cried Ardan just as ready. "For my part, I should think a residence on Mt. Erebus or in Grinnell Land a terrestrial paradise in comparison to either. The *Earth shine* might illuminate the light side of the Moon a little during the long night, but for any practical advantage towards heat or life, it would be perfectly useless!"

"But there is another serious difference between the two sides," said Barbican, "in addition to those enumerated. The dark side is actually more troubled with excessive variations of temperature than the light one."

"That assertion of our worthy President," interrupted Ardan, "with all possible respect for his superior knowledge, I am disposed to question."

"It's as clear as day!" said Barbican.

"As clear as mud, you mean, Mr. President," interrupted Ardan, "the temperature of the light side is excited by two objects at the same time, the Earth and the Sun, whereas—"

—"I beg your pardon, Ardan—" said Barbican.

—"Granted, dear boy—granted with the utmost pleasure!" interrupted the Frenchman.

"I shall probably have to direct my observations altogether to you, Captain," continued Barbican; "friend Michael interrupts me so often that I'm afraid he can hardly understand my remarks."

"I always admired your candor, Barbican," said Ardan; "it's a noble quality, a grand quality!"

"Don't mention it," replied Barbican, turning towards M'Nicholl, still in the dark, and addressing him exclusively; "You see, my dear Captain, the period at which the Moon's invisible side receives at once its light and heat is exactly the period of her *conjunction*, that is to say, when she is lying between the Earth and the Sun. In comparison therefore with the place which she had occupied at her *opposition*, or when her visible side was fully illuminated, she is nearer to the Sun by double her distance from the Earth, or nearly 480 thousand miles. Therefore, my dear Captain, you can see how when the invisible side of the Moon is turned towards the

Sun, she is nearly half a million of miles nearer to him than she had been before. Therefore, her heat should be so much the greater."

"I see it at a glance," said the Captain.

"Whereas—" continued Barbican.

"One moment!" cried Ardan.

"Another interruption!" exclaimed Barbican; "What is the meaning of it, Sir?"

"I ask my honorable friend the privilege of the floor for one moment," cried Ardan.

"What for?"

"To continue the explanation."

"Why so?"

"To show that I can understand as well as interrupt!"

"You have the floor!" exclaimed Barbican, in a voice no longer showing any traces of ill humor.

"I expected no less from the honorable gentleman's well known courtesy," replied Ardan. Then changing his manner and imitating to the life Barbican's voice, articulation, and gestures, he continued: "Whereas, you see, my dear Captain, the period at which the Moon's visible side receives at once its light and heat, is exactly the period of her *opposition*, that is to say, when she is lying on one side of the Earth and the Sun at the other. In comparison therefore with the point which she had occupied in *conjunction*, or when her invisible side was fully illuminated, she is farther from the Sun by double her distance from the Earth, or nearly 480,000 miles. Therefore, my dear Captain, you can readily see how when the Moon's invisible side is turned *from* the Sun, she is nearly half a million miles further from him than she had been before. Therefore her heat should be so much the less."

"Well done, friend Ardan!" cried Barbican, clapping his hands with pleasure. "Yes, Captain, he understood it as well as either of us the whole time. Intelligence, not indifference, caused him to interrupt. Wonderful fellow!"

"That's the kind of a man I am!" replied Ardan, not without some degree of complacency. Then he added simply: "Barbican, my friend, if I understand your explanations so readily, attribute it all to their astonishing lucidity. If I have any faculty, it is that of being able to scent common sense at the first glimmer. Your sentences are so steeped in it that I catch their full meaning long before you end them—hence my apparent inattention. But we're not yet done with the visible face of the

Moon: it seems to me you have not yet enumerated all the advantages in which it surpasses the other side."

"Another of these advantages," continued Barbican, "is that it is from the visible side alone that eclipses of the Sun can be seen. This is self-evident, the interposition of the Earth being possible only between this visible face and the Sun. Furthermore, such eclipses of the Sun would be of a far more imposing character than anything of the kind to be witnessed from our Earth. This is chiefly for two reasons: first, when we, terrestrians, see the Sun eclipsed, we notice that, the discs of the two orbs being of about the same apparent size, one cannot hide the other except for a short time; second, as the two bodies are moving in opposite directions, the total duration of the eclipse, even under the most favorable circumstances, can't last longer than 7 minutes. Whereas to a Selenite who sees the Earth eclipse the Sun, not only does the Earth's disc appear four times larger than the Sun's, but also, as his day is 14 times longer than ours, the two heavenly bodies must remain several hours in contact. Besides, notwithstanding the apparent superiority of the Earth's disc, the refracting power of the atmosphere will never allow the Sun to be eclipsed altogether. Even when completely screened by the Earth, he would form a beautiful circle around her of yellow, red, and crimson light, in which she would appear to float like a vast sphere of jet in a glowing sea of gold, rubies, sparkling carbuncles and garnets."

"It seems to me," said M'Nicholl, "that, taking everything into consideration, the invisible side has been rather shabbily treated."

"I know I should not stay there very long," said Ardan; "the desire of seeing such a splendid sight as that eclipse would be enough to bring me to the visible side as soon as possible."

"Yes, I have no doubt of that, friend Michael," pursued Barbican; "but to see the eclipse it would not be necessary to quit the dark hemisphere altogether. You are, of course, aware that in consequence of her librations, or noddings, or wobblings, the Moon presents to the eyes of the Earth a little more than the exact half of her disc. She has two motions, one on her path around the Earth, and the other a shifting around on her own axis by which she endeavors to keep the same side always turned towards our sphere. This she cannot always do, as while one motion, the latter, is strictly uniform, the other being eccentric, sometimes accelerating her and sometimes retarding, she has not time to shift herself around completely and with perfect correspondence of movement. At her perigee, for instance, she moves forward quicker than she can shift, so that we detect a portion of her western border before she has time to conceal it. Similarly, at her apogee, when her rate of motion is comparatively slow, she shifts a little too quickly for her velocity, and therefore cannot help revealing a certain portion of her eastern border. She shows altogether about 8 degrees of the dark side, about 4 at the east and 4 at the west, so that, out of her 360 degrees, about 188, in other words, a little more than 57 per cent., about 4/7 of the entire surface, becomes visible to human eyes. Consequently a Selenite could catch an occasional glimpse of our Earth, without altogether quitting the dark side."

"No matter for that!" cried Ardan; "if we ever become Selenites we must inhabit the visible side. My weak point is light, and that I must have when it can be got."

"Unless, as perhaps in this case, you might be paying too dear for it," observed M'Nicholl. "How would you like to pay for your light by the loss of the atmosphere, which, according to some philosophers, is piled away on the dark side?"

"Ah! In that case I should consider a little before committing myself," replied Ardan, "I should like to hear your opinion regarding such a notion, Barbican. Hey! Do your hear? Have astronomers any valid reasons for supposing the atmosphere to have fled to the dark side of the Moon?"

"Defer that question till some other time, Ardan," whispered M'Nicholl; "Barbican is just now thinking out something that interests him far more deeply than any empty speculation of astronomers. If you are near the window, look out through it towards the Moon. Can you see anything?"

"I can feel the window with my hand; but for all I can see, I might as well be over head and ears in a hogshead of ink."

The two friends kept up a desultory conversation, but Barbican did not hear them. One fact, in particular, troubled him, and he sought in vain to account for it. Having come so near the Moon—about 30 miles—why had not the Projectile gone all the way? Had its velocity been very great, the tendency to fall could certainly be counteracted. But the velocity being undeniably very moderate, how explain such a decided resistance to Lunar attraction? Had the Projectile come within the sphere of some strange unknown influence? Did the neighborhood of some mysterious body retain it firmly imbedded in ether? That it would never reach the Moon, was now beyond all doubt; but where was it going? Nearer to her or further off? Or was it rushing resistlessly into infinity on the wings of that pitchy night? Who could tell, know, calculate—who could even guess, amid the horror of this gloomy blackness? Questions, like these, left Barbican no rest; in vain he tried to grapple with them; he felt like a child before them, baffled and almost despairing.

In fact, what could be more tantalizing? Just outside their windows, only a few leagues off, perhaps only a few miles, lay the radiant planet of the night, but in every respect as far off from the eyes of himself and his companions as if she was hiding at the other side of Jupiter! And to their ears she was no nearer. Earthquakes of the old Titanic type might at that very moment be upheaving her surface with resistless force, crashing mountain against mountain as fiercely as wave meets wave around the storm-lashed cliffs of Cape Horn. But not the faintest far off murmur even of such a mighty tumult could break the dead brooding silence that surrounded the travellers. Nay, the Moon, realizing the weird fancy of the Arabian poet, who calls her a "giant stiffening into granite, but struggling madly against his doom," might shriek, in a spasm of agony, loudly enough to be heard in Sirius. But our travellers could not hear it. Their ears no sound could now reach. They could no more detect the rending of a continent than the falling of a feather. Air, the propagator and transmitter of sound, was absent from her surface. Her cries, her struggles, her groans, were all smothered beneath the impenetrable tomb of eternal silence!

These were some of the fanciful ideas by which Ardan tried to amuse his companions in the present unsatisfactory state of affairs. His efforts, however well meant, were not successful. M'Nicholl's growls were more savage than usual, and even Barbican's patience was decidedly giving way. The loss of the other face they could have easily borne—with most of its details they had been already familiar. But, no, it must be the dark face that now escaped their observation! The very one that for numberless reasons they were actually dying to see! They looked out of the windows once more at the black Moon beneath them.

There it lay below them, a round black spot, hiding the sweet faces of the stars, but otherwise no more distinguishable by the travellers than if they were lying in the depths of the Mammoth Cave of Kentucky. And just think. Only fifteen days before, that dark face had been splendidly illuminated by the solar beams, every crater lustrous, every peak sparkling, every streak glistening under the vertical ray. In fifteen days later, a day light the most brilliant would have replaced a midnight the most Cimmerian. But in fifteen days later, where would the Projectile be? In what direction would it have been drawn by the forces innumerable of attractions incalculable? To such a question as this, even Ardan would reply only by an ominous shake of the head.

We know already that our travellers, as well as astronomers generally, judging from that portion of the dark side occasionally revealed by the Moon's librations, were *pretty certain* that there is no great difference between her two sides, as far as regards their physical constitutions. This portion, about the seventh part, shows plains and mountains, circles and craters, all of precisely the same nature as those already laid down on the chart. Judging therefore from analogy, the other three-sevenths are, in all probability a world in every respect exactly like the visible face—that is, arid, desert, dead. But our travellers also knew that *pretty certain* is far from *quite certain*, and that arguing merely from analogy may enable you to give a good guess, but can never lead you to an undoubted conclusion. What if the atmosphere had really withdrawn to this dark face? And if air, why not water? Would not this be enough to infuse life into the whole continent? Why should not vegetation flourish on its plains, fish in its seas, animals in its forests, and man in every one of its zones that were capable of sustaining life? To these interesting questions, what a satisfaction it would be to be able to answer positively one way or another! For thousands of difficult problems a mere glimpse at this hemisphere would be enough to furnish a satisfactory reply. How glorious it would be to contemplate a realm on which the eye of man has never yet rested!

Great, therefore, as you may readily conceive, was the depression of our travellers' spirits, as they pursued their way, enveloped in a veil of darkness the most profound. Still even then Ardan, as usual, formed somewhat of an exception. Finding it impossible to see a particle of the Lunar surface, he gave it up for good, and tried to console himself by gazing at the stars, which now fairly blazed in the spangled heavens. And certainly never before had astronomer enjoyed an opportunity for gazing at the heavenly bodies under such peculiar advantages. How Fraye of Paris, Chacornac of Lyons, and Father Secchi of Rome would have envied him!

For, candidly and truly speaking, never before had mortal eye revelled on such a scene of starry splendor. The black sky sparkled with lustrous fires, like the ceiling of a vast hall of ebony encrusted with flashing diamonds. Ardan's eye could take in the whole extent in an easy sweep from the *Southern Cross* to the *Little Bear*, thus embracing within one glance not only the two polar stars of the present day, but also *Campus* and *Vega*, which, by reason of the *precession of the Equinoxes*, are to be our polar stars 12,000 years hence. His imagination, as if intoxicated, reeled wildly through these sublime infinitudes and got lost in them. He forgot all about himself and all about his companions. He forgot even the strangeness of the fate that had sent them wandering through these forbidden regions, like a bewildered comet that had lost its way. With what a soft sweet light every star glowed! No matter what its magnitude, the stream that flowed from it looked calm and holy. No twinkling, no scintillation, no nictitation, disturbed their pure and lambent gleam. No atmosphere here interposed its layers of humidity or of unequal density to interrupt the stately majesty of their effulgence. The longer he gazed upon them, the more absorbing became their attraction. He felt that they were great kindly eyes looking down even yet with benevolence and protection on himself and his companions now driving wildly through space, and lost in the pathless depths of the black ocean of infinity!

He soon became aware that his friends, following his example, had interested themselves in gazing at the stars, and were now just as absorbed as himself in the contemplation of the transcendent spectacle. For a long time all three continued to feast their eyes on all the glories of the starry firmament; but, strange to say, the part that seemed to possess the strangest and weirdest fascination for their wandering glances was the spot where the vast disc of the Moon showed like an enormous round hole, black and soundless, and apparently deep enough to permit a glance into the darkest mysteries of the infinite.

A disagreeable sensation, however, against which they had been for some time struggling, at last put an end to their contemplations, and compelled them to think of themselves. This was nothing less than a pretty sharp cold, at first somewhat endurable, but which soon covered the inside surface of the window panes with a thick coating of ice. The fact was that, the Sun's direct rays having no longer an opportunity of warming up the Projectile, the latter began to lose rapidly by radiation whatever heat it had stored away within its walls. The consequence was a very decided falling of the thermometer, and so thick a condensation of the internal moisture on the window glasses as to soon render all external observations extremely difficult, if not actually impossible.

The Captain, as the oldest man in the party, claimed the privilege of saying he could stand it no longer. Striking a light, he consulted the thermometer and cried out:

"Seventeen degrees below zero, centigrade! that is certainly low enough to make an old fellow like me feel rather chilly!"

"Just one degree and a half above zero, Fahrenheit!" observed Barbican; "I really had no idea that it was so cold."

His teeth actually chattered so much that he could hardly articulate; still he, as well as the others, disliked to entrench on their short supply of gas.

"One feature of our journey that I particularly admire," said Ardan, trying to laugh with freezing lips, "is that we can't complain of monotony. At one time we are frying with the heat and blinded with the light, like Indians caught on a burning prairie; at another, we are freezing in the pitchy darkness of a hyperborean winter, like Sir John Franklin's merry men in the Bay of Boothia. *Madame La Nature*, you don't forget your devotees; on the contrary, you overwhelm us with your attentions!"

"Our external temperature may be reckoned at how much?" asked the Captain, making a desperate effort to keep up the conversation.

"The temperature outside our Projectile must be precisely the same as that of interstellar space in general," answered Barbican.

"Is not this precisely the moment then," interposed Ardan, quickly, "for making an experiment which we could never have made as long as we were in the sunshine?"

"That's so!" exclaimed Barbican; "now or never! I'm glad you thought of it, Ardan. We are just now in the position to find out the temperature of space by actual experiment, and so see whose calculations are right, Fourier's or Pouillet's."

"Let's see," asked Ardan, "who was Fourier, and who was Pouillet?"

"Baron Fourier, of the French Academy, wrote a famous treatise on *Heat*, which I remember reading twenty years ago in Penington's book store," promptly responded the Captain; "Pouillet was an eminent professor of Physics at the Sorbonne, where he died, last year, I think."

"Thank you, Captain," said Ardan; "the cold does not injure your memory, though it is decidedly on the advance. See how thick the ice is already on the window panes! Let it only keep on and we shall soon have our breaths falling around us in flakes of snow."

"Let us prepare a thermometer," said Barbican, who had already set himself to work in a business-like manner.

A thermometer of the usual kind, as may be readily supposed, would be of no use whatever in the experiment that was now about to be made. In an ordinary thermometer Mercury freezes hard when exposed to a temperature of 40° below zero. But Barbican had provided himself with a *Minimum*, *self-recording* thermometer, of a peculiar nature, invented by Wolferdin, a friend of Arago's, which could correctly register exceedingly low degrees of temperature. Before beginning the experiment, this instrument was tested by comparison with one of the usual kind, and then Barbican hesitated a few moments regarding the best means of employing it.

"How shall we start this experiment?" asked the Captain.

"Nothing simpler," answered Ardan, always ready to reply; "you just open your windows, and fling out your thermometer. It follows your Projectile, as a calf follows her mother. In a quarter of an hour you put out your hand—"

"Put out your hand!" interrupted Barbican.

"Put out your hand—" continued Ardan, quietly.

"You do nothing of the kind," again interrupted Barbican; "that is, unless you prefer, instead of a hand, to pull back a frozen stump, shapeless, colorless and lifeless!"

"I prefer a hand," said Ardan, surprised and interested.

"Yes," continued Barbican, "the instant your hand left the Projectile, it would experience the same terrible sensations as is produced by cauterizing it with an iron bar white hot. For heat, whether rushing rapidly out of our bodies or rapidly entering them, is identically the same force and does the same amount of damage. Besides I am by no means certain that we are still followed by the objects that we flung out of the Projectile."

"Why not?" asked M'Nicholl; "we saw them all outside not long ago."

"But we can't see them outside now," answered Barbican; "that may be accounted for, I know, by the darkness, but it may be also by the fact of their not being there at all. In a case like this, we can't rely on uncertainties. Therefore, to make sure of not losing our thermometer, we shall fasten it with a string and easily pull it in whenever we like."

This advice being adopted, the window was opened quickly, and the instrument was thrown out at once by M'Nicholl, who held it fastened by a short stout cord so that it could be pulled in immediately. The window had hardly been open for longer than a second, yet that second had been enough to admit a terrible icy chill into the interior of the Projectile.

"Ten thousand ice-bergs!" cried Ardan, shivering all over; "it's cold enough to freeze a white bear!"

Barbican waited quietly for half an hour; that time he considered quite long enough to enable the instrument to acquire the temperature of the interstellar space. Then he gave the signal, and it was instantly pulled in.

It took him a few moments to calculate the quantity of mercury that had escaped into the little diaphragm attached to the lower part of the instrument; then he said:

"A hundred and forty degrees, centigrade, below zero!"

"Two hundred and twenty degrees, Fahrenheit, below zero!" cried M'Nicholl; "no wonder that we should feel a little chilly!"

"Pouillet is right, then," said Barbican, "and Fourier wrong."

"Another victory for Sorbonne over the Academy!" cried Ardan. "*Vive la Sorbonne!* Not that I'm a bit proud of finding myself in the midst of a temperature so very *distingué*—though it is more than three times colder than Hayes ever felt it at Humboldt Glacier or Nevenoff at Yakoutsk. If Madame the Moon becomes as cold as this every time that her surface is withdrawn from the sunlight for fourteen days, I don't think, boys, that her hospitality is much to hanker after!"

XV

GLIMPSES AT THE INVISIBLE

In spite of the dreadful condition in which the three friends now found themselves, and the still more dreadful future that awaited them, it must be acknowledged that Ardan bravely kept up his spirits. And his companions were just as cheerful. Their philosophy was quite simple and perfectly intelligible. What they could bear, they bore without murmuring. When it became unbearable, they only complained, if complaining would do any good. Imprisoned in an iron shroud, flying through profound darkness into the infinite abysses of space, nearly a quarter million of miles distant from all human aid, freezing with the icy cold, their little stock not only of gas but of *air* rapidly running lower and lower, a near future of the most impenetrable obscurity looming up before them, they never once thought of wasting time in asking such useless questions as where they were going, or what fate was about to befall them. Knowing that no good could possibly result from inaction or despair, they carefully kept their wits about them, making their experiments and recording their observations as calmly and as deliberately as if they were working at home in the quiet retirement of their own cabinets.

Any other course of action, however, would have been perfectly absurd on their part, and this no one knew better than themselves. Even if desirous to act otherwise, what could they have done? As powerless over the Projectile as a baby over a locomotive, they could neither clap brakes to its movement nor switch off its direction. A sailor can turn his ship's head at pleasure; an aeronaut has little trouble, by means of his ballast and his throttle-valve, in giving a vertical movement to his balloon. But nothing of this kind could our travellers attempt. No helm, or ballast, or throttle-valve could avail them now. Nothing in the world could be done to prevent things from following their own course to the bitter end.

If these three men would permit themselves to hazard an expression at all on the subject, which they didn't, each could have done it by his own favorite motto, so admirably expressive of his individual nature. *"Donnez tête baissée!"* (Go it baldheaded!) showed Ardan's uncalculating impetuosity and his Celtic blood. *"Fata quocunque vocant!"* (To its logical consequence!) revealed Barbican's imperturbable stoicism, culture hardening rather than loosening the original British phlegm. Whilst M'Nicholl's "Screw down the valve and let her rip!" betrayed at once his unconquerable Yankee coolness and his old experiences as a Western steamboat captain.

Where were they now, at eight o'clock in the morning of the day called in America the sixth of December? Near the Moon, very certainly; near enough, in fact, for them to perceive easily in the dark the great round screen which she formed between themselves and the Projectile on one side, and the Earth, Sun, and stars on the other. But as to the exact distance at which she lay from them—they had no possible means of calculating it. The Projectile, impelled and maintained by forces inexplicable and even incomprehensible, had come within less than thirty miles from the Moon's north pole. But during those two hours of immersion in the dark shadow, had this distance been increased or diminished? There was evidently no stand-point whereby to estimate either the Projectile's direction or its velocity. Perhaps, moving rapidly away from the Moon, it would be soon out of her shadow altogether. Perhaps, on the contrary, gradually approaching her surface, it might come into contact at any moment with some sharp invisible peak of the Lunar mountains—a catastrophe sure to put a sudden end to the trip, and the travellers too.

An excited discussion on this subject soon sprang up, in which all naturally took part. Ardan's imagination as usual getting the better of his reason, he maintained very warmly that the Projectile, caught and retained by the Moon's attraction, could not help falling on her surface, just as an aerolite cannot help falling on our Earth.

"Softly, dear boy, softly," replied Barbican; "aerolites *can* help falling on the Earth, and the proof is, that few of them *do* fall—most of them don't. Therefore, even granting that we had already assumed the nature of an aerolite, it does not necessarily follow that we should fall on the Moon."

"But," objected Ardan, "if we approach only near enough, I don't see how we can help—"

"You don't see, it may be," said Barbican, "but you can see, if you only reflect a moment. Have you not often seen the November meteors, for instance, streaking the skies, thousands at a time?"

"Yes; on several occasions I was so fortunate."

"Well, did you ever see any of them strike the Earth's surface?" asked Barbican.

"I can't say I ever did," was the candid reply, "but—"

"Well, these shooting stars," continued Barbican, "or rather these wandering particles of matter, shine only from being inflamed by the friction of the atmosphere. Therefore they can never be at a greater distance from the Earth than 30 or 40 miles at furthest, and yet they seldom fall on it. So with our Projectile. It may go very close to the Moon without falling into it."

"But our roving Projectile must pull up somewhere in the long run," replied Ardan, "and I should like to know where that somewhere can be, if not in the Moon."

"Softly again, dear boy," said Barbican; "how do you know that our Projectile must pull up somewhere?"

"It's self-evident," replied Ardan; "it can't keep moving for ever."

"Whether it can or it can't depends altogether on which one of two mathematical curves it has followed in describing its course. According to the velocity with which it was endowed at a certain moment, it must follow either the one or the other; but this velocity I do not consider myself just now able to calculate."

"Exactly so," chimed in M'Nicholl; "it must describe and keep on describing either a parabola or a hyperbola."

"Precisely," said Barbican; "at a certain velocity it would take a parabolic curve; with a velocity considerably greater it should describe a hyperbolic curve."

"I always did like nice corpulent words," said Ardan, trying to laugh; "bloated and unwieldy, they express in a neat handy way exactly what you mean. Of course, I know all about the high—high—those high curves, and those low curves. No matter. Explain them to me all the same. Consider me most deplorably ignorant on the nature of these curves."

"Well," said the Captain, a little bumptiously, "a parabola is a curve of the second order, formed by the intersection of a cone by a plane parallel to one of its sides."

"You don't say so!" cried Ardan, with mouth agape. "Do tell!"

"It is pretty nearly the path taken by a shell shot from a mortar."

"Well now!" observed Ardan, apparently much surprised; "who'd have thought it? Now for the high—high—bully old curve!"

"The hyperbola," continued the Captain, not minding Ardan's antics, "the hyperbola is a curve of the second order, formed from the intersection of a cone by a plane parallel to its axis, or rather parallel to its two *generatrices*, constituting two separate branches, extending indefinitely in both directions."

"Oh, what an accomplished scientist I'm going to turn out, if only left long enough at your feet, illustrious *maestro!*" cried Ardan, with effusion. "Only figure it to yourselves, boys; before the Captain's lucid explanations, I fully expected to hear something about the high curves and the low curves in the back of an Ancient Thomas! Oh, Michael, Michael, why didn't you know the Captain earlier?"

But the Captain was now too deeply interested in a hot discussion with Barbican to notice that the Frenchman was only funning him. Which of the two curves had been the one most probably taken by the Projectile? Barbican maintained it was the parabolic; M'Nicholl insisted that it was the hyperbolic. Their tempers were not improved by the severe cold, and both became rather excited in the dispute. They drew so many lines on the table, and crossed them so often with others, that nothing was left at last but a great blot. They covered bits of paper with x's and y's, which they read out like so many classic passages, shouting them, declaiming them, drawing attention to the strong points by gesticulation so forcible and voice so loud that neither of the disputants could hear a word that the other said. Possibly the very great difference in temperature between the external air in contact with their skin and the blood coursing through their veins, had given rise to magnetic currents as potential in their effects as a superabundant supply of oxygen. At all events, the language they soon began to employ in the enforcement of their arguments fairly made the Frenchman's hair stand on end.

"You probably forget the important difference between a *directrix* and an *axis*," hotly observed Barbican.

"I know what an *abscissa* is, any how!" cried the Captain. "Can you say as much?"

"Did you ever understand what is meant by a *double ordinate*?" asked Barbican, trying to keep cool.

"More than you ever did about a *transverse* and a *conjugate!*" replied the Captain, with much asperity.

"Any one not convinced at a glance that this *eccentricity* is equal to *unity*, must be blind as a bat!" exclaimed Barbican, fast losing his ordinary urbanity.

"*Less* than *unity*, you mean! If you want spectacles, here are mine!" shouted the Captain, angrily tearing them off and offering them to his adversary.

"Dear boys!" interposed Ardan—

—"The *eccentricity* is *equal* to *unity*!" cried Barbican.

—"The *eccentricity* is *less* than *unity*!" screamed M'Nicholl.

"Talking of eccentricity—" put in Ardan.

—"Therefore it's a *parabola*, and must be!" cried Barbican, triumphantly.

—"Therefore it's *hyperbola* and nothing shorter!" was the Captain's quite as confident reply.

"For gracious sake!—" resumed Ardan.

"Then produce your *asymptote*!" exclaimed Barbican, with an angry sneer.

"Let us see the *symmetrical point*!" roared the Captain, quite savagely.

"Dear boys! old fellows!—" cried Ardan, as loud as his lungs would let him.

"It's useless to argue with a Mississippi steamboat Captain," exclaimed Barbican; "he never gives in till he blows up!"

"Never try to convince a Yankee schoolmaster," replied M'Nicholl; "he has one book by heart and don't believe in any other!"

"Here, friend Michael, get me a cord, won't you? It's the only way to convince him!" cried Barbican, hastily turning to the Frenchman.

"Hand me over that ruler, Ardan!" yelled the Captain. "The heavy one! It's the only way now left to bring him to reason!"

"Look here, Barbican and M'Nicholl!" cried Ardan, at last making himself heard, and keeping a tight hold both on the cord and the ruler. "This thing has gone far enough! Come. Stop your talk, and answer me a few questions. What do you want of this cord, Barbican?"

"To describe a parabolic curve!"

"And what are you going to do with the ruler, M'Nicholl!"

"To help draw a true hyperbola!"

"Promise me, Barbican, that you're not going to lasso the Captain!"

"Lasso the Captain! Ha! ha! ha!"

"You promise, M'Nicholl, that you're not going to brain the President!"

"I brain the President! Ho! ho! ho!"

"I want merely to convince him that it is a parabola!"

"I only want to make it clear as day that it is hyperbola!"

"Does it make any real difference whether it is one or the other?" yelled Ardan.

"The greatest possible difference—in the Eye of Science."

"A radical and incontrovertible difference—in the Eye of Science!"

"Oh! Hang the Eye of Science—will either curve take us to the Moon?"

"No!"

"Will either take us back to the Earth?"

"No!"

"Will either take us anywhere that you know of?"

"No!"

"Why not?"

"Because they are both *open* curves, and therefore can never end!"

"Is it of the slightest possible importance which of the two curves controls the Projectile?"

"Not the slightest—except in the Eye of Science!"

"Then let the Eye of Science and her parabolas and hyperbolas, and conjugates, and asymptotes, and the rest of the confounded nonsensical farrago, all go to pot! What's the use of bothering your heads about them here! Have you not enough to trouble you otherwise? A nice pair of scientists you are? 'Stanislow' scientists, probably. Do *real* scientists lose their tempers for a trifle? Am I ever to see my ideal of a true scientific man in the flesh? Barbican came very near realizing my idea perfectly; but I see that Science just has as little effect as Culture in driving the Old Adam out of us! The idea of the only simpleton in the lot having to lecture the others on propriety of deportment! I thought they were going to tear each other's eyes out! Ha! Ha! Ha! It's *impayable*! Give me that cord, Michael! Hand me the heavy ruler, Ardan! It's the only way to bring him to reason! Ho! Ho! Ho! It's too good! I shall never get over it!" and he laughed till his sides ached and his cheeks streamed.

His laughter was so contagious, and his merriment so genuine, that there was really no resisting it, and the next few minutes witnessed nothing but laughing, and handshaking and rib-punching in the Projectile—though Heaven knows there was very little for the poor fellows to be merry about. As they could neither reach the Moon nor return to the Earth, what *was* to befall them? The immediate outlook was the very reverse of exhilarating. If they did not die of hunger, if they did not die of thirst, the reason would simply be that, in a few days, as soon as their gas was exhausted, they would die for want of air, unless indeed the icy cold had killed them beforehand!

By this time, in fact, the temperature had become so exceedingly cold that a further encroachment on their little stock of gas could be put off no longer. The light, of course, they could manage to do without; but a little heat was absolutely necessary to prevent them from freezing to death. Fortunately, however, the caloric developed by the Reiset and Regnault process for purifying the air, raised the internal temperature of the Projectile a little, so that, with an expenditure of gas much less than they had expected, our travellers were able to maintain it at a degree capable of sustaining human life.

By this time, also, all observations through the windows had become exceedingly difficult. The internal moisture condensed so thick and congealed so hard on the glass that nothing short of continued friction could keep up its transparency. But this friction, however laborious they might regard it at other times, they thought very little of just now, when observation had become far more interesting and important than ever.

If the Moon had any atmosphere, our travellers were near enough now to strike any meteor that might be rushing through it. If the Projectile itself were floating in it, as was possible, would not such a good conductor of sound convey to their ears the reflexion of some lunar echo, the roar of some storm raging among the mountains, the rattling of some plunging avalanche, or the detonations of some eructating volcano? And suppose some lunar Etna or Vesuvius was flashing out its fires, was it not even possible that their eye could catch a glimpse of the lurid gleam? One or two facts of this kind, well attested, would singularly elucidate the vexatious question of a lunar atmosphere, which is still so far from being decided. Full of such thoughts and intensely interested in them, Barbican, M'Nicholl and Ardan, patient as astronomers at a transit of Venus, watched steadily at their windows, and allowed nothing worth noticing to escape their searching gaze.

Ardan's patience first gave out. He showed it by an observation natural enough, for that matter, to a mind unaccustomed to long stretches of careful thought:

"This darkness is absolutely killing! If we ever take this trip again, it must be about the time of the New Moon!"

"There I agree with you, Ardan," observed the Captain. "That would be just the time to start. The Moon herself, I grant, would be lost in the solar rays and therefore invisible all the time of our trip, but in compensation, we should have the Full Earth in full view. Besides— and this is your chief point, no doubt, Ardan—if we should happen to be drawn round the Moon, just as we are at the present moment, we should enjoy the inestimable advantage of beholding her invisible side magnificently illuminated!"

"My idea exactly, Captain," said Ardan. "What is your opinion on this point, Barbican?"

"My opinion is as follows:" answered Barbican, gravely. "If we ever repeat this journey, we shall start precisely at the same time and under precisely the same circumstances. You forget that our only object is to reach the Moon. Now suppose we had really landed there, as we expected to do yesterday, would it not have been much more agreeable to behold the lunar continents enjoying the full light of day than to find them plunged in the dismal obscurity of night? Would not our first installation of discovery have been under circumstances decidedly extremely favorable? Your silence shows that you agree with me. As to the invisible side, once landed, we should have the power to visit it when we pleased, and therefore we could always choose whatever time would best suit our purpose. Therefore, if we wanted to land in the Moon, the period of the Full Moon was the best period to select. The period was well chosen, the time was well calculated, the force was well applied, the Projectile was well aimed, but missing our way spoiled everything."

"That's sound logic, no doubt," said Ardan; "still I can't help thinking that all for want of a little light we are losing, probably forever, a splendid opportunity of seeing the Moon's invisible side. How about the other planets, Barbican? Do you think that their inhabitants are as ignorant regarding their satellites as we are regarding ours?"

"On that subject," observed M'Nicholl, "I could venture an answer myself, though, of course, without pretending to speak dogmatically on any such open question. The satellites of the other planets, by their comparative proximity, must be much easier to study than our Moon. The Saturnians, the Uranians, the Jovians, cannot have had very serious difficulty in effecting some communication with their satellites. Jupiter's four moons, for instance, though on an average actually 2-1/2 times farther from their planet's centre than the Moon is from us, are comparatively four times nearer to him on account of his radius being eleven times greater than the Earth's. With Saturn's eight moons, the case is almost precisely similar. Their average distance is nearly three times greater than that of our Moon; but as Saturn's diameter is about 9 times greater than the Earth's, his bodyguards are really between 3 and 4 times nearer to their principal than ours is to us. As to Uranus, his first satellite, *Ariel*, half as far from him as our Moon is from the Earth, is comparatively, though not actually, eight times nearer."

"Therefore," said Barbican, now taking up the subject, "an experiment analogous to ours, starting from either of these three planets, would have encountered fewer difficulties. But the whole question resolves itself into this. *If* the Jovians and the rest have been able to quit their planets, they have probably succeeded in discovering the invisible sides of their satellites. But if they have *not* been able to do so, why, they're not a bit wiser than ourselves—But what's the matter with the Projectile? It's certainly shifting!"

Shifting it certainly was. While the path it described as it swung blindly through the darkness, could not be laid down by any chart for want of a starting point, Barbican and his companions soon became aware of a decided modification of its relative position with regard to the Moon's surface. Instead of its side, as heretofore, it now presented its base to the Moon's disc, and its axis had become rigidly vertical to the lunar horizon. Of this new feature in their journey, Barbican had assured himself by the most undoubted proof towards four o'clock in the morning. What was the cause? Gravity, of course. The heavier portion of the Projectile gravitated towards the Moon's centre exactly as if they were falling towards her surface.

But *were* they falling? Were they at last, contrary to all expectations, about to reach the goal that they had been so ardently wishing for? No! A sight-point, just discovered by M'Nicholl, very soon convinced Barbican that the Projectile was as far as ever from approaching the Moon, but was moving around it in a curve pretty near concentric.

M'Nicholl's discovery, a luminous gleam flickering on the distant verge of the black disc, at once engrossed the complete attention of our travellers and set them to divining its course. It could not possibly be confounded with a star. Its glare was reddish, like that of a distant furnace on a dark night; it kept steadily increasing in size and brightness, thus showing beyond a doubt how the Projectile was moving—in the direction of the luminous point, and *not* vertically falling towards the Moon's surface.

"It's a volcano!" cried the Captain, in great excitement; "a volcano in full blast! An outlet of the Moon's internal fires! Therefore she can't be a burnt out cinder!"

"It certainly looks like a volcano," replied Barbican, carefully investigating this new and puzzling phenomenon with his night-glass. "If it is not one, in fact, what can it be?"

"To maintain combustion," commenced Ardan syllogistically and sententiously, "air is necessary. An undoubted case of combustion lies before us. Therefore, this part of the Moon *must* have an atmosphere!"

"Perhaps so," observed Barbican, "but not necessarily so. The volcano, by decomposing certain substances, gunpowder for instance, may be able to furnish its own oxygen, and thus explode in a vacuum. That blaze, in fact, seems to me to possess the intensity and the blinding glare of objects burning in pure oxygen. Let us therefore be not over hasty in jumping at the conclusion of the existence of a lunar atmosphere."

This fire mountain was situated, according to the most plausible conjecture, somewhere in the neighborhood of the 45th degree, south latitude, of the Moon's invisible side. For a little while the travellers indulged the fond hope that they were directly approaching it, but, to their great disappointment, the path described by the Projectile lay in a different direction. Its nature therefore they had no opportunity of ascertaining. It began to disappear behind the dark horizon within less than half an hour after the time that M'Nicholl had signalled it. Still, the fact of the uncontested existence of such a phenomenon was a grand one, and of considerable importance in selenographic investigations. It proved that heat had not altogether disappeared from the lunar world; and the existence of heat once settled, who can say positively that the vegetable kingdom and even the animal kingdom have not likewise resisted so far every influence tending to destroy them? If terrestrial astronomers could only be convinced, by undoubted evidence, of the existence of this active volcano on the Moon's surface, they would certainly admit of very considerable modifications in the present doubts regarding her inhabitability.

Thoughts of this kind continued to occupy the minds of our travellers even for some time after the little spark of light had been extinguished in the black gloom. But they said very little; even Ardan was silent, and continued to look out of the window. Barbican surrendered himself up to a reverie regarding the mysterious destinies of the lunar world. Was its present condition a foreshadowing of what our Earth is to become? M'Nicholl, too, was lost in speculation. Was the Moon older or younger than the Earth in the order of Creation? Had she ever been a beautiful world of life, and color, and magnificent variety? If so, had her inhabitants—

Great Mercy, what a cry from Ardan! It sounded human, so seldom do we hear a shriek so expressive at once of surprise and horror and even terror! It brought back his startled companions to their senses in a second. Nor did they ask him for the cause of his alarm. It was only too clear. Right in their very path, a blazing ball of fire had suddenly risen up before their eyes, the pitchy darkness all round it rendering its glare still more blinding. Its phosphoric coruscation filled the Projectile with white streams of lurid light, tinging the contents with a pallor indescribably ghastly. The travellers' faces in particular, gleamed with that peculiar livid and cadaverous tinge, blue and yellow, which magicians so readily produce by burning table salt in alcohol.

"*Sacré!*" cried Ardan who always spoke his own language when much excited. "What a pair of beauties you are! Say, Barbican! What thundering thing is coming at us now?"

"Another bolide," answered Barbican, his eye as calm as ever, though a faint tremor was quite perceptible in his voice.

"A bolide? Burning *in vacuo*? You are joking!"

"I was never more in earnest," was the President's quiet reply, as he looked through his closed fingers.

He knew exactly what he was saying. The dazzling glitter did not deceive *him*. Such a meteor seen from the Earth could not appear much brighter than the Full Moon, but here in the midst of the black ether and unsoftened by the veil of the atmosphere, it was absolutely blinding. These wandering bodies carry in themselves the principle of their incandescence. Oxygen is by no means necessary for their combustion. Some of them indeed often take fire as they rush through the layers of our atmosphere, and generally burn out before they strike the Earth. But others, on the contrary, and the greater number too, follow a track through space far more distant from the Earth than the fifty miles supposed to limit our atmosphere. In October, 1844, one of these meteors had appeared in the sky at an altitude calculated to be at least 320 miles; and in August, 1841, another had vanished when it had reached the height of 450 miles. A few even of those seen from the Earth must have been several miles in diameter. The velocity with which some of them have been calculated to move, from east to west, in a direction contrary to that of the Earth, is astounding enough to exceed belief—about fifty miles in a second. Our Earth does not move quite 20 miles in a second, though it goes a thousand times quicker than the fastest locomotive.

Barbican calculated like lightning that the present object of their alarm was only about 250 miles distant from them, and could not be less than a mile and a quarter in diameter. It was coming on at the rate of more than a mile a second or about 75 miles a minute. It lay right in the path of the Projectile, and in a very few seconds indeed a terrible collision was inevitable. The enormous rate at which it grew in size, showed the terrible velocity at which it was approaching.

You can hardly imagine the situation of our poor travellers at the sight of this frightful apparition. I shall certainly not attempt to describe it. In spite of their singular courage, wonderful coolness, extraordinary fortitude, they were now breathless, motionless, almost helpless; their muscles were tightened to their utmost tension; their eyes stared out of their sockets; their faces were petrified with horror. No wonder. Their Projectile, whose course they were powerless as children to guide, was making straight for this fiery mass, whose glare in a few seconds had become more blinding than the open vent of a reverberating furnace. Their own Projectile was carrying them headlong into a bottomless abyss of fire!

Still, even in this moment of horror, their presence of mind, or at least their consciousness, never abandoned them. Barbican had grasped each of his friends by the hand, and all three tried as well as they could to watch through half-closed eyelids the white-hot asteroid's rapid approach. They could utter no word, they could breathe no prayer. They gave themselves up for lost—in the agony of terror that partially interrupted the ordinary functions of their brains, this was absolutely all they could do! Hardly three minutes had elapsed since Ardan had caught the first glimpse of it—three ages of agony! Now it was on them! In a second—in less than a second, the terrible fireball had burst like a shell! Thousands of glittering fragments were flying around them in all directions—but with no more noise than is made by so many light flakes of thistle-down floating about some warm afternoon in summer. The blinding, blasting steely white glare of the explosion almost bereft the travellers of the use of their eyesight forever, but no more report reached their ears than if it had taken place at the bottom of the Gulf of Mexico. In an atmosphere like ours, such a crash would have burst the ear-membranes of ten thousand elephants!

In the middle of the commotion another loud cry was suddenly heard. It was the Captain who called this time. His companions rushed to his window and all looked out together in the same direction.

What a sight met their eyes! What pen can describe it? What pencil can reproduce the magnificence of its coloring? It was a Vesuvius at his best and wildest, at the moment just after the old cone has fallen in. Millions of luminous fragments streaked the sky with their blazing fires. All sizes and shapes of light, all colors and shades of colors, were inextricably mingled together. Irradiations in gold, scintillations in crimson, splendors in emerald, lucidities in ultramarine—a dazzling girandola of every tint and of every hue. Of the enormous fireball, an instant ago such an object of dread, nothing now remained but these glittering pieces, shooting about in all directions, each one an asteroid in its turn. Some flew out straight and gleaming like a steel sword; others rushed here and there irregularly like chips struck off a red-hot rock; and others left long trails of glittering cosmical dust behind them like the nebulous tail of Donati's comet.

These incandescent blocks crossed each other, struck each other, crushed each other into still smaller fragments, one of which, grazing the Projectile, jarred it so violently that the very window at which the travellers were standing, was cracked by the shock. Our friends felt, in fact, as if they were the objective point at which endless volleys of blazing shells were aimed, any of them powerful enough, if it only hit them fair, to make as short work of the Projectile as you could of an egg-shell. They had many hairbreadth escapes, but fortunately the cracking of the glass proved to be the only serious damage of which they could complain.

This extraordinary illumination lasted altogether only a few seconds; every one of its details was of a most singular and exciting nature—but one of its greatest wonders was yet to come. The ether, saturated with luminous matter, developed an intensity of blazing brightness unequalled by the lime light, the magnesium light, the electric light, or any other dazzling source of illumination with which we are acquainted on earth. It flashed out of these asteroids in all directions, and downwards, of course, as well as elsewhere. At one particular instant, it was so very vivid that Ardan, who happened to be looking downwards, cried out, as if in transport:

"Oh!! The Moon! Visible at last!"

And the three companions, thrilling with indescribable emotion, shot a hasty glance through the openings of the coruscating field beneath them. Did they really catch a glimpse of the mysterious invisible disc that the eye of man had never before lit upon? For a second or so they gazed with enraptured fascination at all they could see. What did they see, what could they see at a distance so uncertain that Barbican has never been able even to guess at it? Not much. Ardan was reminded of the night he had stood on the battlements of Dover Castle, a few years before, when the fitful flashes of a thunder storm gave him occasional and very uncertain glimpses of the French coast at the opposite side of the strait. Misty strips long and narrow, extending over one portion of the disc—probably cloud-scuds sustained by a highly rarefied atmosphere—permitted only a very dreamy idea of lofty mountains stretching beneath them in shapeless proportions, of smaller reliefs, circuses, yawning craters, and the other capricious, sponge-like formations so common on the visible side. Elsewhere the watchers became aware for an instant of immense spaces, certainly not arid plains, but seas, real oceans, vast and calm, reflecting from their placid depths the dazzling fireworks of the weird and wildly flashing meteors. Farther on, but very darkly as if behind a screen, shadowy continents revealed themselves, their surfaces flecked with black cloudy masses, probably great forests, with here and there a—

Nothing more! In less than a second the illumination had come to an end, involving everything in the Moon's direction once more in pitchy darkness.

But had the impression made on the travellers' eyes been a mere vision or the result of a reality? an optical delusion or the shadow of a solid fact? Could an observation so rapid, so fleeting, so superficial, be really regarded as a genuine scientific affirmation? Could such a feeble glimmer of the invisible disc justify them in pronouncing a decided opinion on the inhabitability of the Moon? To such questions as these, rising spontaneously and simultaneously in the minds of our travellers, they could not reply at the moment; they could not reply to them long afterwards; even to this day they can give them no satisfactory answer. All they could do at the moment, they did. To every sight and sound they kept their eyes and ears open, and, by observing the most perfect silence, they sought to render their impressions too vivid to admit of deception.

There was now, however, nothing to be heard, and very little more to be seen. The few coruscations that flashed over the sky, gradually became fewer and dimmer; the asteroids sought paths further and further apart, and finally disappeared altogether. The ether resumed its original blackness. The stars, eclipsed for a moment, blazed out again on the firmament, and the invisible disc, that had flashed into view for an instant, once more relapsed forever into the impenetrable depths of night.

XVI

The Southern Hemisphere

Exceedingly narrow and exceedingly fortunate had been the escape of the Projectile. And from a danger too the most unlikely and the most unexpected. Who would have ever dreamed of even the possibility of such an encounter? And was all danger over? The sight of one of these erratic bolides certainly justified the gravest apprehensions of our travellers regarding the existence of others. Worse than the sunken reefs of the Southern Seas or the snags of the Mississippi, how could the Projectile be expected to avoid them? Drifting along blindly through the boundless ethereal ocean, *her* inmates, even if they saw the danger, were totally powerless to turn her aside. Like a ship without a rudder, like a runaway horse, like a collapsed balloon, like an iceberg in an Atlantic storm, like a boat in the Niagara rapids, she moved on sullenly, recklessly, mechanically, mayhap into the very jaws of the most frightful danger, the bright intelligences within no more able to modify her motions even by a finger's breadth than they were able to affect Mercury's movements around the Sun.

But did our friends complain of the new perils now looming up before them? They never thought of such a thing. On the contrary, they only considered themselves (after the lapse of a few minutes to calm their nerves) extremely lucky in having witnessed this fresh glory of exuberant nature, this transcendent display of fireworks which not only cast into absolute insignificance anything of the kind they had ever seen on Earth, but had actually enabled them by its dazzling illumination to gaze for a second or two at the Moon's mysterious invisible disc. This glorious momentary glance, worth a whole lifetime of ordinary existence, had revealed to mortal ken her continents, her oceans, her forests. But did it also convince them of the existence of an atmosphere on her surface whose vivifying molecules would render *life* possible? This question they had again to leave unanswered—it will hardly ever be answered in a way quite satisfactory to human curiosity. Still, infinite was their satisfaction at having hovered even for an instant on the very verge of such a great problem's solution.

It was now half-past three in the afternoon. The Projectile still pursued its curving but otherwise unknown path over the Moon's invisible face. Had this path been disturbed by that dangerous meteor? There was every reason to fear so—though, disturbance or no disturbance, the curve it described should still be one strictly in accordance with the laws of Mechanical Philosophy. Whether it was a parabola or a hyperbola, however, or whether it was disturbed or not, made very little difference as, in any case, the Projectile was bound to quit pretty soon the cone of the shadow, at a point directly opposite to where it had entered it. This cone could not possibly be of very great extent, considering the very slight ratio borne by the Moon's diameter when compared with the Sun's. Still, to all appearances, the Projectile seemed to be quite as deeply immersed in the shadow as ever, and there was apparently not the slightest sign of such a state of things coming soon to an end. At what rate was the Projectile now moving? Hard to say, but certainly not slowly, certainly rapidly enough to be out of the shadow by this time, if describing a curve rigidly parabolic. Was the curve therefore *not* parabolic? Another puzzling problem and sadly bewildering to poor Barbican, who had now almost lost his reason by attempting to clear up questions that were proving altogether too profound for his overworked brains.

Not that he ever thought of taking rest. Not that his companions thought of taking rest. Far from it. With senses as high-strung as ever, they still watched carefully for every new fact, every unexpected incident that might throw some light on the sidereal investigations. Even their dinner, or what was called so, consisted of only a few bits of bread and meat, distributed by Ardan at five o'clock, and swallowed mechanically. They did not even turn on the gas full head to see what they were eating; each man stood solidly at his window, the glass of which they had enough to do in keeping free from the rapidly condensing moisture.

At about half-past five, however, M'Nicholl, who had been gazing for some time with his telescope in a particular direction, called the attention of his companions to some bright specks of light barely discernible in that part of the horizon towards which the Projectile was evidently moving. His words were hardly uttered when his companions announced the same discovery. They could soon all see the glittering specks not only becoming more and more numerous, but also gradually assuming the shape of an extremely slender, but extremely brilliant crescent. Rapidly more brilliant and more decided in shape the profile gradually grew, till it soon resembled the first faint sketch of the New Moon that we catch of evenings in the western sky, or rather the first glimpse we get of her limb as it slowly moves out of eclipse. But it was inconceivably brighter than either, and was furthermore strangely relieved by the pitchy blackness both of sky and Moon. In fact, it soon became so brilliant as to dispel in a moment all doubt as to its particular nature. No meteor could present such a perfect shape; no volcano, such dazzling splendor.

"The Sun!" cried Barbican.

"The Sun?" asked M'Nicholl and Ardan in some astonishment.

"Yes, dear friends; it is the Sun himself that you now see; these summits that you behold him gilding are the mountains that lie on the Moon's southern rim. We are rapidly nearing her south pole."

"After doubling her north pole!" cried Ardan; "why, we must be circumnavigating her!"

"Exactly; sailing all around her."

"Hurrah! Then we're all right at last! There's nothing more to fear from your hyperbolas or parabolas or any other of your open curves!"

"Nothing more, certainly, from an open curve, but every thing from a closed one."

"A closed curve! What is it called? And what is the trouble?"

"An eclipse it is called; and the trouble is that, instead of flying off into the boundless regions of space, our Projectile will probably describe an elliptical orbit around the Moon—"

—"What!" cried M'Nicholl, in amazement, "and be her satellite for ever!"

"All right and proper," said Ardan; "why shouldn't she have one of her own?"

"Only, my dear friend," said Barbican to Ardan, "this change of curve involves no change in the doom of the Projectile. We are as infallibly lost by an ellipse as by a parabola."

"Well, there was one thing I never could reconcile myself to in the whole arrangement," replied Ardan cheerfully; "and that was destruction by an open curve. Safe from that, I could say, 'Fate, do your worst!' Besides, I don't believe in the infallibility of your ellipsic. It may prove just as unreliable as the hyperbola. And it is no harm to hope that it may!"

From present appearances there was very little to justify Ardan's hope. Barbican's theory of the elliptic orbit was unfortunately too well grounded to allow a single reasonable doubt to be expressed regarding the Projectile's fate. It was to gravitate for ever around the Moon—a sub-satellite. It was a new born individual in the astral universe, a microcosm, a little world in itself, containing, however, only three inhabitants and even these destined to perish pretty soon for want of air. Our travellers, therefore, had no particular reason for rejoicing over the new destiny reserved for the Projectile in obedience to the inexorable laws of the centripetal and centrifugal forces. They were soon, it is true, to have the opportunity of beholding once more the illuminated face of the Moon. They might even live long enough to catch a last glimpse of the distant Earth bathed in the glory of the solar rays. They might even have strength enough left to be able to chant one solemn final eternal adieu to their dear old Mother World, upon whose features their mortal eyes should never again rest in love and longing! Then, what was their Projectile to become? An inert, lifeless, extinct mass, not a particle better than the most defunct asteroid that wanders blindly through the fields of ether. A gloomy fate to look forward to. Yet, instead of grieving over the inevitable, our bold travellers actually felt thrilled with delight at the prospect of even a momentary deliverance from those gloomy depths of darkness and of once more finding themselves, even if only for a few hours, in the cheerful precincts illuminated by the genial light of the blessed Sun!

The ring of light, in the meantime, becoming brighter and brighter, Barbican was not long in discovering and pointing out to his companions the different mountains that lay around the Moon's south pole.

"There is *Leibnitz* on your right," said he, "and on your left you can easily see the peaks of *Doerfel*. Belonging rather to the Moon's dark side than to her Earth side, they are visible to terrestrial astronomers only when she is in her highest northern latitudes. Those faint peaks beyond them that you can catch with such difficulty must be those of *Newton* and *Curtius*."

"How in the world can you tell?" asked Ardan.

"They are the highest mountains in the circumpolar regions," replied Barbican. "They have been measured with the greatest care; *Newton* is 23,000 feet high."

"More or less!" laughed Ardan. "What Delphic oracle says so?"

"Dear friend," replied Barbican quietly, "the visible mountains of the Moon have been measured so carefully and so accurately that I should hardly hesitate in affirming their altitude to be as well known as that of Mont Blanc, or, at least, as those of the chief peaks in the Himalayahs or the Rocky Mountain Range."

"I should like to know how people set about it," observed Ardan incredulously.

"There are several well known methods of approaching this problem," replied Barbican; "and as these methods, though founded on different principles, bring us constantly to the same result, we may pretty safely conclude that our calculations are right. We have no time, just now to draw diagrams, but, if I express myself clearly, you will no doubt easily catch the general principle."

"Go ahead!" answered Ardan. "Anything but Algebra."

"We want no Algebra now," said Barbican, "It can't enable us to find principles, though it certainly enables us to apply them. Well. The Sun at a certain altitude shines on one side of a mountain and flings a shadow on the other. The length of this shadow is easily found by means of a telescope, whose object glass is provided with a micrometer. This consists simply of two parallel spider threads, one of which is stationary and the other movable. The Moon's real diameter being known and occupying a certain space on the object glass, the exact space occupied by the shadow can be easily ascertained by means of the movable thread. This space, compared with the Moon's space, will give us the length of the shadow. Now, as under the same circumstances a certain height can cast only a certain shadow, of course a knowledge of the one must give you that of the other, and *vice versa*. This method, stated roughly, was that followed by Galileo, and, in our own day, by Beer and Maedler, with extraordinary success."

"I certainly see some sense in this method," said Ardan, "if they took extraordinary pains to observe correctly. The least carelessness would set them wrong, not only by feet but by miles. We have time enough, however, to listen to another method before we get into the full blaze of the glorious old Sol."

"The other method," interrupted M'Nicholl laying down his telescope to rest his eyes, and now joining in the conversation to give himself something to do, "is called that of the *tangent rays*. A solar ray, barely passing the edge of the Moon's surface, is caught on the peak of a mountain the rest of which lies in shadow. The distance between this starry peak and the line separating the light from the darkness, we measure carefully by means of our telescope. Then—"

"I see it at a glance!" interrupted Ardan with lighting eye; "the ray, being a tangent, of course makes right angles with the radius, which is known: consequently we have two sides and one angle—quite enough to find the other parts of the triangle. Very ingenious—but now, that I think of it—is not this method absolutely impracticable for every mountain except those in the immediate neighborhood of the light and shadow line?"

"That's a defect easily remedied by patience," explained Barbican— the Captain, who did not like being interrupted, having withdrawn to his telescope—"As this line is continually changing, in course of time all the mountains must come near it. A third method—to measure the mountain profile directly by means of the micrometer—is evidently applicable only to altitudes lying exactly on the lunar rim."

"That is clear enough," said Ardan, "and another point is also very clear. In Full Moon no measurement is possible. When no shadows are made, none can be measured. Measurements, right or wrong, are possible only when the solar rays strike the Moon's surface obliquely with regard to the observer. Am I right, Signor Barbicani, maestro illustrissimo?"

"Perfectly right," replied Barbican. "You are an apt pupil."

"Say that again," said Ardan. "I want Mac to hear it."

Barbican humored him by repeating the observation, but M'Nicholl would only notice it by a grunt of doubtful meaning.

"Was Galileo tolerably successful in his calculations?" asked Ardan, resuming the conversation.

Before answering this question, Barbican unrolled the map of the Moon, which a faint light like that of day-break now enabled him to examine. He then went on: "Galileo was wonderfully successful— considering that the telescope which he employed was a poor instrument of his own construction, magnifying only thirty times. He gave the lunar mountains a height of about 26,000 feet—an altitude cut down by Hevelius, but almost doubled by Riccioli. Herschel was the first to come pretty close to the truth, but Beer and Maedler, whose *Mappa Selenographica* now lies before us, have left really nothing more to be done for lunar astronomy—except, of course, to pay a personal visit to the Moon—which we have tried to do, but I fear with a very poor prospect of success."

"Cheer up! cheer up!" cried Ardan. "It's not all over yet by long odds. Who can say what is still in store for us? Another bolide may shunt us off our ellipse and even send us to the Moon's surface."

Then seeing Barbican shake his head ominously and his countenance become more and more depressed, this true friend tried to brighten him up a bit by feigning to take deep interest in a subject that to him was absolutely the driest in the world.

"Meer and Baedler—I mean Beer and Maedler," he went on, "must have measured at least forty or fifty mountains to their satisfaction."

"Forty or fifty!" exclaimed Barbican. "They measured no fewer than a thousand and ninety-five lunar mountains and crater summits with a perfect success. Six of these reach an altitude of upwards of 18,000 feet, and twenty-two are more than 15,000 feet high."

"Which is the highest in the lot?" asked Ardan, keenly relishing Barbican's earnestness.

"*Doerfel* in the southern hemisphere, the peak of which I have just pointed out, is the highest of the lunar mountains so far measured," replied Barbican. "It is nearly 25,000 feet high."

"Indeed! Five thousand feet lower than Mount Everest—still for a lunar mountain, it is quite a respectable altitude."

"Respectable! Why it's an enormous altitude, my dear friend, if you compare it with the Moon's diameter. The Earth's diameter being more than 3-1/2 times greater than the Moon's, if the Earth's mountains bore the same ratio to those of the Moon, Everest should be more than sixteen miles high, whereas it is not quite six."

"How do the general heights of the Himalayahs compare with those of the highest lunar mountains?" asked Ardan, wondering what would be his next question.

"Fifteen peaks in the eastern or higher division of the Himalayahs, are higher than the loftiest lunar peaks," replied Barbican. "Even in the western, or lower section of the Himalayahs, some of the peaks exceed *Doerfel*."

"Which are the chief lunar mountains that exceed Mont Blanc in altitude?" asked Ardan, bravely suppressing a yawn.

"The following dozen, ranged, if my memory does not fail me, in the exact order of their respective heights;" replied Barbican, never wearied in answering such questions: "*Newton, Curtius, Casatus, Rheita, Short, Huyghens, Biancanus, Tycho, Kircher, Clavius, Endymion*, and *Catharina*."

"Now those not quite up to Mont Blanc?" asked Ardan, hardly knowing what to say.

"Here they are, about half a dozen of them: *Moretus, Theophilus, Harpalus, Eratosthenes, Werner*, and *Piccolomini*," answered Barbican as ready as a schoolboy reciting his lesson, and pointing them out on the map as quickly as a compositor distributing his type.

"The next in rank?" asked Ardan, astounded at his friend's wonderful memory.

"The next in rank," replied Barbican promptly, "are those about the size of the Matterhorn, that is to say about 2-3/4 miles in height. They are *Macrobius*, *Delambre*, and *Conon*. Come," he added, seeing Ardan hesitating and at a loss what other question to ask, "don't you want to know what lunar mountains are about the same height as the Peak of Teneriffe? or as Ætna? or as Mount Washington? You need not be afraid of puzzling me. I studied up the subject thoroughly, and therefore know all about it."

"Oh! I could listen to you with delight all day long!" cried Ardan, enthusiastically, though with some embarrassment, for he felt a twinge of conscience in acting so falsely towards his beloved friend. "The fact is," he went on, "such a rational conversation as the present, on such an absorbing subject, with such a perfect master—"

"The Sun!" cried M'Nicholl starting up and cheering. "He's cleared the disc completely, and he's now himself again! Long life to him! Hurrah!"

"Hurrah!" cried the others quite as enthusiastically (Ardan did not seem a bit desirous to finish his sentence).

They tossed their maps aside and hastened to the window.

XVII

TYCHO

It was now exactly six o'clock in the evening. The Sun, completely clear of all contact with the lunar disc, steeped the whole Projectile in his golden rays. The travellers, vertically over the Moon's south pole, were, as Barbican soon ascertained, about 30 miles distant from it, the exact distance they had been from the north pole—a proof that the elliptic curve still maintained itself with mathematical rigor.

For some time, the travellers' whole attention was concentrated on the glorious Sun. His light was inexpressibly cheering; and his heat, soon penetrating the walls of the Projectile, infused a new and sweet life into their chilled and exhausted frames. The ice rapidly disappeared, and the windows soon resumed their former perfect transparency.

"Oh! how good the pleasant sunlight is!" cried the Captain, sinking on a seat in a quiet ecstasy of enjoyment. "How I pity Ardan's poor friends the Selenites during that night so long and so icy! How impatient they must be to see the Sun back again!"

"Yes," said Ardan, also sitting down the better to bask in the vivifying rays, "his light no doubt brings them to life and keeps them alive. Without light or heat during all that dreary winter, they must freeze stiff like the frogs or become torpid like the bears. I can't imagine how they could get through it otherwise."

"I'm glad *we're* through it anyhow," observed M'Nicholl. "I may at once acknowledge that I felt perfectly miserable as long as it lasted. I can now easily understand how the combined cold and darkness killed Doctor Kane's Esquimaux dogs. It was near killing me. I was so miserable that at last I could neither talk myself nor bear to hear others talk."

"My own case exactly," said Barbican—"that is," he added hastily, correcting himself, "I tried to talk because I found Ardan so interested, but in spite of all we said, and saw, and had to think of, Byron's terrible dream would continually rise up before me:

> *"The bright Sun was extinguished, and the Stars*
> *Wandered all darkling in the eternal space,*

Rayless and pathless, and the icy Earth
Swung blind and blackening in the Moonless air.
Morn came and went, and came and brought no day!
And men forgot their passions in the dread
Of this their desolation, and all hearts
Were chilled into a selfish prayer for light!"

As he pronounced these words in accents at once monotonous and melancholy, Ardan, fully appreciative, quietly gesticulated in perfect cadence with the rhythm. Then the three men remained completely silent for several minutes. Buried in recollection, or lost in thought, or magnetized by the bright Sun, they seemed to be half asleep while steeping their limbs in his vitalizing beams.

Barbican was the first to dissolve the reverie by jumping up. His sharp eye had noticed that the base of the Projectile, instead of keeping rigidly perpendicular to the lunar surface, turned away a little, so as to render the elliptical orbit somewhat elongated. This he made his companions immediately observe, and also called their attention to the fact that from this point they could easily have seen the Earth had it been Full, but that now, drowned in the Sun's beams, it was quite invisible. A more attractive spectacle, however, soon engaged their undivided attention—that of the Moon's southern regions, now brought within about the third of a mile by their telescopes. Immediately resuming their posts by the windows, they carefully noted every feature presented by the fantastic panorama that stretched itself out in endless lengths beneath their wondering eyes.

Mount *Leibnitz* and Mount *Doerfel* form two separate groups developed in the regions of the extreme south. The first extends westwardly from the pole to the 84th parallel; the second, on the southeastern border, starting from the pole, reaches the neighborhood of the 65th. In the entangled valleys of their clustered peaks, appeared the dazzling sheets of white, noted by Father Secchi, but their peculiar nature Barbican could now examine with a greater prospect of certainty than the illustrious Roman astronomer had ever enjoyed.

"They're beds of snow," he said at last in a decided tone.

"Snow!" exclaimed M'Nicholl.

"Yes, snow, or rather glaciers heavily coated with glittering ice. See how vividly they reflect the Sun's rays. Consolidated beds of lava could never shine with such dazzling uniformity. Therefore there must be both water and air on the Moon's surface. Not much—perhaps very little if you insist on it—but the fact that there is some can now no longer be questioned."

This assertion of Barbican's, made so positively by a man who never decided unless when thoroughly convinced, was a great triumph for Ardan, who, as the gracious reader doubtless remembers, had had a famous dispute with M'Nicholl on that very subject at Tampa. His eyes brightened and a smile of pleasure played around his lips, but, with a great effort at self-restraint, he kept perfectly silent and would not permit himself even to look in the direction of the Captain. As for M'Nicholl, he was apparently too much absorbed in *Doerfel* and *Leibnitz* to mind anything else.

These mountains rose from plains of moderate extent, bounded by an indefinite succession of walled hollows and ring ramparts. They are the only chains met in this region of ridge-brimmed craters and circles; distinguished by no particular feature, they project a few pointed peaks here and there, some of which exceed four miles and a half in height. This altitude, however, foreshortened as it was by the vertical position of the Projectile, could not be noticed just then, even if correct observation had been permitted by the dazzling surface.

Once more again before the travellers' eyes the Moon's disc revealed itself in all the old familiar features so characteristic of lunar landscapes— no blending of tones, no softening of colors, no graduation of shadows, every line glaring in white or black by reason of the total absence of refracted light. And yet the wonderfully peculiar character of this desolate world imparted to it a weird attraction as strangely fascinating as ever.

Over this chaotic region the travellers were now sweeping, as if borne on the wings of a storm; the peaks defiled beneath them; the yawning chasms revealed their ruin-strewn floors; the fissured cracks untwisted themselves; the ramparts showed all their sides; the mysterious holes presented their impenetrable depths; the clustered mountain summits and rings rapidly decomposed themselves: but in a moment again all had become more inextricably entangled than ever. Everything appeared to be the finished handiwork of volcanic agency, in the utmost purity and highest perfection. None of the mollifying effects of air or water could here be noticed. No smooth-capped mountains, no gently winding river channels, no vast prairie-lands of deposited sediment, no traces of vegetation, no signs of agriculture, no vestiges of a great city. Nothing but vast beds of glistering lava, now rough like immense piles of scoriae and clinker, now smooth like crystal mirrors, and reflecting the Sun's rays with the same intolerable glare. Not the faintest speck of life. A world absolutely and completely dead, fixed, still, motionless—save when a gigantic land-slide, breaking off the vertical wall of a crater, plunged down into the soundless depths, with all the fury too of a crashing avalanche, with all the speed of a Niagara, but, in the total absence of atmosphere, noiseless as a feather, as a snow flake, as a grain of impalpable dust.

Careful observations, taken by Barbican and repeated by his companions, soon satisfied them that the ridgy outline of the mountains on the Moon's border, though perhaps due to different forces from those acting in the centre, still presented a character generally uniform. The same bulwark-surrounded hollows, the same abrupt projections of surface. Yet a different arrangement, as Barbican pointed out to his companions, might be naturally expected. In the central portion of the disc, the Moon's crust, before solidification, must have been subjected to two attractions—that of the Moon herself and that of the Earth—acting, however, in contrary directions and therefore, in a certain sense, serving to neutralize each other. Towards the border of her disc, on the contrary, the terrestrial attraction, having acted in a direction perpendicular to that of the lunar, should have exerted greater power, and therefore given a different shape to the general contour. But no remarkable difference had so far been perceived by terrestrial observers; and none could now be detected by our travellers. Therefore the Moon must have found in herself alone the principle of her shape and of her superficial development—that is, she owed nothing to external influences. "Arago was perfectly right, therefore," concluded Barbican, "in the remarkable opinion to which he gave expression thirty years ago:

'No external action whatever has contributed to the formation of the Moon's diversified surface.'"

"But don't you think, Barbican," asked the Captain, "that every force, internal or external, that might modify the Moon's shape, has ceased long ago?"

"I am rather inclined to that opinion," said Barbican; "it is not, however, a new one. Descartes maintained that as the Earth is an extinct Sun, so is the Moon an extinct Earth. My own opinion at present is that the Moon is now the image of death, but I can't say if she has ever been the abode of life."

"The abode of life!" cried Ardan, who had great repugnance in accepting the idea that the Moon was no better than a heap of cinders and ashes; "why, look there! If those are not as neat a set of the ruins of an abandoned city as ever I saw, I should like to know what they are!"

He pointed to some very remarkable rocky formations in the neighborhood of *Short*, a ring mountain rising to an altitude considerably higher than that of Mont Blanc. Even Barbican and M'Nicholl could detect some regularity and semblance of order in the arrangement of these rocks, but this, of course, they looked on as a mere freak of nature, like the Lurlei Rock, the Giant's Causeway, or the Old Man of the Franconia Mountains. Ardan, however, would not accept such an easy mode of getting rid of a difficulty.

"See the ruins on that bluff," he exclaimed; "those steep sides must have been washed by a great river in the prehistoric times. That was the fortress. Farther down lay the city. There are the dismantled ramparts; why, there's the very coping of a portico still intact! Don't you see three broken pillars lying beside their pedestals? There! a little to the left of those arches that evidently once bore the pipes of an aqueduct! You don't see them? Well, look a little to the right, and there is something that you can see! As I'm a living man I have no difficulty in discerning the gigantic butments of a great bridge that formerly spanned that immense river!"

Did he really see all this? To this day he affirms stoutly that he did, and even greater wonders besides. His companions, however, without denying that he had good grounds for his assertion on this subject or questioning the general accuracy of his observations, content themselves with saying that the reason why they had failed to discover the wonderful city, was that Ardan's telescope was of a strange and peculiar construction. Being somewhat short-sighted, he had had it manufactured expressly for his own use, but it was of such singular power that his companions could not use it without hurting their eyes.

But, whether the ruins were real or not, the moments were evidently too precious to be lost in idle discussion. The great city of the Selenites soon disappeared on the remote horizon, and, what was of far greater importance, the distance of the Projectile from the Moon's disc began to increase so sensibly that the smaller details of the surface were soon lost in a confused mass, and it was only the lofty heights, the wide craters, the great ring mountains, and the vast plains that still continued to give sharp, distinctive outlines.

A little to their left, the travellers could now plainly distinguish one of the most remarkable of the Moon's craters, *Newton*, so well known to all lunar astronomers. Its ramparts, forming a perfect circle, rise to such a height, at least 22,000 feet, as to seem insurmountable.

"You can, no doubt, notice for yourselves," said Barbican, "that the external height of this mountain is far from being equal to the depth of its crater. The enormous pit, in fact, seems to be a soundless sea of pitchy black, the bottom of which the Sun's rays have never reached. There, as Humboldt says, reigns eternal darkness, so absolute that Earth-shine or even Sunlight is never able to dispel it. Had Michael's friends the old mythologists ever known anything about it, they would doubtless have made it the entrance to the infernal regions. On the whole surface of our Earth, there is no mountain even remotely resembling it. It is a perfect type of the lunar crater. Like most of them, it shows that the peculiar formation of the Moon's surface is due, first, to the cooling of the lunar crust; secondly, to the cracking from internal pressure; and, thirdly, to the violent volcanic action in consequence. This must have been of a far fiercer nature than it has ever been with us. The matter was ejected to a vast height till great mountains were formed; and still the action went on, until at last the floor of the crater sank to a depth far lower than the level of the external plain."

"You may be right," said Ardan by way of reply; "as for me, I'm looking out for another city. But I'm sorry to say that our Projectile is increasing its distance so fast that, even if one lay at my feet at this moment, I doubt very much if I could see it a bit better than either you or the Captain."

Newton was soon passed, and the Projectile followed a course that took it directly over the ring mountain *Moretus*. A little to the west the travellers could easily distinguish the summits of *Blancanus*, 7,000 feet high, and, towards seven o'clock in the evening, they were approaching the neighborhood of *Clavius*.

This walled-plain, one of the most remarkable on the Moon, lies 55° S. by 15° E. Its height is estimated at 16,000 feet, but it is considered to be about a hundred and fifty miles in diameter. Of this vast crater, the travellers now at a distance of 250 miles, reduced to 2-1/2 by their telescopes, had a magnificent bird's-eye view.

"Our terrestrial volcanoes," said Barbican, "as you can now readily judge for yourselves, are no more than molehills when compared with those of the Moon. Measure the old craters formed by the early eruptions of Vesuvius and Ætna, and you will find them little more than three miles in diameter. The crater of Cantal in central France is only about six miles in width; the famous valley in Ceylon, called the *Crater*, though not at all due to volcanic action, is 44 miles across and is considered to be the greatest in the world. But even this is very little in comparison to the diameter of *Clavius* lying beneath us at the present moment."

"How much is its diameter?" asked the Captain.

"At least one hundred and forty-two miles," replied Barbican; "it is probably the greatest in the Moon, but many others measure more than a hundred miles across."

"Dear boys," said Ardan, half to himself, half to the others, "only imagine the delicious state of things on the surface of the gentle Moon when these craters, brimming over with hissing lava, were vomiting forth, all at the same time, showers of melted stones, clouds of blinding smoke, and sheets of blasting flame! What an intensely overpowering spectacle was here presented once, but now, how are the mighty fallen! Our Moon, as at present beheld, seems to be nothing more than the skinny spectre left after a brilliant display of fireworks, when the spluttering crackers, the glittering wheels, the hissing serpents, the revolving suns, and the dazzling stars, are all 'played out', and nothing remains to tell of the gorgeous spectacle but a few blackened sticks and half a dozen half burned bits of pasteboard. I should like to hear one of you trying to explain the cause, the reason, the principle, the philosophy of such tremendous cataclysms!"

Barbican's only reply was a series of nods, for in truth he had not heard a single word of Ardan's philosophic explosion. His ears were with his eyes, and these were obstinately bent on the gigantic ramparts of *Clavius*, formed of concentric mountain ridges, which were actually leagues in depth. On the floor of the vast cavity, could be seen hundreds of smaller craters, mottling it like a skimming dish, and pierced here and there by sharp peaks, one of which could hardly be less than 15,000 feet high.

All around, the plain was desolate in the extreme. You could not conceive how anything could be barrener than these serrated outlines, or gloomier than these shattered mountains—until you looked at the plain that encircled them. Ardan hardly exaggerated when he called it the scene of a battle fought thousands of years ago but still white with the hideous bones of overthrown peaks, slaughtered mountains and mutilated precipices!

"Hills amid the air encountered hills,
Hurled to and fro in jaculation dire,"

murmured M'Nicholl, who could quote you Milton quite as readily as the Bible.

"This must have been the spot," muttered Barbican to himself, "where the brittle shell of the cooling sphere, being thicker than usual, offered greater resistance to an eruption of the red-hot nucleus. Hence these piled up buttresses, and these orderless heaps of consolidated lava and ejected scoriæ."

The Projectile advanced, but the scene of desolation seemed to remain unchanged. Craters, ring mountains, pitted plateaus dotted with shapeless wrecks, succeeded each other without interruption. For level plain, for dark "sea," for smooth plateau, the eye here sought in vain. It was a Swiss Greenland, an Icelandic Norway, a Sahara of shattered crust studded with countless hills of glassy lava.

At last, in the very centre of this blistered region, right too at its very culmination, the travellers came on the brightest and most remarkable mountain of the Moon. In the dazzling *Tycho* they found it an easy matter to recognize the famous lunar point, which the world will for ever designate by the name of the distinguished astronomer of Denmark.

This brilliant luminosity of the southern hemisphere, no one that ever gazes at the Full Moon in a cloudless sky, can help noticing. Ardan, who had always particularly admired it, now hailed it as an old friend, and almost exhausted breath, imagination and vocabulary in the epithets with which he greeted this cynosure of the lunar mountains.

"Hail!" he cried, "thou blazing focus of glittering streaks, thou coruscating nucleus of irradiation, thou starting point of rays divergent, thou egress of meteoric flashes! Hub of the silver wheel that ever rolls in silent majesty over the starry plains of Night! Paragon of jewels enchased in a carcanet of dazzling brilliants! Eye of the universe, beaming with heavenly resplendescence!

"Who shall say what thou art? Diana's nimbus? The golden clasp of her floating robes? The blazing head of the great bolt that rivets the lunar hemispheres in union inseverable? Or cans't thou have been some errant bolide, which missing its way, butted blindly against the lunar face, and there stuck fast, like a Minie ball mashed against a cast-iron target? Alas! nobody knows. Not even Barbican is able to penetrate thy mystery. But one thing *I* know. Thy dazzling glare so sore my eyes hath made that longer on thy light to gaze I do not dare. Captain, have you any smoked glass?"

In spite of this anti-climax, Ardan's companions could hardly consider his utterings either as ridiculous or over enthusiastic. They could easily excuse his excitement on the subject. And so could we, if we only remember that *Tycho*, though nearly a quarter of a million miles distant, is such a luminous point on the lunar disc, that almost any moonlit night it can be easily perceived by the unaided terrestrial eye. What then must have been its splendor in the eyes of our travellers whose telescopes brought it actually four thousand times nearer! No wonder that with smoked glasses, they endeavored to soften off its effulgent glare! Then in hushed silence, or at most uttering at intervals a few interjections expressive of their intense admiration, they remained for some time completely engrossed in the overwhelming spectacle. For the time being, every sentiment, impression, thought, feeling on their part, was concentrated in the eye, just as at other times under violent excitement every throb of our life is concentrated in the heart.

Tycho belongs to the system of lunar craters that is called *radiating*, like *Aristarchus* or *Copernicus*, which had been already seen and highly admired by our travellers at their first approach to the Moon. But it is decidedly the most remarkable and conspicuous of them all. It occupies the great focus of disruption, whence it sends out great streaks thousands of miles in length; and it gives the most unmistakable evidence of the terribly eruptive nature of those forces that once shattered the Moon's solidified shell in this portion of the lunar surface.

Situated in the southern latitude of 43° by an eastern longitude of 12°, *Tycho's* crater, somewhat elliptical in shape, is 54 miles in diameter and upwards of 16,000 feet in depth. Its lofty ramparts are buttressed by other mountains, Mont Blancs in size, all grouped around it, and all streaked with the great divergent fissures that radiate from it as a centre.

Of what this incomparable mountain really is, with all these lines of projections converging towards it and with all these prominent points of relief protruding within its crater, photography has, so far, been able to give us only a very unsatisfactory idea. The reason too is very simple: it is only at Full Moon that *Tycho* reveals himself in all his splendor. The shadows therefore vanishing, the perspective foreshortenings disappear and the views become little better than a dead blank. This is the more to be regretted as this wonderful region is well worthy of being represented with the greatest possible photographic accuracy. It is a vast agglomeration of holes, craters, ring formations, a complicated intersection of crests—in short, a distracting volcanic network flung over the blistered soil. The ebullitions of the central eruption still evidently preserve their original form. As they first appeared, so they lie. Crystallizing as they cooled, they have stereotyped in imperishable characters the aspect formerly presented by the whole Moon's surface under the influences of recent plutonic upheaval.

Our travellers were far more fortunate than the photographers. The distance separating them from the peaks of *Tycho's* concentric terraces was not so considerable as to conceal the principal details from a very satisfactory view. They could easily distinguish the annular ramparts of the external circumvallation, the mountains buttressing the gigantic walls internally as well as externally, the vast esplanades descending irregularly and abruptly to the sunken plains all around. They could even detect a difference of a few hundred feet in altitude in favor of the western or right hand side over the eastern. They could also see that these dividing ridges were actually inaccessible and completely unsurmountable, at least by ordinary terrestrial efforts. No system of castrametation ever devised by Polybius or Vauban could bear the slightest comparison with such vast fortifications, A city built on the floor of the circular cavity could be no more reached by the outside Lunarians than if it had been built in the planet Mars.

This idea set Ardan off again. "Yes," said he, "such a city would be at once completely inaccessible, and still not inconveniently situated in a plateau full of aspects decidedly picturesque. Even in the depths of this immense crater, Nature, as you can see, has left no flat and empty void. You can easily trace its special oreography, its various mountain systems which turn it into a regular world on a small scale. Notice its cones, its central hills, its valleys, its substructures already cut and dry and therefore quietly prepared to receive the masterpieces of Selenite architecture. Down there to the left is a lovely spot for a Saint Peter's; to the right, a magnificent site for a Forum; here a Louvre could be built capable of entrancing Michael Angelo himself; there a citadel could be raised to which even Gibraltar would be a molehill! In the middle rises a sharp peak which can hardly be less than a mile in height—a grand pedestal for the statue of some Selenite Vincent de Paul or George Washington. And around them all is a mighty mountain-ring at least 3 miles high, but which, to an eye looking from the centre of our vast city, could not appear to be more than five or six hundred feet. Enormous circus, where mighty Rome herself in her palmiest days, though increased tenfold, would have no reason to complain for want of room!"

He stopped for a few seconds, perhaps to take breath, and then resumed:

"Oh what an abode of serene happiness could be constructed within this shadow-fringed ring of the mighty mountains! O blessed refuge, unassailable by aught of human ills! What a calm unruffled life could be enjoyed within thy hallowed precincts, even by those cynics, those haters of humanity, those disgusted reconstructors of society, those misanthropes and misogynists old and young, who are continually writing whining verses in odd corners of the newspapers!"

"Right at last, Ardan, my boy!" cried M'Nicholl, quietly rubbing the glass of his spectacles; "I should like to see the whole lot of them carted in there without a moment's delay!"

"It couldn't hold the half of them!" observed Barbican drily.

XVIII

Puzzling Questions

It was not until the Projectile had passed a little beyond *Tycho's* immense concavity that Barbican and his friends had a good opportunity for observing the brilliant streaks sent so wonderfully flying in all directions from this celebrated mountain as a common centre. They examined them for some time with the closest attention.

What could be the nature of this radiating aureola? By what geological phenomena could this blazing coma have been possibly produced? Such questions were the most natural things in the world for Barbican and his companions to propound to themselves, as indeed they have been to every astronomer from the beginning of time, and probably will be to the end.

What *did* they see? What you can see, what anybody can see on a clear night when the Moon is full—only our friends had all the advantages of a closer view. From *Tycho*, as a focus, radiated in all directions, as from the head of a peeled orange, more than a hundred luminous streaks or channels, edges raised, middle depressed—or perhaps *vice versa*, owing to an optical illusion—some at least twelve miles wide, some fully thirty. In certain directions they ran for a distance of at least six hundred miles, and seemed—especially towards the west, northwest, and north—to cover half the southern hemisphere. One of these flashes extended as far as *Neander* on the 40th meridian; another, curving around so as to furrow the *Mare Nectaris*, came to an end on the chain of the *Pyrenees*, after a course of perhaps a little more than seven hundred miles. On the east, some of them barred with luminous network the *Mare Nubium* and even the *Mare Humorum*.

The most puzzling feature of these glittering streaks was that they ran their course directly onward, apparently neither obstructed by valley, crater, or mountain ridge however high. They all started, as said before, from one common focus, *Tycho's* crater. From this they certainly all seemed to emanate. Could they be rivers of lava once vomited from that centre by resistless volcanic agency and afterwards crystallized into glassy rock? This idea of Herschel's, Barbican had no hesitation in qualifying as exceedingly absurd. Rivers running in perfectly straight lines, across plains, and *up* as well as *down* mountains!

"Other astronomers," he continued, "have looked on these streaks as a peculiar kind of *moraines*, that is, long lines of erratic blocks belched forth with mighty power at the period of *Tycho's* own upheaval."

"How do you like that theory, Barbican," asked the Captain.

"It's not a particle better than Herschel's," was the reply; "no volcanic action could project rocks to a distance of six or seven hundred miles, not to talk of laying them down so regularly that we can't detect a break in them."

"Happy thought!" cried Ardan suddenly; "it seems to me that I can tell the cause of these radiating streaks!"

"Let us hear it," said Barbican.

"Certainly," was Ardan's reply; "these streaks are all only the parts of what we call a 'star,' as made by a stone striking ice; or by a ball, a pane of glass."

"Not bad," smiled Barbican approvingly; "only where is the hand that flung the stone or threw the ball?"

"The hand is hardly necessary," replied Ardan, by no means disconcerted; "but as for the ball, what do you say to a comet?"

Here M'Nicholl laughed so loud that Ardan was seriously irritated. However, before he could say anything cutting enough to make the Captain mind his manners, Barbican had quickly resumed:

"Dear friend, let the comets alone, I beg of you; the old astronomers fled to them on all occasions and made them explain every difficulty—"

—"The comets were all used up long ago—" interrupted M'Nicholl.

—"Yes," went on Barbican, as serenely as a judge, "comets, they said, had fallen on the surface in meteoric showers and crushed in the crater cavities; comets had dried up the water; comets had whisked off the atmosphere; comets had done everything. All pure assumption! In your case, however, friend Michael, no comet whatever is necessary. The shock that gave rise to your great 'star' may have come from the interior rather than the exterior. A violent contraction of the lunar crust in the process of cooling may have given birth to your gigantic 'star' formation."

"I accept the amendment," said Ardan, now in the best of humor and looking triumphantly at M'Nicholl.

"An English scientist," continued Barbican, "Nasmyth by name, is decidedly of your opinion, especially ever since a little experiment of his own has confirmed him in it. He filled a glass globe with water, hermetically sealed it, and then plunged it into a hot bath. The enclosed water, expanding at a greater rate than the glass, burst the latter, but, in doing so, it made a vast number of cracks all diverging in every direction

JULES VERNE

from the focus of disruption. Something like this he conceives to have taken place around *Tycho*. As the crust cooled, it cracked. The lava from the interior, oozing out, spread itself on both sides of the cracks. This certainly explains pretty satisfactorily why those flat glistening streaks are of much greater width than the fissures through which the lava had at first made its way to the surface."

"Well done for an Englishman!" cried Ardan in great spirits.

"He's no Englishman," said M'Nicholl, glad to have an opportunity of coming off with some credit. "He is the famous Scotch engineer who invented the steam hammer, the steam ram, and discovered the 'willow leaves' in the Sun's disc."

"Better and better," said Ardan—"but, powers of Vulcan! What makes it so hot? I'm actually roasting!"

This observation was hardly necessary to make his companions conscious that by this time they felt extremely uncomfortable. The heat had become quite oppressive. Between the natural caloric of the Sun and the reflected caloric of the Moon, the Projectile was fast turning into a regular bake oven. This transition from intense cold to intense heat was already about quite as much as they could bear.

"What shall we do, Barbican?" asked Ardan, seeing that for some time no one else appeared inclined to say a word.

"Nothing, at least yet awhile, friend Ardan," replied Barbican, "I have been watching the thermometer carefully for the last few minutes, and, though we are at present at 38° centigrade, or 100° Fahrenheit, I have noticed that the mercury is slowly falling. You can also easily remark for yourself that the floor of the Projectile is turning away more and more from the lunar surface. From this I conclude quite confidently, and I see that the Captain agrees with me, that all danger of death from intense heat, though decidedly alarming ten minutes ago, is over for the present and, for some time at least, it may be dismissed from further consideration."

"I'm not very sorry for it," said Ardan cheerfully; "neither to be baked like a pie in an oven nor roasted like a fat goose before a fire is the kind of death I should like to die of."

"Yet from such a death you would suffer no more than your friends the Selenites are exposed to every day of their lives," said the Captain, evidently determined on getting up an argument.

"I understand the full bearing of your allusion, my dear Captain," replied Ardan quickly, but not at all in a tone showing that he was disposed to second M'Nicholl's expectations.

He was, in fact, fast losing all his old habits of positivism. Latterly he had seen much, but he had reflected more. The deeper he had reflected, the more inclined he had become to accept the conclusion that the less he knew. Hence he had decided that if M'Nicholl wanted an argument it should not be with him. All speculative disputes he should henceforth avoid; he would listen with pleasure to all that could be urged on each side; he might even skirmish a little here and there as the spirit moved him; but a regular pitched battle on a subject purely speculative he was fully determined never again to enter into.

"Yes, dear Captain," he continued, "that pointed arrow of yours has by no means missed its mark, but I can't deny that my faith is beginning to be what you call a little 'shaky' in the existence of my friends the Selenites. However, I should like to have your square opinion on the matter. Barbican's also. We have witnessed many strange lunar phenomena lately, closer and clearer than mortal eye ever rested on them before. Has what we have seen confirmed any theory of yours or confounded any hypothesis? Have you seen enough to induce you to adopt decided conclusions? I will put the question formally. Do you, or do you not, think that the Moon resembles the Earth in being the abode of animals and intelligent beings? Come, answer, *messieurs*. Yes, or no?"

"I think we can answer your question categorically," replied Barbican, "if you modify its form a little."

"Put the question any way you please," said Ardan; "only you answer it! I'm not particular about the form."

"Good," said Barbican; "the question, being a double one, demands a double answer. First: *Is the Moon inhabitable?* Second: *Has the Moon ever been inhabited?*"

"That's the way to go about it," said the Captain. "Now then, Ardan, what do *you* say to the first question? Yes, or no?"

"I really can't say anything," replied Ardan. "In the presence of such distinguished scientists, I'm only a listener, a 'mere looker on in Vienna' as the Divine Williams has it. However, for the sake of argument, suppose I reply in the affirmative, and say that *the Moon is inhabitable*."

"If you do, I shall most unhesitatingly contradict you," said Barbican, feeling just then in splendid humor for carrying on an argument, not, of course, for the sake of contradicting or conquering or crushing or showing off or for any other vulgar weakness of lower minds, but for the noble and indeed the only motive that should impel a philosopher—

that of *enlightening* and *convincing*, "In taking the negative side, however, or saying that the Moon is not inhabitable, I shall not be satisfied with merely negative arguments. Many words, however, are not required. Look at her present condition: her atmosphere dwindled away to the lowest ebb; her 'seas' dried up or very nearly so; her waters reduced to next to nothing; her vegetation, if existing at all, existing only on the scantiest scale; her transitions from intense heat to intense cold, as we ourselves can testify, sudden in the extreme; her nights and her days each nearly 360 hours long. With all this positively against her and nothing at all that we know of positively for her, I have very little hesitation in saying that the Moon appears to me to be absolutely uninhabitable. She seems to me not only unpropitious to the development of the animal kingdom but actually incapable of sustaining life at all—that is, in the sense that we usually attach to such a term."

"That saving clause is well introduced, friend Barbican," said M'Nicholl, who, seeing no chance of demolishing Ardan, had not yet made up his mind as to having another little bout with the President. "For surely you would not venture to assert that the Moon is uninhabitable by a race of beings having an organization different from ours?"

"That question too, Captain," replied Barbican, "though a much more difficult one, I shall try to answer. First, however, let us see, Captain, if we agree on some fundamental points. How do we detect the existence of life? Is it not by *movement*? Is not *motion* its result, no matter what may be its organization?"

"Well," said the Captain in a drawling way, "I guess we may grant that."

"Then, dear friends," resumed Barbican, "I must remind you that, though we have had the privilege of observing the lunar continents at a distance of not more than one-third of a mile, we have never yet caught sight of the first thing moving on her surface. The presence of humanity, even of the lowest type, would have revealed itself in some form or other, by boundaries, by buildings, even by ruins. Now what *have* we seen? Everywhere and always, the geological works of *nature*; nowhere and never, the orderly labors of *man*. Therefore, if any representatives of animal life exist in the Moon, they must have taken refuge in those bottomless abysses where our eyes were unable to track them. And even this I can't admit. They could not always remain in these cavities. If there is any atmosphere at all in the Moon, it must be found in her immense low-lying plains. Over those plains her inhabitants must have often passed, and on those plains they must in some way or other have left some mark, some trace, some vestige of their existence, were it even only a road. But you both know well that nowhere are any such traces visible: therefore, they don't exist; therefore, no lunar inhabitants exist—except, of course, such a race of beings, if we can imagine any such, as could exist without revealing their existence by *movement*."

"That is to say," broke in Ardan, to give what he conceived a sharper point to Barbican's cogent arguments, "such a race of beings as could exist without existing!"

"Precisely," said Barbican: "Life without movement, and no life at all, are equivalent expressions."

"Captain," said Ardan, with all the gravity he could assume, "have you anything more to say before the Moderator of our little Debating Society gives his opinion on the arguments regarding the question before the house?"

"No more at present," said the Captain, biding his time.

"Then," resumed Ardan, rising with much dignity, "the Committee on Lunar Explorations, appointed by the Honorable Baltimore Gun Club, solemnly assembled in the Projectile belonging to the aforesaid learned and respectable Society, having carefully weighed all the arguments advanced on each side of the question, and having also carefully considered all the new facts bearing on the case that have lately come under the personal notice of said Committee, unanimously decides negatively on the question now before the chair for investigation— namely, 'Is the Moon inhabitable?' Barbican, as chairman of the Committee, I empower you to duly record our solemn decision—*No, the Moon is not inhabitable*."

Barbican, opening his note-book, made the proper entry among the minutes of the meeting of December 6th.

"Now then, gentlemen," continued Ardan, "if you are ready for the second question, the necessary complement of the first, we may as well approach it at once. I propound it for discussion in the following form: *Has the Moon ever been inhabited?* Captain, the Committee would be delighted to hear your remarks on the subject."

"Gentlemen," began the Captain in reply, "I had formed my opinion regarding the ancient inhabitability of our Satellite long before I ever dreamed of testing my theory by anything like our present journey. I will now add that all our observations, so far made, have only served to confirm me in my opinion. I now venture to assert, not only with every kind of probability in my favor but also on what I consider most excellent arguments, that the Moon was once inhabited by a race of beings possessing an organization similar to our own, that she once produced animals anatomically resembling our terrestrial animals, and that all these living organizations, human and animal, have had their day, that that day vanished ages and ages ago, and that, consequently, *Life*, extinguished forever, can never again reveal its existence there under any form."

"Is the Chair," asked Ardan, "to infer from the honorable gentleman's observations that he considers the Moon to be a world much older than the Earth?"

"Not exactly that," replied the Captain without hesitation; "I rather mean to say that the Moon is a world that grew old more rapidly than the Earth; that it came to maturity earlier; that it ripened quicker, and was stricken with old age sooner. Owing to the difference of the volumes of the two worlds, the organizing forces of matter must have been comparatively much more violent in the interior of the Moon than in the interior of the Earth. The present condition of its surface, as we see it lying there beneath us at this moment, places this assertion beyond all possibility of doubt. Wrinkled, pitted, knotted, furrowed, scarred, nothing that we can show on Earth resembles it. Moon and Earth were called into existence by the Creator probably at the same period of time. In the first stages of their existence, they do not seem to have been anything better than masses of gas. Acted upon by various forces and various influences, all of course directed by an omnipotent intelligence, these gases by degrees became liquid, and the liquids grew condensed into solids until solidity could retain its shape. But the two heavenly bodies, though starting at the same time, developed at a very different ratio. Most undoubtedly, our globe was still gaseous or at most only liquid, at the period when the Moon, already hardened by cooling, began to become inhabitable."

"*Most undoubtedly* is good!" observed Ardan admiringly.

"At this period," continued the learned Captain, "an atmosphere surrounded her. The waters, shut in by this gaseous envelope, could no longer evaporate. Under the combined influences of air, water, light, and solar heat as well as internal heat, vegetation began to overspread the continents by this time ready to receive it, and most undoubtedly—I mean—a—incontestably—it was at this epoch that *life* manifested itself on the lunar surface. I say *incontestably* advisedly, for Nature never exhausts herself in producing useless things, and therefore a world, so wonderfully inhabitable, *must* of necessity have had inhabitants."

"I like *of necessity* too," said Ardan, who could never keep still; "I always did, when I felt my arguments to be what you call a little shaky."

"But, my dear Captain," here observed Barbican, "have you taken into consideration some of the peculiarities of our Satellite which are decidedly opposed to the development of vegetable and animal existence? Those nights and days, for instance, 354 hours long?"

"I have considered them all," answered the brave Captain. "Days and nights of such an enormous length would at the present time, I grant, give rise to variations in temperature altogether intolerable to any ordinary organization. But things were quite different in the era alluded to. At that time, the atmosphere enveloped the Moon in a gaseous mantle, and the vapors took the shape of clouds. By the screen thus formed by the hand of nature, the heat of the solar rays was tempered and the nocturnal radiation retarded. Light too, as well as heat, could be modified, tempered, and *genialized* if I may use the expression, by the air. This produced a healthy counterpoise of forces, which, now that the atmosphere has completely disappeared, of course exists no longer. Besides—friend Ardan, you will excuse me for telling you something new, something that will surprise you—"

—"Surprise me, my dear boy, fire away surprising me!" cried Ardan. "I like dearly to be surprised. All I regret is that you scientists have surprised me so much already that I shall never have a good, hearty, genuine surprise again!"

—"I am most firmly convinced," continued the Captain, hardly waiting for Ardan to finish, "that, at the period of the Moon's occupancy by living creatures, her days and nights were by no means 354 hours long."

"Well! if anything could surprise me," said Ardan quickly, "such an assertion as that most certainly would. On what does the honorable gentleman base his *most firm conviction*?"

"We know," replied the Captain, "that the reason of the Moon's present long day and night is the exact equality of the periods of her rotation on her axis and of her revolution around the Earth. When she has turned once around the Earth, she has turned once around herself. Consequently, her back is turned to the Sun during one-half of the month; and her face during the other half. Now, I don't believe that this state of things existed at the period referred to."

"The gentleman does not believe!" exclaimed Ardan. "The Chair must be excused for reminding the honorable gentleman that it can not accept his incredulity as a sound and valid argument. These two movements have certainly equal periods now; why not always?"

"For the simple reason that this equality of periods is due altogether to the influence of terrestrial attraction," replied the ready Captain. "This attraction at present, I grant, is so great that it actually disables the Moon from revolving on herself; consequently she must always keep the same face turned towards the Earth. But who can assert that this attraction was powerful enough to exert the same influence at the epoch when the Earth herself was only a fluid substance? In fact, who can even assert that the Moon has always been the Earth's satellite?"

"Ah, who indeed?" exclaimed Ardan. "And who can assert that the Moon did not exist long before the Earth was called into being at all? In fact, who can assert that the Earth itself is not a great piece broken off the Moon? Nothing like asking absurd questions! I've often found them passing for the best kind of arguments!"

"Friend Ardan," interposed Barbican, who noticed that the Captain was a little too disconcerted to give a ready reply; "Friend Ardan, I must say you are not quite wrong in showing how certain methods of reasoning, legitimate enough in themselves, may be easily abused by being carried too far. I think, however, that the Captain might maintain his position without having recourse to speculations altogether too gigantic for ordinary intellect. By simply admitting the insufficiency of the primordeal attraction to preserve a perfect balance between the movements of the lunar rotation and revolution, we can easily see how the nights and days could once succeed each other on the Moon exactly as they do at present on the Earth."

"Nothing can be clearer!" resumed the brave Captain, once more rushing to the charge. "Besides, even without this alternation of days and nights, life on the lunar surface was quite possible."

"Of course it was possible," said Ardan; "everything is possible except what contradicts itself. It is possible too that every possibility is a fact; therefore, it *is* a fact. However," he added, not wishing to press the Captain's weak points too closely, "let all these logical niceties pass for the present. Now that you have established the existence of your humanity in the Moon, the Chair would respectfully ask how it has all so completely disappeared?"

"It disappeared completely thousands, perhaps millions, of years ago," replied the unabashed Captain. "It perished from the physical impossibility of living any longer in a world where the atmosphere had become by degrees too rare to be able to perform its functions as the great resuscitating medium of dependent existences. What took place on the Moon is only what is to take place some day or other on the Earth, when it is sufficiently cooled off."

"Cooled off?"

"Yes," replied the Captain as confidently and with as little hesitation as if he was explaining some of the details of his great machine-shop in Philadelphia; "You see, according as the internal fire near the surface was extinguished or was withdrawn towards the centre, the lunar shell naturally cooled off. The logical consequences, of course, then gradually took place: extinction of organized beings; and then extinction of vegetation. The atmosphere, in the meantime, became thinner and thinner—partly drawn off with the water evaporated by the terrestrial attraction, and partly sinking with the solid water into the crust-cracks caused by cooling. With the disappearance of air capable of respiration, and of water capable of motion, the Moon, of course, became uninhabitable. From that day it became the abode of death, as completely as it is at the present moment."

"That is the fate in store for our Earth?"

"In all probability."

"And when is it to befall us?"

"Just as soon as the crust becomes cold enough to be uninhabitable."

"Perhaps your philosophership has taken the trouble to calculate how many years it will take our unfortunate *Terra Mater* to cool off?"

"Well; I have."

"And you can rely on your figures?"

"Implicitly."

"Why not tell it at once then to a fellow that's dying of impatience to know all about it? Captain, the Chair considers you one of the most tantalizing creatures in existence!"

"If you only listen, you will hear," replied M'Nicholl quietly. "By careful observations, extended through a series of many years, men have been able to discover the average loss of temperature endured by the Earth in a century. Taking this as the ground work of their calculations, they have ascertained that our Earth shall become an uninhabitable planet in about—"

"Don't cut her life too short! Be merciful!" cried Ardan in a pleading tone half in earnest. "Come, a good long day, your Honor! A good long day!"

"The planet that we call the Earth," continued the Captain, as grave as a judge, "will become uninhabitable to human beings, after a lapse of 400 thousand years from the present time."

"Hurrah!" cried Ardan, much relieved. "*Vive la Science!* Henceforward, what miscreant will persist in saying that the Savants are good for nothing? Proudly pointing to this calculation, can't they exclaim to all defamers: 'Silence, croakers! Our services are invaluable! Haven't we insured the Earth for 400 thousand years?' Again I say *vive la Science!*"

"Ardan," began the Captain with some asperity, "the foundations on which Science has raised—"

"I'm half converted already," interrupted Ardan in a cheery tone; "I do really believe that Science is not altogether unmitigated homebogue! *Vive—*"

—"But what has all this to do with the question under discussion?" interrupted Barbican, desirous to keep his friends from losing their tempers in idle disputation.

"True!" said Ardan. "The Chair, thankful for being called to order, would respectfully remind the house that the question before it is: *Has the Moon been inhabited?* Affirmative has been heard. Negative is called on to reply. Mr. Barbican has the *parole*."

But Mr. Barbican was unwilling just then to enter too deeply into such an exceedingly difficult subject. "The probabilities," he contented himself with saying, "would appear to be in favor of the Captain's speculations. But we must never forget that they *are* speculations— nothing more. Not the slightest evidence has yet been produced that the Moon is anything else than 'a dead and useless waste of extinct volcanoes.' No signs of cities, no signs of buildings, not even of ruins, none of anything that could be reasonably ascribed to the labors of intelligent creatures. No sign of change of any kind has been established. As for the agreement between the Moon's rotation and her revolution, which compels her to keep the same face constantly turned towards the Earth, we don't know that it has not existed from the beginning. As for what is called the effect of volcanic agency upon her surface, we don't know that her peculiar blistered appearance may not have been brought about altogether by the bubbling and spitting that blisters molten iron when cooling and contracting. Some close observers have even ventured to account for her craters by saying they were due to pelting showers of meteoric rain. Then again as to her atmosphere—why should she have lost her atmosphere? Why should it sink into craters? Atmosphere is gas, great in volume, small in matter; where would there be room for it? Solidified by the intense cold? Possibly in the night time. But would not the heat of the long day be great enough to thaw it back again? The same trouble attends the alleged disappearance of the water. Swallowed up in the cavernous cracks, it is said. But why are there cracks? Cooling is not always attended by cracking. Water cools without cracking; cannon balls cool without cracking. Too much stress has been laid on the great difference between the *nucleus* and the *crust*: it is really impossible to say where one ends and the other begins. In fact, no theory explains satisfactorily anything regarding the present state of the Moon's surface. In fact, from the day that Galileo compared her clustering craters to 'eyes on a peacock's tail' to the present time, we must acknowledge that we know nothing more than we can actually see, not one particle more of the Moon's history than our telescopes reveal to our corporal eyes!"

"In the lucid opinion of the honorable and learned gentleman who spoke last," said Ardan, "the Chair is compelled to concur. Therefore, as to the second question before the house for deliberation, *Has the Moon been ever inhabited?* the Chair gets out of its difficulty, as a Scotch jury does when it has not evidence enough either way, by returning a solemn verdict of *Not Proven!*"

"And with this conclusion," said Barbican, hastily rising, "of a subject on which, to tell the truth, we are unable as yet to throw any light worth speaking of, let us be satisfied for the present. Another question of greater moment to us just now is: where are we? It seems to me that we are increasing our distance from the Moon very decidedly and very rapidly."

It was easy to see that he was quite right in this observation. The Projectile, still following a northerly course and therefore approaching the lunar equator, was certainly getting farther and farther from the Moon. Even at 30° S., only ten degrees farther north than the latitude of *Tycho*, the travellers had considerable difficulty, comparatively, in observing the details of *Pitatus*, a walled mountain on the south shores of the *Mare Nubium*. In the "sea" itself, over which they now floated, they could see very little, but far to the left, on the 20th parallel, they could discern the vast crater of *Bullialdus*, 9,000 feet deep. On the right, they had just caught a glimpse of *Purbach*, a depressed valley almost square in shape with a round crater in the centre, when Ardan suddenly cried out:

"A Railroad!"

And, sure enough, right under them, a little northeast of *Purbach*, the travellers easily distinguished a long line straight and black, really not unlike a railroad cutting through a low hilly country.

This, Barbican explained, was of course no railway, but a steep cliff, at least 1,000 feet high, casting a very deep shadow, and probably the result of the caving in of the surface on the eastern edge.

Then they saw the immense crater of *Arzachel* and in its midst a cone mountain shining with dazzling splendor. A little north of this, they could detect the outlines of another crater, *Alphonse*, at least 70 miles in diameter. Close to it they could easily distinguish the immense crater or, as some observers call it, Ramparted Plain, *Ptolemy*, so well known to lunar astronomers, occupying, as it does, such a favorable position near the centre of the Moon, and having a diameter fully, in one direction at least, 120 miles long.

The travellers were now in about the same latitude as that at which they had at first approached the Moon, and it was here that they began most unquestionably to leave her. They looked and looked, readjusting their glasses, but the details were becoming more and more difficult to catch. The reliefs grew more and more blurred and the outlines dimmer and dimmer. Even the great mountain profiles began to fade away, the dazzling colors to grow duller, the jet black shadows greyer, and the general effect mistier.

At last, the distance had become so great that, of this lunar world so wonderful, so fantastic, so weird, so mysterious, our travellers by degrees lost even the consciousness, and their sensations, lately so vivid, grew fainter and fainter, until finally they resembled those of a man who is suddenly awakened from a peculiarly strange and impressive dream.

XIX

In Every Fight, The Impossible Wins

No matter what we have been accustomed to, it is sad to bid it farewell forever. The glimpse of the Moon's wondrous world imparted to Barbican and his companions had been, like that of the Promised Land to Moses on Mount Pisgah, only a distant and a dark one, yet it was with inexpressibly mournful eyes that, silent and thoughtful, they now watched her fading away slowly from their view, the conviction impressing itself deeper and deeper in their souls that, slight as their acquaintance had been, it was never to be renewed again. All doubt on the subject was removed by the position gradually, but decidedly, assumed by the Projectile. Its base was turning away slowly and steadily from the Moon, and pointing surely and unmistakably towards the Earth.

Barbican had been long carefully noticing this modification, but without being able to explain it. That the Projectile should withdraw a long distance from the Moon and still be her satellite, he could understand; but, being her satellite, why not present towards her its heaviest segment, as the Moon does towards the Earth? That was the point which he could not readily clear up.

By carefully noting its path, he thought he could see that the Projectile, though now decidedly leaving the Moon, still followed a curve exactly analogous to that by which it had approached her. It must therefore be describing a very elongated ellipse, which might possibly extend even to the neutral point where the lunar and terrestrial attractions were mutually overcome.

With this surmise of Barbican's, his companions appeared rather disposed to agree, though, of course, it gave rise to new questions.

"Suppose we reach this dead point," asked Ardan; "what then is to become of us?"

"Can't tell!" was Barbican's unsatisfactory reply.

"But you can form a few hypotheses?"

"Yes, two!"

"Let us have them."

"The velocity will be either sufficient to carry us past the dead point, or it will not: sufficient, we shall keep on, just as we are now, gravitating forever around the Moon—"

—"Hypothesis number two will have at least one point in its favor," interrupted as usual the incorrigible Ardan; "it can't be worse than hypothesis number one!"

—"Insufficient," continued Barbican, laying down the law, "we shall rest forever motionless on the dead point of the mutually neutralizing attractions."

"A pleasant prospect!" observed Ardan: "from the worst possible to no better! Isn't it, Barbican?"

"Nothing to say," was Barbican's only reply.

"Have you nothing to say either, Captain?" asked Ardan, beginning to be a little vexed at the apparent apathy of his companions.

"Nothing whatever," replied M'Nicholl, giving point to his words by a despairing shake of his head.

"You don't mean surely that we're going to sit here, like bumps on a log, doing nothing until it will be too late to attempt anything?"

"Nothing whatever can be done," said Barbican gloomily. "It is vain to struggle against the impossible."

"Impossible! Where did you get that word? I thought the American schoolboys had cut it out of their dictionaries!"

"That must have been since my time," said Barbican smiling grimly.

"It still sticks in a few old copies anyhow," drawled M'Nicholl drily, as he carefully wiped his glasses.

"Well! it has no business *here*!" said Ardan. "What! A pair of live Yankees and a Frenchman, of the nineteenth century too, recoil before an old fashioned word that hardly scared our grandfathers!"

"What can we do?"

"Correct the movement that's now running away with us!"

"Correct it?"

"Certainly, correct it! or modify it! or clap brakes on it! or take some advantage of it that will be in our favor! What matters the exact term so you comprehend me?"

"Easy talking!"

"As easy doing!"

"Doing what? Doing how?"

"The what, and the how, is your business, not mine! What kind of an artillery man is he who can't master his bullets? The gunner who cannot command his own gun should be rammed into it head foremost himself and blown from its mouth! A nice pair of savants *you* are! There you sit as helpless as a couple of babies, after having inveigled me—"

"Inveigled!!" cried Barbican and M'Nicholl starting to their feet in an instant; "WHAT!!!"

"Come, come!" went on Ardan, not giving his indignant friends time to utter a syllable; "I don't want any recrimination! I'm not the one to complain! I'll even let up a little if you consider the expression too strong! I'll even withdraw it altogether, and assert that the trip delights me! that the Projectile is a thing after my own heart! that I was never in better spirits than at the present moment! I don't complain, I only appeal to your own good sense, and call upon you with all my voice to do everything possible, so that we may go *somewhere*, since it appears we can't get to the Moon!"

"But that's exactly what we want to do ourselves, friend Ardan," said Barbican, endeavoring to give an example of calmness to the impatient M'Nicholl; "the only trouble is that we have not the means to do it."

"Can't we modify the Projectile's movement?"

"No."

"Nor diminish its velocity?"

"No."

"Not even by lightening it, as a heavily laden ship is lightened, by throwing cargo overboard?"

"What can we throw overboard? We have no ballast like balloon-men."

"I should like to know," interrupted M'Nicholl, "what would be the good of throwing anything at all overboard. Any one with a particle of common sense in his head, can see that the lightened Projectile should only move the quicker!"

"Slower, you mean," said Ardan.

"Quicker, I mean," replied the Captain.

"Neither quicker nor slower, dear friends," interposed Barbican, desirous to stop a quarrel; "we are floating, you know, in an absolute void, where specific gravity never counts."

"Well then, my friends," said Ardan in a resigned tone that he evidently endeavored to render calm, "since the worst is come to the worst, there is but one thing left for us to do!"

"What's that?" said the Captain, getting ready to combat some new piece of nonsense.

"To take our breakfast!" said the Frenchman curtly.

It was a resource he had often fallen back on in difficult conjunctures. Nor did it fail him now.

Though it was not a project that claimed to affect either the velocity or the direction of the Projectile, still, as it was eminently practicable and not only unattended by no inconvenience on the one hand but evidently fraught with many advantages on the other, it met with decided and instantaneous success. It was rather an early hour for breakfast, two o'clock in the morning, yet the meal was keenly relished. Ardan served it up in charming style and crowned the dessert with a few bottles of a wine especially selected for the occasion from his own private stock. It was a *Tokay Imperial* of 1863, the genuine *Essenz*, from Prince Esterhazy's own wine cellar, and the best brain stimulant and brain clearer in the world, as every connoisseur knows.

It was near four o'clock in the morning when our travellers, now well fortified physically and morally, once more resumed their observations with renewed courage and determination, and with a system of recording really perfect in its arrangements.

Around the Projectile, they could still see floating most of the objects that had been dropped out of the window. This convinced them that, during their revolution around the Moon, they had not passed through any atmosphere; had anything of the kind been encountered, it would have revealed its presence by its retarding effect on the different objects that now followed close in the wake of the Projectile. One or two that were missing had been probably struck and carried off by a fragment of the exploded bolide.

Of the Earth nothing as yet could be seen. She was only one day Old, having been New the previous evening, and two days were still to elapse before her crescent would be sufficiently cleared of the solar rays to be capable of performing her ordinary duty of serving as a time-piece for the Selenites. For, as the reflecting reader need hardly be reminded, since she rotates with perfect regularity on her axis, she can make such rotations visible to the Selenites by bringing some particular point on her surface once every twenty-four hours directly over the same lunar meridian.

Towards the Moon, the view though far less distinct, was still almost as dazzling as ever. The radiant Queen of Night still glittered in all her splendor in the midst of the starry host, whose pure white light seemed to borrow only additional purity and silvery whiteness from the gorgeous contrast. On her disc, the "seas" were already beginning to assume the ashy tint so well known to us on Earth, but the rest of her surface sparkled with all its former radiation, *Tycho* glowing like a sun in the midst of the general resplendescence.

Barbican attempted in vain to obtain even a tolerable approximation of the velocity at which the Projectile was now moving. He had to content himself with the knowledge that it was diminishing at a uniform rate—of which indeed a little reflection on a well known law of Dynamics readily convinced him. He had not much difficulty even in explaining the matter to his friends.

"Once admitting," said he, "the Projectile to describe an orbit round the Moon, that orbit must of necessity be an ellipse. Every moving body circulating regularly around another, describes an ellipse. Science has proved this incontestably. The satellites describe ellipses around the planets, the planets around the Sun, the Sun himself describes an ellipse around the unknown star that serves as a pivot for our whole solar system. How can our Baltimore Gun Club Projectile then escape the universal law?

"Now what is the consequence of this law? If the orbit were a *circle*, the satellite would always preserve the same distance from its primary, and its velocity should therefore be constant. But the orbit being an *ellipse*, and the attracting body always occupying one of the foci, the satellite must evidently lie nearer to this focus in one part of its orbit than in another. The Earth when nearest to the Sun, is in her *perihelion*; when most distant, in her *aphelion*. The Moon, with regard to the Earth, is similarly in her *perigee*, and her *apogee*. Analogous expressions denoting the relations of the Projectile towards the Moon, would be *periselene* and *aposelene*. At its *aposelene* the Projectile's velocity would have reached its minimum; at the *periselene*, its maximum. As it is to the former point that we are now moving, clearly the velocity must keep on diminishing until that point is reached. Then, *if it does not die out altogether*, it must spring up again, and even accelerate as it reapproaches the Moon. Now the great trouble is this: If the *Aposelenetic* point should coincide with the point of lunar attraction, our velocity must certainly become *nil*, and the Projectile must remain relatively motionless forever!"

"What do you mean by 'relatively motionless'?" asked M'Nicholl, who was carefully studying the situation.

"I mean, of course, not absolutely motionless," answered Barbican; "absolute immobility is, as you are well aware, altogether impossible, but motionless with regard to the Earth and the—"

"By Mahomet's jackass!" interrupted Ardan hastily, "I must say we're a precious set of *imbéciles!*"

"I don't deny it, dear friend," said Barbican quietly, notwithstanding the unceremonious interruption; "but why do you say so just now?"

"Because though we are possessed of the power of retarding the velocity that takes us from the Moon, we have never thought of employing it!"

"What do you mean?"

"Do you forget the rockets?"

"It's a fact!" cried M'Nicholl. "How have we forgotten them?"

"I'm sure I can't tell," answered Barbican, "unless, perhaps, because we had too many other things to think about. Your thought, my dear friend, is a most happy one, and, of course, we shall utilize it."

"When? How soon?"

"At the first favorable opportunity, not sooner. For you can see for yourselves, dear friends," he went on explaining, "that with the present obliquity of the Projectile with regard to the lunar disc, a discharge of our rockets would be more likely to send us away from the Moon than towards her. Of course, you are both still desirous of reaching the Moon?"

"Most emphatically so!"

"Then by reserving our rockets for the last chance, we may possibly get there after all. In consequence of some force, to me utterly inexplicable, the Projectile still seems disposed to turn its base towards the Earth. In fact, it is likely enough that at the neutral point its cone will point vertically to the Moon. That being the moment when its velocity will most probably be *nil*, it will also be the moment for us to discharge our rockets, and the possibility is that we may force a direct fall on the lunar disc."

"Good!" cried Ardan, clapping hands.

"Why didn't we execute this grand manoeuvre the first time we reached the neutral point?" asked M'Nicholl a little crustily.

"It would be useless," answered Barbican; "the Projectile's velocity at that time, as you no doubt remember, not only did not need rockets, but was actually too great to be affected by them."

"True!" chimed in Ardan; "a wind of four miles an hour is very little use to a steamer going ten."

"That assertion," cried M'Nicholl, "I am rather dis—"

—"Dear friends," interposed Barbican, his pale face beaming and his clear voice ringing with the new excitement; "let us just now waste no time in mere words. We have one more chance, perhaps a great one. Let us not throw it away! We have been on the brink of despair—"

—"Beyond it!" cried Ardan.

—"But I now begin to see a possibility, nay, a very decided probability, of our being able to attain the great end at last!"

"Bravo!" cried Ardan.

"Hurrah!" cried M'Nicholl.

"Yes! my brave boys!" cried Barbican as enthusiastically as his companions; "all's not over yet by a long shot!"

What had brought about this great revulsion in the spirits of our bold adventurers? The breakfast? Prince Esterhazy's Tokay? The latter, most probably. What had become of the resolutions they had discussed so ably and passed so decidedly a few hours before? *Was the Moon inhabited? No! Was the Moon habitable? No!* Yet in the face of all this—or rather as coolly as if such subjects had never been alluded to—here were the reckless scientists actually thinking of nothing but how to work heaven and earth in order to get there!

One question more remained to be answered before they played their last trump, namely: "At what precise moment would the Projectile reach the neutral point?"

To this Barbican had very little trouble in finding an answer. The time spent in proceeding from the south pole to the dead point being evidently equal to the time previously spent in proceeding from the dead point to the north pole—to ascertain the former, he had only to calculate the latter. This was easily done. To refer to his notes, to check off the different rates of velocity at which they had readied the different parallels, and to turn these rates into time, required only a very few minutes careful calculation. The Projectile then was to reach the point of neutral attraction at one o'clock in the morning of December 8th. At the present time, it was five o'clock in the morning of the 7th; therefore, if nothing unforeseen should occur in the meantime, their great and final effort was to be made about twenty hours later.

The rockets, so often alluded to as an idea of Ardan's and already fully described, had been originally provided to break the violence of the Projectile's fall on the lunar surface; but now the dauntless travellers were about to employ them for a purpose precisely the reverse. In any case, having been put in proper order for immediate use, nothing more now remained to be done till the moment should come for firing them off.

"Now then, friends," said M'Nicholl, rubbing his eyes but hardly able to keep them open, "I'm not over fond of talking, but this time I think I may offer a slight proposition."

"We shall be most happy to entertain it, my dear Captain," said Barbican.

"I propose we lie down and take a good nap."

"Good gracious!" protested Ardan; "What next?"

"We have not had a blessed wink for forty hours," continued the Captain; "a little sleep would recuperate us wonderfully."

"No sleep now!" exclaimed Ardan.

"Every man to his taste!" said M'Nicholl; "mine at present is certainly to turn in!" and suiting the action to the word, he coiled himself on the sofa, and in a few minutes his deep regular breathing showed his slumber to be as tranquil as an infant's.

Barbican looked at him in a kindly way, but only for a very short time; his eyes grew so filmy that he could not keep them open any longer. "The Captain," he said, "may not be without his little faults, but for good practical sense he is worth a ship-load like you and me, Ardan. By Jove, I'm going to imitate him, and, friend Michael, you might do worse!"

In a short time he was as unconscious as the Captain.

Ardan gazed on the pair for a few minutes, and then began to feel quite lonely. Even his animals were fast asleep. He tried to look out, but observing without having anybody to listen to your observations, is dull work. He looked again at the sleeping pair, and then he gave in.

"It can't be denied," he muttered, slowly nodding his head, "that even your practical men sometimes stumble on a good idea."

Then curling up his long legs, and folding his arms under his head, his restless brain was soon forming fantastic shapes for itself in the mysterious land of dreams.

But his slumbers were too much disturbed to last long. After an uneasy, restless, unrefreshing attempt at repose, he sat up at about half-past seven o'clock, and began stretching himself, when he found his companions already awake and discussing the situation in whispers.

The Projectile, they were remarking, was still pursuing its way from the Moon, and turning its conical point more and more in her direction. This latter phenomenon, though as puzzling as ever, Barbican regarded with decided pleasure: the more directly the conical summit pointed to the Moon at the exact moment, the more directly towards her surface would the rockets communicate their reactionary motion.

Nearly seventeen hours, however, were still to elapse before that moment, that all important moment, would arrive.

The time began to drag. The excitement produced by the Moon's vicinity had died out. Our travellers, though as daring and as confident as ever, could not help feeling a certain sinking of heart at the approach of the moment for deciding either alternative of their doom in this world—their fall to the Moon, or their eternal imprisonment in a changeless orbit. Barbican and M'Nicholl tried to kill time by revising their calculations and putting their notes in order; Ardan, by feverishly walking back and forth from window to window, and stopping for a second or two to throw a nervous glance at the cold, silent and impassive Moon.

Now and then reminiscences of our lower world would flit across their brains. Visions of the famous Gun Club rose up before them the oftenest, with their dear friend Marston always the central figure. What was his bustling, honest, good-natured, impetuous heart at now? Most probably he was standing bravely at his post on the Rocky Mountains, his eye glued to the great Telescope, his whole soul peering through its tube. Had he seen the Projectile before it vanished behind the Moon's north pole? Could he have caught a glimpse of it at its reappearance? If so, could he have concluded it to be the satellite of a satellite! Could Belfast have announced to the world such a startling piece of intelligence? Was that all the Earth was ever to know of their great enterprise? What were the speculations of the Scientific World upon the subject? etc., etc.

In listless questions and desultory conversation of this kind the day slowly wore away, without the occurrence of any incident whatever to relieve its weary monotony. Midnight arrived, December the seventh was dead. As Ardan said: "*Le Sept Decembre est mort; vive le Huit!*" In one hour more, the neutral point would be reached. At what velocity was the Projectile now moving? Barbican could not exactly tell, but he felt quite certain that no serious error had slipped into his calculations. At one o'clock that night, *nil* the velocity was to be, and *nil* it would be!

Another phenomenon, in any case, was to mark the arrival of the exact moment. At the dead point, the two attractions, terrestrial and lunar, would again exactly counterbalance each other. For a few seconds, objects would no longer possess the slightest weight. This curious circumstance, which had so much surprised and amused the travellers at its first occurrence, was now to appear again as soon as the conditions should become identical. During these few seconds then would come the moment for striking the decisive blow.

They could soon notice the gradual approach of this important instant. Objects began to weigh sensibly lighter. The conical point of the Projectile had become almost directly under the centre of the lunar surface. This gladdened the hearts of the bold adventurers. The recoil of the rockets losing none of its power by oblique action, the chances pronounced decidedly in their favor. Now, only supposing the Projectile's velocity to be absolutely annihilated at the dead point, the slightest force directing it towards the Moon would be *certain* to cause it finally to fall on her surface.

Supposing!—but supposing the contrary!

—Even these brave adventurers had not the courage to suppose the contrary!

"Five minutes to one o'clock," said M'Nicholl, his eyes never quitting his watch.

"Ready?" asked Barbican of Ardan.

"Ay, ay, sir!" was Ardan's reply, as he made sure that the electric apparatus to discharge the rockets was in perfect working order.

"Wait till I give the word," said Barbican, pulling out his chronometer.

The moment was now evidently close at hand. The objects lying around had no weight. The travellers felt their bodies to be as buoyant as a hydrogen balloon. Barbican let go his chronometer, but it kept its place as firmly in empty space before his eyes as if it had been nailed to the wall!

"One o'clock!" cried Barbican in a solemn tone.

Ardan instantly touched the discharging key of the little electric battery. A dull, dead, distant report was immediately heard, communicated probably by the vibration of the Projectile to the internal air. But Ardan saw through the window a long thin flash, which vanished in a second. At the same moment, the three friends became instantaneously conscious of a slight shock experienced by the Projectile.

They looked at each other, speechless, breathless, for about as long as it would take you to count five: the silence so intense that they could easily hear the pulsation of their hearts. Ardan was the first to break it.

"Are we falling or are we not?" he asked in a loud whisper.

"We're not!" answered M'Nicholl, also hardly speaking above his breath. "The base of the Projectile is still turned away as far as ever from the Moon!"

Barbican, who had been looking out of the window, now turned hastily towards his companions. His face frightened them. He was deadly pale; his eyes stared, and his lips were painfully contracted.

"We *are* falling!" he shrieked huskily.

"Towards the Moon?" exclaimed his companions.

"No!" was the terrible reply. "Towards the Earth!"

"*Sacré!*" cried Ardan, as usually letting off his excitement in French.

"Fire and fury!" cried M'Nicholl, completely startled out of his habitual *sang froid*.

"Thunder and lightning!" swore the usually serene Barbican, now completely stunned by the blow. "I had never expected this!"

Ardan was the first to recover from the deadening shock: his levity came to his relief.

"First impressions are always right," he muttered philosophically. "The moment I set eyes on the confounded thing, it reminded me of the Bastille; it is now proving its likeness to a worse place: easy enough to get into, but no redemption out of it!"

There was no longer any doubt possible on the subject. The terrible fall had begun. The Projectile had retained velocity enough not only to carry it beyond the dead point, but it was even able to completely overcome the feeble resistance offered by the rockets. It was all clear now. The same velocity that had carried the Projectile beyond the neutral point on its way to the Moon, was still swaying it on its return to the Earth. A well known law of motion required that, in the path which it was now about to describe, *it should repass, on its return through all the points through which it had already passed during its departure.*

No wonder that our friends were struck almost senseless when the fearful fall they were now about to encounter, flashed upon them in all its horror. They were to fall a clear distance of nearly 200 thousand miles! To lighten or counteract such a descent, the most powerful springs, checks, rockets, screens, deadeners, even if the whole Earth were engaged in their construction—would produce no more effect than so many spiderwebs. According to a simple law in Ballistics, *the Projectile was to strike the Earth with a velocity equal to that by which it had been animated when issuing from the mouth of the Columbiad*—a velocity of at least seven miles a second!

To have even a faint idea of this enormous velocity, let us make a little comparison. A body falling from the summit of a steeple a hundred and fifty feet high, dashes against the pavement with a velocity of fifty five miles an hour. Falling from the summit of St. Peter's, it strikes the earth at the rate of 300 miles an hour, or five times quicker than the rapidest express train. Falling from the neutral point, the Projectile should strike the Earth with a velocity of more than 25,000 miles an hour!

"We are lost!" said M'Nicholl gloomily, his philosophy yielding to despair.

"One consolation, boys!" cried Ardan, genial to the last. "We shall die together!"

"If we die," said Barbican calmly, but with a kind of suppressed enthusiasm, "it will be only to remove to a more extended sphere of our investigations. In the other world, we can pursue our inquiries under far more favorable auspices. There the wonders of our great Creator, clothed in brighter light, shall be brought within a shorter range. We shall require no machine, nor projectile, nor material contrivance of any kind to be enabled to contemplate them in all their grandeur and to appreciate them fully and intelligently. Our souls, enlightened by the emanations of the Eternal Wisdom, shall revel forever in the blessed rays of Eternal Knowledge!"

"A grand view to take of it, dear friend Barbican;" replied Ardan, "and a consoling one too. The privilege of roaming at will through God's great universe should make ample amends for missing the Moon!"

M'Nicholl fixed his eyes on Barbican admiringly, feebly muttering with hardly moving lips:

"Grit to the marrow! Grit to the marrow!"

Barbican, head bowed in reverence, arms folded across his breast, meekly and uncomplainingly uttered with sublime resignation:

"Thy will be done!"

"Amen!" answered his companions, in a loud and fervent whisper.

THEY WERE SOON FALLING THROUGH the boundless regions of space with inconceivable rapidity!

XX

Off the Pacific Coast

"Well, Lieutenant, how goes the sounding?"

"Pretty lively, Captain; we're nearly through;" replied the Lieutenant. "But it's a tremendous depth so near land. We can't be more than 250 miles from the California coast."

"The depression certainly is far deeper than I had expected," observed Captain Bloomsbury. "We have probably lit on a submarine valley channelled out by the Japanese Current."

"The Japanese Current, Captain?"

"Certainly; that branch of it which breaks on the western shores of North America and then flows southeast towards the Isthmus of Panama."

"That may account for it, Captain," replied young Brownson; "at least, I hope it does, for then we may expect the valley to get shallower as we leave the land. So far, there's no sign of a Telegraphic Plateau in this quarter of the globe."

"Probably not, Brownson. How is the line now?"

"We have paid out 3500 fathoms already, Captain, but, judging from the rate the reel goes at, we are still some distance from bottom."

As he spoke, he pointed to a tall derrick temporarily rigged up at the stern of the vessel for the purpose of working the sounding apparatus, and surrounded by a group of busy men. Through a block pulley strongly lashed to the derrick, a stout cord of the best Italian hemp, wound off a large reel placed amidships, was now running rapidly and with a slight whirring noise.

"I hope it's not the 'cup-lead' you are using, Brownson?" said the Captain, after a few minutes observation.

"Oh no, Captain, certainly not," replied the Lieutenant. "It's only Brooke's apparatus that is of any use in such depths."

"Clever fellow that Brooke," observed the Captain; "served with him under Maury. His detachment of the weight is really the starting point for every new improvement in sounding gear. The English, the French, and even our own, are nothing but modifications of that fundamental principle. Exceedingly clever fellow!"

"Bottom!" sang out one of the men standing near the derrick and watching the operations.

The Captain and the Lieutenant immediately advanced to question him.

"What's the depth, Coleman?" asked the Lieutenant.

"21,762 feet," was the prompt reply, which Brownson immediately inscribed in his note-book, handing a duplicate to the Captain.

"All right, Lieutenant," observed the Captain, after a moment's inspection of the figures. "While I enter it in the log, you haul the line aboard. To do so, I need hardly remind you, is a task involving care and patience. In spite of all our gallant little donkey engine can do, it's a six hours job at least. Meanwhile, the Chief Engineer had better give orders for firing up, so that we may be ready to start as soon as you're through. It's now close on to four bells, and with your permission I shall turn in. Let me be called at three. Good night!"

"Goodnight, Captain!" replied Brownson, who spent the next two hours pacing backward and forward on the quarter deck, watching the hauling in of the sounding line, and occasionally casting a glance towards all quarters of the sky.

It was a glorious night. The innumerable stars glittered with the brilliancy of the purest gems. The ship, hove to in order to take the soundings, swung gently on the faintly heaving ocean breast. You felt you were in a tropical clime, for, though no breath fanned your cheek, your senses easily detected the delicious odor of a distant garden of sweet roses. The sea sparkled with phosphorescence. Not a sound was heard except the panting of the hard-worked little donkey-engine and the whirr of the line as it came up taut and dripping from the ocean depths. The lamp, hanging from the mast, threw a bright glare on deck, presenting the strongest contrast with the black shadows, firm and motionless as marble. The 11th day of December was now near its last hour.

The steamer was the *Susquehanna*, a screw, of the United States Navy, 4,000 in tonnage, and carrying 20 guns. She had been detached to take soundings between the Pacific coast and the Sandwich Islands, the initiatory movement towards laying down an Ocean Cable, which the *Pacific Cable Company* contemplated finally extending to China. She lay just now a few hundred miles directly south of San Diego, an old Spanish town in southwestern California, and the point which is expected to be the terminus of the great *Texas and Pacific Railroad*.

The Captain, John Bloomsbury by name, but better known as 'High-Low Jack' from his great love of that game—the only one he was ever known to play—was a near relation of our old friend Colonel Bloomsbury of the Baltimore Gun Club. Of a good Kentucky family, and educated at Annapolis, he had passed his meridian without ever being heard of, when suddenly the news that he had run the gauntlet in a little gunboat past the terrible batteries of Island Number Ten, amidst a perfect storm of shell, grape and canister discharged at less than a hundred yards distance, burst on the American nation on the sixth of April, 1862, and inscribed his name at once in deep characters on the list of the giants of the Great War. But war had never been his vocation. With the return of peace, he had sought and obtained employment on the Western Coast Survey, where every thing he did he looked on as a labor of love. The Sounding Expedition he had particularly coveted, and, once entered upon it, he discharged his duties with characteristic energy.

He could not have had more favorable weather than the present for a successful performance of the nice and delicate investigations of sounding. His vessel had even been fortunate enough to have lain altogether out of the track of the terrible wind storm already alluded to, which, starting from somewhere southwest of the Sierra Madre, had swept away every vestige of mist from the summits of the Rocky Mountains and, by revealing the Moon in all her splendor, had enabled Belfast to send the famous despatch announcing that he had seen the Projectile. Every feature of the expedition was, in fact, advancing so favorably that the Captain expected to be able, in a month or two, to submit to the *P.C. Company* a most satisfactory report of his labors.

Cyrus W. Field, the life and soul of the whole enterprise, flushed with honors still in full bloom (the Atlantic Telegraph Cable having been just laid), could congratulate himself with good reason on having found a treasure in the Captain. High-Low Jack was the congenial spirit by whose active and intelligent aid he promised himself the pleasure of seeing before long the whole Pacific Ocean covered with a vast reticulation of electric cables. The practical part, therefore, being in such safe hands, Mr. Field could remain with a quiet conscience in Washington, New York or London, seeing after the financial part of the grand undertaking, worthy of the Nineteenth Century, worthy of the Great Republic, and eminently worthy of the illustrious CYRUS W. himself!

As already mentioned, the *Susquehanna* lay a few hundred miles south of San Diego, or, to be more accurate, in 27° 7′ North Latitude and 118° 37′ West Longitude (Greenwich).

It was now a little past midnight. The Moon, in her last quarter, was just beginning to peep over the eastern horizon. Lieutenant Brownson, leaving the quarter deck, had gone to the forecastle, where he found a crowd of officers talking together earnestly and directing their glasses towards her disc. Even here, out on the ocean, the Queen of the night, was as great an object of attraction as on the North American Continent generally, where, that very night and that very hour, at least 40 million pairs of eyes were anxiously gazing at her. Apparently forgetful that even the very best of their glasses could no more see the Projectile than angulate Sirius, the officers held them fast to their eyes for five minutes at a time, and then took them away only to talk with remarkable fluency on what they had not discovered.

"Any sign of them yet, gentlemen?" asked Brownson gaily as he joined the group. "It's now pretty near time for them to put in an appearance. They're gone ten days I should think."

"They're there, Lieutenant! not a doubt of it!" cried a young midshipman, fresh from Annapolis, and of course "throughly posted" in the latest revelations of Astronomy. "I feel as certain of their being there as I am of our being here on the forecastle of the *Susquehanna*!"

"I must agree with you of course, Mr. Midshipman," replied Brownson with a slight smile; "I have no grounds whatever for contradicting you."

"Neither have I," observed another officer, the surgeon of the vessel. "The Projectile was to have reached the Moon when at her full, which was at midnight on the 5th. To-day was the 11th. This gives them six days of clear light—time enough in all conscience not only to land safely but to install themselves quite comfortably in their new home. In fact, I see them there already—"

"In my mind's eye, Horatio!" laughed one of the group. "Though the Doc wears glasses, he can see more than any ten men on board."

—"Already"—pursued the Doctor, heedless of the interruption. "*Scene*, a stony valley near a Selenite stream; the Projectile on the right, half buried in volcanic *scoriae*, but apparently not much the worse for the wear; ring mountains, craters, sharp peaks, etc. all around; old Mac discovered taking observations with his levelling staff; Barbican perched on the summit of a sharp pointed rock, writing up his note-book; Ardan, eye-glass on nose, hat under arm, legs apart, puffing at his *Imperador*, like a—"

—"A locomotive!" interrupted the young Midshipman, his excitable imagination so far getting the better of him as to make him forget his manners. He had just finished Locke's famous Moon Hoax, and his brain was still full of its pictures. "In the background," he went on, "can be seen thousands of *Vespertiliones-Homines* or *Man-Bats*, in all the various attitudes of curiosity, alarm, or consternation; some of them peeping around the rocks, some fluttering from peak to peak, all gibbering a language more or less resembling the notes of birds. *Enter* Lunatico, King of the Selenites—"

"Excuse us, Mr. Midshipman," interrupted Brownson with an easy smile, "Locke's authority may have great weight among the young Middies at Annapolis, but it does not rank very high at present in the estimation of practical scientists." This rebuff administered to the conceited little Midshipman, a rebuff which the Doctor particularly relished, Brownson continued: "Gentlemen, we certainly know nothing whatever regarding our friends' fate; guessing gives no information. How we ever are to hear from the Moon until we are connected with it by a lunar cable, I can't even imagine. The probability is that we shall never—"

"Excuse me, Lieutenant," interrupted the unrebuffed little Midshipman; "Can't Barbican write?"

A shout of derisive comments greeted this question.

"Certainly he can write, and send his letter by the Pony Express!" cried one.

"A Postal Card would be cheaper!" cried another.

"The *New York Herald* will send a reporter after it!" was the exclamation of a third.

"Keep cool, just keep cool, gentlemen," persisted the little Midshipman, not in the least abashed by the uproarious hilarity excited by his remarks. "I asked if Barbican couldn't write. In that question I see nothing whatever to laugh at. Can't a man write without being obliged to send his letters?"

"This is all nonsense," said the Doctor. "What's the use of a man writing to you if he can't send you what he writes?"

"What's the use of his sending it to you if he can have it read without that trouble?" answered the little Midshipman in a confident tone. "Is there not a telescope at Long's Peak? Doesn't it bring the Moon within a few miles of the Rocky Mountains, and enable us to see on her surface, objects as small as nine feet in diameter? Well! What's to prevent

JULES VERNE

Barbican and his friends from constructing a gigantic alphabet? If they write words of even a few hundred yards and sentences a mile or two long, what is to prevent us from reading them? Catch the idea now, eh?"

They did catch the idea, and heartily applauded the little Middy for his smartness. Even the Doctor saw a certain kind of merit in it, and Brownson acknowledged it to be quite feasible. In fact, expanding on it, the Lieutenant assured his hearers that, by means of large parabolic reflectors, luminous groups of rays could be dispatched from the Earth, of sufficient brightness to establish direct communication even with Venus or Mars, where these rays would be quite as visible as the planet Neptune is from the Earth. He even added that those brilliant points of light, which have been quite frequently observed in Mars and Venus, are perhaps signals made to the Earth by the inhabitants of these planets. He concluded, however, by observing that, though we might by these means succeed in obtaining news from the Moon, we could not possibly send any intelligence back in return, unless indeed the Selenites had at their disposal optical instruments at least as good as ours.

All agreed that this was very true, and, as is generally the case when one keeps all the talk to himself, the conversation now assumed so serious a turn that for some time it was hardly worth recording.

At last the Chief Engineer, excited by some remark that had been made, observed with much earnestness:

"You may say what you please, gentlemen, but I would willingly give my last dollar to know what has become of those brave men! Have they done anything? Have they seen anything? I hope they have. But I should dearly like to know. Ever so little success would warrant a repetition of the great experiment. The Columbiad is still to the good in Florida, as it will be for many a long day. There are millions of men to day as curious as I am upon the subject. Therefore it will be only a question of mere powder and bullets if a cargo of visitors is not sent to the Moon every time she passes our zenith.

"Marston would be one of the first of them," observed Brownson, lighting his cigar.

"Oh, he would have plenty of company!" cried the Midshipman. "I should be delighted to go if he'd only take me."

"No doubt you would, Mr. Midshipman," said Brownson, "the wise men, you know, are not all dead yet."

"Nor the fools either, Lieutenant," growled old Frisby, the fourth officer, getting tired of the conversation.

"There is no question at all about it," observed another; "every time a Projectile started, it would take off as many as it could carry."

"I wish it would only start often enough to improve the breed!" growled old Frisby.

"I have no doubt whatever," added the Chief Engineer, "that the thing would get so fashionable at last that half the inhabitants of the Earth would take a trip to the Moon."

"I should limit that privilege strictly to some of our friends in Washington," said old Frisby, whose temper had been soured probably by a neglect to recognize his long services; "and most of them I should by all means insist on sending to the Moon. Every month I would ram a whole raft of them into the Columbiad, with a charge under them strong enough to blow them all to the—But—Hey!—what in creation's that?"

Whilst the officer was speaking, his companions had suddenly caught a sound in the air which reminded them immediately of the whistling scream of a Lancaster shell. At first they thought the steam was escaping somewhere, but, looking upwards, they saw that the strange noise proceeded from a ball of dazzling brightness, directly over their heads, and evidently falling towards them with tremendous velocity. Too frightened to say a word, they could only see that in its light the whole ship blazed like fireworks, and the whole sea glittered like a silver lake. Quicker than tongue can utter, or mind can conceive, it flashed before their eyes for a second, an enormous bolide set on fire by friction with the atmosphere, and gleaming in its white heat like a stream of molten iron gushing straight from the furnace. For a second only did they catch its flash before their eyes; then striking the bowsprit of the vessel, which it shivered into a thousand pieces, it vanished in the sea in an instant with a hiss, a scream, and a roar, all equally indescribable. For some time the utmost confusion reigned on deck. With eyes too dazzled to see, ears still ringing with the frightful combination of unearthly sounds, faces splashed with floods of sea water, and noses stifled with clouds of scalding steam, the crew of the *Susquehanna* could hardly realize that their marvellous escape by a few feet from instant and certain destruction was an accomplished fact, not a frightful dream. They were still engaged in trying to open their eyes and to get the hot water out of their ears, when they suddenly heard the trumpet voice of Captain Bloomsbury crying, as he stood half dressed on the head of the cabin stairs:

"What's up, gentlemen? In heaven's name, what's up?"

The little Midshipman had been knocked flat by the concussion and stunned by the uproar. But before any body else could reply, his voice was heard, clear and sharp, piercing the din like an arrow:

"It's THEY, Captain! Didn't I tell you so?"

XXI

News for Marston!

In a few minutes, consciousness had restored order on board the *Susquehanna*, but the excitement was as great as ever. They had escaped by a hairsbreadth the terrible fate of being both burned and drowned without a moment's warning, without a single soul being left alive to tell the fatal tale; but on this neither officer nor man appeared to bestow the slightest thought. They were wholly engrossed with the terrible catastrophe that had befallen the famous adventurers. What was the loss of the *Susquehanna* and all it contained, in comparison to the loss experienced by the world at large in the terrible tragic *dénouement* just witnessed? The worst had now come to the worst. At last the long agony was over forever. Those three gallant men, who had not only conceived but had actually executed the grandest and most daring enterprise of ancient or modern times, had paid by the most fearful of deaths, for their sublime devotion to science and their unselfish desire to extend the bounds of human knowledge! Before such a reflection as this, all other considerations were at once reduced to proportions of the most absolute insignificance.

But was the death of the adventurers so very certain after all? Hope is hard to kill. Consciousness had brought reflection, reflection doubt, and doubt had resuscitated hope.

"It's they!" had exclaimed the little Midshipman, and the cry had thrilled every heart on board as with an electric shock. Everybody had instantly understood it. Everybody had felt it to be true. Nothing could be more certain than that the meteor which had just flashed before their eyes was the famous projectile of the Baltimore Gun Club. Nothing could be truer than that it contained the three world renowned men and that it now lay in the black depths of the Pacific Ocean.

But here opinions began to diverge. Some courageous breasts soon refused to accept the prevalent idea.

"They're killed by the shock!" cried the crowd.

"Killed?" exclaimed the hopeful ones; "Not a bit of it! The water here is deep enough to break a fall twice as great."

"They're smothered for want of air!" exclaimed the crowd.

"Their stock may not be run out yet!" was the ready reply. "Their air apparatus is still on hand."

"They're burned to a cinder!" shrieked the crowd.

"They had not time to be burned!" answered the Band of Hope. "The Projectile did not get hot till it reached the atmosphere, through which it tore in a few seconds."

"If they're neither burned nor smothered nor killed by the shock, they're sure to be drowned!" persisted the crowd, with redoubled lamentations.

"Fish 'em up first!" cried the Hopeful Band. "Come! Let's lose no time! Let's fish 'em up at once!"

The cries of Hope prevailed. The unanimous opinion of a council of the officers hastily summoned together by the Captain was to go to work and fish up the Projectile with the least possible delay. But was such an operation possible? asked a doubter. Yes! was the overwhelming reply; difficult, no doubt, but still quite possible. Certainly, however, such an attempt was not immediately possible as the *Susquehanna* had no machinery strong enough or suitable enough for a piece of work involving such a nicety of detailed operations, not to speak of its exceeding difficulty. The next unanimous decision, therefore, was to start the vessel at once for the nearest port, whence they could instantly telegraph the Projectile's arrival to the Baltimore Gun Club.

But what *was* the nearest port? A serious question, to answer which in a satisfactory manner the Captain had to carefully examine his sailing charts. The neighboring shores of the California Peninsula, low and sandy, were absolutely destitute of good harbors. San Diego, about a day's sail directly north, possessed an excellent harbor, but, not yet having telegraphic communication with the rest of the Union, it was of course not to be thought of. San Pedro Bay was too open to be approached in winter. The Santa Barbara Channel was liable to the same objection, not to mention the trouble often caused by kelp and wintry fogs. The bay of San Luis Obispo was still worse in every respect; having no islands to act as a breakwater, landing there in winter was often impossible. The harbor of the picturesque old town of Monterey was safe enough, but some uncertainty regarding sure telegraphic communications with San Francisco, decided the council not to venture it. Half Moon Bay, a little to the north, would be just as risky, and in moments like the present when every minute was worth a day, no risk involving the slightest loss of time could be ventured.

Evidently, therefore, the most advisable plan was to sail directly for the bay of San Francisco, the Golden Gate, the finest harbor on the Pacific Coast and one of the safest in the world. Here telegraphic communication with all parts of the Union was assured beyond a doubt. San Francisco, about 750 miles distant, the *Susquehanna* could probably make in three days; with a little increased pressure, possibly in two days and a-half. The sooner then she started, the better.

The fires were soon in full blast. The vessel could get under weigh at once. In fact, nothing delayed immediate departure but the consideration that two miles of sounding line were still to be hauled up from the ocean depths. Rut the Captain, after a moment's thought, unwilling that any more time should be lost, determined to cut it. Then marking its position by fastening its end to a buoy, he could haul it up at his leisure on his return.

"Besides," said he, "the buoy will show us the precise spot where the Projectile fell."

"As for that, Captain," observed Brownson, "the exact spot has been carefully recorded already: 27° 7′ north latitude by 41° 37′ west longitude, reckoning from the meridian of Washington."

"All right, Lieutenant," said the Captain curtly. "Cut the line!"

A large cone-shaped metal buoy, strengthened still further by a couple of stout spars to which it was securely lashed, was soon rigged up on deck, whence, being hoisted overboard, the whole apparatus was carefully lowered to the surface of the sea. By means of a ring in the small end of the buoy, the latter was then solidly attached to the part of the sounding line that still remained in the water, and all possible precautions were taken to diminish the danger of friction, caused by the contrary currents, tidal waves, and the ordinary heaving swells of ocean.

It was now a little after three o'clock in the morning. The Chief Engineer announced everything to be in perfect readiness for starting. The Captain gave the signal, directing the pilot to steer straight for San Francisco, north-north by west. The waters under the stern began to boil and foam; the ship very soon felt and yielded to the power that animated her; and in a few minutes she was making at least twelve knots an hour. Her sailing powers were somewhat higher than this, but it was necessary to be careful in the neighborhood of such a dangerous coast as that of California.

Seven hundred and fifty miles of smooth waters presented no very difficult task to a fast traveller like the *Susquehanna*, yet it was not till

JULES VERNE

two days and a-half afterwards that she sighted the Golden Gate. As usual, the coast was foggy; neither Point Lobos nor Point Boneta could be seen. But Captain Bloomsbury, well acquainted with every portion of this coast, ran as close along the southern shore as he dared, the fog-gun at Point Boneta safely directing his course. Here expecting to be able to gain a few hours time by signalling to the outer telegraph station on Point Lobos, he had caused to be painted on a sail in large black letters: "THE MOONMEN ARE BACK!" but the officers in attendance, though their fog-horn could be easily heard—the distance not being quite two miles—were unfortunately not able to see it. Perhaps they did see it, but feared a hoax.

Giving the Fort Point a good wide berth, the *Susquehanna* found the fog gradually clearing away, and by half-past three the passengers, looking under it, enjoyed the glorious view of the Contra Costa mountains east of San Francisco, which had obtained for this entrance the famous and well deserved appellation of the Golden Gate. In another half hour, they had doubled Black Point, and were lying safely at anchor between the islands of Alcatraz and Yerba Buena. In less than five minutes afterwards the Captain was quickly lowered into his gig, and eight stout pairs of arms were pulling him rapidly to shore.

The usual crowd of idlers had collected that evening on the summit of Telegraph Hill to enjoy the magnificent view, which for variety, extent, beauty and grandeur, is probably unsurpassed on earth. Of course, the inevitable reporter, hot after an item, was not absent. The *Susquehanna* had hardly crossed the bar, when they caught sight of her. A government vessel entering the bay at full speed, is something to look at even in San Francisco. Even during the war, it would be considered rather unusual. But they soon remarked that her bowsprit was completely broken off. *Very* unusual. Something decidedly is the matter. See! The vessel is hardly anchored when the Captain leaves her and makes for Megg's Wharf at North Point as hard as ever his men can pull! Something *must* be the matter—and down the steep hill they all rush as fast as ever their legs can carry them to the landing at Megg's Wharf.

The Captain could hardly force his way through the dense throng, but he made no attempt whatever to gratify their ill dissembled curiosity.

"Carriage!" he cried, in a voice seldom heard outside the din of battle.

In a moment seventeen able-bodied cabmen were trying to tear him limb from limb.

"To the telegraph office! Like lightning!" were his stifled mutterings, as he struggled in the arms of the Irish giant who had at last succeeded in securing him.

"To the telegraph office!" cried most of the crowd, running after him like fox hounds, but the more knowing ones immediately began questioning the boatmen in the Captain's gig. These honest fellows, nothing loth to tell all that they knew and more that they invented, soon had the satisfaction of finding themselves the centrepoint of a wonder stricken audience, greedily swallowing up every item of the extraordinary news and still hungrily gaping for more.

By this time, however, an important dispatch was flying east, bearing four different addresses: To the Secretary of the U.S. Navy, Washington; To Colonel Joseph Wilcox, Vice-President *pro tem.*, Baltimore Gun Club, Md; To J.T. Marston, Esq. Long's Peak, Grand County, Colorado; and To Professor Wenlock, Sub-Director of the Cambridge Observatory, Mass.

This dispatch read as follows:

> "In latitude twenty-seven degrees seven minutes north and
> longitude forty-one degrees thirty-seven minutes west
> shortly after one o'clock on the morning of twelfth instant
> Columbiad Projectile fell in Pacific—send instructions—
>
> BLOOMSBURY,
> *Captain*, SUSQUEHANNA

In five minutes more all San Francisco had the news. An hour later, the newspaper boys were shrieking it through the great cities of the States. Before bed-time every man, woman, and child in the country had heard it and gone into ecstasies over it. Owing to the difference in longitude, the people of Europe could not hear it till after midnight. But next morning the astounding issue of the great American enterprise fell on them like a thunder clap.

We must, of course, decline all attempts at describing the effects of this most unexpected intelligence on the world at large.

The Secretary of the Navy immediately telegraphed directions to the *Susquehanna* to keep a full head of steam up night and day so as to be ready to give instant execution to orders received at any moment.

The Observatory authorities at Cambridge held a special meeting that very evening, where, with all the serene calmness so characteristic of learned societies, they discussed the scientific points of the question in all its bearings. But, before committing themselves to any decided opinion, they unanimously resolved to wait for the development of further details.

At the rooms of the Gun Club in Baltimore there was a terrible time. The kind reader no doubt remembers the nature of the dispatch sent one day previously by Professor Belfast from the Long's Peak observatory, announcing that the Projectile had been seen but that it had become the Moon's satellite, destined to revolve around her forever and ever till time should be no more. The reader is also kindly aware by this time that such dispatch was not supported by the slightest foundations in fact. The learned Professor, in a moment of temporary cerebral excitation, to which even the greatest scientist is just as liable as the rest of us, had taken some little meteor or, still more probably, some little fly-speck in the telescope for the Projectile. The worst of it was that he had not only boldly proclaimed his alleged discovery to the world at large but he had even explained all about it with the well known easy pomposity that "Science" sometimes ventures to assume. The consequences of all this may be readily guessed. The Baltimore Gun Club had split up immediately into two violently opposed parties. Those gentlemen who regularly conned the scientific magazines, took every word of the learned Professor's dispatch for gospel—or rather for something of far higher value, and more strictly in accordance with the highly advanced scientific developments of the day. But the others, who never read anything but the daily papers and who could not bear the idea of losing Barbican, laughed the whole thing to scorn. Belfast, they said, had seen as much of the Projectile as he had of the "Open Polar Sea," and the rest of the dispatch was mere twaddle, though asserted with all the sternness of a religious dogma and enveloped in the usual scientific slang.

The meeting held in the Club House, 24 Monument Square, Baltimore, on the evening of the 13th, had been therefore disorderly in the highest degree. Long before the appointed hour, the great hall was densely packed and the greatest uproar prevailed. Vice-President Wilcox took the chair, and all was comparatively quiet until Colonel Bloomsbury, the Honorary Secretary in Marston's absence, commenced to read Belfast's dispatch. Then the scene, according to the account given in the next day's *Sun*, from whose columns we condense our report, actually "beggared description." Roars, yells, cheers, counter-cheers, clappings, hissings, stampings, squallings, whistlings, barkings, mewings, cock crowings, all of the most fearful and demoniacal character, turned the immense hall into a regular pandemonium. In vain did President Wilcox fire off his detonating bell, with a report on ordinary occasions as loud as the roar of a small piece of ordnance. In the dreadful noise then prevailing it was no more heard than the fizz of a lucifer match.

Some cries, however, made themselves occasionally heard in the pauses of the din. "Read! Read!" "Dry up!" "Sit down!" "Give him an egg!" "Fair play!" "Hurrah for Barbican!" "Down with his enemies!" "Free Speech!" "Belfast won't bite you!" "He'd like to bite Barbican, but his teeth aren't sharp enough!" "Barbican's a martyr to science, let's hear his fate!" "Martyr be hanged; the Old Man is to the good yet!" "Belfast is the grandest name in Science!" "Groans for the grandest name!" (Awful groans.) "Three cheers for Old Man Barbican!" (The exceptional strength alone of the walls saved the building, from being blown out by an explosion in which at least 5,000 pairs of lungs participated.)

"Three cheers for M'Nicholl and the Frenchman!" This was followed by another burst of cheering so hearty, vigorous and long continued that the scientific party, or *Belfasters* as they were now called, seeing that further prolongation of the meet was perfectly useless, moved to adjourn. It was carried unanimously. President Wilcox left the chair, the meeting broke up in the wildest disorder— the scientists rather crest fallen, but the Barbican men quite jubilant for having been so successful in preventing the reading of that detested dispatch.

Little sleeping was done that night in Baltimore, and less business next day. Even in the public schools so little work was done by the children that S.T. Wallace, Esq., President of the Education Board, advised an anticipation of the usual Christmas recess by a week. Every one talked of the Projectile; nothing was heard at the corners but discussions regarding its probable fate. All Baltimore was immediately rent into two parties, the *Belfasters* and the *Barbicanites*. The latter was the most enthusiastic and noisy, the former decidedly the most numerous and influential.

Science, or rather pseudo-science, always exerts a mysterious attraction of an exceedingly powerful nature over the generality—that is, the more ignorant portion of the human race. Assert the most absurd nonsense, call it a scientific truth, and back it up with strange words which, like *potentiality*, etc., sound as if they had a meaning but in reality have none, and nine out of every ten men who read your book will believe you. Acquire a remarkable name in one branch of human knowledge, and presto! you are infallible in all. Who can contradict you, if you only wrap up your assertions in specious phrases that not one man in a million attempts to ascertain the real meaning of? We like so much to be saved the trouble of thinking, that it is far easier and more comfortable to be led than to contradict, to fall in quietly with the great flock of sheep that jump blindly after their leader than to remain apart, making one's self ridiculous by foolishly attempting to argue. Real argument, in fact, is very difficult, for several reasons: first, you must understand your subject *well*, which is hardly likely; secondly, your opponent must also understand it well, which is even less likely; thirdly, you must listen patiently to his arguments, which is still less likely; and fourthly, he must listen to yours, the least likely of all. If a quack advertises a panacea for all human ills at a dollar a bottle, a hundred will buy the bottle, for one that will try how many are killed by it. What would the investigator gain by charging the quack with murder? Nobody would believe him, because nobody would take the trouble to follow his arguments. His adversary, first in the field, had gained the popular ear, and remained the unassailable master of the situation. Our love of "Science" rests upon our admiration of intellect, only unfortunately the intellect is too often that of other people, not our own.

The very sound of Belfast's phrases, for instance, "satellite," "lunar attraction," "immutable path of its orbit," etc, convinced the greater part of the "intelligent" community that he who used them so flippantly must be an exceedingly great man. Therefore, he had completely proved his case. Therefore, the great majority of the ladies and gentlemen that regularly attend the scientific lectures of the Peabody Institute, pronounced Barbican's fate and that of his companions to be sealed. Next morning's newspapers contained lengthy obituary notices of the Great Balloon-attics as the witty man of the *New York Herald* phrased it, some of which might be considered quite complimentary. These, all industriously copied into the evening papers, the people were carefully reading over again, some with honest regret, some deriving a great moral lesson from an attempt exceedingly reprehensible in every point of view, but most, we are sorry to acknowledge, with a feeling of ill concealed pleasure. Had not they always said how it was to end? Was there anything more absurd ever conceived? Scientific men too! Hang such science! If you want a real scientific man, no wind bag, no sham, take Belfast! *He* knows what he's talking about! No taking *him* in! Didn't he by means of the Monster Telescope, see the Projectile, as large as life, whirling round and round the Moon? Anyway, what else could have happened? Wasn't it what anybody's common sense expected? Don't you remember a conversation we had with you one day? etc., etc.

The *Barbicanites* were very doleful, but they never though of giving in. They would die sooner. When pressed for a scientific reply to a scientific argument, they denied that there was any argument to reply to. What! Had not Belfast seen the Projectile? No! Was not the Great Telescope then good for anything? Yes, but not for everything! Did not Belfast know his business? No! Did they mean to say that he had seen nothing at all? Well, not exactly that, but those scientific gentlemen can seldom be trusted; in their rage for discovery, they make a mountain out of a molehill, or, what is worse, they start a theory and then distort facts to support it. Answers of this kind either led directly to a fight, or the *Belfasters* moved away thoroughly disgusted with the ignorance of their opponents, who could not see a chain of reasoning as bright as the noonday sun.

Things were in this feverish state on the evening of the 14th, when, all at once, Bloomsbury's dispatch arrived in Baltimore. I need not say that it dropped like a spark in a keg of gun powder. The first question all asked was: Is it genuine or bogus? real or got up by the stockbrokers? But a few flashes backwards and forwards over the wires soon settled that point. The stunning effects of the new blow were hardly over when the *Barbicanites* began to perceive that the wonderful intelligence was decidedly in their favor. Was it not a distinct contradiction of the whole story told by their opponents? If Barbican and his friends were lying at the bottom of the Pacific, they were certainly not circumgyrating around the Moon. If it was the Projectile that had broken off the bowsprit of the *Susquehanna*, it could not certainly be the Projectile that Belfast had seen only the day previous doing the duty of a satellite. Did not the truth of one incident render the other an absolute impossibility? If Bloomsbury was right, was not Belfast an ass? Hurrah!

The new revelation did not improve poor Barbican's fate a bit—no matter for that! Did not the *party* gain by it? What would the *Belfasters* say now? Would not they hold down their heads in confusion and disgrace?

The *Belfasters*, with a versatility highly creditable to human nature, did nothing of the kind. Rapidly adopting the very line of tactics they had just been so severely censuring, they simply denied the whole thing. What! the truth of the Bloomsbury dispatch? Yes, every word of it! Had not Bloomsbury seen the Projectile? No! Were not his eyes good for anything? Yes, but not for everything! Did not the Captain know his business? No! Did they mean to say that the bowsprit of the *Susquehanna* had not been broken off? Well, not exactly that, but those naval gentlemen are not always to be trusted; after a pleasant little supper, they often see the wrong light-house, or, what is worse, in their desire to shield their negligence from censure, they dodge the blame by trying to show that the accident was unavoidable. The *Susquehanna's* bowsprit had been snapped off, in all probability, by some sudden squall, or, what was still more likely, some little aerolite had struck it and frightened the crew into fits. When answers of this kind did not lead to blows, the case was an exceptional one indeed. The contestants were so numerous and so excited that the police at last began to think of letting them fight it out without any interference. Marshal O'Kane, though ably assisted by his 12 officers and 500 patrolmen, had a terrible time of it. The most respectable men in Baltimore, with eyes blackened, noses bleeding, and collars torn, saw the inside of a prison that night for the first time in all their lives. Men that even the Great War had left the warmest of friends, now abused each other like fishwomen. The prison could not hold the half of those arrested. They were all, however, discharged next morning, for the simple reason that the Mayor and the aldermen had been themselves engaged in so many pugilistic combats during the night that they were altogether disabled from attending to their magisterial duties next day.

Our readers, however, may be quite assured that, even in the wildest whirl of the tremendous excitement around them, all the members of the Baltimore Gun Club did not lose their heads. In spite of the determined opposition of the *Belfasters* who would not allow the Bloomsbury dispatch to be read at the special meeting called that evening, a few succeeded in adjourning to a committee-room, where Joseph Wilcox, Esq., presiding, our old friends Colonel Bloomsbury, Major Elphinstone, Tom Hunter, Billsby the brave, General Morgan, Chief Engineer John Murphy, and about as many more as were sufficient to form a quorum, declared themselves to be in regular session, and proceeded quietly to debate on the nature of Captain Bloomsbury's dispatch.

Was it of a nature to justify immediate action or not? Decided unanimously in the affirmative. Why so? Because, whether actually true or untrue, the incident it announced was not impossible. Had it indeed announced the Projectile to have fallen in California or in South America, there would have been good valid reasons to question its accuracy. But by taking into consideration the Moon's distance, and the time elapsed between the moment of the start and that of the presumed fall (about 10 days), and also the Earth's revolution in the meantime, it was soon calculated that the point at which the Projectile should strike our globe, if it struck it at all, would be somewhere about 27° north latitude, and 42° west longitude—the very identical spot given in the Captain's dispatch! This certainly was a strong point in its favor, especially as there was positively nothing valid whatever to urge against it.

A decided resolution was therefore immediately taken. Everything that man could do was to be done at once, in order to fish up their brave associates from the depths of the Pacific. That very night, in fact, whilst the streets of Baltimore were still resounding with the yells of contending *Belfasters* and *Barbicanites*, a committee of four, Morgan, Hunter, Murphy, and Elphinstone, were speeding over the Alleghanies in a special train, placed at their disposal by the *Baltimore and Ohio Railroad Company*, and fast enough to land them in Chicago pretty early on the following evening.

Here a fresh locomotive and a Pullman car taking charge of them, they were whirled off to Omaha, reaching that busy locality at about supper time on the evening of December 16th. The Pacific Train, as it was called though at that time running no further west than Julesburg, instead of waiting for the regular hour of starting, fired up that very night, and was soon pulling the famous Baltimore Club men up the slopes of the Nebraska at the rate of forty miles an hour. They were awakened before light next morning by the guard, who told them that Julesburg, which they were just entering, was the last point so far reached by the rails. But their regret at this circumstance was most unexpectedly and joyfully interrupted by finding their hands warmly clasped and their names cheerily cried out by their old and beloved friend, J.T. Marston, the illustrious Secretary of the Baltimore Gun Club.

At the close of the first volume of our entertaining and veracious history, we left this most devoted friend and admirer of Barbican established firmly at his post on the summit of Long's Peak, beside the Great Telescope, watching the skies, night and day, for some traces of his departed friends. There, as the gracious Reader will also remember, he had come a little too late to catch that sight of the Projectile which Belfast had at first reported so confidently, but of which the Professor by degrees had begun to entertain the most serious doubts.

In these doubts, however, Marston, strange to say, would not permit himself for one moment to share. Belfast might shake his head as much as he pleased; he, Marston, was no fickle reed to be shaken by every wind; he firmly believed the Projectile to be there before him, actually in sight, if he could only see it. All the long night of the 13th, and even for several hours of the 14th, he never quitted the telescope for a single instant. The midnight sky was in magnificent order; not a speck dimmed its azure of an intensely dark tint. The stars blazed out like fires; the Moon refused none of her secrets to the scientists who were gazing at her so intently that night from the platform on the summit of Long's Peak. But no black spot crawling over her resplendent surface rewarded their eager gaze. Marston indeed would occasionally utter a joyful cry announcing some discovery, but in a moment after he was confessing with groans that it was all a false alarm. Towards morning, Belfast gave up in despair and went to take a sleep; but no sleep for Marston. Though he was now quite alone, the assistants having also retired, he kept on talking incessantly to himself, expressing the most unbounded confidence in the safety of his friends, and the absolute certainty of their return. It was not until some hours after the Sun had risen and the Moon had disappeared behind the snowy peaks of the west, that he at last withdrew his weary eye from the glass through which every image formed by the great reflector was to be viewed. The countenance he turned on Belfast, who had now come back, was rueful in the extreme. It was the image of grief and despair.

"Did you see nothing whatever during the night, Professor?" he asked of Belfast, though he knew very well the answer he was to get.

"Nothing whatever."

"But you saw them once, didn't you?"

"Them! Who?"

"Our friends."

"Oh! the Projectile—well—I think I must have made some oversight."

"Don't say that! Did not Mr. M'Connell see it also?"

"No. He only wrote out what I dictated."

"Why, you must have seen it! I have seen it myself!"

"You shall never see it again! It's shot off into space."

"You're as wrong now as you thought you were right yesterday."

"I'm sorry to say I was wrong yesterday; but I have every reason to believe I'm right to-day."

"We shall see! Wait till to-night!"

"To-night! Too late! As far as the Projectile is concerned, night is now no better than day."

The learned Professor was quite right, but in a way which he did not exactly expect. That very evening, after a weary day, apparently a month long, during which Marston sought in vain for a few hours' repose, just as all hands, well wrapped up in warm furs, were getting ready to assume their posts once more near the mouth of the gigantic Telescope, Mr. M'Connell hastily presented himself with a dispatch for Belfast.

The Professor was listlessly breaking the envelope, when he uttered a sharp cry of surprise.

"Hey!" cried Marston quickly. "What's up now?"

"Oh!! The Pro—pro—projectile!!"

"What of it? What? Oh what?? Speak!!"

"It's Back!!"

Marston uttered a wild yell of mingled horror, surprise, and joy, jumped a little into the air, and then fell flat and motionless on the platform. Had Belfast shot him with a ten pound weight, right between the two eyes, he could not have knocked him flatter or stiffer. Having neither slept all night, nor eaten all day, the poor fellow's system had become so weak that such unexpected news was really more than he could bear. Besides, as one of the Cambridge men of the party, a young medical student, remarked: the thin, cold air of these high mountains was extremely enervating.

The astronomers, all exceedingly alarmed, did what they could to recover their friend from his fit, but it was nearly ten minutes before they had the satisfaction of seeing his limbs moving with a slight quiver and his breast beginning to heave. At last the color came back to his face and his eyes opened. He stared around for a few seconds at his friends, evidently unconscious, but his senses were not long in returning.

"Say!" he uttered at last in a faint voice.

"Well!" replied Belfast.

"Where is that infernal Pro—pro—jectile?"

"In the Pacific Ocean."

"What??"

He was on his feet in an instant.

"Say that again!"

"In the Pacific Ocean."

"Hurrah! All right! Old Barbican's not made into mincemeat yet! No, sirree! Let's start!"

"Where for?"

"San Francisco!"

"When?"

"This instant!"

"In the dark?"

"We shall soon have the light of the Moon! Curse her! it's the least she can do after all the trouble she has given us!"

XXII

On the Wings of the Wind

Leaving M'Connell and a few other Cambridge men to take charge of the Great Telescope, Marston and Belfast in little more than an hour after the receipt of the exciting dispatch, were scudding down the slopes of Long's Peak by the only possible route—the inclined railroad. This mode of travelling, however, highly satisfactory as far as it went, ceased altogether at the mountain foot, at the point where the Dale River formed a junction with Cache la Poudre Creek. But Marston, having already mapped out the whole journey with some care and forethought, was ready for almost every emergency. Instinctively feeling that the first act of the Baltimore Gun Club would be to send a Committee to San Francisco to investigate matters, he had determined to meet this deputation on the route, and his only trouble now was to determine at what point he would be most likely to catch them. His great start, he knew perfectly well, could not put him more than a day in advance of them: they having the advantage of a railroad nearly all the way, whilst himself and Belfast could not help losing much time in struggling through ravines, canyons, mountain precipices, and densely tangled forests, not to mention the possibility of a brush or two with prowling Indians, before they could strike the line of the Pacific Railroad, along which he knew the Club men to be approaching. After a few hours rest at La Porte, a little settlement lately started in the valley, early in the morning they took the stage that passed through from Denver to Cheyenne, a town at that time hardly a year old but already flourishing, with a busy population of several thousand inhabitants.

Losing not a moment at Cheyenne, where they arrived much sooner than they had anticipated, they took places in Wells, Fargo and Co.'s *Overland Stage Mail* bound east, and were soon flying towards Julesburg at the rate of twelve miles an hour. Here Marston was anxious to meet the Club men, as at this point the Pacific Railroad divided into two branches—one bearing north, the other south of the Great Salt Lake—and he feared they might take the wrong one.

But he arrived in Julesburg fully 10 hours before the Committee, so that himself and Belfast had not only ample time to rest a little after their rapid flight from Long's Peak, but also to make every possible preparation for the terrible journey of more than fifteen hundred miles that still lay before them.

This journey, undertaken at a most unseasonable period of the year, and over one of the most terrible deserts in the world, would require a volume for itself. Constantly presenting the sharpest points of contrast between the most savage features of wild barbaric nature on the one hand, and the most touching traits of the sweetest humanity on the other, the story of our Club men's adventures, if only well told, could hardly fail to be highly interesting. But instead of a volume, we can give it only a chapter, and that a short one.

From Julesburg, the last station on the eastern end of the Pacific Railroad, to Cisco, the last station on its western end, the distance is probably about fifteen hundred miles, about as far as Constantinople is from London, or Moscow from Paris. This enormous stretch of country had to be travelled all the way by, at the best, a six horse stage tearing along night and day at a uniform rate, road or no road, of ten miles an hour. But this was the least of the trouble. Bands of hostile Indians were a constant source of watchfulness and trouble, against which even a most liberal stock of rifles and revolvers were not always a reassurance. Whirlwinds of dust often overwhelmed the travellers so completely that they could hardly tell day from night, whilst blasts of icy chill, sweeping down from the snowy peaks of the Rocky Mountains, often made them imagine themselves in the midst of the horrors of an Arctic winter.

The predominant scenery gave no pleasure to the eye or exhilaration to the mind. It was of the dreariest description. Days and days passed with hardly a house to be seen, or a tree or a blade of grass. I might even add, or a mountain or a river, for the one was too often a heap of agglomerated sand and clay cut into unsightly chasms by the rain, and the other generally degenerated into a mere stagnant swamp, its shallowness and dryness increasing regularly with its length. The only houses were log ranches, called Relays, hardly visible in their sandy surroundings, and separate from each other by a mean distance of ten miles. The only trees were either stunted cedars, so far apart, as to be often denominated Lone Trees; and, besides wormwood, the only plant was the sage plant, about two feet high, gray, dry, crisp, and emitting a sharp pungent odor by no means pleasant.

In fact, Barbican and his companions had seen nothing drearier or savager in the dreariest and savagest of lunar landscapes than the scenes occasionally presented to Marston and his friends in their headlong journey on the track of the great Pacific Railroad. Here, bowlders, high, square, straight and plumb as an immense hotel, blocked up your way; there, lay an endless level, flat as the palm of your hand, over which your eye might roam in vain in search of something green like a meadow, yellow like a cornfield, or black like ploughed ground—a mere boundless waste of dirty white from the stunted wormwood, often rendered misty with the clouds of smarting alkali dust.

Occasionally, however, this savage scenery decidedly changed its character. Now, a lovely glen would smile before our travellers, traversed by tinkling streams, waving with sweet grasses, dotted with little groves, alive with hares, antelopes, and even elks, but apparently never yet trodden by the foot of man. Now, our Club men felt like travelling on clouds, as they careered along the great plateau west of the Black Hills, fully 8,000 feet above the level of the sea, though even there the grass was as green and fresh as if it grew in some sequestered valley of Pennsylvania. Again,

"In this untravelled world whose margin fades
For ever and for ever as they moved,"

they would find themselves in an immense, tawny, treeless plain, outlined by mountains so distant as to resemble fantastic cloud piles. Here for days they would have to skirt the coasts of a Lake, vast, unruffled, unrippled, apparently of metallic consistency, from whose sapphire depths rose pyramidal islands to a height of fully three thousand feet above the surface.

In a few days all would change. No more sand wastes, salt water flats, or clouds of blinding alkali dust. The travellers' road, at the foot of black precipitous cliffs, would wind along the brink of a roaring torrent, whose devious course would lead them into the heart of the Sierras, where misty peaks solemnly sentinelled the nestling vales still smiling in genial summer verdure. Across these they were often whirled through immense forests of varied character, here dense enough to obscure the track, there swaying in the sweet sunlight and vocal with joyous birds of bright and gorgeous plumage. Then tropical vegetation would completely hide the trail, crystal lakes would obstruct it, cascades shooting down from perpendicular rocks would obliterate it, mountain passes barricaded by basaltic columns would render it uncertain, and on one occasion it was completely covered up by a fall of snow to a depth of more than twenty feet.

But nothing could oppose serious delay to our travellers. Their motto was ever "onward!" and what they lost in one hour by some mishap they endeavored to recover on the next by redoubled speed. They felt that they would be no friends of Barbican's if they were discouraged by impossibilities. Besides, what would have been real impossibilities at another time, several concurrent circumstances now rendered comparatively easy.

The surveys, the gradings, the cuttings, and the other preliminary labors in the great Pacific Railroad, gave them incalculable aid. Horses, help, carriages, provisions were always in abundance. Their object being well known, they had the best wishes of every hand on the road. People remained up for them all hours of the night, no matter at what station they were expected. The warmest and most comfortable of meals were always ready for them, for which no charge would be taken on any account. In Utah, a deputation of Mormons galloped alongside them for forty miles to help them over some points of the road that had been often found difficult. The season was the finest known for many years. In short, as an old Californian said as he saw them shooting over the rickety bridge that crossed the Bear River at Corinne: "they had everything in their favor—*luck* as well as *pluck!*"

The rate at which they performed this terrible ride across the Continent and the progress they made each day, some readers may consider worthy of a few more items for the sake of future reference. Discarding the ordinary overland mail stage as altogether too slow for their purpose, they hired at Julesburg a strong, well built carriage, large enough to hold them all comfortably; but this they had to replace twice before they came to their journey's end. Their team always consisted of the best six horses that could be found, and their driver was the famous Hank Monk of California, who, happening to be in Julesburg about that time, volunteered to see them safely landed in Cisco on the summit of the Sierra Nevada. They were enabled to change horses as near as possible every hour, by telegraphing ahead in the morning, during the day, and often far into the hours of night.

Starting from Julesburg early in the morning of the 17th, their first resting place for a few hours at night was Granite Canyon, twenty miles west of Cheyenne, and just at the foot of the pass over the Black Hills. On the 18th, night-fall found them entering St. Mary's, at the further end of the pass between Rattle Snake Hills and Elk Mountain. It was after 5 o'clock and already dark on the 19th, when the travellers, hurrying with all speed through the gloomy gorge of slate formation leading to the banks of the Green River, found the ford too deep to be ventured before morning. The 20th was a clear cold day very favorable for brisk locomotion, and the bright sun had not quite disappeared behind the Wahsatch Mountains when the Club men, having crossed the Bear River, began to leave the lofty plateau of the Rocky Mountains by the great inclined plane marked by the lines of the Echo and the Weber Rivers on their way to the valley of the Great American Desert.

Quitting Castle Rock early on the morning of the 21st, they soon came in sight of the Great Salt Lake, along the northern shores of which they sped all day, taking shelter after night-fall at Terrace, in a miserable log cabin surrounded by piles of drifting sand. The 22d was a terrible day. The sand was blinding, the alkali dust choking, the ride for five or six hours was up considerable grade; still they had accomplished their 150 miles before resting for the night at Elko, even at this period a flourishing little village on the banks of the Humboldt. After another smothering ride on the 23d, they rested, at Winnemucca, another flourishing village, situated at the precise point in the desert where the Little Humboldt joins Humboldt River, without, however, making the channel fuller or wider. The 24th was decidedly the hardest day, their course lying through the worst part of the terrible Nevada desert. But a glimpse of the Sierras looming in the western horizon gave them courage and strength enough to reach Wadsworth, at their foot, a little before midnight. Our travellers had now but one day's journey more to make before reaching the railroad at Cisco, but, this being a very steep ascent nearly all the way up, each mile cost almost twice as much time and exertion.

At last, late in the evening of Christmas Day, amidst the most enthusiastic cheers of all the inhabitants of Cisco, who welcomed them with a splendid pine brand procession, Marston and his friends, thoroughly used up, feet swelled, limbs bruised, bones aching, stomachs seasick, eyes bleared, ears ringing, and brains on fire for want of rest, took their places in the State Car waiting for them, and started without a moment's delay for Sacramento, about a hundred miles distant. How delicious was the change to our poor travellers! Washed, refreshed, and lying at full length on luxurious sofas, their sensations, as the locomotive spun them down the ringing grooves of the steep Sierras, can be more easily imagined than described. They were all fast asleep when the train entered Sacramento, but the Mayor and the other city authorities who had waited up to receive them, had them carried carefully, so as not to disturb their slumbers, on board the *Yo Semite*, a fine steamer belonging to the California Navigation Company, which landed them safely at San Francisco about noon on the 26th, after accomplishing the extraordinary winter journey of 1500 miles over land in little more than nine days, only about 200 miles being done by steam.

Half-past two P.M. found our travellers bathed, dressed, shaved, dined, and ready to receive company in the grand parlor of the *Occidental Hotel*. Captain Bloomsbury was the first to call.

Marston hobbled eagerly towards him and asked:

"What have you done towards fishing them up, Captain?"

"A good deal, Mr. Marston; indeed almost everything is ready."

"Is that really the case, Captain?" asked all, very agreeably surprised.

"Yes, gentlemen, I am most happy to state that I am quite in earnest."

"Can we start to-morrow?" asked General Morgan. "We have not a moment to spare, you know."

"We can start at noon to-morrow at latest," replied the Captain, "if the foundry men do a little extra work to-night."

"We must start this very day, Captain Bloomsbury," cried Marston resolutely; "Barbican has been lying two weeks and thirteen hours in the depths of the Pacific! If he is still alive, no thanks to Marston! He must by this time have given me up! The grappling irons must be got on board at once, Captain, and let us start this evening!"

At half-past four that very evening, a shot from the Fort and a lowering of the Stars and Stripes from its flagstaff saluted the *Susquehanna*, as she steamed proudly out of the Golden Gate at the lively rate of fifteen knots an hour.

XXIII

The Club Men Go a Fishing

Captain Bloomsbury was perfectly right when he said that almost everything was ready for the commencement of the great work which the Club men had to accomplish. Considering how much was required, this was certainly saying a great deal; but here also, as on many other occasions, fortune had singularly favored the Club men.

San Francisco Bay, as everybody knows, though one of the finest and safest harbors in the world, is not without some danger from hidden rocks. One of these in particular, the Anita Rock as it was called, lying right in mid channel, had become so notorious for the wrecks of which it was the cause, that, after much time spent in the consideration of the subject, the authorities had at last determined to blow it up. This undertaking having been very satisfactorily accomplished by means of *dynamite* or giant powder, another improvement in the harbor had been also undertaken with great success. The wrecks of many vessels lay scattered here and there pretty numerously, some, like that of the *Flying Dragon*, in spots so shallow that they could be easily seen at low water, but others sunk at least twenty fathoms deep, like that of the *Caroline*, which had gone down in 1851, not far from Blossom Rock, with a treasure on board of 20,000 ounces of gold. The attempt to clear away these wrecks had also turned out very well; even sufficient treasure had been recovered to repay all the expense, though the preparations for the purpose by the contractors, M'Gowan and Co. had been made on the most extensive scale, and in accordance with the latest improvements in the apparatus for submarine operations.

Buoys, made of huge canvas sacks, coated with India rubber, and guarded by a net work of strong cordage, had been manufactured and provided by the *New York Submarine Company*. These buoys, when inflated and working in pairs, had a lifting capacity of 30 tons a pair. Reservoirs of air, provided with powerful compression pumps, always accompanied the buoys. To attach the latter, in a collapsed condition, with strong chains to the sides of the vessels which were to be lifted, a diving apparatus was necessary. This also the *New York Company* had provided, and it was so perfect in its way that, by means of peculiar appliances of easy management, the diver could walk about on the bottom, take his own bearings, ascend to the surface at pleasure, and open his helmet without assistance. A few sets likewise of Rouquayrol and Denayrouze's famous submarine armor had been provided. These would prove of invaluable advantage in all operations performed at great sea depths, as its distinctive feature, "the regulator," could maintain, what is not done by any other diving armor, a constant equality of pressure on the lungs between the external and the internal air.

But perhaps the most useful article of all was a new form of diving bell called the *Nautilus*, a kind of submarine boat, capable of lateral as well as vertical movement at the will of its occupants. Constructed with double sides, the intervening chambers could be filled either with water or air according as descent or ascent was required. A proper supply of water enabled the machine to descend to depths impossible to be reached otherwise; this water could then be expelled by an ingenious contrivance, which, replacing it with air, enabled the diver to rise towards the surface as fast as he pleased.

All these and many other portions of the submarine apparatus which had been employed that very year for clearing the channel, lifting the wrecks and recovering the treasure, lay now at San Francisco, unused fortunately on account of the season of the year, and therefore they could be readily obtained for the asking. They had even been generously offered to Captain Bloomsbury, who, in obedience to a telegram from Washington, had kept his crew busily employed for nearly two weeks night and day in transferring them all safely on board the *Susquehanna*.

Marston was the first to make a careful inspection of every article intended for the operation.

"Do you consider these buoys powerful enough to lift the Projectile, Captain?" he asked next morning, as the vessel was briskly heading southward, at a distance of ten or twelve miles from the coast on their left.

"You can easily calculate that problem yourself, Mr. Marston," replied the Captain. "It presents no difficulty. The Projectile weighs about 20 thousand pounds, or 10 tons?"

"Correct!"

"Well, a pair of these buoys when inflated can raise a weight of 30 tons."

"So far so good. But how do you propose attaching them to the Projectile?"

"We simply let them descend in a state of collapse; the diver, going down with them, will have no difficulty in making a fast connection. As soon as they are inflated the Projectile will come up like a cork."

"Can the divers readily reach such depths?"

"That remains to be seen Mr. Marston."

"Captain," said Morgan, now joining the party, "you are a worthy member of our Gun Club. You have done wonders. Heaven grant it may not be all in vain! Who knows if our poor friends are still alive?"

"Hush!" cried Marston quickly. "Have more sense than to ask such questions. Is Barbican alive! Am *I* alive? They're all alive, I tell you, only we must be quick about reaching them before the air gives out. That's what's the matter! Air! Provisions, water—abundance! But air—oh! that's their weak point! Quick, Captain, quick—They're throwing the reel—I must see her rate!" So saying, he hurried off to the stern, followed by General Morgan. Chief Engineer Murphy and the Captain of the *Susquehanna* were thus left for awhile together.

These two men had a long talk on the object of their journey and the likelihood of anything satisfactory being accomplished. The man of the sea candidly acknowledged his apprehensions. He had done everything in his power towards collecting suitable machinery for fishing up the Projectile, but he had done it all, he said, more as a matter of duty than because he believed that any good could result from it; in fact, he never expected to see the bold adventurers again either living or dead. Murphy, who well understood not only what machinery was capable of effecting, but also what it would surely fail in, at first expressed the greatest confidence in the prosperous issue of the undertaking. But when he learned, as he now did for the first time, that the ocean bed on which the Projectile was lying could be hardly less than 20,000 feet below the surface, he assumed a countenance as grave as the Captain's, and at once confessed that, unless their usual luck stood by them, his poor friends had not the slightest possible chance of ever being fished up from the depths of the Pacific.

The conversation maintained among the officers and the others on board the *Susquehanna*, was pretty much of the same nature. It is almost needless to say that all heads—except Belfast's, whose scientific mind rejected the Projectile theory with the most serene contempt—were filled with the same idea, all hearts throbbed with the same emotion. Wouldn't it be glorious to fish them up alive and well? What were they doing just now? Doing? *Doing!* Their bodies most probably were lying in a shapeless pile on the floor of the Projectile, like a heap of clothes, the uppermost man being the last smothered; or perhaps floating about in the water inside the Projectile, like dead gold fish in an aquarium; or perhaps burned to a cinder, like papers in a "champion" safe after a great fire; or, who knows? perhaps at that very moment the poor fellows were making their last and almost superhuman struggles to burst their watery prison and ascend once more into the cheerful regions of light and air! Alas! How vain must such puny efforts prove! Plunged into ocean depths of three or four miles beneath the surface, subjected to an inconceivable pressure of millions and millions of tons of sea water, their metallic shroud was utterly unassailable from within, and utterly unapproachable from without!

Early on the morning of December 29th, the Captain calculating from his log that they must now be very near the spot where they had witnessed the extraordinary phenomenon, the *Susquehanna* hove to. Having to wait till noon to find his exact position, he ordered the steamer to take a short circular course of a few hours' duration, in hope of sighting the buoy. But though at least a hundred telescopes scanned the calm ocean breast for many miles in all directions, it was nowhere to be seen.

Precisely at noon, aided by his officers and in the presence of Marston, Belfast, and the Gun Club Committee, the Captain took his observations. After a moment or two of the most profound interest, it was a great gratification to all to learn that the *Susquehanna* was on the right parallel, and only about 15 miles west of the precise spot where the Projectile had disappeared beneath the waves. The steamer started at once in the direction indicated, and a minute or two before one o'clock the Captain said they were "there." No sign of the buoy could yet be seen in any direction; it had probably been drifted southward by the Mexican coast current which slowly glides along these shores from December to April.

"At last!" cried Marston, with a sigh of great relief.

"Shall we commence at once?" asked the Captain.

"Without losing the twenty thousandth part of a second!" answered Marston; "life or death depends upon our dispatch!"

The *Susquehanna* again hove to, and this time all possible precautions were taken to keep her in a state of perfect immobility—an operation easily accomplished in these pacific latitudes, where cloud and wind and water are often as motionless as if all life had died out of the world. In fact, as the boats were quietly lowered, preparatory for beginning the operations, the mirror like calmness of sea, sky, and ship so impressed the Doctor, who was of a poetical turn of mind, that he could not help exclaiming to the little Midshipman, who was standing nearest:

"Coleridge realized, with variations:

> *The breeze drops down, the sail drops down,*
> *All's still as still can be;*
> *If we speak, it is only to break*
> *The silence of the sea.*
> *Still are the clouds, still are the shrouds,*
> *No life, no breath, no motion;*
> *Idle are all as a painted ship*
> *Upon a painted ocean!"*

Chief Engineer Murphy now took command. Before letting down the buoys, the first thing evidently to be done was to find out, if possible, the precise point where the Projectile lay. For this purpose, the Nautilus was clearly the only part of the machinery that could be employed with advantage. Its chambers were accordingly soon filled with water, its air reservoirs were also soon completely charged, and the Nautilus itself, suspended by chains from the end of a yard, lay quietly on the ocean surface, its manhole on the top remaining open for the reception of those who were willing to encounter the dangers that awaited it in the fearful depths of the Pacific. Every one looking on was well aware that, after a few hundred feet below the surface, the pressure would grow more and more enormous, until at last it became quite doubtful if any line could bear the tremendous strain. It was even possible that at a certain depth the walls of the Nautilus might be crushed in like an eggshell, and the whole machine made as flat as two leaves of paper pasted together.

Perfectly conscious of the nature of the tremendous risk they were about to run, Marston, Morgan, and Murphy quietly bade their friends a short farewell and were lowered into the manhole. The Nautilus having room enough for four, Belfast had been expected to be of the party but, feeling a little sea sick, the Professor backed out at the last moment, to the great joy of Mr. Watkins, the famous reporter of the *N.Y. Herald*, who was immediately allowed to take his place.

Every provision against immediate danger had been made. By means of preconcerted signals, the inmates could have themselves drawn up, let down, or carried laterally in whatever direction they pleased. By barometers and other instruments they could readily ascertain the pressure of the air and water, also how far they had descended and at what rate they were moving. The Captain, from his bridge, carefully superintended every detail of the operation. All signals he insisted on attending to himself personally, transmitting them instantly by his bell to the engineer below. The whole power of the steam engine had been brought to bear on the windlass; the chains could withstand an enormous strain. The wheels had been carefully oiled and tested beforehand; the signalling apparatus had been subjected to the rigidest examination; and every portion of the machinery had been proved to be in admirable working order.

The chances of immediate and unforeseen danger, it is true, had been somewhat diminished by all these precautions. The risk, nevertheless, was fearful. The slightest accident or even carelessness might easily lead to the most disastrous consequence.

Five minutes after two o'clock, the manhole being closed, the lamps lit, and everything pronounced all right, the signal for the descent was given, and the Nautilus immediately disappeared beneath the waters. A double anxiety now possessed all on board the *Susquehanna*: the prisoners in the Nautilus were in danger as well as the prisoners in the Projectile. Marston and his friends, however, were anything but disquieted on their own account, and, pencil in hand and noses flattened on the glass plates, they examined carefully everything they could see in the liquid masses through which they were descending.

For the first five hundred feet, the descent was accomplished with little trouble. The Nautilus sank rather slowly, at a uniform rate of a foot to the second. It had not been two minutes under water when the light of day completely disappeared. But for this the occupants were fully prepared, having provided themselves with powerful lamps, whose brilliant light, radiating from polished reflectors, gave them an opportunity of seeing clearly around it for a distance of eight or ten feet in all directions. Owing to the superlatively excellent construction of the Nautilus, also on account of the *scaphanders*, or suits of diving armor, with which Marston and his friends had clothed themselves, the disagreeable sensations to which divers are ordinarily exposed, were hardly felt at all in the beginning of the descent.

Marston was about to congratulate his companions on the favorable auspices inaugurating their trip, when Murphy, consulting the instrument, discovered to his great surprise that the Nautilus was not making its time. In reply to their signal "faster!" the downward movement increased a little, but it soon relaxed again. Instead of less than two minutes, as at the beginning, it now took twelve minutes to make a hundred feet. They had gone only seven hundred feet in thirty-seven minutes. In spite of repeated signalling, their progress during the next hour was even still more alarming, one hundred feet taking exactly 59 minutes. To shorten detail, it required two hours more to make another hundred feet; and then the Nautilus, after taking ten minutes to crawl an inch further, came to a perfect stand still. The pressure of the water had evidently now become too enormous to allow further descent.

The Clubmen's distress was very great; Marston's, in particular, was indescribable. In vain, catching at straws, he signalled "eastwards!" "westwards!" "northwards!" or "southwards!" the Nautilus moved readily every way but downwards.

"Oh! what shall we do?" he cried in despair; "Barbican, must we really give you up though separated from us by the short distance of only a few miles?"

At last, nothing better being to be done, the unwilling signal "heave upwards!" was given, and the hauling up commenced. It was done very slowly, and with the greatest care. A sudden jerk might snap the chains; an incautious twist might put a kink on the air tube; besides, it was well known that the sudden removal of heavy pressure resulting from rapid ascent, is attended by very disagreeable sensations, which have sometimes even proved fatal.

It was near midnight when the Clubmen were lifted out of the manhole. Their faces were pale, their eyes bloodshot, their figures stooped. Even the *Herald* Reporter seemed to have got enough of exploring. But Marston was as confident as ever, and tried to be as brisk.

He had hardly swallowed the refreshment so positively enjoined in the circumstances, when he abruptly addressed the Captain:

"What's the weight of your heaviest cannon balls?"

"Thirty pounds, Mr. Marston."

"Can't you attach thirty of them to the Nautilus and sink us again?"

"Certainly, Mr. Marston, if you wish it. It shall be the first thing done to-morrow."

"To-night, Captain! At once! Barbican has not an instant to lose."

"At once then be it, Mr. Marston. Just as you say."

The new sinkers were soon attached to the Nautilus, which disappeared once more with all its former occupants inside, except the *Herald* Reporter, who had fallen asleep over his notes, or at least seemed to be. He had probably made up his mind as to the likelihood of the Nautilus ever getting back again.

The second descent was quicker than the first, but just as futile. At 1152 feet, the Nautilus positively refused to go a single inch further. Marston looked like a man in a stupor. He made no objection to the signal given by the others to return; he even helped to cut the ropes by which the cannon balls had been attached. Not a single word was spoken by the party, as they slowly rose to the surface. Marston seemed to be struggling against despair. For the first time, the impossibility of the great enterprise seemed to dawn upon him. He and his friends had undertaken a great fight with the mighty Ocean, which now played with them as a giant with a pigmy. To reach the bottom was evidently completely out of their power; and what was infinitely worse, there was nothing to be gained by reaching it. The Projectile was not on the bottom; it could not even have got to the bottom. Marston said it all in a few words to the Captain, as the Clubmen stepped on deck a few hours later:

"Barbican is floating midway in the depths of the Pacific, like Mahomet in his coffin!"

Blindly yielding, however, to the melancholy hope that is born of despair, Marston and his friends renewed the search next day, the 30th, but they were all too worn out with watching and excitement to be able to continue it longer than a few hours. After a night's rest, it was renewed the day following, the 31st, with some vigor, and a good part of the ocean lying between Guadalupe and Benito islands was carefully investigated to a depth of seven or eight hundred feet. No traces whatever of the Projectile. Several California steamers, plying between San Francisco and Panama, passed the *Susquehanna* within hailing distance. But to every question, the invariable reply one melancholy burden bore:

"No luck!"

All hands were now in despair. Marston could neither eat nor drink. He never even spoke the whole day, except on two occasions. Once, when somebody heard him muttering:

"He's now seventeen days in the ocean!"

The second time he spoke, the words seemed to be forced out of him. Belfast admitted, for the sake of argument, that the Projectile had fallen into the ocean, but he strongly denounced the absurd idea of its occupants being still alive. "Under such circumstances," went on the learned Professor, "further prolongation of vital energy would be simply impossible. Want of air, want of food, want of courage—"

"No, sir!" interrupted Marston quite savagely. "Want of air, of meat, of drink, as much as you like! But when you speak of Barbican's want of courage, you don't know what you are talking about! No holy martyr ever died at the stake with a loftier courage than my noble friend Barbican!"

That night he asked the Captain if he would not sail down as far as Cape San Lucas. Bloomsbury saw that further search was all labor lost, but he respected such heroic grief too highly to give a positive refusal. He consented to devote the following day, New Year's, to an exploring expedition as far as Magdalena Bay, making the most diligent inquiries in all directions.

But New Year's was just as barren of results as any of its predecessors, and, a little before sunset, Captain Bloomsbury, regardless of further entreaties and unwilling to risk further delay, gave orders to 'bout ship and return to San Francisco.

The *Susquehanna* was slowly turning around in obedience to her wheel, as if reluctant to abandon forever a search in which humanity at large was interested, when the look-out man, stationed in the forecastle, suddenly sang out:

"A buoy to the nor'east, not far from shore!"

All telescopes were instantly turned in the direction indicated. The buoy, or whatever object it was, could be readily distinguished. It certainly did look like one of those buoys used to mark out the channel that ships follow when entering a harbor. But as the vessel slowly approached it, a small flag, flapping in the dying wind—a strange feature in a buoy— was seen to surmount its cone, which a nearer approach showed to be emerging four or five feet from the water. And for a buoy too it was exceedingly bright and shiny, reflecting the red rays of the setting sun as strongly as if its surface was crystal or polished metal!

"Call Mr. Marston on deck at once!" cried the Captain, his voice betraying unwonted excitement as he put the glass again to his eye.

Marston, thoroughly worn out by his incessant anxiety during the day, had been just carried below by his friends, and they were now trying to make him take a little refreshment and repose. But the Captain's order brought them all on deck like a flash.

They found the whole crew gazing in one direction, and, though speaking in little more than whispers, evidently in a state of extraordinary excitement.

What could all this mean? Was there any ground for hope? The thought sent a pang of delight through Marston's wildly beating heart that almost choked him.

The Captain beckoned to the Club men to take a place on the bridge beside himself. They instantly obeyed, all quietly yielding them a passage.

The vessel was now only about a quarter of a mile distant from the object and therefore near enough to allow it to be distinguished without the aid of a glass.

What! The flag bore the well known Stars and Stripes!

An electric shudder of glad surprise shot through the assembled crowd. They still spoke, however, in whispers, hardly daring to utter their thoughts aloud.

The silence was suddenly startled by a howl of mingled ecstasy and rage from Marston.

He would have fallen off the bridge, had not the others held him firmly. Then he burst into a laugh loud and long, and quite as formidable as his howl.

Then he tore away from his friends, and began beating himself over the head.

"Oh!" he cried in accents between a yell and a groan, "what chuckleheads we are! What numskulls! What jackasses! What double-treble-barrelled gibbering idiots!" Then he fell to beating himself over the head again.

"What's the matter, Marston, for heaven's sake!" cried his friends, vainly trying to hold him.

"Speak for yourself!" cried others, Belfast among the number.

"No exception, Belfast! You're as bad as the rest of us! We're all a set of unmitigated, demoralized, dog-goned old lunatics! Ha! Ha! Ha!"

"Speak plainly, Marston! Tell us what you mean!"

"I mean," roared the terrible Secretary, "that we are no better than a lot of cabbage heads, dead beats, and frauds, calling ourselves scientists! O Barbican, how you must blush for us! If we were schoolboys, we should all be skinned alive for our ignorance! Do you forget, you herd of ignoramuses, that the Projectile weighs only ten tons?"

"We don't forget it! We know it well! What of it?"

"This of it: it can't sink in water without displacing its own volume in water; its own volume in water weighs thirty tons! Consequently, it can't sink; more consequently, it hasn't sunk; and, most consequently, there it is before us, bobbing up and down all the time under our very noses! O Barbican, how can we ever venture to look at you straight in the face again!"

Marston's extravagant manner of showing it did not prevent him from being perfectly right. With all their knowledge of physics, not a single one of those scientific gentlemen had remembered the great fundamental law that governs sinking or floating bodies. Thanks to its slight specific gravity, the Projectile, after reaching unknown depths of ocean through the terrific momentum of its fall, had been at last arrested in its course and even obliged to return to the surface.

By this time, all the passengers of the *Susquehanna* could easily recognize the object of such weary longings and desperate searches, floating quietly a short distance before them in the last rays of the declining day!

The boats were out in an instant. Marston and his friends took the Captain's gig. The rowers pulled with a will towards the rapidly nearing Projectile. What did it contain? The living or the dead? The living certainly! as Marston whispered to those around him; otherwise how could they have ever run up that flag?

The boats approached in perfect silence, all hearts throbbing with the intensity of newly awakened hope, all eyes eagerly watching for some sign to confirm it. No part of the windows appeared over the water, but the trap hole had been thrown open, and through it came the pole that bore the American flag. Marston made for the trap hole and, as it was only a few feet above the surface, he had no difficulty in looking in.

At that moment, a joyful shout of triumph rose from the interior, and the whole boat's crew heard a dry drawling voice with a nasal twang exclaiming:

"Queen! How is that for high?"

It was instantly answered by another voice, shriller, louder, quicker, more joyous and triumphant in tone, but slightly tinged with a foreign accent:

"King! My brave Mac! How is that for high?"

The deep, clear, calm voice that spoke next thrilled the listeners outside with an emotion that we shall not attempt to portray. Except that their ears could detect in it the faintest possible emotion of triumph, it was in all respects as cool, resolute, and self-possessed as ever:

"Ace! Dear friends, how is that for high?"

They were quietly enjoying a little game of High-Low-Jack!

How they must have been startled by the wild cheers that suddenly rang around their ocean-prison! How madly were these cheers re-echoed from the decks of the *Susquehanna*! Who can describe the welcome that greeted these long lost, long beloved, long despaired of Sons of Earth, now so suddenly and unexpectedly rescued from destruction, and restored once more to the wonderstricken eyes of admiring humanity? Who can describe the scenes of joy and exuberant happiness, and deep felt gratitude, and roaring rollicking merriment, that were witnessed on board the steamer that night and during the next three days!

As for Marston, it need hardly be said that he was simply ecstatic, but it may interest both the psychologist and the philologist to learn that the expression *How is that for high?* struck him at once as with a kind of frenzy. It became immediately such a favorite tongue morsel of his that ever since he has been employing it on all occasions, appropriate or otherwise. Thanks to his exertions in its behalf all over the country, the phrase is now the most popular of the day, well known and relished in every part of the Union. If we can judge from its present hold on the popular ear it will continue to live and flourish for many a long day to come; it may even be accepted as the popular expression of triumph in those dim, distant, future years when the memory not only of the wonderful occasion of its formation but also of the illustrious men themselves who originated it, has been consigned forever to the dark tomb of oblivion!

XXIV

Farewell to the Baltimore Gun Club

The intense interest of our extraordinary but most veracious history having reached its culmination at the end of the last chapter, our absorbing chronicle might with every propriety have been then and there concluded; but we can't part from our gracious and most indulgent reader before giving him a few more details which may be instructive perhaps, if not amusing.

No doubt he kindly remembers the world-wide sympathy with which our three famous travellers had started on their memorable trip to the Moon. If so, he may be able to form some idea of the enthusiasm universally excited by the news of their safe return. Would not the millions of spectators that had thronged Florida to witness their departure, now rush to the other extremity of the Union to welcome them back? Could those innumerable Europeans, Africans and Asiatics, who had visited the United States simply to have a look at M'Nicholl, Ardan and Barbican, ever think of quitting the country without having seen those wonderful men again? Certainly not! Nay, more—the reception and the welcome that those heroes would everywhere be greeted with, should be on a scale fully commensurate with the grandeur of their own gigantic enterprise. The Sons of Earth who had fearlessly quitted this terrestrial globe and who had succeeded in returning after accomplishing a journey inconceivably wonderful, well deserved to be received with every extremity of pride, pomp and glorious circumstance that the world is capable of displaying.

To catch a glimpse of these demi-gods, to hear the sound of their voices, perhaps even to touch their hands—these were the only emotions with which the great heart of the country at large was now throbbing.

To gratify this natural yearning of humanity, to afford not only to every foreigner but to every native in the land an opportunity of beholding the three heroes who had reflected such indelible glory on the American name, and to do it all in a manner eminently worthy of the great American Nation, instantly became the desire of the American People.

To desire a thing, and to have it, are synonymous terms with the great people of the American Republic.

A little thinking simplified the matter considerably: as all the people could not go to the heroes, the heroes should go to all the people.

So decided, so done.

It was nearly two months before Barbican and his friends could get back to Baltimore. The winter travelling over the Rocky Mountains had been very difficult on account of the heavy snows, and, even when they found themselves in the level country, though they tried to travel as privately as possible, and for the present positively declined all public receptions, they were compelled to spend some time in the houses of the warm friends near whom they passed in the course of their long journey.

The rough notes of their Moon adventures—the only ones that they could furnish just then—circulating like wild fire and devoured with universal avidity, only imparted a keener whet to the public desire to feast their eyes on such men. These notes were telegraphed free to every newspaper in the country, but the longest and best account of the "*Journey to the Moon*" appeared in the columns of the *New York Herald*, owing to the fact that Watkins the reporter had had the adventurers all to himself during the whole of the three days' trip of the *Susquehanna* back to San Francisco. In a week after their return, every man, woman, and child in the United States knew by heart some of the main facts and incidents in the famous journey; but, of course, it is needless to say that they knew nothing at all about the finer points and the highly interesting minor details of the astounding story. These are now all laid before the highly favored reader for the first time. I presume it is unnecessary to add that they are worthy of his most implicit confidence, having been industriously and conscientiously compiled from the daily journals of the three travellers, revised, corrected, and digested very carefully by Barbican himself.

It was, of course, too early at this period for the critics to pass a decided opinion on the nature of the information furnished by our travellers. Besides, the Moon is an exceedingly difficult subject. Very few newspaper men in the country are capable of offering a single opinion regarding her that is worth reading. This is probably also the reason why half-scientists talk so much dogmatic nonsense about her.

Enough, however, had appeared in the notes to warrant the general opinion that Barbican's explorations had set at rest forever several pet theories lately started regarding the nature of our satellite. He and his friends had seen her with their own eyes, and under such favorable circumstances as to be altogether exceptional. Regarding her formation, her origin, her inhabitability, they could easily tell what system *should* be rejected and what *might* be admitted. Her past, her present, and her future, had been alike laid bare before their eyes. How can you object to the positive assertion of a conscientious man who has passed within a few hundred miles of *Tycho*, the culminating point in the strangest of all the strange systems of lunar oreography? What reply can you make to a man who has sounded the dark abysses of the *Plato* crater? How can you dare to contradict those men whom the vicissitudes of their daring journey had swept over the dark, Invisible Face of the Moon, never before revealed to human eye? It was now confessedly the privilege and the right of these men to set limits to that selenographic science which had till now been making itself so very busy in reconstructing the lunar world. They could now say, authoritatively, like Cuvier lecturing over a fossil skeleton: "Once the Moon was this, a habitable world, and inhabitable long before our Earth! And now the Moon is that, an uninhabitable world, and uninhabitable ages and ages ago!"

We must not even dream of undertaking a description of the grand *fête* by which the return of the illustrious members of the Gun Club was to be adequately celebrated, and the natural curiosity of their countrymen to see them was to be reasonably gratified. It was one worthy in every way of its recipients, worthy of the Gun Club, worthy of the Great Republic, and, best of all, every man, woman, and child in the United States could take part in it. It required at least three months to prepare it: but this was not to be regretted as its leading idea could not be properly carried out during the severe colds of winter.

All the great railroads of the Union had been closely united by temporary rails, a uniform gauge had been everywhere adopted, and every other necessary arrangement had been made to enable a splendid palace car, expressly manufactured for the occasion by Pullman himself, to visit every chief point in the United States without ever breaking connection. Through the principal street in each city, or streets if one was not large enough, rails had been laid so as to admit the passage of the triumphal car. In many cities, as a precaution against unfavorable weather, these streets had been arched over with glass, thus becoming grand arcades, many of which have been allowed to remain so to the present day. The houses lining these streets, hung with tapestry, decorated with flowers, waving with banners, were all to be illuminated at night time in a style at once both the most brilliant and the most tasteful. On the sidewalks, tables had been laid, often miles and miles long, at the public expense; these were to be covered with every kind of eatables, exquisitely cooked, in the greatest profusion, and free to everyone for twelve hours before the arrival of the illustrious guests and also for twelve hours after their departure. The idea mainly aimed at was that, at the grand national banquet about to take place, every inhabitant of the United States, without exception, could consider Barbican and his companions as his own particular guests for the time being, thus giving them a welcome the heartiest and most unanimous that the world has ever yet witnessed.

Evergreens were to deck the lamp-posts; triumphal arches to span the streets; fountains, squirting *eau de cologne*, to perfume and cool the air; bands, stationed at proper intervals, to play the most inspiring music; and boys and girls from public and private schools, dressed in picturesque attire, to sing songs of joy and glory. The people, seated at the banquetting tables, were to rise and cheer and toast the heroes as they passed; the military companies, in splendid uniforms, were to salute them with presented arms; while the bells pealed from the church towers, the great guns roared from the armories, *feux de joie* resounded from the ships in the harbor, until the day's wildest whirl of excitement was continued far into the night by a general illumination and a surpassing display of fireworks. Right in the very heart of the city, the slowly moving triumphal car was always to halt long enough to allow the Club men to join the cheering citizens at their meal, which was to be breakfast, dinner or supper according to that part of the day at which the halt was made.

The number of champagne bottles drunk on these occasions, or of the speeches made, or of the jokes told, or of the toasts offered, or of the hands shaken, of course, I cannot now weary my kind reader by detailing, though I have the whole account lying before me in black and white, written out day by day in Barbican's own bold hand. Yet I should like to give a few extracts from this wonderful journal. It is a perfect model of accuracy and system. Whether detailing his own doings or those of the innumerable people he met, Caesar himself never wrote anything more lucid or more pointed. But nothing sets the extraordinary nature of this great man in a better light than the firm, commanding, masterly character of the handwriting in which these records are made. The elegant penmanship all through might easily pass for copper plate engraving—

except on one page, dated "*Boston, after dinner*," where, candor compels me to acknowledge, the "Solid Men" appear to have succeeded in rendering his iron nerves the least bit wabbly.

The palace car had been so constructed that, by turning a few cranks and pulling out a few bolts, it was transformed at once into a highly decorated and extremely comfortable open barouche. Marston took the seat usually occupied by the driver: Ardan and M'Nicholl sat immediately under him, face to face with Barbican, who, in order that everyone might be able to distinguish him, was to keep all the back seat for himself, the post of honor.

On Monday morning, the fifth of May, a month generally the pleasantest in the United States, the grand national banquet commenced in Baltimore, and lasted twenty-four hours. The Gun Club insisted on paying all the expenses of the day, and the city compromised by being allowed to celebrate in whatever way it pleased the reception of the Club men on their return.

They started on their trip that same day in the midst of one of the grandest ovations possible to conceive. They stopped for a little while at Wilmington, but they took dinner in Philadelphia, where the splendor of Broad Street (at present the finest boulevard in the world, being 113 feet wide and five miles long) can be more easily alluded to than even partially described.

The house fronts glittered with flowers, flags, pictures, tapestries, and other decorations; the chimneys and roofs swarmed with men and boys cheerfully risking their necks every moment to get one glance at the "Moon men"; every window was a brilliant bouquet of beautiful ladies waving their scented handkerchiefs and showering their sweetest smiles; the elevated tables on the sidewalks, groaning with an abundance of excellent and varied food, were lined with men, women, and children, who, however occupied in eating and drinking, never forgot to salute the heroes, cheering them lustily as they slowly moved along; the spacious street itself, just paved from end to end with smooth Belgian blocks, was a living moving panorama of soldiers, temperance men, free masons, and other societies, radiant in gorgeous uniforms, brilliant in flashing banners, and simply perfect in the rhythmic cadence of their tread, wings of delicious music seeming to bear them onward in their proud and stately march.

A vast awning, spanning the street from ridge to ridge, had been so prepared and arranged that, in case of rain or too strong a glare from the summer sun, it could be opened out wholly or partially in the space of a very few minutes. There was not, however, the slightest occasion for using it, the weather being exceedingly fine, almost paradisiacal, as Marston loved to phrase it.

The "Moon men" supped and spent the night in New York, where they were received with even greater enthusiasm than at Philadelphia. But no detailed description can be given of their majestic progress from city to city through all portions of the mighty Republic. It is enough to say that they visited every important town from Portland to San Francisco, from Salt Lake City to New Orleans, from Mobile to Charleston, and from Saint Louis to Baltimore; that, in every section of the great country, preparations for their reception were equally as enthusiastic, their arrival was welcomed with equal *furore*, and their departure accompanied with an equal amount of affectionate and touching sympathy.

The *New York Herald* reporter, Mr. Watkins, followed them closely everywhere in a palace car of his own, and kept the public fully enlightened regarding every incident worth regarding along the route, almost as soon as it happened. He was enabled to do this by means of a portable telegraphic machine of new and most ingenious construction. Though its motive power was electricity, it could dispense with the ordinary instruments and even with wires altogether, yet it managed to transmit messages to most parts of the world with an accuracy that, considering how seldom it failed, is almost miraculous. The principle actuating it, though guessed at by many shrewd scientists, is still a profound secret and will probably remain so for some time longer, the *Herald* having purchased the right to its sole and exclusive use for fifteen years, at an enormous cost.

Who shall say that the apotheosis of our three heroes was not worthy of them, or that, had they lived in the old prehistoric times, they would not have taken the loftiest places among the demi-gods?

As the tremendous whirl of excitement began slowly to die away, the more thoughtful heads of the Great Republic began asking each other a few questions:

Can this wonderful journey, unprecedented in the annals of wonderful journeys, ever lead to any practical result?

Shall we ever live to see direct communication established with the Moon?

Will any Air Line of space navigation ever undertake to start a system of locomotion between the different members of the solar system?

Have we any reasonable grounds for ever expecting to see trains running between planet and planet, as from Mars to Jupiter and, possibly afterwards, from star to star, as from Polaris to Sirius?

Even to-day these are exceedingly puzzling questions, and, with all our much vaunted scientific progress, such as "no fellow can make out." But if we only reflect a moment on the audacious go-a-headiveness of the Yankee branch of the Anglo Saxon race, we shall easily conclude that the American people will never rest quietly until they have pushed to its last result and to every logical consequence the astounding step so daringly conceived and so wonderfully carried out by their great countryman Barbican.

In fact, within a very few months after the return of the Club men from the Continental Banquet, as it was called in the papers, the country was flooded by a number of little books, like Insurance pamphlets, thrust into every letter box and pushed under every door, announcing the formation of a new company called *The Grand Interstellar Communication Society.* The Capital was to be 100 million dollars, at a thousand dollars a share: J.P. BARBICAN, ESQ., P.G.C. was to be President; Colonel JOSHUA D. M'NICHOLL, Vice-President; Hon. J.T. MARSTON, Secretary; Chevalier MICHAEL ARDAN, General Manager; JOHN MURPHY, ESQ., Chief Engineer; H. PHILLIPS COLEMAN, ESQ. (Philadelphia lawyer), Legal Adviser; and the Astrological Adviser was to be Professor HENRY of Washington. (Belfast's blunder had injured him so much in public estimation, his former partisans having become his most merciless revilers, that it was considered advisable to omit his name altogether even in the list of the Directors.)

From the very beginning, the moneyed public looked on the G.I.C.S, with decided favor, and its shares were bought up pretty freely. Conducted on strictly honorable principles, keeping carefully aloof from all such damaging connection as the *Credit Mobilier*, and having its books always thrown open for public inspection, its reputation even to-day is excellent and continually improving in the popular estimation. Holding out no utopian inducements to catch the unwary, and making no wheedling promises to blind the guileless, it states its great objects with all their great advantages, without at the same time suppressing its enormous and perhaps insuperable difficulties. People know exactly what to think of it, and, whether it ever meets with perfect success or proves a complete failure, no one in the country will ever think of casting a slur on the bright name of its peerless President, J.P. Barbican.

For a few years this great man devoted every faculty of his mind to the furthering of the Company's objects. But in the midst of his labors, the rapid approach of the CENTENNIAL surprised him. After a long and careful consultation on the subject, the Directors and Stockholders of the G.I.C.S. advised him to suspend all further labors in their behalf for a few years, in order that he might be freer to devote the full energies of his giant intellect towards celebrating the first hundredth anniversary of his country's Independence—as all true Americans would wish to see it celebrated—in a manner every way worthy of the GREAT REPUBLIC OF THE WEST!

Obeying orders instantly and with the single-idea'd, unselfish enthusiasm of his nature, he threw himself at once heart and soul into the great enterprise. Though possessing no official prominence—this he absolutely insists upon—he is well known to be the great fountain head whence emanate all the life, order, dispatch, simplicity, economy, and wonderful harmony which, so far, have so eminently characterized the magnificent project. With all operations for raising the necessary funds—further than by giving some sound practical advice—he positively refused to connect himself (this may be the reason why subscriptions to the Centennial stock are so slow in coming in), but in the proper apportionment of expenses and the strict surveillance of the mechanical, engineering, and architectural departments, his services have proved invaluable. His experience in the vast operations at Stony Hill has given him great skill in the difficult art of managing men. His voice is seldom heard at the meetings, but when it is, people seem to take a pleasure in readily submitting to its dictates.

In wet weather or dry, in hot weather or cold, he may still be seen every day at Fairmount Park, Philadelphia, leisurely strolling from building to building, picking his steps quietly through the bustling crowds of busy workmen, never speaking a word, not even to Marston his faithful shadow, often pencilling something in his pocket book, stopping occasionally to look apparently nowhere, but never, you may be sure, allowing a single detail in the restless panorama around him to escape the piercing shaft of his eagle glance.

He is evidently determined on rendering the great CENTENNIAL of his country a still greater and more wonderful success than even his own world-famous and never to be forgotten JOURNEY through the boundless fields of ether, and ALL AROUND THE MOON!

END.

A Note About the Author

Jules Verne (1828–1905) was a French novelist, poet, and playwright. Verne is considered a major French and European author, as he has a wide influence on avant-garde and surrealist literary movements, and is also credited as one of the primary inspirations for the steampunk genre. However, his influence does not stop in the literary sphere. Verne's work has also provided an invaluable impact on scientific fields as well. Verne is best known for his series of bestselling adventure novels, which earned him such an immense popularity that he is one of the world's most translated authors.

A Note from the Publisher

Spanning many genres, from non-fiction essays to literature classics to children's books and lyric poetry, Mint Edition books showcase the master works of our time in a modern new package. The text is freshly typeset, is clean and easy to read, and features a new note about the author in each volume. Many books also include exclusive new introductory material. Every book boasts a striking new cover, which makes it as appropriate for collecting as it is for gift giving. Mint Edition books are only printed when a reader orders them, so natural resources are not wasted. We're proud that our books are never manufactured in excess and exist only in the exact quantity they need to be read and enjoyed.

Discover more of your favorite classics with Bookfinity™.

- Track your reading with custom book lists.
- Get great book recommendations for your personalized Reader Type.
- Add reviews for your favorite books.
- AND MUCH MORE!

Visit **bookfinity.com** and take the fun Reader Type quiz to get started.

Enjoy our classic and modern companion pairings!

Printed in the USA
CPSIA information can be obtained
at www.ICGtesting.com
JSHW022220140824
68134JS00018B/1161

9 781513 270449